THE LAND IS BRIGHT

Katrina

THE LAND IS BRIGHT

Elizabeth Murphy

HEADLINE

To Ted and our family, with love.

First published in Great Britain in 1989
by HEADLINE BOOK PUBLISHING PLC

British Library Cataloguing in Publication Data

Murphy, Elizabeth
The land is bright.
I Title
823'.914[F]

ISBN 0-7472-0092-0

Typeset in 11/12 pt English Times
by Colset Pte Ltd, Singapore

Printed and bound in Great Britain by
Richard Clay Ltd, Bungay, Suffolk

HEADLINE BOOK PUBLISHING PLC
Headline House
79 Great Titchfield Street
London W1P 7FN

And not by eastern windows only
When daylight comes, comes in the light
In front the sun climbs slow, how slowly
But westward look, the land is bright.

Arthur Hugh Clough

Acknowledgements

I would like to thank Mr. Roger Hull, Reference Librarian, and staff of Crosby Central Library, and the staff of the Local History Department, Picton Library, Liverpool for their help. My brother John Savage, for finding old books and photographs for research for this book, Freda Collins and members of Crosby Writers' Club, other friends, and my husband and family for their unstinting help and encouragement, for which I am truly grateful.

Chapter One

Darkness came early to the narrow streets of Liverpool in 1886, but although the March afternoon was made even more dreary by fog, the tiny living room of number nine, Gell Street was bright with the flames of a huge coal fire.

A wooden cradle stood on the rag rug before the fire, and twelve-year-old Sally Palin was rocking it, and peering anxiously at her sleeping baby sister.

Two young boys with mourning bands on their shabby jackets were sitting by the table. The elder boy came over to the cradle and looked at the baby.

'D'yer think we should get Mrs Malloy, Sal?' he asked, but Sally shook her head.

'No. Da left *me* in charge of our Emily,' she said. 'He'll be home soon, anyhow.'

In an effort to look grown up she had scraped back her red-brown hair, and wrapped one of her dead mother's white aprons around her thin body, high under her armpits, but her childish voice trembled, and her blue eyes were wide with fear.

'But she looks awful poorly,' John was persisting, when suddenly their father lifted the latch of the door. It opened directly into the living room, and his face paled as he saw the frightened children. Swiftly he crossed to the cradle, and turned back the blanket from the sleeping baby.

'She's sweating, Da,' Sally said nervously, but her father smiled.

'No wonder,' he said. 'She's roasting hot.' He drew the cradle further away from the fire.

'Oh, Da, I thought she had the fever!' Sally said. 'Her cheeks were so red. I built up the fire to cook the scouse, but it's ready now, anyway.'

'Aye, well, you didn't need to cook the baby too,' Matthew Palin said drily.

Sally glanced at him, wondering whether or not she should smile. Since her mother's death two weeks earlier, he had been like an unpredictable stranger instead of the loving father she had always known. Feeling lighthearted with relief about Emily, she drew the black pan on to the hob beside the fire, and said impulsively, 'Our John wanted to call Mrs Mal, Da, but she's already been in and out of the house all day like a fiddler's elbow. I was sick of seeing her.'

'That's enough now, Sally,' her father said sternly. 'Yer should be showing a good example to the lads. Speak respectful about anyone older than yerself, and remember, Mrs Mal was a good neighbour to Mam when the baby was born and – and at the end.'

1

'But Da, *we* looked after Mam,' Sally protested.

'Aye, but Mrs Malloy done things for Mam that I couldn't do, and you wasn't old enough for. Now think on, all of yer. I don't want none of yer to ferget a good turn. And you, Sally, don't yer ferget we've got a long road to travel yet with the baby. Yer'll be glad of Mrs Mal many a time.'

He hung his cap and jacket behind the door, and sat down in the wooden armchair to unlace his boots. Sally hung her head.

'There's a letter for you, Da,' she said in a subdued voice, hoping to change the subject. I never know when I'm doing right, she thought resentfully. Doing all the work and cooking a nice tea, and he bites me head off for nothing.

Matthew opened the letter and read it slowly, then sat with his lips pursed and a worried frown on his face, as Sally began to serve the meal, and John cut slices of bread. As they sat down to eat, the baby woke and began to cry loudly, and Sally jumped up to lift her from the cradle.

A moment later there was a tap at the door, and Mrs Malloy from next door came in. She was a tiny woman with bright blue eyes, and greying dark hair drawn back in a bun. Over her long black skirt she wore a spotless white apron, and a black shawl.

'Ah, Matt,' she said in a soft Irish brogue, 'are ye all right, lad? I heard the little wan cry. Will I take her across to Maggie Connolly's?'

'If yer will, Mrs Mal,' he said. 'She's maybe hungry.'

Sally took a blanket from the cradle to wrap round the baby, and Mrs Malloy chuckled.

'God bless ye, child,' she said. 'Sure it's only a few steps across the street, and she'll be under me shawl. She'll not take cold.' Sally opened the door, and as Mrs Malloy carried the baby out, a young woman carrying a basket on her head came stepping down the street. She stopped beside them.

'Is the babby orl right?' she asked. 'Our Molly's just 'ad 'er fifth, an' she's got plenty of milk if yer needin' it.'

'Ah, no, Maggie Connolly has full and plenty,' Mrs Malloy said shortly, and Sally timidly added, 'Thanks all the same, Katie.' The girl showed her broken teeth in a smile, and moved gracefully away, her ragged skirts swinging about her bare feet, and a strong smell of fish wafting back from her. Mrs Malloy screwed up her mouth in disgust.

'The impidence of thim, the dirty tinkers!' she exclaimed. 'Sure I couldn't face yer poor mam when me time comes, if I let the child be nourished be the like of them. At least Maggie's clean. Go you in now, girl, and ate yer scouse before it gets cold on yer.'

She carried the baby across the narrow street to the neighbour whose baby had been born a few days before Julia Palin's, and who had offered to share her abundant breast milk with the bereaved child.

When Sally turned back to the kitchen her father was sitting, spoon in hand, staring into the distance, and seven-year-old Alfred had taken advantage of his preoccupation to dip a crust into Sally's plate of scouse. His own plate had been wiped clean.

'Alfred,' Sally shouted indignantly. He jumped back, and Matthew looked up sharply.

2

'What's the matter with yer, girl?' he exclaimed. 'Screeching like that. Enough to frighten the daylights out of anyone.'

'Sorry, Da,' Sally muttered, picking up her spoon. Her father began to eat his neglected meal, and Sally made fierce grimaces at Alfred. He grinned back, peeping at her mischievously under lowered eyelids, and child though she was herself, a wave of thankfulness swept over her, to see signs of the merry little boy he had been until his mother's death two weeks earlier. Since then he had crept about like a sad little ghost, stunned by the suddenness of his loss.

After the meal the boys helped Sally to clear away, and to wash the dishes, and by the time that Mrs Malloy returned with Emily, now replete and fast asleep, John and Alfred were in bed.

Sally took the baby upstairs. When she came down Mrs Malloy had gone, and Matthew was sitting in his chair, smoking and staring into the fire, the letter in his hand. Sally moved quietly about the kitchen, glancing at her father's abstracted face from time to time, as she cut bread and made sandwiches for his 'carry out'.

Finally, when she sat down opposite to him and took up a sock to darn, she said timidly, 'Is something wrong, Da?'

He leaned forward and knocked out his pipe, shaking his head, then a thought seemed to strike him. He held out the letter to Sally.

'Ee are, girl. Yer can read it. It's got to do with you, anyroad. It's from yer mam's sister, yer Aunt Hester, from Ormesdale.' Sally laid down the sock and opened the letter.

> *My Dear Brother,*
> *I hope this finds you all well as it leaves us at present. Me and Walter have been thinking about your poor motherless children, living in that place, since we came back from the funeral. As you know we have not been blessed with children, although we are well blessed with this world's goods, owing to our hard work on the smallholding. We have talked things over, and Walter is willing to train the eldest lad up to the farming, and I will take the baby. I will give her a mother's love and care for the sake of my poor sister. R.I.P.*
> *I hope this will help you and lift the burden from young Sally,*
> *Your affec. Sister,*
> *Hester.*

Sally dropped the letter.

'Oh, Da, you wouldn't!' she exclaimed. 'You wouldn't let her take our Emily and our John.'

Matthew sighed. 'I don't know what to do, girl, and that's the God's truth,' he said. He got up and walked over to stand at the door. Foggy air laden with the fumes of sulphur from a nearby match works drifted in.

Tugs on the river hooted mournfully, and there were screams and shouts as two women fought outside a gin palace further down the hill. Matthew slammed the door shut, and came back to the fireplace.

' "Living in that place" yer aunt says, and maybe she's right,' he said

3

bitterly. 'We was always hopin' to flit from 'ere. I don't want to part with none of yer, Sally, but it'd be a chanst for John, and the baby'd have a good home and every care.'

Sally's face was red, and her eyes were bright with tears. 'But I'll give her every care, Da, and I *will* ask Mrs Malloy, honest I will. Our John'd fret and so would Emily, because she's used to us already. Mam wouldn't want them to go, Da.'

'Well, God knows I don't want us split up,' her father said, staring into the fire, and rubbing the bowl of his pipe up and down his cheek. Sally watched him anxiously, and finally he sighed deeply and eased his shoulders back against the chair. Before he could speak there was a knock at the door, and Mrs Malloy came in with a pile of clean napkins for the baby.

'Off to bed now, Sally,' her father ordered, and she said goodnight to him and to Mrs Malloy, and went up obediently, taking care to leave the door at the foot of the stairs ajar. She felt sure that her father intended to consult Mrs Malloy and she was anxious to hear what was said.

As she crouched at the top of the stairs she heard him say, 'Will ye take a look at that, Mrs Mal, and tell me what yer think.'

'God bless ye, lad, sure ye know I've no schooling,' Mrs Malloy replied, and then Sally heard her father reading the letter aloud. For a moment Mrs Malloy said nothing, then she asked quietly, 'But yerself now, Matt. How do ye feel about it yerself, lad?'

'I don't know, Mrs Mal, and that's the truth. It's a chanst for our John, right enough, and the baby'd never know the difference, but I don't want to part with none of them. Our Sal said just now that her Mam wouldn't want them parted.'

'That's true for Sally,' Mrs Malloy sighed. 'Sure Julie would be broken hearted at the idea, and the baby couldn't go yet anyhow, without Hester had a wet nurse for her.'

'Oh, she'll have everything organised, the same one,' Matthew said bitterly. 'There's nothing she likes better than bossing people around.'

'Aye, ye'd never take herself and Julie for sisters. Julie never raised her voice, but Lord ha' mercy on her, she could charm the birds off the trees, and as blithe as a bird herself. But I won't make your trouble worse be talking about her, lad.'

Sally heard paper rustle, then her father read aloud, ' "Your poor motherless children, living in that place", she says. Well, we know this is a rough sort of place to rear children, Mrs Mal. There's decent people round here but there's plenty of riff raff too.'

'Outside the house, lad, but there's nothing wrong between these four walls. Ye've reared a grand family, thank God, and made a good home for them.'

'So yer don't think I should let them go, Mrs Mal? Tell me straight now.'

'Well, if ye were desperate, lad, I'd say yes – but sure, ye're far from desperate. Ye have a grand steady job, and Sally's a good reliable girl. I'll help all I can.'

'Yer've helped us already, Mrs Mal. I don't know what we'd do with-

4

out yer. I don't think Julie'd like the children to go to Hester, anyroad. They never saw eye to eye.'

Sally heard Mrs Malloy chuckle. 'Me and Walter "have talked it over", says she. Poor little omadhaun, he'd be lucky if he got a word in edgeways. I don't think he opened his mouth, except to eat, from the minute they came that day, until they went home. Mind you, she'd make two of him, wouldn't she?'

'Aye, but he knows how to make the money,' Matthew said bitterly. 'Still, I'll tell them I'll make me own arrangements for me own children, without them putting their oar in.'

'But mind what ye say, Mattie lad. Ye don't want to be falling out with them. No sense in shutting the door.'

'Oh, I'll be careful. I'll take me time over the letter.' Sally heard the click of the latch as Mrs Malloy left, and with a sigh of relief she stole into the bedroom, and kissed the baby's soft cheek.

'I'm your mam now, Emmie,' she whispered. 'No one will ever take you away from me.' She climbed into bed and was asleep within minutes.

The following morning when Mrs Malloy had taken the baby to Maggie Connolly's, Sally went out to scrub her step and that of her neighbour on the other side, Mrs Hart.

It was a bright morning with a fresh breeze, and most of the tiny houses had freshly scrubbed steps, and clean windows. Sally looked around her, feeling angry as she thought of her aunt's phrase, 'living in that place'. Without being able to express her thoughts, she felt instinctively that the people of Gell Street, although poorly clad and often hungry, had an innate decency, and a striving for respectability. The shadow of the pawnshop and the public house fell more heavily on most of the other homes than on her own, but all their lives were far different to those lived in the filthy courts and dilapidated houses, swarming with people, and with vermin, further down the hill.

Mrs Malloy was respectable, Sally thought indignantly, and so were John and James Duggan, the Irish brothers who lodged with her. Mrs Hart, whose step she was now scrubbing, had been born a lady, far superior to Aunt Hester.

When the steps were finished, she went in and moved the black kettle over the fire to make tea. It was ready when Mrs Malloy came in, smiling, with Emily wrapped in her shawl.

'If ye'd see the cut of Maggie, girl,' she said, 'ye'd split yer sides. She's just after whitewashing the bedrooms and she was like a snowman. I declare to God, she'd as much whitewash on herself as on the walls.'

'She keeps her house nice and clean though, doesn't she, Mrs Mal? I was thinking what Aunt Hester said about round here,' Sally said.

'Ah, bad luck to her. Boasting and bragging, and upsetting your poor da with the ould letter, as if he hasn't enough on his plate, God help him. She's had a grand aisy life and never known a poor day, but she was always black jealous of your Mam, all the same.'

Sally almost dropped the teapot in surprise.

'Aunt Hester was? But why, Mrs Mal?'

'Because your mam had a real man for a husband, and there was

5

love and happiness in this house, Sally, for all they'd a struggle to make the two ends meet between paydays. But I shouldn't be talking to ye this way, girl. Don't let on to your da, now.'

'Da didn't like her saying that about Gell Street, anyway, I could tell,' said Sally. Mrs Malloy sipped her tea, and sighed.

'Well, God knows we're all strivers, Sal, and yet we're all living on the edge of a pit. It only needs a bit of misfortune to be knocking us over the edge.'

'Yes, but we're all respectable, aren't we, Mrs Mal, and there are posh people here too, like Mrs Hart.'

Mrs Malloy gave a short laugh. 'Mrs Hart, is it?' she said. 'There's one now that should be a lesson to ye, Sally. Hadn't she the great life, travelling the world with her mother, and coming home to a grand mansion, with servants to wait on her hand and foot, but then didn't she run off with Tom Hart, and him the gardener? Her poor mother was that heartbroken she had the gates shut behind them, and she swore they'd never be opened until she was carried through them in her coffin.'

Sally was wide-eyed.

'I never knew,' she said. 'I used to go in with Mam to help Mrs Hart, and Mam used to tell me to listen to Mrs Hart, and try to talk like her. I'm going in tomorrow to scrub out for her.'

'Yer da doesn't mind ye going in to do for her then? I know he thinks nothing of the quality. I remember him giving out about the ould Queen when she was here in May for the Exhibition.'

Sally looked puzzled. 'Da said Mam helped Mrs Hart as a neighbour because she wasn't strong enough to do her own housework, and Mr Hart is away on the tugs, and I should do the same.'

Mrs Malloy nodded her head with a satisfied air. 'Well, if ye never have a penny, any of youse, ye're well off with the father and mother God gave ye, girl, and the way they've reared ye.' She put down her teacup and stood up, drawing her shawl around her, and bending to look into the cradle.

'This little wan has a look of your Mam, Lord ha' mercy on her,' she said. 'The dark curls and the lovely brown eyes, and so has young Alfie. Yerself and John, now, ye take after yer Da, tall and thin, but maybe not so red-haired. Please God, he's the kind of man ye'll find someday for a husband, girlie. A good, steady man.'

'I'm not going to get married,' Sally said. 'I'm just going to look after Emily and Da and the lads.'

Mrs Malloy laughed. 'Ah, well, time will tell, child,' she said. 'There's wan thing, yer da won't be able to close any gates after ye.'

She left, smiling, and Sally picked up the baby and cuddled her.

'I mean it, Emmy,' she whispered. 'I'll never leave you. I'll always be here to look after you.'

Chapter Two

As time passed, life fell into a different pattern for the Palin family. Sally sometimes felt that the years before her mother's death belonged to another life, when she had no responsibilities and her mother was always about the house, whistling and singing.

'A whistling woman, a crowing hen, would frighten the devil out of his den', her father had been used to say, when her mother whistled one of the tunes played by the barrel organ in the street, but how happy he would be if he could hear that merry sound now.

He had become quiet and morose, rarely speaking except to reprove one of the children, or to comment bitterly on some item in the newspaper, which he read from cover to cover each night; but he was always just, and as before, nearly all that he earned was used for his family. Four ounces of thin twist a week, and the nightly *Liverpool Echo* were his only indulgences, except for half a pint of rum and coffee in a Birkenhead coffee house, before starting his day's work in the shipyard at six o'clock.

John had started work as a messenger boy for a grocer in Brunswick Road, after school and all day Saturday, and at the end of the first week he proudly handed his father his wages of one shilling and sixpence, and fourpence he had earned in tips. Sally felt proud too, when her father said, 'Keep threepence out of yer wages, lad, and any tips yer make, and give our Sally the one and threepence. She lays out the money now.'

She put the money into her mother's shabby purse, which already held the twenty-one shillings which her father gave her for housekeeping, but later she took out a shilling and put it into the old teapot on the mantelpiece. The housekeeping money had seemed enormous to her at first, even after she had paid the four shillings rent money, but it seemed to dwindle alarmingly. She knew how to buy food economically because she had so often shopped for her mother, but soap, candles, lamp oil and coal devoured money – especially coal, and yet there seemed no hope of using less. Good fires were needed for cooking, and for drying clothes, as well as for providing a warm room for Emily, and for the boys and her father when they came home wet and cold. Sally often wondered how her mother had managed to provide clothes and boots for the family, and worried about what she would do when they were needed. The shilling would be a start and every week she would try to save something more, she decided.

Emily was rapidly outgrowing her baby clothes, and it was Mrs Hart who solved that problem for Sally. When she went in to do Mrs Hart's scrubbing one day there were two short baby dresses and two flannel petticoats lying on the table. The dresses were beautifully embroidered, and even the petticoats had feather stitching round the neck.

'I've made these a little large to allow for growth, Sally,' Mrs Hart said. 'Emily seems to be growing so rapidly.'

Sally stood gazing at the dresses, speechless with delight for a moment, then she burst out, 'Oh, Mrs Hart, they're lovely. She'll look a real lady. I'm going to shorten her on Sunday.'

'I'm pleased to hear that, Sally,' Mrs Hart said quietly. 'Short dresses are much healthier for babies, I feel. Their limbs have more freedom.' She was more animated than usual and her pale face was pink with pleasure at Sally's delight. For a moment Sally could see traces of the lively girl she must have been. Since Mrs Malloy's revelations she had often looked curiously at Mrs Hart, wondering how the pale, thin woman, sitting so quietly with folded hands and straight back, could ever have been the headstrong girl described by Mrs Malloy.

The dresses were admired by Matthew and the boys, but Mrs Malloy was less enthusiastic.

'It's a kind thought in her, right enough, to make the dresses,' she said. 'But sure, all that stitchery is out of place.'

'You mean it's too good for Emily,' Sally said angrily.

'Now don't be firing up, girlie. Haven't we all to live in the station God calls us, and it's no kindness to be making the child different.'

'*Nothing's* too good for Emily,' Sally said. 'And she's going to be a lady anyhow, when she grows up.'

Mrs Malloy smiled and sighed. 'Dream yer dreams, child,' she said. 'Life will be knocking ye down soon enough.'

Emily had become the adored heart of the household. She was a placid baby, and even when Maggie Connolly's milk dwindled, and the child was passed round the nursing mothers in the street, she accepted her various wet nurses with equanimity, and smiled on everyone.

Sally spent hours every day cuddling and talking to her. She had time to lavish on the baby because she had so few other interests, but she was conscientious about maintaining her mother's standards in cooking, cleaning and washing.

The houses in Gell Street were regarded as superior in that neighbourhood. They were tall and narrow, and the front door opened into the living room/kitchen. Behind that there was a narrow back kitchen with a sink with a cold tap, and a washing boiler. Stairs from the living kitchen led to the two small bedrooms, and above them was the attic where the boys slept.

Twice a year Matthew whitewashed every wall in the house. Sally hated the smell of the lime, and envied Mary Duncan who lived across the street, because her house had wallpaper on the walls, until she sat behind Mary in school one day, and saw two bugs on her neck.

The lime wash kept the bugs at bay, and Sally's mother had waged unremitting war on the cockroaches which swarmed in all the houses. She had filled in all the cracks in the skirting boards and floor boards with a mixture of carbolic soap and brown sugar, and sprinkled

Keating's Powder in the hearth to deal with those that came from behind the grate.

Sally continued to do this, and every Friday she blackleaded the grate, and polished the steel fender and the jockey bar, which hooked on to the firebars to hold the pans, with emery paper. A big black kettle constantly on the hob supplied hot water, and the oven on the other side was used for baking.

It was a bright and comfortable room, with a rag rug before the fireplace, and a horsehair sofa in addition to Matthew's Windsor chair and the white scrubbed table and kitchen chairs. Sally felt that Emily need never be ashamed of it no matter how high she rose.

Without the baby her life would have been very lonely at this time. All her friends had now left school, and either departed into service, or were working long hours. She saw little of John, as he had time for only a hasty snack after school before dashing off to work. It was late when he came home, to eat his meal and fall into bed.

Alfred spent much of his time in Mrs Malloy's house. He had become very attached to her two lodgers, who made much of him and brought him gifts of sweets or small toys. They were brothers from the west of Ireland, who had worked on building sites and lodged with Mrs Malloy for many years. She came in to see Sally one day, smiling.

'I declare to God, Sally,' she said, 'I didn't think they had a tongue between them, all the years they're with me, and if ye'd hear them rattling away to young Alfie! Telling him all about their mammy, and their sisters, and the little ass they have for drawing up seaweed from the strand. Ah, well, 'tis a good thing. He'll not miss your poor mam so much, so.'

Although Sally missed her mother, she drew comfort from a feeling of closeness to her when she wore her aprons, or used her shabby old purse.

Sometimes when she thought of the old days before her mother's death, she would suddenly be filled with a fierce longing for her. Then she would ferociously scrub the kitchen floor, or hack pieces from the block of salt and roll them out to fill the salt box, until the longing died down.

Sally rarely went far from home at this time, as Emily was becoming too heavy for her to carry far, even when she wore her mother's shawl and supported the baby in it.

Once a week she walked down the hill to Great Homer Street to pay the Burial Club, past the filthy courts and alleys where starving half-naked children swarmed, and girls sat on the pavement chopping firewood. Often fights broke out between the girls, who tore at each other's hair and lashed out with dirty bare feet, but the next moment they were screaming with laughter, their quarrel forgotten.

Once she saw a woman who had formerly lived in Gell Street, sitting apathetically on some broken steps with her children around her. Sally remembered that the woman's husband had broken his back in a fall in a ship's hold. Was this what Mrs Malloy meant, she wondered, when she spoke of the pit that they could so easily fall into?

On other afternoons she avoided such worrying sights by walking up the hill towards Shaw Street. Occasionally she went in to St. Francis Xavier's Church in Langsdale Street, and sat quietly satisfying her love of beauty by gazing at the soaring columns on either side of the main aisle, or at the stained glass windows.

Sometimes there would be a smell of incense from an earlier service, or perfume from the flowers on the altar. Sally would unwrap her shawl and sit Emily up on her knee, hoping that the baby would absorb some of the beauty around her. The religious aspect meant little to Sally. Her father was a man of independent thought who cared little for any religion, and his cynical outlook had been absorbed by his wife, and through her by Sally.

Shortly after her mother's death two ladies of the parish had visited the family, and Matthew had arrived home early from work to find one cross-examining Sally, and the other prowling round, looking in the oven and the cupboard. His face had grown white with anger as they greeted him patronizingly, and he had civilly enquired the name of the prowler.

When he was told it, he replied quietly, 'Someone of that name owns them slums further down. Why don't you go there, Missis, or do you only go in clean houses? They might need yer. I can look after me own. Good day to yer.'

Even their arrogance had failed them, in the face of his anger, and they had scuttled away. Mrs Malloy, of course, was in the house within minutes, to find out what had happened. She shook her head when Matthew told her in a few terse words.

'Ye were maybe a bit hasty, lad,' she said. 'Ye have to hould a candle to the divil sometimes, and ye can do well out of the likes of them.'

'I'd sooner starve,' Matthew said forcefully. 'Poking and prying without a by your leave. Let them go to them as needs them, but no. Yer won't find *them* in Back Phoebe Anne Street.'

Mrs Malloy said no more, and after she had gone Matthew said irritably to Sally, 'She's a good woman, but don't take too many of your notions from her. She's overfond of creeping to the gentry to suit me.'

Sally only nodded, because she knew in her heart that there was no problem. Emily was going to *be* one of the gentry.

When Emily grew old enough to walk Sally took her further afield. On fine Sundays she took Emily and Alfred down to the Landing Stage, to watch the parade of people and to see the shipping crowded in the river. Her father always took a nap on Sunday afternoons and John preferred to be with his friends, but the two younger children enjoyed the outings. Sometimes on Saturdays she took them to Lewis's, the Mecca of children at that time. Clean and respectably dressed as they were, they passed the eagle-eyed scrutiny of the doorman, but Sally watched cynically as the man bent deferentially to answer a query by a small boy in a smart sailor suit, then roughly altered his manner to order away a barefoot child who tried to enter. Wealth, it seemed, could always command respect.

Aunt Hester had accepted Matthew's decision. She continued to

10

write to them, but now it was Sally who answered the letters. She wrote of John's job, and the family's health, even about Alfie's friendship with the Duggan brothers, but she said as little as possible about Emily. She was always afraid that if Hester saw Emily, she would find some way of persuading Da to part with her, even though all the family idolized her.

Alfred was always ready to carry her on his back, or to push her in the swing which their father had rigged up in the doorway, and John spent much of his scanty pocket money on her. Every evening Matthew went through a ritual of pretending to cut her toenails, and dandling her on his foot, before she was carried up to bed by Sally, but Emily remained unspoilt, and repaid them all with exuberant and demonstrative affection.

Sally had become a clever needlewoman, and Mrs Hart had shown her how to do the intricate embroidery she had learned at her exclusive school. The money saved in the teapot was used by Sally to buy second hand clothes in Paddy's Market, which she turned and altered for herself and Matthew and the boys, but for Emily she always contrived to buy new material which she used to make beautifully trimmed and embroidered dresses and pinafores.

The neighbours commented freely on Sally's devotion to Emily.

'Eh, she won't let the wind blow on that child,' said one as the sisters passed, Emily's white pinafore crackling with starch and Sally proudly holding her hand.

'Aye, she watches over 'er like a jewel,' another woman said enviously. 'It's flyin' in the face of God, to make so much of a child.' But Emily was a general favourite. Even Mrs Hart, nervous and withdrawn with other people, would always unbend to Emily.

When Sally went in to help Mrs Hart she always took Emily with her, and the child stood by Mrs Hart's chair, being taught the nursery rhymes and poems which she had learned in her own nursery.

Later at home Sally would listen proudly as Emily repeated what she had learned in exactly the clear, unaccented tones used by Mrs Hart. The two boys who spent more time than Sally outside the house both spoke with the thick Liverpool accents of their companions, and this led to a rare quarrel between Sally and John.

'I wish you two would try to speak better,' she said one day. 'I don't want Emily to copy you.' John's face grew red with anger.

'Wharrabout when she goes to school?' he said. 'D'yer want her to be skitted at?'

'I want her to be a lady,' said Sally.

Alfred grinned but John said angrily, 'Talkin' posh won't make our Emmie a lady, an' talkin' ordinary doesn't make us scruffs, neither.'

'You can do what you like,' Sally said. 'But our Emily's going to have nice friends, and talk like them. She's got a nice voice too. Maybe she'll even get in the choir.'

'Them snobs,' John said scornfully. 'Wharra 'ope you've got.'

Sally was about to make an angry reply when Emily suddenly burst into loud sobs.

'You shouted, you shouted,' she cried, running to fling her arms

11

around John's legs and then back to Sally. The quarrel was forgotten as they both tried to comfort her, but Sally realised that she had hurt John, and later she said to him, 'I'm sorry, John. I suppose I'm like Katie Boyle from Stitt Street, the one who stuck feathers in her hair. Mrs Hart said she had delusions of grandeur.'

'What's them when they're a' 'ome?' John said with a grin, and the incident passed, but afterwards Sally was careful to keep her dreams for Emily's future to herself, except sometimes to hint of them to the child. On fine days when she took Emily to the Landing Stage to watch the parade of wealth and privilege as ladies and gentlemen were assisted aboard the tender which would take them out to the liner lying in the river, there was always an unspoken resolve in her mind that one day Emily would be among their number.

Sometimes they took the horse tram to the southern end of the city, and walked through the leafy avenues and squares of the residences of the merchant princes of Liverpool. One day they stood looking wistfully into the gardens in the centre of one of the squares, where nursemaids wheeled perambulators, and children played among the flowers and trees.

'Can we go in, Sal?' Emily asked, but Sally shook her head.

'No, love,' she said. 'You have to live in one of those big houses, then you get a key to go in.'

Emily's brown eyes looked up trustfully. 'Should we live there then, Sal?' she asked.

Sally hugged her fiercely. 'Someday you will, my pet,' she promised. 'Someday you'll be a greater lady than any of them.'

Chapter Three

They walked on, and Emily's attention soon turned to the other sights. The organ grinder and his sad-eyed monkey, the chestnut seller, a pair of grey horses pulling a splendid carriage, all delighted the child.

Sally had forgotten that it was the Twelfth of July, until their homeward bound omnibus passed several Orange Lodge processions. She hurried Emily along Shaw Street, when they alighted, but as they turned in to Langsdale Street a procession appeared at the bottom of the hill. Crowds were milling about on the pavement, and Sally tried to cross to the other side of the road to where their home lay, but she was too late. She managed to push through the crowds on the left hand pavement, and to place Emily against the high wall which surrounded St. Francis Xavier's, so that she could stand in front of her and protect her.

As the procession drew nearer, the mood of the crowd seemed to worsen, especially among some of the women who muttered and folded their arms outside their shawls belligerently. Police were pushing the crowd back. Sally turned towards Emily, and arched her back over the child as the crowd swayed.

The procession reached the church and the noise of the drum became deafening, then a woman in the procession thrust a long pole into the air. A kipper dangled from it, with a placard bearing the words 'Cured at Lourdes'. Instantly pandemonium broke out, as several of the bystanders plunged into the procession.

'Bad luck to ye, ye Orange whore,' an old woman screamed, darting past the police and burying her hands in the placard carrier's hair. Screams and yells filled the air and fights broke out along the length of the procession, while the police plunged among the marchers and spectators, laying about indiscriminately with their batons. Sally hung over Emily, bracing her arms against the wall, as bodies were flung against her and fell away again.

As the screams died down, she peered round cautiously. Most of the crowd had gone, and the police were lining up at the edge of the pavement. A broken boot and a torn orange sash lay near Sally's feet, but the procession, looking tattered and dishevelled, was forming up again. A police sergeant jerked Sally's arm, and she put her other arm protectively round Emily.

'What are you doing here with that child?' he asked roughly.

'I'm trying to get home. We live in Gell Street,' replied Sally, drawing Emily closer to her.

'Clear off then, before they start up again, and don't be hanging round looking for trouble,' he said. 'Think yourself lucky you're not locked up.'

He stepped into the middle of the street and waved them across. Sally hurried home, her cheeks burning with indignation. She was still furious when she told her father about it later.

'Aye, I know that fellow,' Matthew said. 'He's a dab hand at bullying the poor and creeping to the rich. That's how he got to be sergeant.'

'As if I'd have taken Emily among that scum if I'd remembered the day!' Sally said. 'Why do they do it, Da? Fight like that, I mean. They're all as bad as one another'.

'Not for the love of God, girl, you may be sure,' Matthew said sardonically. 'But for one thing, they don't know any better, and for another, it's the only bit of excitement in their miserable lives. A fight on the Twelfth of July, and another on the Seventeenth of March, gives them something to look forward to.'

'But why doesn't someone stop it?' persisted Sally.

'Who, girl? The rich won't, you may be sure. It suits them. While the poor are fighting among themselves, they won't gang up on the real enemy – the rich who exploit them, and tread them down. I tell you, Sally, if the poor had the sense to unite there'd be bloody revolution in this country, but it'll never come while they're fighting among themselves about religion. Religion! God save the mark. They're nothing better than heathen savages, every last one of them.'

Sally was astounded. She had never heard her father make such a speech or give his opinions so definitely. He often smiled when Mrs Malloy aired her views, but he rarely made any comment. I suppose he talked like this to Mam, she thought, realising suddenly in how many ways he missed her mother.

Emily had seemed unperturbed by the commotion, standing quietly against the wall, then trotting home holding tightly to Sally's hand, but later as Sally tucked her up in bed she suddenly clung to her.

'Can we go now, Sal?' she asked tearfully, 'all of us.'

'Go where, pet?'

'To the big house where the trees and the little birdies were.'

'Oh, Emmie, pet, if only we could. We will someday, I promise you. Why do you want to go now, love? Were you frightened by the fighting?'

'The man with the stick shouted at us,' the child said, her lip trembling. Sally hugged her.

'He didn't mean it, love, he thought we were somebody else. Don't worry, the same man will be licking your boots before I've done. Go to sleep now, love, and the next time we'll go to see the seagulls, and the ships in the river.'

She kissed the child tenderly and went downstairs, seething with anger. Da's right, she thought bitterly. That fellow wouldn't have dared to speak like that if we were rich, but that's the last time anyone treats Emily like that. She's going to be treated with respect by everyone.

Mrs Malloy was at her door when Sally and Emily returned from their walk the following day, and Sally told her of the policeman's behaviour.

'The way he snarled at me,' she said. ' "What are you doing here with that child?" As though I would have taken Emily among them if I'd known.'

Mrs Malloy pursed her lips. 'He maybe thought ye were a nursemaid. Wouldn't he think, now, the child belonged somewhere else from the style of her?'

Sally blushed with pleasure. 'I never thought of that,' she said.

'Ah, sure he wouldn't have been worried about Maggie Connolly's little wan, for all she's the wan age with Emily.' They both looked at Emily, who smiled shyly, aware that she was being discussed. Her glossy ringlets fell on the shoulders of her spotless white muslin frock, and her tiny button boots shone like glass.

'She's a pattern of class, so she is,' said Mrs Malloy but there was a sharp note in her voice as she went on, 'I seen young John going out to his work in the teems of rain the other night. The boots were dropping off his feet, God help him.'

Sally's face grew red but she said nothing, and Mrs Malloy continued, ' 'Tis a good thing young Alfie can wear the Duggans' cast offs, or sure, he'd be in the same state, and this little wan with Sunday boots, no less.'

'The lads don't begrudge Emily anything,' Sally muttered.

'All credit to them then,' Mrs Malloy said, 'but shame on ye, Sally, that takes advantage of their good nature. It's not good for the child, either. Your poor Mam, Lord ha' mercy on her, she'd never make fish of wan and fowl of the other.'

Sally seized Emily's hand and jerked her indoors, then she banged the door shut and stood in the middle of the kitchen, her breast heaving and tears of mortification filling her eyes.

'The old besom,' she muttered. 'The nosy old besom.' She went into the back kitchen and began to fling potatoes into the bowl for peeling. Emily followed her, throwing her arms round Sally's legs and putting her face against her skirt. Sally wiped her hands and bent over the child.

'Don't cry, my pet,' she said fondly. 'Come upstairs now and we'll change your clothes.' She felt calmer by the time she had taken off Emily's best clothes and dressed her in her everyday dress, but the child still seemed upset. Sally lifted her on to her knee.

'You mustn't cry when people shout at each other, love,' she said gently. 'They don't always mean it, you know.'

Emily looked thoughtful. 'What about Johnny Andrews and Maggie?' she said, referring to a drunken couple who lived in the corner house. 'And the "chip" girls, and –'

'Oh, Emily, you know I don't mean them!' Sally exclaimed. 'Come on down now, and play with your dolly. I've got work to do.'

As the afternoon wore on she began to regret flinging away from Mrs Malloy, and to wonder if the older woman had been right. Perhaps I do spend too much on Emily, and not enough on the lads, she thought. Mrs Malloy's remarks about her mother worried her particularly.

She remembered a neighbour saying to her mother, 'Which is your best child, Julie?' and her mother's reply: 'Each one means as much to me as the other. I wouldn't give one a raisin without I had enough for all, and that way there's no jealousy.'

She was bending to put away the ironing blanket when John came in. She cast a hurried glance at his boots before she straightened up.

His sock showed where the sole had parted from the upper, and the heels were worn right down.

'Oh, John, I didn't realise your boots were so bad!' she exclaimed. He lifted his foot.

'Yeh, they're done,' he said. 'But it doesn't marrer. I'm gettin' new ones termorrer.'

Sally drew in her breath. Mrs Malloy! The interfering old . . . she thought, but before she could speak John said proudly, 'I've saved one and threepence, and Da give me a shillun towards them, so I'll go to the market termorrer.'

'Da did?' Sally said. So Da had noticed the state of John's boots, too.

'You can have my new boots, John' Emily suddenly piped up.

John laughed. 'Ta, girl,' he said. 'But I don't think they'll fit me, thanks all the same.'

Sally escaped into the back kitchen and stood pressing her hands against her burning cheeks. Everybody seems to be rubbing it into me, she thought, even the baby. I've been a right fool, but why didn't Da say something?

After a few minutes she pulled herself together, and began to make a cup of tea for John, and cut some bread and dripping for him before he went to work. She was wondering how she could approach Mrs Malloy, but when John had gone, and Alfred had run out to see a fallen horse, there was a tap on the door, and her neighbour came in.

'Ye've been crying, girlie,' she said. 'Sure, I wouldn't upset yiz for the world, any one of yiz, but I had to speak out.'

'You were quite right, Mrs Mal,' Sally said. She stood with down-bent head, picking at a loose thread on the tablecloth. 'Our John's getting new boots, but no thanks to me. He saved up and Da put to it. Will you have a cup of tea, Mrs Mal?'

'I will indeed, girl, thank ye.' She sat down. 'I'm glad ye don't hould it against me, Sal, for opening me mouth, but yiz are like me own flesh and blood to me.'

'Maybe I do spoil you know who,' Sally said, jerking her head towards Emily, 'but she's so lovable.'

'Indeed and she is, God love her, but I'll just say one thing more, and then I'll close up me mouth. Are ye not trying to make her too grand for the life she'll have and the place she'll live? That would be no kindness at all, girlie.'

'I have plans,' Sally said stubbornly. 'I just want Emily to be ready, that's all.'

Mrs Malloy sighed. 'Ah, well, I'll say no more. Only remember, Sally, there's grand ladies that never know a happy day. Look at the ould Queen. Hasn't she a power of troubles with her children and one thing and another? And only the other side of that wall there's one that had money and class, and hasn't she supped sorrow, and her mother too?'

Sally was anxious to change the subject.

'Mrs Hart told me that her mother used to buy penny readings at Lewis's, and they used to take turn about to read them to each other,' she said.

Mrs Malloy leaned forward.

'Indeed, and does she often talk about her home to ye?' she asked eagerly. Sally shook her head. She admired and pitied Mrs Hart, and she was unwilling to discuss her with Mrs Malloy. She admired her for her clear voice, and her long, aristocratic hands, and she pitied her for her fragility and for the lines of suffering in her face. Most of all she pitied Mrs Hart for the days in every quarter when her door was firmly closed against the world.

'Not at home,' she would reply to every knock on the door, then drunken singing would be heard, followed later by loud lamentations and the crashing of furniture. After a few days Mrs Hart would reappear, white-faced and shaking, but no reference was ever made to the lost days.

Mr Hart was employed on the tugboats, so he came home only infrequently, but even when his days off coincided with the arrival of Mrs Hart's quarterly cheque her outbreak was only postponed until he went back to sea. Still Sally's admiration for Mrs Hart was undiminished, and she tried to teach Emily to imitate her speech and her manner of sitting and walking.

'Sit up straight like Mrs Hart, Emily,' she would say, or, 'Don't shout, love, speak quietly like Mrs Hart.'

When Mrs Malloy had left to cook a meal for her lodgers, and Sally's father came home, she was wondering how to broach the subject of John's boots when Emily solved the problem. She looked at Matthew's boots as he took them off and said suddenly, 'Johnny's boots broke and Sally cried.'

Matthew looked up at Sally, but she shook her head.

'Little pitchers, Da,' she said.

But when Emily had been put to bed he said, 'Now, Sally, what's this about our John's boots?'

'I didn't realise his boots were so bad, and I bought new boots for Emily,' Sally said. He said nothing, and she added resentfully, 'Mrs Malloy told me off about it.' He was still silent, puffing reflectively at his pipe, and finally Sally asked, 'Why didn't *you* say something to me, Da?'

Matthew took the pipe from his mouth. 'If yer'd spent the money on yerself I'd have spoke out quick enough, girl, but it was only a misjudgement like. Yer seen to the baby, but our John would 'a got his boots when ye could manage it.'

'Mrs Mal said I was making fish of one and fowl of the other,' Sally muttered.

'Don't fret yerself. Yer put yerself last, and do yer best for the lot of us, girl, and I'm suited.' He gave her his rare smile, and Sally sat back, her spirits lifting.

'You're good to us, too, Da,' she said. The next moment the door was flung open, and the moment of closeness had passed. Alfred stood there, grinning, his face covered in smuts.

'Yer should see the fire. Another cotton warehouse – it's great. Flames right up in the sky.'

'I hope the owners agree with yer, lad, or the insurance,' Matthew said drily, as he shook out his newspaper.

17

'Aren't yer comin, Da? Can I go back?' asked Alfie.

'Aye, go on, but don't get too close, and be back here in half an hour.' Alfie sped away, and Matthew shook his head.

'There's too many of these fires,' he said. 'That cotton steamer in the Hornby Dock last November, an' a warehouse fire in Bootle only a couple a' weeks after, and that big one in Regent Road in May.'

'It's just excitement to lads like Alfie,' Sally said.

'Everything's excitement to him,' Matthew said, but he spoke indulgently. Cheerful, happy go lucky Alfie never caused any friction, unlike John who often infuriated his father by repeating comments he heard in the shop, and arguing about them. Sally could sometimes divert them by a remark about Emily, but often she thought that it was their likeness to each other which caused the trouble, when neither of them would concede a point to the other. Mrs Malloy often commented on the likeness between John and herself and their father, and the difference in Alfie and Emily.

'Isn't it strange, now? Emily, God love her, with yer Mam's lovely brown eyes and black curls, and the same way with her that'd charm the birds off the trees. Young Alfie the same, and yerself and John now, the model of your Da. Tall and thin made, and hair the same colour though they're more reddish than you, and yer eyes maybe a darker blue than your Da's. All three of yiz though, that would worry over a pin, and the two young ones, God bless them, sure they wouldn't care if it snowed.'

'You always say I'm a worrier, Mrs Mal, but I don't think I am,' Sally said.

'Of course ye are, girl, but there, ye can't help the way God made yer. Still, God between us and all harm, Sally, isn't it grand now the way things is going so smooth for yiz?'

It was true that there was little for Sally to worry about at this time. By the summer of 1890 life was better for all the family. John had taken the examination which allowed him to leave school at thirteen years of age and was now working full-time in the grocer's, while Alfie had taken his place as messenger. Even though Matthew's wages had been reduced because of falling orders, there was enough money coming into the house for Sally's careful housekeeping to ensure comfort for all of them.

Sally worked hard to create a happy home, and cared deeply for her father, and her brothers, but an extra measure of her love and care was poured out on Emily. She tried to shield her from the harsh reality of life in the poverty stricken area in which they lived, and to prepare her for the higher standard of life which she was determined Emily would achieve.

So many children in nearby houses died young, that Sally's greatest fear was that Emily would be stricken by illness. The child was nearly five years old when tragedy struck, but it came from an unexpected quarter.

18

Chapter Four

One day in late July 1890 John came home from work, complaining of a sore throat and a headache. He was unable to eat his meal, and wanted only to go to bed. Sally put a hot brick in the bed because he seemed so cold, and made a lemon drink for him, but later he became so feverish that she went in alarm for Mrs Malloy. The older woman poulticed his chest and dosed him with blackcurrant and quinine, trying to hide her uneasiness from Sally, but he grew steadily worse. The following morning Alfred developed the same symptoms, and by nightfall both boys were so ill that Matthew went for a doctor.

The doctor was a plump young man with a full brown beard and a pompous manner, but he spoke kindly to Sally and Mrs Malloy after he had examined the boys.

'They are having excellent nursing,' he said. 'You are doing all that's possible to help them.'

To Matthew he was more forthright. 'I'm sorry, my man,' he said. 'I can ease the suffering of these boys, but I can give you little hope that they will recover.'

The medicine he prescribed gave the boys brief periods of respite from their fevered tossing, and delirious rambling, but they both grew weaker.

Matthew was despairing, but Sally and Mrs Malloy refused to accept the verdict and laboured day and night to relieve the boys with poultices and infusions of Friar's Balsam. On the seventh night John opened his eyes and smiled at Sally, as he drank from the glass she held for him.

Sally turned to Mrs Malloy and put her arms around her.

'Oh, Mrs Mal, thank God, thank God,' she exclaimed, but the older woman shook her head.

'Don't raise your hopes, now, girlie,' she said sorrowfully. 'Haven't I seen this many and many a time. 'Tis but the last flicker before the lamp goes out, child.'

Sally refused to believe it, but at two o'clock the following morning, John's life slipped quietly away. Four hours later Alfred died without regaining consciousness.

At first Sally was too exhausted to realise fully what had happened, and Matthew went about like a man stunned. Mrs Malloy was invaluable, taking charge of everything and steering Matthew through the funeral arrangements. Emily had stayed with Mrs Hart while the boys were ill, and on the day of the funeral they set out early in the morning for a picnic in Eastham Woods, so that the sad business would be concluded before the child was aware of it.

Aunt Hester and Uncle Walter came from Ormesdale for the funeral, and after it was over, and the neighbours had gone, they sat talking to Matthew while Sally went next door to collect Emily from Mrs Hart. She stayed for a time to talk, relieved to escape for a short time from the tragic atmosphere in her own house, which had been made worse that day by Hester's noisy and unrestrained displays of grief.

When she returned home with Emily, Hester clicked her tongue in disapproval.

'Nay, Sally, I thowt ye'd have getten a black dress for the child. Her two brothers gone, and nowt but a bit of black ribbon in her hair.'

Sally's face flushed and she drew Emily close to her. 'We don't need outward show, Aunt. Emmie's only a baby yet, and we'll explain things to her later,' she said angrily.

Hester tossed her head. 'Dearie me, I nowt but asked,' she said, then with a change of expression she leaned forward and patted Sally's knee.

'Nay, love, I'm none vexed. I know as you're wore out wi' everything. I've just been telling your da as he's not bein' fair to ye, and we've decided to tek Emily home wi' us.'

Sally's head jerked up.

'Emily's all right' she said. 'She doesn't need a holiday. She's better at home with us just now.'

'Nay, not a holiday, lass. To live wi' us. You don't want same thing to happen to her, as happened to the poor lads.'

'But it won't,' Sally cried. 'The doctor said she was the healthiest child in the neighbourhood.'

Hester laughed bitterly. 'Aye mebbe, but that's not saying owt, is it?' She smoothed her black silk dress over her ample stomach.

'I've allus said as children didn't stand a chance round here, and I've been proved right. If your Da had listened to me, John and Alfred would be alive this minute.'

'That's not fair,' Sally said. 'It wasn't his fault –' She burst into angry tears.

'Now, now, Sally,' Matthew said. An air of defeat and sadness hung about him as he slumped in his chair like an old man.

'Yer aunt's right,' he said in a low voice. 'If I'd of let John go he'd be a healthy farmhand now, and he wouldn't have fetched the illness to Alfie neither. I've learned me lesson, girl.'

'But Emmie's safe here, Da. Oh, don't let her go! What would we do without her?' She snatched Emily into her arms, and the child looked in dismay at Sally's flushed face and tear-filled eyes. She patted Sally's cheek.

'Don't cry, Sal,' she said. 'Emily will make it better.' At this Sally's tears burst out afresh, and Emily began to sob noisily in fright. The jet ornaments on Hester's bonnet tinkled as she tossed her head angrily, then smoothed her dress with short, sharp movements.

'Eh, dear, what a to-do. We're not tekkin' child to China, tha' knows, or t' workhouse,' she said. 'She's coming to a good home, and tha' should be reet pleased for her.'

Sally jumped to her feet.

'You planned this, didn't you?' she said. 'You haven't just thought of it. And all fixed up in a few minutes while I was out of the way.'

Two bright red spots appeared in Hester's cheeks, and she thrust her head forward.

'Watch tha' tongue,' she began furiously, but Walter cleared his throat warningly, and Hester resumed her bland expression.

'You're upset, lass, but old heads are wise heads, think on. It's up to tha Da, anyroad.'

Matthew was staring into the fire like a man in a dream, and Sally dropped to her knees beside him, hugging Emily to her. She shook his arm.

'Look at her, Da. Look at our Emmie. Can you let her go to strangers, away from us – now of all times?'

'I must, girl,' he said. 'For her sake and yours.'

'I've towd him,' Hester broke in. 'He's got to study you and all. You'll be wantin' to get wed, and lads 'll not want to be saddled wi' a young 'un.'

'I'm not getting married,' Sally said fiercely. 'I'm staying here.'

'Eh, don't talk daft, lass. I've heard that before, and they were allus fust to goo. Well, tha'd best put child's clothes together. We mun get home and get her t'bed. Walter, goo and get trap round.'

Walter, thin and grey-haired, rose obediently to his feet, but before leaving the room, he spoke to Sally for the first time.

'Sithee, it's all fo' t'best, lass,' he said gently. 'Us'll mek little lass happy, and her'll like th' animals and poultry, an' us'll fetch her to see thee now and agin.'

'Get the pony, do, Walter,' Hester said sharply. 'Eh, well, if you won't shape to get child's clothes, *I* mun.' She bustled up the narrow stairway to the bedroom, and a few moments later she came down, with the straw bassinet from the corner of the bedroom filled with Emily's clothes.

'Well, tha's kept her nice, I must say. These little things is made and laundered a treat. Coom here, Emily love, let Auntie tie tha bonnet.'

Walter had come to stand silently by the door and she handed the bassinet to him, then turned to Matthew.

'Well, we're off. Look after thyself, Matt. Tha's doin' reet thing, lad. Kiss tha' da, Emily.'

The child held up her face to Matthew, looking at him with large, wondering eyes. He kissed her and held her close for a moment.

'God bless you, my little pet,' he said, then turned her back to Hester and covered his face with his hands. Sally had sunk back in her chair, stunned by the suddenness of the blow. Hester approached her, holding Emily by the hand.

'Say goodbye to tha sister, Emily,' she said. Sally held out her arms like someone in a trance, and Emily clung to her.

'Pony's waitin',' said Walter.

'Aye, coom along now, Emily, do,' said Hester, as the sisters clung together speechlessly.

Sally's wide eyes gazed in frantic appeal at her father. 'Da, Da,' she gasped, but he turned away his face.

'Now, now, coom wi' Auntie and see th' chucky hens,' Hester said, pulling Emily from Sally's arms.

'Sally come too,' Emily said tearfully, but Walter came foward and took her in his arms.

'Nay, lass, Sally has to cook tha' da's tea. Coom now and hold t' reins wi' me.'

The next moment they were gone, and Matthew and Sally were left staring at each other over the gulf which had opened between them. When Mrs Malloy burst in a few moments later, Matthew was huddled in his chair like an old man, staring at the fire, and Sally was wandering about like a lost soul.

'So she's taken the child, bad luck to her!' Mrs Malloy exclaimed. 'Without so much as a goodbye to me that helped to rear her. God knows, she was as dear to me as me own flesh an' blood, the darlin'.' She lifted her apron to wipe the tears which poured down her cheeks, and Matthew looked at her with a haggard face.

'I had to,' he muttered. 'Yer didn't tell me there were three children dead in the street, and dozens more round about.'

'Ah, the quare one'd be quick to tell ye,' Mrs Malloy said bitterly. 'True for her, there were three children dead, and more in the courts below, and Maggie Connolly's little wan died last night, but wasn't she alwis sickly? Emily would have taken no harm. Didn't Sally keep her in a glass case itself?'

The torrent of words poured over Matthew, but he turned away his head.

'Leave me be, woman,' he growled.

'Come away with me now, girlie,' said Mrs Malloy to Sally, alarmed by her white face and staring eyes. She took Sally's unresisting arm and drew her in to her own house.

'Bad luck to the bloody ould faggot,' she muttered, 'that'd take advantage of people's troubles.'

She placed Sally in an armchair, and quickly stirred up the fire.

'I'll have a cup of tea for ye in a minute, girl. It's all been too much for ye, this on top of everything else.'

Sally sat unmoving, as Mrs Malloy made the tea and added something from a black bottle to the cup, but she was unable to grip it. Even when Mrs Malloy held the cup to her lips, her teeth chattered so much that she was unable to drink from it. The older woman soon realised that a merciful numbness had overtaken Sally, and putting the cup down, she helped the girl back to her own house and into bed. She stayed until Sally had fallen into an exhausted sleep, then came downstairs. She was still too angry with Matthew to spare him more than a glance and, sunk in misery, he seemed oblivious to all that was happening.

During the following weeks Matthew and Sally scarcely spoke to each other. Matthew left the meals prepared by Sally almost untouched. He came in from work each night and sat huddled in his chair, lost in his own world of misery, as Sally was lost in hers.

She went about with a face like stone during the day, clamping down on all thought of Emily and cleaning the house ferociously, but at night, alone in the bed she had shared with the child, she let her grief and misery break through. Her sorrow at the death of the boys was swallowed up in her greater grief at the loss of Emily.

22

Every night she lay in bed sobbing and biting at the pillow in an agony of longing for the child. She tossed and turned, wondering whether Emily was fretting, and whether Hester would be kind to her and understand her little ways. What if Emily was afraid of the animals and the chickens? Would they laugh at her fears and force her to go near them? Would she be afraid of the dark if she had to sleep alone?

Each morning she came downstairs, dry-eyed but exhausted, seeming to grow thinner and paler every day. In that area, almost every one of the neighbours had known bereavement and they did what they could to comfort her, with gifts from their small store. A bit of cowheel in a basin, an apple, and once some wild flowers which a child had gathered.

'She's fretting herself to death about them lads,' they said. 'When she's 'ad as much trouble as what we've 'ad, she won't take it so much to 'eart.'

Only Mrs Malloy suspected the truth. She grieved for her at the loss of all the children, but she realised although Sally would have grieved deeply for John and Alfred if Emily had still been with her, her sorrow for the boys had been swallowed up in her greater grief for Emily. Mrs Malloy realised, too, how bitterly Matthew was reproaching himself for not letting John and Emily go to the farm after their mother's death. Her own anger with Matthew had soon vanished, but she worried about the situation between Sally and her father.

When several weeks had passed and there was no sign of any improvement, she spoke to Sally one morning.

'What are ye going to do about yer poor da, Sally? Sure he's dwindlin' away, God help him. That heavy work, and him hardly ating a bite.'

'What can *I* do?' Sally asked sullenly, twisting the strings of her apron. 'He won't eat what I cook for him, and anyhow I'm miserable myself.'

'Aye, but it's Emmy yer grieving for, not the poor lads,' Mrs Malloy said shrewdly. 'D'ye not realise why it's worse for yer da? When yer after losing someone, sure the worst part is thinking of what ye've done wrong with them, and yer da's not thinking of a cross word, or a trifle of neglect. He's blaming himself for their deaths, and it's wearing him away, God help him. Isn't it twice as hard for him too, without yer mam beside him to comfort him?'

Sally was silent, feeling all the force of Mrs Malloy's argument. How often had she bitterly regretted that she had let John go to work on that first day, and disregarded Alfred at first because she was worried about John? After a moment she said slowly, 'Da shouldn't have sent Emily away though, Mrs Mal. She'd be a comfort to both of us now.'

'Ah, poor Matt. He always put his children first. Isn't it a pity now, the one he has left doesn't give tuppence for him?'

Sally's eyes opened wide with shock.

'Oh, I do, Mrs Mal, but I think he shouldn't have sent Emily away without even asking me how I felt.'

Mrs Malloy nodded her head.

'Ah, now, Sally, ye shouldn't be blaming him for that. Ye know yerself he was nearly out of his mind between losing the lads and thinking he was to blame for not letting John go away, and yer aunt, the crafty ould faggot, played on that to get her own way, God stiffen her. Yer da was trying to do what was best for yiz.'

Sally was suddenly shaken by sobs. She covered her face with her apron and cried bitterly.

'There, there now, childie.' Mrs Malloy said. 'Come into the house.'

She drew Sally into her house, and swung the black kettle over the fire.

'We'll have a cup of tea, and I'll tell ye what I was thinking.' She poured out the tea, and when Sally seemed more composed, sat down beside her.

'Now, girlie,' she said. 'I was talking to Jinny Philbin the other day, that's on the tripe stall in the Market, and she was telling me that the girl on the sweet stall is leaving. Wouldn't that be a grand job for ye now, if ye could get it? I'm sure Jinny would speak for ye.'

'Would she, Mrs Mal? I've been thinking I should get a job now there's not so much to do –' Her lip trembled and she took a gulp of her tea.

'I'll see Jinny then,' Mrs Malloy said, well content with the result of her words. She felt that a new interest would help Sally to recover more quickly from her own loss, and make her better able to help her father in his.

Sally went to splash her face with cold water, then she went to the shops and bought bacon and cabbage for her father's tea. She was bending over the fire when he came in. When she looked round, she saw with a stab of fear how old and haggard he looked.

'I got bacon and cabbage for your tea, Da,' she said. 'I got a newspaper too. I know you like to read the paper.'

'Aye, I did, girl,' Matthew said, hanging his cap behind the door. 'But I've no heart for it lately, and that's the truth.'

'Sit in, Da,' Sally urged, hoping that the savoury smell of the food would tempt him to eat. Matthew gave the ghost of a smile.

'Yer a good girl, Sally,' he said. His eyes strayed to the newspaper by his plate, and Sally toyed with her food, wondering whether to tell him about the job before he became engrossed in the newspaper, or whether to risk asking him something which had been on her mind since she had spoken to Mrs Malloy. She plucked up her courage.

'Da,' she began. 'I've been thinking. Aunt Hester rushed you into parting with our Emily, didn't she? D' you think we could get her back?'

Matthew's expression hardened and he pushed away his plate.

'No one forced me to send the child away. It was me own doin'. I'll decide what's best, Sally. I took notice of yer once, and look what happened.'

'But, Da, –' began Sally. Matthew turned away from the table and picked up his paper.

'That's enough,' he said. 'I don't want to hear another word.'

Sally's eyes filled with tears, and she clashed the dishes angrily as

24

she cleared away and washed up. I just don't count, she thought. It doesn't matter what I think or want. For two pins I'd get a living in job and let him get on without me . . . but an image of her mother rose in her mind, and she knew that she would never walk out on her father.

The following morning Mrs Malloy came in before eight o'clock.

'I'm just after seeing Jinny Philbin, Sally,' she said. 'She says they're getting mad busy in the Market, and Christmas only a coupl'a weeks away. If ye go along this morning she'll put in the good word for ye.'

'Oh, thanks, Mrs Mal. I'll tidy myself up and go right away,' Sally said in a subdued voice. 'I didn't realise that Christmas was so near.'

'What did yer da say about the job?'

'I didn't mention it, Mrs Mal. I asked him about getting Emily back, and he jumped down my throat. I'd made him a tea he likes, too, and got a paper for him, but he left the meal and just read the paper all night.'

'It must be grand now, to be able to read,' Mrs Malloy said diplomatically. 'I'll leave ye to get ready.' She lifted the latch and paused.

'I didn't know ye had that in mind about Emily, child. Ye'll face things better now, knowing as she's gone for good. Sure, she'll be having a grand time there, and yer uncle and aunt just mats beneath her feet, so don't be frettin' yerself, girlie.'

She went out, and Sally swiftly brushed and braided her hair, then put on a clean bodice, and took her mother's shawl from the tin trunk in the corner of the bedroom. Before leaving she peered into the spotted mirror. Her blue eyes stared back, looking unnaturally large in her thin white face. She pinched her cheeks, and bit her lips to give them some colour, hoping that the market woman would not consider her too delicate for the job.

Jinny Philbin was looking out for her, and took her to the proprietor of the sweet stall.

'This is Sally Palin, wor' I told yer about, Mrs Gregson,' she said. The woman's glance swept swiftly over Sally. She was a stout woman, with heavy lidded eyes and a deceptively lethargic manner. She seemed to be satisfied with her scrutiny.

'Have you worked with sweets before?' she asked.

'No, M'm, I've never worked anywhere before,' Sally said nervously. 'I keep house for my father.'

'Aye, so Jinny told me. Well, I'll give you a trial. Be here at half past seven tomorrow, and bring a clean apron. 4/6 a week to start.' She turned away to a customer.

'Thank you, thank you,' stammered Sally, amazed at the swiftness of the transaction. She stopped at the tripe stall to tell Jinny that she was to start work, and to thank her.

'She's a bi'rova slave driver, but she's orl right,' Jinny said. 'See yer termorrer.'

Chapter Five

Mrs Malloy was pleased to hear of Sally's success, and promised to help by keeping the fire in and looking after the meals Sally planned to leave cooking in the oven.

Later Sally went to see Mrs Hart. Since the death of the boys, and Emily's departure, the readings had been discontinued. Sally did the work in silence, too sunk in misery to bother with conversation.

Mrs Hart sat quietly, except to say one day, 'It will pass, Sally. The sharp edge of sorrow will become dull, and perhaps that is the greatest tragedy of all.'

Sally remembered what Mrs Malloy had told her, that Mrs Hart's only child, a delicate little girl, had lost her precarious hold on life at nine months old.

Now she told Mrs Hart about her new job, and suggested that she should ask a neighbour's child to do the scrubbing.

'Lily Dolan is a good girl, Mrs Hart,' she said. 'She's only twelve but she does most of the work in the Dolans' house since Mary and Ada have gone into service. She looks after the young ones, too, because Mrs Dolan is drunk half the time.' She stopped, appalled by her gaffe, but Mrs Hart smiled sadly.

'She sounds eminently suitable, Sally, if her mother will allow her to do it. I'll pay her, of course.'

She unpinned the watch that she wore, and held it out to Sally.

'I'd like you to have this, Sally. I'm so grateful for all you have done for me, and it would make me happy if you would accept it.'

'Oh, I couldn't,' Sally exclaimed. 'It's your own watch that you've always had, Mrs Hart.'

'Please, Sally. Please take it.' She put the watch into Sally's hand. 'I've always regretted that I was never able to tell your dear mother how much her kindness meant to me. She seemed to be recovering and I was – indisposed when her illness suddenly became fatal. She made life bearable for me, Sally.' She took Sally's hand and held it, looking into the fire as though seeing pictures there.

'I was so distressed when I came here. My mother – but no matter. I'd always been considered delicate and I had no stamina. Tom worried that the housework would be beyond me, and he went to ask your mother to help. He offered her some small sum, and she refused it, so when she came to help I apologized for having offended her.

'I've never forgotten her words, Sally. She looked at me with those lovely brown eyes and said so kindly, "I'm not offended, but there's no need for payment between neighbours. We all help each other any way we can, and if I can help you now, maybe you'll be able to help someone else one day, and that's how it goes." '

Mrs Hart sighed, pressing Sally's hand between her own. 'I can't tell you what her friendship meant to me, Sally, and then, child though you were, you took her place. You helped me not only with the housework, but in so many other ways, and I've been powerless to help you in your grief, except to pray for you. Please take the watch. Let me at least show that I appreciate kindness.'

Tears were running down Sally's face, but she took the watch and carefully pinned it to her blouse.

'Thank you,' she said. Then wiping her eyes, she took a deep breath.

'What Mam said, Mrs Hart. About passing help on. You've helped us. I always – Mam told me to take you as a model, and I told Emily the same. You showed us how to speak and behave, and the readings –' She stopped, unable to say any more.

Tears filled Mrs Hart's eyes, and she said in a low voice, 'Oh, Sally my dear, never as a model, but if I helped at all, I'm so glad.'

Later when Matthew came home, he seemed to be in a black mood, and Sally waited until she had served their meal before she told him about her job. He showed little interest, staring ahead as he chewed his food.

'Do you like the tripe and onions, Da?' Sally asked, determined to gain his attention. He glanced down at his plate and nodded indifferently, as though unaware of what he had been eating. She began to tell him about Mrs Hart's gift, but he paid no attention until she said: 'Mrs Hart said Mam was very kind to her. She said she apologized to Mam for offering her money, and Mam said she helped her as a neighbour, and perhaps Mrs Hart could help someone else sometime.'

'Aye, that was Julie,' Matthew said, with a groan, pushing his plate away.

'Never mind, Da,' Sally said sympathetically. 'Mrs Malloy said the other day that at least Mam was spared knowing about the lads.'

'What does she know about it?' Matthew snarled. 'It's easy said. I wouldn't have lost me lads if Mam'd been here to look after them.' He dropped his face into his hands. 'Me wife and then me lads,' he groaned.

Sally could scarcely speak for anger.

'So you blame me?' she said furiously. 'Mam couldn't have done more to save them than I did! And you've got two daughters, too, but they don't count. You couldn't wait to push Emily out of the house. I suppose you wish I'd died instead of the lads.'

Matthew's hand shot out and struck Sally on the side of the head, jerking her back in her chair.

'Yer bloody impident bitch!' he said. Then he jumped to his feet and leaned his arm on the mantelpiece and his head on his arm.

'Oh, Julie girl,' Sally heard him moan, as she wrenched open the door at the foot of the stairs and fled up to her bedroom.

'I hate him, I hate him,' she cried, flinging herself upon the bed and sobbing wildly. 'All I've done, and now this.' She could never remember her father striking her before.

I'm getting out of this, she thought. He wishes I was dead, so I'll *be* dead to him, and see how he likes it. I've suffered more than him, but I'm not allowed to have moods. I'm supposed just to put up with his. I'll never forgive him, never.

Presently her sobs grew quieter and she sat up. Her head ached, partly because of the blow, and partly because of her tears, and she went to the rickety washstand to pour some water into the bowl and wash her face.

The house was quiet. She vaguely recalled hearing her father's step on the stairs, but she had no idea how long she had been lying on the bed.

She opened the tiny window and sat by it, trying to plan. The night was cold and frost glittered on the nearby roofs, under the frosty blue light of the moon. Farm carts were beginning to rattle over the cobbled streets, on their way to market, and Sally thought of Ormesdale. Should she go there, and ask if she could work on the farm, or help Aunt Hester in the house? Her commonsense told her that she would not be welcome, even if she could bring herself to ask them for a favour, and then what of Jinny Philbin? It would be unfair if she failed to turn up, after Jinny speaking for her, but where could she live on 4/6d a week? Perhaps she could go into service, but at her age she would probably need references.

Round and round in her head the arguments raged. If only she was a boy, and could take the 'Pier Head Jump', and go to sea.

Finally she lay down again, and sleep overcame her. The sound of her father moving about downstairs woke her. The next moment there was a step on the stairs, and he came into the room with a cup of tea.

' 'Ere, drink this, girl,' he said gruffly. 'I'm sorry I hit yer last night. The black dog was on me.'

Tears spurted from Sally's eyes. 'Oh, Da,' she said. 'I'm sorry too.'

Her father stood, smiling awkwardly for a moment, then he nodded and went downstairs.

Sally sipped her tea, wishing that she could have been more demonstrative. Emily or Alfie, she thought, would have flung their arms around him, but she consoled herself with the realization that she and her father were alike, and understood each other. In a strange way, she felt, the incident had drawn them closer together.

The following morning she set off for the Market with a light heart, thankful that there was no need for a drastic change in her life. She accepted that her father was sorry that he had hurt her, and she was young enough to be excited by the prospect of meeting new people in different surroundings.

The stall was in a popular position, so that there were many customers, and any waverers were encouraged by Mrs Gregson's calls of: 'Come on, now. Cinnamon balls a penny a quarter, humbugs three ha'pence, last you all day.'

Sally was kept busy, and although her legs ached the time passed quickly, but just after twelve o'clock she suddenly felt exhausted. Mrs Gregson's heavy lidded eyes missed little, and she pulled out some money from the fishwives' pocket she wore beneath her apron.

'Here, Sally,' she said. 'Go and get yourself a pasty and a cup of tea.' She pointed to a wooden box wedged in the corner behind the stall.

'Sit there to have them, and when you're finished, I'll have mine.' Thankfully Sally hurried over to the tea stall.

'Don't let her work you to death, love,' the man who served her advised.

'She's very good. She's letting me have my dinner first,' Sally said defensively. The man was small and fat, with a drooping moustache, and his eyes twinkled as he leaned over the counter and handed Sally a mug of tea.

'Watch yerself, girl,' he said. 'She's like that ould feller Shylock, him that wanted a pound of flesh.' He winked. 'Yer 'aven't gorrit ter spare.'

Sally was smiling as she carried her tea back to the stall, and Mrs Gregson looked at her sharply.

'What's he been saying to you?' she asked, and then before Sally could reply, she raised her voice to carry to the tea stall.

'I hope you don't come to no harm with that tea, Sally. He's laid out everyone in the market with it before now.'

'Don't you believe it,' the man shouted back jovially, 'It was your brandy balls done that, missis.'

There were shouts of laughter from the other stallholders, and from the customers who were milling about, and Sally smiled to herself as she munched her pasty and drank the strong, sweet tea. I'm going to like it here, she thought happily. Already the sorrows which had threatened to overwhelm her at home, seemed smaller and more manageable.

At the end of the day Mrs Gregson spoke approvingly to Sally as they cleared up the stall.

'You made a good shape today,' she said. 'I seen you were careful with the change too. Were you good at arithmetic at school?'

Sally blushed with pleasure.

'Yes, I was,' she admitted. 'I've handled the money at home too, since my mother died.'

'Well, if you keep on like today you'll suit me,' said Mrs Gregson. 'Don't be late in the morning.'

Sally was too excited to think of her aching feet as she walked home, but she was glad to open the house door, and to find the fire alight, and the kitchen filled with the savoury smell of the hotpot in the oven. Mrs Malloy had banked down the fire with slack, so Sally poked it into a blaze and swung the kettle over it, before sitting down in her father's chair and resting her feet on a stool. Suddenly she realised how tired she was, but after making a cup of tea and resting for a few minutes, she went upstairs to make the beds and empty the slops. I'll have to do this before I leave for work in future, she thought. I'd be disgraced if something happened like Da being brought home from work ill, and no beds made.

Matthew looked depressed and weary when he came in from work, but he made an effort to seem cheerful as he asked Sally about her job.

Her impressions of the day were too chaotic for her to describe it well, but she told him about the man on the tea stall, and Mrs Gregson saying that she had done well.

'So she buys yer dinner then?' he said. 'Yer seem to have fallen on yer feet there, girl.' Sally agreed, but as soon as the meal was finished, Matthew turned his chair towards the fire, and sat smoking, and reading his paper.

He seemed to have forgotten her presence, but Sally was satisfied that he had shown some interest in her affairs, no matter how little. She was sadly aware that the old loving relationship between them had gone forever, but at least they were closer than they had been since Emily's departure.

She did the necessary chores as quickly as possible, as she was anxious to go to bed as soon as she had been in to thank Mrs Malloy, but there was a tap at the door and the old woman came in.

'I was just going in to thank you, Mrs Mal,' Sally exclaimed.

'Aye, well, I slipped in here to see how ye got on, for those Duggan lads are either side of the fire like a pair of Marley horses. Mind ye, they're grand lads. Twice a week they're at the Devotions and then out for a pint, and four nights a week at the Irish Club, so they're usually no trouble to me, God love them. How did it go, Sal?'

'Oh, it was splendid, Mrs Mal. It was so exciting, all the different people, and the jokes. Mrs Gregson said I'd done well.'

'Well, now, isn't that grand, girlie. "Well begun is half done", as they say. The money side would come aisy to ye, the way ye've been handlin' the house money these years.'

'Thanks for doing the dinner and the fire. It was lovely to come in and find it ready.'

'Ah, sure, it was only the fire. Ye had the hotpot ready to put in the oven. What will ye do tomorrow?'

'I've boiled a shank, and I'm making pea soup. Do you mind watching it for me tomorrow, Mrs Mal?'

'Not at all,' She turned to Matthew.

'Hasn't she the fine head for planning, Matthew? Sure, she should be running the army.'

'She couldn't do worse than the ones they have now, God knows,' said Matthew. 'Trouble is, they get the job because they're someone's son or nephew. They're planted because of their families, even if they're half witted.'

'Ah, there's plenty of them among the gentry. When I was a girl in service the village was full of cripples and idiots, and the housekeeper said it was because they were all married to cousins and the like, but they had their share in the Big House for the self same reason. The eldest lad was away somewhere. With a servant, they said, but he was more a class of keeper, and the last little one was born blind and helpless. It was a mercy when God took her.' She glanced at Sally who was slumped wearily against the table.

'Ah, Sally girl, yer eyes are closing on ye, and me nattering. Away to bed now, child. I'll finish the soup.'

Sally was glad to obey, and fell asleep as soon as she lay down in

31

bed. She slept soundly and woke refreshed, and this she found was the pattern of her nights as time went on.

Although Emily was never far from her thoughts, and she still grieved for the boys, the hard work and the changing scene in the market, combined with her youthful resilience, meant that she never again experienced the nights of misery and frenzied longing which she had previously known.

Chapter Six

As Christmas approached the stall became even more busy, and although Sally's legs had become accustomed to the long hours of standing, she was very tired by the time she returned home, and very glad of Mrs Malloy's help.

She offered her first week's wages to her father, but he told her brusquely to use them as she wished. With some of the money she bought and dressed a doll for Emily, and the following week bought wool to make socks for her father, and neck shawls for Mrs Hart and Mrs Malloy, as Christmas presents.

As she walked wearily up the street a few days before Christmas, Mrs Malloy was standing by her open front door. She drew Sally into her house.

'Yer Da has had his meal, girlie,' she said. She pointed dramatically to the table which was covered with boxes and packages.

'Ye've had a visitor, yer Uncle Walter. He left all this with me as yiz were out, but I haven't said a word to yer Da yet.'

'Uncle Walter! Was Emily with him?' Sally asked eagerly. Mrs Malloy shook her head.

'No, child. I asked about her, but sure it was like getting blood from a stone to get any news.'

'He didn't say how she liked the doll then?'

'No, just left down the parcels and away with him.' They turned to the table and began to open the packages. There was a straw-filled box containing a parcel of sausages, and two dozen eggs, and a muslin-wrapped leg of pork.

'Will ye look at the bloom on them eggs?' Mrs Malloy exclaimed. 'They're never above a day old.' Sally was opening the other packages. They contained a bottle of rum and a box of crystallized fruits, but Sally seized on a kettle holder worked by Emily in bright wool, with a note in uneven letters pinned to it. *'To Sally, with love from Emily'*.

'Look at this, Mrs Mal. Isn't she clever, and not five yet?'

'She is indeed, God love her. This is fine and generous of yer aunt, Sally.'

Sally's face darkened, and she pushed the parcels away. 'I want nothing from her, only this from Emily. She can't buy me off like that.'

'Sally, girl,' exclaimed Mrs Malloy. 'I expected that class of talk from your father with the moods he has, but I thought ye'd more sense. Yer aunt's thankful to ye, and trying to show it, that's all.'

'Thankful for Emily. Well, she's worth more than this to me. There's *nothing* they could give to make up for stealing Emily from us.' Mrs Malloy shook her head, then changed her ground as she looked at Sally's angry face.

'Now I think the child will be the reason for all this. Wasn't she always wanting to share what she had, and it shows she has the whip hand over those two.'

'I don't think that's the reason, Mrs Mal. Da won't have any truck with it, I know.'

'I'll come in with ye now while ye tell him. It's maybe the best time, when he's just had his meal.'

'He won't have it, Mrs Mal.'

'We'll see. Doesn't he know as well as meself that good food's not easy come by, and yer aunt took the trouble to teach the child to make the kettle holder and write the note.'

Sally was silent as they went in to the Palin house, but she kept the kettle holder in her hand. Matthew raised his head from his newspaper when they went in.

'That was tasty, ta, Mrs Mal,' he said.

Mrs Malloy nudged Sally. 'I'm just telling Sally, Matt, Walter came today, an' he came to me with your house being empty.'

'Look, Da,' Sally said, 'he brought this kettle holder from Emily. Hasn't she made it well?'

Matthew leaned forward to look at it. 'Aye, and she'd get no help from Hester. Yer mam was clever with her needle, but Hester – she used to say she could do anything with a needle bar sew with it.'

Mrs Malloy broke in swiftly, 'The child must have them under her thumb entirely, Matt. She wanted stuff sent to you and Sally, and didn't the little feller bring a box of pork and stuff. It seems she has only to give her orders.'

Matthew's brows drew together.

'What d'yer mean, pork and stuff? We want no charity.'

'Oh, a bottle of rum and some food for Sally. I'll bring them in when she's had her tea, and the table's cleared. I laughed to meself. The poor little feller, it isn't enough he's bossed be Hester, he has the child giving him his orders now.'

Matthew smiled doubtfully. 'I can't see them taking orders from her, the age of her,' he said. 'I don't know what the game is.'

'Wasn't she always wanting to share,' Mrs Malloy demanded, deliberately misunderstanding him. 'I gave her a sugar butty once, and she only a baby, and she broke half off for me.' She turned to Sally. 'You're nearly too tired to eat, child, but try to get it down. Ye need to keep up your strength. Ye've busier days yet to come.'

No more was said about the food, but later when Sally went in to Mrs Malloy she protested about the way she had twisted the truth.

'You only said to me that Emily might have suggested the presents, but the way you told Da, he thinks Uncle Walter told you that,' she said.

'Aye, I'm a wicked woman,' Mrs Malloy said, her eyes twinkling. 'Never mind, child, I'll tell it in Confession.'

Sally still had reservations about the gifts. She was delighted with the kettle holder, which she hung proudly above the fireplace, continuing to use the old one, but she took the crystallized fruit to Mrs Hart. The eggs and sausages she divided between herself and Mrs Malloy, but she was determined that she would eat none of them herself.

The following night she fried eggs and sausages for her father's tea, not saying that they came from Ormesdale, but she ate only fried bread herself. The bitterness she felt towards her aunt seemed to be increased rather than diminished by the gifts, although she knew that she was being unfair.

After some argument, Mrs Malloy agreed to have the leg of pork, but only if Sally and Matthew would come to her for their Christmas dinner. She pointed out to Matthew how exhausted Sally was by her long hours of work, and although reluctant, he had finally agreed. Sally was grateful for the suggestion. She had been dreading Christmas Day, with only herself and her father instead of the happy family of the previous years.

During the last few days before Christmas, the atmosphere in the Market grew more and more hilarious, and in spite of her weariness, Sally enjoyed the long hours on the sweet stall. On Christmas Eve the noise was deafening, as the men on the butchers' stalls began to auction off the remaining meat and poultry, with much good-humoured repartee between the stallholders and the crowds of customers. The cries of 'Sage er mint er parsley' from the 'Mary Ellens' by the door grew louder in competition.

The sweet stall was crowded with young men buying sweets for their girl friends, and mothers with hoarded pennies choosing sweets as a Christmas treat for their children. Mrs Gregson, Sally and Agnes, the girl who worked on the stall on Saturday nights, were kept frantically busy.

It was very late when Agnes and Sally left, and walked along to where their ways parted. Both were drunk with fatigue, but Agnes was too happy to care as she clutched the bag of sweets given to her by Mrs Gregson, and a parcel of beef and sausages, and some fruit, given to her by other stallholders.

She had also been given two shillings and sixpence, instead of the shilling she had expected, and Sally felt a vicarious pleasure at the happiness of the younger girl.

'Me mam'll be made up,' Agnes said. 'She managed to get some pork pieces for our Christmas dinner, but wait till she sees all this.' Sally knew that Agnes's mother was a widow with several children younger than Agnes, and she could imagine the relief that the extra food would bring.

The happy feeling carried her home, but once indoors she almost collapsed into a chair. Her father placed a stool so that she could rest her swollen legs, and made her a cup of tea, but she was falling asleep as she tried to drink it. He took it gently from her hand.

'Never mind the tea, Sally,' he said. 'Bed's the only place for yer. God knows you've earned yer money this week.' He helped her to her feet, and she staggered upstairs, throwing off her clothes, and falling into the blessed haven of her bed.

On Christmas morning she woke to the sound of church bells and the smell of frying bacon. A clock struck, and she lay and counted the strokes. Nine. She jumped out of bed and quickly washed and dressed in her Sunday dress, then tied a clean white apron around her waist and braided and pinned her hair in a neat coil at the back of her head. Her father looked up approvingly when she ran downstairs.

'That's better, he said. 'Yer looked as if ye'd had the stuffing knocked out of yer altogether last night. Good job yer've got two days to get over it.'

'I was just tired, Da,' Sally said. She went to him, and kissed him shyly.

'Happy Christmas, Da,' she said.

'Happy Christmas, girl,' he said gruffly. He had laid the table and put the bacon to fry, but Sally took over the cooking. She was chattering about Agnes's spoils when suddenly her father interrupted her.

'Listen, Sally, I'm not going in next door. You go in and bring me a plate of dinner if yer like, but I'll eat it here.'

'Oh, Da,' Sally said in dismay. 'Mrs Mal's gone to a lot of trouble. She'll be hurt.'

He shook his head impatiently. 'I can't sit there talking. I've too much on me mind. Troubles lie light on yer when yer young, but I can't ferget so easy.'

Sally's face was flushed, and her throat was tight with tears, but she swallowed and lifted her head.

'I haven't forgotten Mam and the lads, and Emily, Da,' she said quietly. 'I've dreaded Christmas but I've tried to put a good face on it for your sake, and I think you should do the same for me.'

Matthew's mouth opened in amazement and he half rose from his chair, then sank back again. He picked up the poker and poked furiously at the fire for a moment, then he turned and looked at Sally, standing defiantly by the table.

'Well, ye're very ready with yer tongue these days, I'll say that for yer, girl,' he said. 'Still, I'm a fair man. I've always tried to be a just father to ye, and maybe you've spoken the truth.'

She bent her head and smoothed the tablecloth.

'I know, Da,' she said quietly. 'I know it's hard for you, but Mrs Mal's made up because she thinks she's found a way to get us through the day. I wouldn't like to throw it back in her face.'

'Aye. She's a good-hearted woman, right enough,' Matthew agreed. He pursed his lips, and glanced sideways at Sally. 'Although sometimes I think she'd make a good boss ganger.' They laughed together, and Matthew shrugged his shoulders.

'I suppose I'd better go then,' he said.

After breakfast they went by tram to the cemetery, and Sally laid a posy of flowers on the plot where her mother and brothers were buried. She slipped her hand through her father's arm and wiped her eyes.

'Sometimes I can't believe it, Da,' she said. 'It just seems like a bad dream.'

'It's real, right enough, Sal,' he said heavily. They stood in silence for a few moments, then turned to go. Near the gate of the cemetery they passed a group of children sitting on a flat gravestone, and Sally looked at them pityingly. There was a small boy in a sailor suit, and two girls of about ten and twelve years of age bending anxiously over a third girl who lay back as though exhausted, with a pair of crutches propped beside her. Her back was grotesquely curved, and her thin white face marked by suffering. All the children wore deep mourning, but their cloaks and dresses were of rich material, heavily braided, and their hats and boots of the best quality.

'Look, Da,' Sally whispered. 'They look as though they've lost their mother and she'd be badly needed by that poor little cripple. No one seems to escape, no matter how well off they are.'

'Aye, but money makes all the difference,' Matthew said. He began to walk more quickly as the tramcar approached, and as they stepped on board he said more cheerfully, 'I'm glad I could buy a grave, anyroad. It was a struggle many a time for the Burial Club money, but I'm glad we kept it up.'

They had not been home for long when there was a knock at the door, and Sally opened it to find the Duggan brothers, the lodgers from next door. They came in and stood turning their caps round and round in their hands.

'Good day to ye, sor, good day to ye, mam,' said one. 'A Merry Christmas to ye. We were wondering, sor, if ye'd take a walk with us to Everton Road for a pint.'

Sally looked eagerly at Matthew, hoping he would agree.

'To Everton Road, yer said?'

'Aye, sor. We go up the hill as a rule, but if ye'd rather go down into the town –' the other brother said.

'No, no, Everton Road'll suit me fine,' Matthew said, taking his jacket and cap from the nail behind the door.

'I'll go in to Mrs Mal and give her a hand.'

Sally banked up the fire with slack, and turned back the rag rug before going in next door.

'Did you ask John and James to ask Da out, Mrs Mal?' she said, but Mrs Malloy shook her head.

'Ah, no, it was their own idea. They're grand lads, and grieving themselves because they can't get home to see their mammy and the little sisters.'

'I suppose most people have some trouble, but then there are good things happening, too,' said Sally. She began to tell Mrs Malloy about Agnes's delight, sure this time of an appreciative audience.

'Aye, I know the mother well,' Mrs Malloy said. 'A grand woman. She had the best of husbands that carried her round, yet when he died she turned to and battled for her children. Will ye look at that pork, Sally? Isn't it a grand sight?'

The leg of pork was indeed an appetizing sight as it lay on the plate, covered in golden crackling, and Sally felt a pang as she thought how much John and Alfred and Emily would have enjoyed it the previous Christmas.

As if in answer to her thoughts Mrs Malloy said, 'Sure, Emily will be having the likes of this every day of the week. They must have full and plenty to be able to send this to yer.' Sally made no reply and Mrs

Malloy added quickly, 'I see yer neighbour the other side has her husband home for Christmas. She'll be thankful to see him.'

'Mrs Hart?' said Sally. 'Yes, I haven't seen Mr Hart yet, but she told me yesterday that the tug was in the river, waiting to dock the Blue Funnel liner. I must slip in there later.'

When the table was laid and all was ready, she went back to her house for the bag of sweets given to her by Mrs Gregson. She left some for Mrs Malloy, and took the rest to the Dolans across the street.

She was warmly welcomed by Mrs Dolan, who put down a handleless cup on the hob and tried to rise to her feet when Sally entered.

'Come in, come in,' she said. 'I'm just having a cup of tea while I'm waiting on himself coming in with a goose.' But Sally had seen the black bottle hastily pushed under the chair, and she knew that the cup contained something stronger than tea. There seemed to be no preparation for a meal, and she was glad to cheer the children with sweets. She warned the eldest, Ada, not to let the baby have anything hard from the bag of sweets in case it choked, and asked in a whisper if Mary was expected home, as Mrs Dolan had sunk back in to her chair, smiling vacantly.

'She's getting two hours off and the cook's promised her something,' Ada whispered. 'When she' – nodding at her mother – 'goes asleep I'll give the kids sugar butties to keep them going till our Mary comes. Me da won't be coming, y'know, Sal. She's only kidding herself.'

Sally felt sad as she left the house, but she was cheered by the sight of her father walking down the street with the Duggans. The porter had loosened their tongues, and they had brought a bottle for Mrs Malloy, so it was a cheerful meal, enjoyed by all of them. Afterwards Matthew went home to bank up the fire and brought back the bottle of rum, then they sat around the fire talking.

John and James told of the farm in Ireland, and Mrs Malloy of her years in service, then Matthew told them of the days when he used to go courting Sally's mother, with a bunch of flowers concealed under his bowler hat.

Sally listened entranced, feeling happier than she had felt since her brothers' death and Emily's departure, and even Matthew seemed more like his old self as he talked of his youth and joked with the Irishmen. Later, at home, Matthew told Sally of the plans which James and John had confided to him.

'They're hoping to go back to Sligo in the spring,' he said. 'Seems the next farm is for sale. The farmer died, and his widow wants to emigrate to Chicago to a daughter there, and take the two little girls she has at home.'

'And they're buying the farm,' Sally said. 'They must have saved a lot of money.'

'Well, farm – God save the mark. It's probably a few poor fields like they've got already, but they've saved enough to buy it for James. John owns the other one as the eldest son, and they'll work the two farms together.'

He leaned forward and knocked out his pipe.

'They've always been so quiet, but they opened up this morning.

Talked sense, too. John said they'd work harder for less, but as he said, 'It'll be our own land, and we'll be back where we belong so it'll be all worth while.'

'Mrs Malloy will miss them,' Sally said. 'She's always saying how good they are. It'll make a great change in her life.'

Matthew agreed. Neither of them realised that the Duggans' departure would change their own lives far more than Mrs Malloy's.

Chapter Seven

After Christmas life became more flat and dreary for Sally. The Market was quiet and trade poor, and as the novelty of her surroundings wore off, Sally found some of her misery returning, even when she was at work. The weather was atrocious, and although she was now accustomed to the long hours of standing, she was plagued by chilblains on her hands and feet.

The only bright spot was the company of Agnes on Saturday nights. After a week of grim silence or petty fault-finding by Mrs Gregson, who was worried about trade, it was a relief to Sally to see Agnes's cheerful face on Saturday. Mrs Gregson sometimes left the stall to talk to other stallholders, and they were free to talk.

Sally was often doubled up with laughter as Agnes told tales of the Jewish tailor's shop, where she worked as a messenger girl during the week, and gave impersonations of the other girls who worked there. Her employer was an Orthodox Jew, who lived over his business, and Agnes earned coppers by lighting his fire on the Sabbath. Sally listened spellbound as Agnes described the preparations for the Friday evening meal, and told her of the time when the family 'mourned in ashes' on the death of the beloved eldest son.

In late February there was a spell of almost spring-like weather, and Sally felt restless and less content to stay at home every night, preparing for the next day.

She had a routine now, and she felt that she had time to spare, so she agreed eagerly when Agnes invited her to visit her home.

'It's not posh, you know,' Agnes warned her. 'There's me and our Tom working, and five younger ones. I turn up me wages to me mam, and keep the market shilling for meself. Our Tom gives me mam his wages from the woodyard, and he washes dishes in the Unicorn for his spend. We'll learn ye to dance.'

Sally thoroughly enjoyed her first visit to the Cassidy household, and spent many happy hours there during the following weeks. Tom played the mouth organ, and Agnes tried to teach Sally the waltz, and the steps of the Lancers. They planned to visit the Irish Club, but Sally was anxious to learn something about dancing before she went there.

After a few weeks, when Sally was reasonably proficient in the waltz, Agnes decided to teach her the four hand reel. One of the children was detailed to play the mouth organ, and Sally and Agnes, Tom and Mrs Cassidy, took their places.

Mrs Cassidy, a tall, gaunt woman, was the only one of the four who knew the steps of the dance, and she flew about, as light as a feather, while the others bumped into each other, and grabbed wildly at the

41

wrong hands. Mrs Cassidy screeched instructions, and the young musician fell about, helpless with laughter, until the dancers broke up in confusion, and Sally, Agnes and Tom fell breathlessly into chairs. Mrs Cassidy, undaunted, swung the kettle over the fire.

'We'll be the better for a cup of tea, after that,' she said. 'But, Mother of God, I think youse have all got two left feet.'

'Doesn't matter, anyhow,' Tom growled. 'They're all the same in the Irish Club, especially the bog men who stand round the door all night.'

'How do you know?' Agnes retorted. 'You never go.'

'I'll go with yer on Paddy's night,' he said. Later, when he had gone out, Agnes turned to Sally.

'I think our Tom must have fell for yer, Sal. He never goes to the Irish Club. He says he was born in England so he's English, and he hates the Irish.'

'But-but,' Sally stuttered, staring at Mrs Cassidy who only smiled placidly.

'Ah, he's young, and maybe thinking it makes him different, and him with the map of Ireland stamped on his face, God help him.'

She was sitting on a wooden chair, with her feet on a stool which one of the children had brought for her.

'Haven't I grand children, thank God, Sally?' she said. 'A bright fire, a good cup of tea, and my children round me – aren't I the envy of all?'

Sally felt tears prick her eyes as she looked at the gaunt woman in her patched and shabby dress, with her lined face and her hands red and swollen from years of scrubbing, who could yet count herself fortunate. She had only the few shillings her children earned, and the little she earned herself by scrubbing a public house, to keep her large family, yet she was content and Sally envied her.

She envied Agnes her happy home, too, especially when she compared it with her own. Matthew had again become morose and withdrawn, only speaking when she went in to reproach her.

'Ye're out too late these days, Sally. Get in earlier than this tomorrow.'

Still, it took more than that to dampen her spirits now, and on Saint Patrick's Night she went joyfully to the Irish Club with the Cassidys. She was flattered by Tom's attentions, even though she liked him least of the Cassidy family, and she was even more flattered when the accordion player swaggered over to talk to her during the interval. Agnes was proud of her success.

'There's a few of them there got their eyes on Pat Roach,' she said, as they walked home. 'But I've never seen him come and talk to no one before. He might have asked to walk you home if our Tom hadn't been standing guard on us.'

'And I'm not even pretty,' Sally said. 'I was just thinking, Ag, if our Emily was grown up she'd cause havoc there. She's so lovely.'

Tom was slouching along behind them, and Agnes turned to say sharply, 'I'm seein' Sally to her door. Her da won't let her out again if he sees her with a feller, so you'd better mizzle.'

Tom turned away, and Agnes turned back to Sally.

'Does Emily speak nice like you?' she said.

'She did, but I don't know how she'll speak now. I used to tell her to try to talk like Mrs Hart from next door, but my aunt and uncle speak awful broad Lancashire, especially my uncle. She might have picked it up.'

'You're always thinking about her, aren't you?' Agnes said.

'I think about my brothers, too,' Sally said defensively, 'but well, they're dead, so I try to close my mind. I worry about Emily though, in case she's unhappy there. She was like my own child, Ag, because I brought her up from when she was a few weeks old, and when she was taken away – well, it was worse in a way than if she died, because I still worry about what's happening to her.'

'Well, why don't you go and see?' Agnes said practically. 'You'd get to Ormesdale and back in a day, easy.'

They were walking along the street, and Sally stopped dead. 'I must be going daft!' she exclaimed. 'The way I've been worrying about her, and I never thought of going to see her! Honestly, I must be going crazy.'

'They couldn't stop you seeing her, and if you seen her and she was all right, you could stop worrying. It's not that far,' said Agnes. Sally thought of her aunt's words: 'We're not tekkin' child to China.' Why had she been content with scraps of information in her aunt's letters instead of asking to see Emily?

When she reached home from the market the next day, she spoke to Mrs Malloy about it.

'Yer were just confused, and no wonder, child, the way everything fell in on yer. Didn't I often think of it meself, but ye know, Sally, I'm not one to interfere.'

Sally repressed a smile. 'It's a wonder Da hasn't suggested it, though, isn't it, Mrs Malloy?' she said.

'He'll have his reasons, Sally,' Mrs Malloy said, nodding her head. 'He's a deep thinking man, your da, but don't start tackling him about it the minute his foot is in the door. Let him get his tea first.'

Sally realised that this was good advice, but she waited impatiently for the meal to be over, determined to open the subject before her father became engrossed in his newspaper.

'Da,' she said quickly, as he drained his mug of tea and picked up his pipe, 'I was thinking, why don't we go to Ormesdale one day? Aunt Hester said herself we could go to see Emily.'

Matthew made no reply until he had lit a spill at the fire, and his pipe was drawing well, then he turned and looked keenly at Sally.

'What's in yer mind, girl?' he said.

'I – I don't know what you mean, Da,' Sally stammered.

'I mean I don't want any more of that carry on about bringing the child home,' he said. 'I've made up me mind, Sally. She's being reared in a healthier place than this, and there she stays.'

'I only want to see her, Da,' Sally protested. 'Just to be able to picture her there, and know she's all right. It's nearly a year –' She stopped, her throat tight with tears. Matthew sat puffing his pipe and staring in to the fire. After a moment he turned back again to Sally.

'Aye well, that makes sense, girl, but I don't want yer upsetting her, or upsetting yerself, either. Still, she's had time to settle there.'

'I won't upset her, Da,' Sally said earnestly. 'I just want to see her.'

Matthew nodded, and picked up his newspaper dismissively. 'All right. Write a line to yer aunt and ask her to come here, or tell her we'll go there some Sunday.'

Sally joyfully cleared away the dishes, and got out the pen and ink and the packet of notepaper. It took only a short time for her to write the letter, and in case her father changed his mind, she walked down immediately to the druggist in Byrom Street, to buy a stamp and post the letter.

Chapter Eight

The reply from Hester came a week later, inviting them to visit the farm on the first Sunday in May. Sally felt nervous and excited as they set out. She was still in mourning for her brothers, but she wore her best black dress and jacket, and a black straw hat on her neatly braided hair, and pinned her mother's brooch to her dress. Her father wore the suit which he had worn for his wedding, which was carefully hoarded for special occasions. It still fitted his spare frame, and with the stiff collar which Sally had bought, and his boots shining like glass, Sally felt proud of him, and sure that the wealthy relatives need not be ashamed of them.

The first part of the journey was by train, and Walter met them at the station in a smart pony trap. It was a bright sunny day, with small white clouds in the blue sky, and the fields and hedges fresh and green, but Matthew sat staring ahead in silence, and Sally was too anxious for her first sight of Emily to enjoy the beauty around her.

At every turn in the lane she looked eagerly for the house, and at long last the trap turned in to a side lane, and stopped before a solidly built farmhouse, with two figures standing before it. Sally's eyes passed swiftly over the stout, well corseted figure of Aunt Hester, resplendent in black silk, to the child standing beside her. Could this be Emily, looking so different after less than a year? She looked much taller, and all her baby chubbiness had gone.

The ringlets which Sally had so lovingly tended had gone too, and Emily's dark hair had been arranged to hang down her back in a shining plait. She drew shyly behind her aunt as the trap drew up, but Sally jumped down, and gathered the child into her arms and kissed her, even as Hester was saying in a loud, hearty voice, 'Nay, lass, don't mek strange with your da and Sally.'

Emily flung her arms around Sally's neck, smiling a gap-toothed smile.

'Why, you've lost your teeth, love!' Sally exclaimed.

'Well, they're nobbut milk teeth,' said Hester. She turned to Matthew, who had come round the trap and lifted Emily in his arms.

'Now, what dost think of her, Matty?'

'She's grown,' Matthew said shortly, kissing Emily and putting her down.

'Aye, she has that,' said Hester. 'Walter, tek trap round.' Walter went off obediently, and Hester led the way into the kitchen, with Sally holding tightly to Emily's hand as they followed her.

'Emily, tek Sally to tha bedroom to tek off her hat and coat,' Hester commanded. 'Sit down, Matt. Tha must be clemmed after tha journey.'

Emily took Sally into a hallway, then up a flight of stairs to her bedroom. Sally looked about her in amazement. The room was not very large, but to Sally it seemed enormous. Small windows with deep windowsills were set in two of the walls, and a bed covered with a hand-crocheted spread was against the third wall.

The windows were open, and starched white muslin curtains fluttered in the sweet-smelling air. There was a mahogany tallboy, and a wash-stand with a marble top and a tiled back, with white muslin curtains like a skirt around it. Sally took off her hat and jacket as though in a dream, and Emily went to the washstand. A basin, ewer, and soapdish patterned with roses stood on it, and a huckaback towel was folded over the side.

'Dost want to get washed, Sal?' she asked, and when Sally nodded, she stood on tiptoe to pour water into the basin. Sally washed her hands, and splashed water on to her hot face. Emily handed her the towel, then drew back the curtains round the washstand. There was a broad shelf beneath it, on which stood a flower-sprigged chamber pot, and a slop pail.

'Dirty water goes in t'bucket,' she said. 'Chamber's for neet time.'

Sally was astounded to hear the accent which Emily had so quickly acquired. She sat down on a cane-bottomed chair and drew the child to her.

'Listen, love,' she said. 'Do you remember Mrs Hart who used to teach you nursery rhymes?' Emily nodded, and Sally said earnestly, 'I used to tell you to try to talk like Mrs Hart, love, and you did. Will you still try to talk like that? It's all right for Aunt Hester and Uncle Walter to talk the way they do because they've always lived here, but will you always try to talk like Mrs Hart?'

Emily played with a button on Sally's dress, her brow furrowed.

'Aunt Hester said I mustn't talk la di da i' school, but Uncle Walter said, 'Tha'll have to learn to talk posh, Hester, before Ah've done. Farm'll be nobbut a sideline to me e'er long.'

Sally's eyes widened, as much to hear Walter's voice so faithfully copied, as at what the child had said. She asked curiously, 'What did Aunt Hester say to that?'

'Sommat about pudding,' Emily said. 'I know: "T'proof of pudding's i' the eating".'

At that moment Hester's voice could be heard calling them, and Sally hastily emptied the ewer and set the room to rights before they went downstairs. Walter and Matthew were leaving the kitchen and Hester poured glasses of home-made lemonade for the two girls.

'When that's gone, tek Sally to see outside, lass,' she said, 'while I dish up dinner.'

'Can I help, Aunt?' Sally asked, but Hester was already tying a white apron around her ample waist.

'Nay, lass,' she said with a hearty laugh, 'the day as I can't manage a meal for five people wi'out help, is the day they put me six feet under.'

Emily proudly escorted Sally round the garden, her excitement growing as they approached a small plot at the side of the house.

'Now, Sally, what dost think of that?' she asked, in a fair if unconscious echo of her aunt's voice. 'Them's all mine.'

Sally smiled ruefully. She realised now that it was unrealistic to expect Emily to speak differently from the way that those around her spoke, especially as she seemed to have a quick ear for speech, as she had proved by her apt imitation of Mrs Hart. She suddenly realised that Emily was telling her what she had grown.

'Them's peas, and them's carrots,' she said. 'And that's mint, and thyme, and parsley.' She broke off leaves of mint and thyme, and Sally sniffed their aromatic scent.

'My word, you've soon learned all this, love,' she said admiringly. 'You must be a born gardener.' They strolled on and Emily told Sally proudly of how she helped to feed the hens, and to pick out small potatoes for the pig swill.

Sally listened with mingled feelings of pride and sadness, but later when Hester called them, and she saw the table laden with a huge leg of pork and tureens of vegetables, the sadness predominated.

She looked at the home-grown, plentiful food on Emily's plate, and the tall glass of milk beside it, then her gaze wandered to the hams hanging from the kitchen ceiling, and through an open door to the parlour, furnished in plush and mahogany, and her sadness increased.

She should be glad that Emily was living in such comfort – she *was* glad, she told herself – but the realisation of how unfair it would be to take Emily from such surroundings to her old home in Gell Street depressed her. No matter how Sally tried, she could not provide these living conditions, the secure background of affluence, and sadly she acknowledged it.

Her father was sitting opposite her, and their eyes met. He had been quiet and withdrawn all day, obviously surprised and irritated by Walter's bragging, but as he looked into Sally's eyes he suddenly smiled, the old loving smile that she had not seen for so long. It was as though he understood, and was trying to help her to face the end of a dream. In an unconscious gesture of courage, she straightened her shoulders and flung back her head as she returned his smile.

Hester was demanding her opinion of the vegetables, and Sally was able to turn to her and praise the flavour of them.

'Aye, all home-grown,' Hester said with a satisfied air. 'They say as you shouldn't eat pork wi'out there's an R i' the month, but that's oo'er own, and I can vouch for it.'

'Aye, nowt but t' best for me,' Walter chimed in. 'It's well known i' market as I only sell t'best and buy t'best. Oo'er Emily's best scholar i' school, too, isn't that reet, lass?'

Emily blushed and hung her head, and Matthew said sharply, 'That's not fer the child ter say.'

Before Walter could reply, Hester said swiftly, 'Now, Sally, how about tha job? Dost still like it?'

Sally began to talk about the market, and to tell them about Agnes Cassidy and her visits to the Irish Club.

After dinner Emily was sent upstairs for a rest, and Matthew sat on the wall outside, smoking, while Walter went to attend to his

47

livestock. Sally helped Hester to wash the dishes, and her aunt took the opportunity to cross-question her about the Irish Club, and the men she met there.

Sally answered her questions guilelessly, and Hester clicked her tongue and shook her head.

'Eh, I can see as I'll have to tek thee in hand, Sally, being as tha's been told nowt about what can happen to tha.'

'What do you mean, Aunt?' Sally asked in alarm.

'Well, dost tha know how babies are made?' Hester demanded.

'I – I thought they grew inside their mam,' Sally stammered, her face crimson.

'Ah, but they have to get theer first, tha knows,' said Hester. 'So, Sally, never do owt with a lad but what thy mam could watch tha doing. Don't let a lad touch tha breast, and sithee, don't let him press up against thee or lift tha skirt.' She stood back from the sink and surveyed Sally.

'You're a smart-looking lass, Sally, with a good head on thi' for keeping house and sewing, and a nice way of talking. Tha should be mixing in good company, and looking about thi' for a steady, older man, wi' a bit of brass behind him.'

'I'm not thinking of getting married, Auntie,' Sally said, her face burning, as she bent her head over the plate she was agitatedly rubbing.

'Eh, I wish I'd a pound for every time as I've heard that, lass, but think on – look above thyself when it comes to marrying. Don't be throwing thyself away on some rough lad, without two pennies to rub together, as'll come home drunk and knock thee about.'

'But I only *dance* with the lads in the Irish Club,' Sally protested. 'That's all.'

'Well, see as it is, lass. I mun speak out, Sally, seeing as thi' father's not bothered. He'd do better to tek his head out of t'paper, worrying about ills of t'world, and worry about what's under his nose. He should be seeing as you mix wi' someone different to them roughs, someone as could give you a good home, better than what you've got.'

'My da's very strict,' Sally said angrily. 'And there's nothing wrong with our home. Da does his best for us, and Mrs Malloy says there's love and happiness in our house.'

'Nay, nay, lass, no need to flare up,' Hester said, realising that she had gone too far, 'I'm saying nowt against your da, only men don't think of these things. I don't want one of these lads to tek advantage because tha knows nowt, and then tha'd find thyself i' trouble, and it'd be marriage or worse for thee.'

'You needn't worry, Aunt,' Sally was beginning, but Hester hung up the dishcloth with an air of finality.

'I'll say no more, lass. I just don't want to see thee dragged down for want of a word, that's all.'

They were both relieved when Emily appeared in the doorway, her pinafore over her arm.

'I've been asleep a long time,' she announced. 'Can I get up now?'

Sally was glad to escape into the garden again with the child, to recover from the anger and embarrassment she felt at her aunt's warnings and criticism of her father, but she decided to put them to the back of her mind and to enjoy her day with Emily.

All too soon for Sally the day drew to a close, and after a lavish tea she mounted the stairs again with Emily, to collect her hat and jacket. She stared hungrily at the child, trying to store up pictures of her for the days ahead, but when Emily looked back at her with a puzzled expression, she said hastily, 'They're good strong boots you're wearing, love, aren't they?'

Emily opened the tallboy to show several dresses and starched pinafores hanging up, then she took a small pair of buttoned boots from the shelf.

'These are my Sunday boots,' she said proudly.

Memories swept over Sally like scalding water, and she buried her face in her hands. Mrs Mal saying: 'Sunday boots, no less'; John smiling ruefully and holding up his broken boot, with Alfie laughing beside him. She groaned aloud, and tears dripped through her fingers as she wept for her brothers and for the happy times that had gone forever.

She came back to the present to find Emily pulling anxiously at her arm, her lips trembling, and Sally dropped to her knees, and took the child in her arms.

'It's all right, pet,' she said, hastily wiping away her tears. 'I just thought of something. I'm made up to see all these clothes. What's in the box?'

Emily smiled again as she drew out a box of hair ribbons, then she opened the bottom drawer to show Sally her underwear. By that time Sally had recovered enough to wipe the traces of tears from her face, and the sisters went downstairs, hand in hand. In the hall Sally hugged Emily again.

'Don't forget me or Da, will you, love?' she said. 'Do you remember John and Alfie?' Emily nodded. 'Don't forget them either, love, or all I told you about Mam. I'll leave a picture of Mam with you.'

They went into the kitchen where Hester waited with Matthew, and Sally said immediately, 'Da, have you got that picture of Mam that Mrs Hart drew for Emily?'

Matthew took it from his pocket, and Sally said to Hester, 'I always talked about Mam to Emily, and Mrs Hart drew this picture so that Emily would know what Mam looked like.'

Hester tossed her head. 'I don't think child should be upset about someone as she never knew,' she said.

'It didn't upset her, aunt,' Sally said. 'The lads and I used to talk about Mam, so I explained about her to Emily. She used to love to hear about her.'

'Eh, that's downright strange, is that. Child were nobbut a few weeks old when she died.'

Matthew's quiet voice cut in. 'Julie gave her life for the child. It's right she should know about her.'

Hester clicked her tongue, then bustled forward as the trap drew up outside. 'Now, Sally,' she said, holding up a basket, 'I've put some fresh eggs, and one of my cheeses in. Tha looks to need feeding up. Some of my sausages, too.'

49

'Thank you, Aunt Hester,' Sally said quietly, kissing her aunt's cheek, but Hester held on to her arm.

'Think on what I told thee, lass. Watch thysen.' She lowered her voice. 'Men! They're all nobbut wanting one thing, but see as tha finds someone with a bit behind them.'

Sally blushed, but said only, 'Goodbye, Aunt Hester. Thank you for the meal and everything.'

She dropped to her knees to take Emily in her arms again. 'Goodbye, my little love,' she whispered. 'I'll see you again soon. Be a good girl.'

Emily hugged her, nodding and smiling, and Sally climbed into the trap, blinded by tears. Matthew soon followed her, and the next moment they were away, leaving Hester and Emily smiling and waving.

As they drove along Walter pointed out how well his farm was doing, and how badly his neighbours managed by comparison. Matthew sat grimly silent, but Sally tried to make suitable replies. When they reached the station, Walter stood at the open carriage door, thumbs in his waistcoat armholes.

'Now think on,' he said. 'Tha's always welcome. Hester can always lay on a good meal wi' what she's got to coom at.'

'We came to see the child,' Matthew said. 'We can eat at home.' For a moment Walter seemed taken aback, but he soon recovered.

'Aye, well, tha must be pleased to see as how little lass has grown,' he said.

'She comes of tall parents,' Matthew said, surveying Walter's diminutive figure, but Sally broke in swiftly, 'She looks well, Uncle. She showed me her garden.'

Walter preened himself again until he was thrust aside by the guard closing the doors, and blowing his whistle.

'Oh, Da,' Sally said reproachfully, 'you were awful nasty to him, and they're doing their best for Emily.'

Matthew made an impatient gesture. 'Aah, he's getting a right little cock o' the walk,' he said. 'Anyhow, you've changed your tune, girl.'

Sally made no reply, and the carriage filled with people at the next stop, so the journey was completed in silence.

Chapter Nine

As they walked from the station Sally's mind was filled with a tumult of impressions – of Emily, of the farmhouse, of Hester and Walter – and thoughts of Hester's questions and advice. She craved solitude to sort out her thoughts, so she was relieved to see that Mrs Malloy's door was closed. She was able to hurry through the necessary jobs then went up to bed, but not to sleep.

For hours she lay thinking of the events of the day, sometimes weeping as she thought of Emily, or feeling angry as she remembered Hester's probing questions. In spite of herself, her curiosity was aroused by Hester's talk of sex, and she turned on to her back and ran her hands over her breasts, down over her flat stomach and to her thighs. I'd like to have a baby, she thought dreamily, one that was all my own, that no one could take away from me.

Strange feelings and desires invaded her body, but as her thoughts turned to Hester's warnings and her salacious expression as she uttered them, Sally's face suddenly burned. She jerked her nightdress down and turned on her side, determined to try to sleep, but it was a long time before sleep came to her. When she woke the following morning, she felt years older than the innocent girl who had set out for Ormesdale.

In the Market she found herself looking at the men appraisingly, thinking of them as possible husbands and rejecting them immediately.

The man from the fruit stall brought her an apple, with his usual joke.

'Ee are, love. This is the wrong way round, like. It's you what should be temptin' me with an apple.' But she was unable to respond with her customary giggle, and stood blushing and tongue-tied. He moved away, looking puzzled, and Mrs Gregson, who missed nothing, said sharply, 'Don't be working yourself up over Billy. He gives apples to all the young girls, but he's a happily married man.'

'I didn't – I wasn't,' Sally stammered. 'He just gave me a shock. I was miles away.'

'Well, don't be daydreaming. Get on with your work,' Mrs Gregson said. Bad-minded old faggot, Sally thought furiously, and Aunt Hester too! Who's she to be giving advice about husbands? Look at Uncle Walter. Her anger gave her courage to call over to the fruit stall.

'No wonder you crept up behind me with that apple, Billy. There's a maggot in it.'

'Is there, queen?' Billy shouted, obviously delighted to see her back to normal. ' 'Ere, I'll change it.'

'No, I'm only joking,' Sally laughed. For the rest of the day she put all thought of Hester firmly to the back of her mind.

In the evening she went in to see Mrs Malloy, but for once the older woman's questions were perfunctory. John and James Duggan were due to leave on the Tuesday night boat for Dublin, and Mrs Malloy was subdued and red-eyed with weeping.

'Haven't they been like sons to me these years, girl,' she said. 'Sure, I never valued them enough until I knew they were going from me.'

'But you must be happy for them, Mrs Mal,' Sally said. 'To be going home, and having the other farm.'

'Oh, I am, girl, indeed I am, and the mammy and the little girls will be thankful to God to see them.' She lifted the corner of her apron and wiped her eyes. 'I'll have to be washing me face. The cut of me, and the lads are bringing two fellers they work with, to see will they suit me.'

Sally had put some eggs and cheese on the table and the sight of the food reminded Mrs Malloy of the trip to Ormesdale. As they went to the door she patted Sally's arm.

'Thanks be to God ye saw the child with every comfort, girl. Didn't I tell you she'd be living like a queen. Ye'll be more aisy in yer mind about her now.'

Sally smiled and left without replying, but later on she went in to see her other neighbour, Mrs Hart, who listened with keen interest to Sally's account of Emily's progress, and her description of the farmhouse. More perceptive than Mrs Malloy, Mrs Hart could see that Sally was grieved that she herself had been able to provide so much less for Emily than she enjoyed now.

'You gave Emily a gift beyond price, Sally,' she said in her clear, sweet voice. 'The love you poured out on her will give her a sense of security which she will never lose.'

'Do you think so, Mrs Hart?' Sally said eagerly. 'She was always a happy child, wasn't she?' She paused, uncertain how to express her fears.

'It's just – Aunt Hester – she doesn't seem to love Emmie as *Emmie*. I feel she wants a daughter to be proud of, but anyone would do. I mean, I wonder would she still love our Emily if she couldn't boast about her.'

'You fear that she regards Emily more as a possession than a person. Perhaps so. For some people, Sally, it is the only love that they are capable of, but the child will still be their first concern.'

'Oh, they look after Emily, right enough. They couldn't do more for her, or give her more, but – it's just – somehow, I don't want Emily to grow up thinking like that.'

'To value possessions more than people, you mean, Sally? No. The early years are the formative ones. As the twig is bent, so the tree will grow. I think it was a Jesuit priest who said, 'Give me a child until he is seven, and then do with him what you will.' But Sally, my dear, don't worry so constantly about what *might* happen. Enjoy what you have, and expect happiness.'

I seem to be getting advice from everyone lately, Sally thought ruefully as she returned home, but I suppose I'm lucky that people take the trouble.

On Thursday Mrs Gregson decided that the stall must be spring cleaned, and it was late when Sally walked wearily up Gell Street. She had forgotten about Mrs Malloy's new lodgers, but as she reached the door it opened, and two men came out.

One was a small, grey-haired man with a weatherbeaten face, but the man who followed him, and came face to face with Sally, was young, with dark eyes and dark curly hair, and white teeth showing as he smiled at Sally.

Neither of them ever forgot that moment. The girls playing hopscotch, the boys fighting over a hoop, and the women gossiping at their doors all seemed to vanish as Sally and the young man stood lost in a world of their own, gazing into each other's eyes.

Mrs Malloy broke the spell as she came to her open door.

'Ah, there you are, girlie, and dead on·yer feet be the look of yer. God forgive that ould slavedriver! These are the new lads, Sally. That's Paddy Ryan.' The older man held out his hand, and Sally took it, smiling vaguely. 'And this is Lawrie Ward,' Mrs Malloy went on. 'They're just off now for a pint.'

Lawrie raised his cap, and took Sally's hand, holding it until Mrs Malloy stepped into the street, pulling her door closed behind her.

'I'll come in with ye, Sal,' she said. 'Yer da is after having his tea and then off out with some man's wages that had a fall from a ship today.'

'I'll see you later,' Lawrie said, as Sally was swept away from him into her own house.

Her weariness had vanished. She went into the scullery to wash her hands and face, and to peer anxiously into the bit of mirror that her father used for shaving.

Mrs Malloy had lifted Sally's meal from the oven, and settled down for a gossip while it was eaten. She smiled as she saw Sally's pink cheeks and bright eyes.

'Ye look a bit better than when ye came home, girlie,' she said. 'What kept ye so late?'

'Spring cleaning,' Sally said briefly, then before Mrs Malloy could ask any other questions she said eagerly, 'The new men seem nice, Mrs Mal.'

'Aye, well, if they're as good as the ones that are over the sea this minute, they'll do well enough,' Mrs Malloy said with a sigh.

'Did you say Lawrie Ward was a seaman? He's only young, isn't he?'

'Yes, Paddy Ryan is a lot older than him. He's twenty years in England, he tells me, and he's a widower. Didn't he lose his wife over the first child, God help him, and the child too.' She glanced at Sally's face and relented.

'Lawrie Ward seems a nice enough lad,' she said. 'And full of life. He did a Pier Head jump when he was only a bit of a lad, but he never liked the sea. He's been away two years to China, he tells me, but he made up his mind he'd find a shore job when he got back.'

Sally's meal grew cold as she sat engrossed, drinking in all the details about Lawrie, and Mrs Malloy began to look thoughtful.

'Ate yer tea, girl,' she said. 'Before it goes cold on ye. What I know about that lad is only what he told me himself, mind ye.'

'But the Duggans recommended him,' Sally said.

'Well, they knew Paddy Ryan for years, and knew him as a sober respectable man, but this other lad now, they told me straight that he was new come to the site and they knew nothing about him, only that he seemed clean and polite and they thought he'd suit me. Time will tell, anyhow.'

She picked up her shawl.

'I'll be going now, Sal, down to Benediction. I'll say a prayer for you, girlie, that ye find the rich young man yer aunt is after recommending.'

'Rich *old* man, Mrs Mal,' Sally laughed.

'Aye well, there's many a true word spoken in jest, and there's sense in what yer aunt says. Pay heed to her, girl.'

Sally nodded, but when Mrs Malloy had gone, and she was free to sit and think of the merry brown eyes and gentle smile of Lawrie Ward, she realised that her search was over before it had really begun. For good or ill, she had met the man she wanted to spend her life with.

In a happy dream she made her preparations for the morning, then escaped to bed as soon as her father came home. She had hoped to lie awake thinking about Lawrie, but nagging doubts crept in. Had it really happened as she thought it had? Had Lawrie felt as she did, that nothing would ever be the same again, and that they were linked together forever?

Perhaps this was what had happened to Mrs Hart. She had wandered into the garden one day, and looked at Tom Hart, then felt that nothing mattered but to be with him always. And yet . . . .

She remembered one day when Mrs Hart had been reading aloud, and when she came to the lines 'In that moment her fate was sealed. Heart spoke to heart', she had closed the book, saying that it was melodramatic and foolish.

'But that can happen, can't it, Mrs Hart?' Sally recalled saying. 'People can fall in love at first sight.' She remembered that Mrs Hart had smiled sadly.

'Perhaps, Sally, but I wouldn't wish you to be influenced by a book like that. There are other factors, unrecognized at the time. A longing for an escape from a dull life, the charm of difference.'

Sally turned these words over and over in her mind. Were there also other reasons for her feeling for Lawrie? Was it because Aunt Hester had talked about marriage, so that it was in her thoughts? Were she and Lawrie really meant for each other, and would they be happy together?

Then as she lay tense, a worried frown on her face, the absurdity of all her self questioning struck her, and she began to laugh. No wonder people told her that she worried too much. She turned her pillow over and settled down to sleep, her last thoughts happy memories of Lawrie's brown eyes smiling into hers.

Chapter Ten

When Paddy Ryan and Lawrie returned to Mrs Malloy's house, she was sitting by the fire, knitting, with a plate of bread and cheese on the table for their supper, and the kettle on the fire for cocoa.

'Thank ye, M'm. You're spoiling us entirely,' said Paddy Ryan, and then relapsed into silence, but Lawrie immediately began to talk about Sally.

'Has she just lost her mother?' he asked, and Mrs Malloy shook her head.

'Ah, no, her mother's dead these years, Lord ha' mercy on her. Sally's in mourning for her two brothers. God took the two of them on the one day, but sure, she's grieving as much for the little sister she reared, that was taken to live in the country with her mother's sister.'

'She seemed tired,' Lawrie said. 'Does she have to work very hard?' He jumped to his feet as the kettle began to sing, and poured the boiling water into the mugs of cocoa.

'Ah, thank ye, lad,' said Mrs Malloy. 'I suppose the years at sea have made ye handy. Mind you, there's not many settle ashore when once they've been seafaring.'

'I know. My father would never have settled, but he was a seven seas sailor, and it was in his blood. I never liked the life, and this last trip made up my mind for me. Where does Sally work?'

'In the market. Ye say yer mother and father are long dead?' said Mrs Malloy, determined to find out as much as possible about her new lodger.

'Yes. My mother died of consumption,' Lawrie said. 'All the children she had after me died at birth or soon after. I was twelve when she died and my father was ashore at the time, so he arranged for me to live with an aunt, and he went back to sea. I went to see him off, but then I saw a lad I knew working on a barque in Wapping Dock, and I signed on.'

'Glory be to God. What did your da say about that?'

A shadow crossed Lawrie's face. 'He never knew,' he said. 'His ship went down off the Manacles with all hands.'

'Lord ha' mercy on them,' said Mrs Malloy, crossing herself. 'There's many a one been lost that way. So ye've been on yer own since then, and ye've just finished a China run?'

'Yes, a two-year trip, but I'd had enough of the sea. I was lucky to get on to the building, and luckier still that the Duggans spoke for me here. Is there just Sally and her father next door then?'

'Aye. She looked after them all when her mam died, and she only a child herself. Now she looks after her da, and works in the market.'

55

Mrs Malloy leaned forward and looked meaningly at Lawrie. 'She's supped sorrow, lad, young as she is,' she said. 'I wouldn't want any more trouble to come to her.'

Lawrie's tanned face grew red. 'It won't through me, Mrs Malloy,' he said. 'I can promise you.'

She nodded. 'As long as we understand each other, lad,' she said.

'I want to ask Sally out. Do y'think I should ask her da first? I want to do it properly, Mrs Mal.'

Mrs Malloy rolled up the sock she was knitting, and thrust the needles into it, pursing her lips as she considered the question.

'Well, now, it might be as well, lad. Matthew's a strict man, but mind how ye go about it. Sally's a girl that has a mind of her own, too. Of course they know well that I never interfere.'

Lawrie turned to Paddy Ryan, who was sitting quietly puffing at a clay pipe.

'You don't mind, Paddy? There'll be plenty of other fellers down at the pub.'

Paddy removed the pipe from his mouth. 'Not at all,' he said, and replaced it.

Mrs Malloy stood up and began to gather up the dishes, smiling at Paddy. A man of few words, she thought, but wasn't it just as well, for the other lad could talk enough for two. Still, he'd answered her questions straightforward enough, and she felt more easy in her mind, seeing the way things seemed to be shaping with him and Sally.

Rain poured down the following day, and at midday the building workers were 'rained off' and sent home. In the late afternoon Sally was astonished to see Lawrie, freshly washed and changed, walking towards the stall, carrying a bunch of flowers. He had been in her thoughts throughout the day, and a burning blush spread over her face. She turned away and began hurriedly to fill a jar of pear drops. Mrs Gregson was busy with a customer, and when Lawrie stood by the stall, she said sharply, 'Serve, Sally.'

'Half a pound of those, please,' Lawrie said, pointing to the nearest sweets and laying the flowers on the counter. Sally weighed out the sweets with shaking hands, her head downbent, but as Lawrie handed her the money he held on to her hand.

'I really came to ask you, Sally, would you mind if I asked your father if we could go out together?' he said quietly.

Sally's blush deepened. She made no reply as she turned away to place the money in a drawer.

'I'm sorry to bother you here,' Lawrie said earnestly, 'but I didn't want to ask your father before I'd asked you.'

'Mrs Gregson's looking vexed,' Sally whispered. 'I'll have to go.'

Lawrie released her hand, which he had taken again. 'I'm sorry. I'll go, but is it all right, Sally?'

She nodded, then lifted her head and looked at him. Instantly the feeling of wonder returned, of being isolated in a ring of magic, as they stood smiling into each other's eyes – until Mrs Gregson's sharp cry of 'Sally' brought them down to earth again. Lawrie left, and as Sally carefully put the flowers beneath the counter Mrs Gregson approached.

'Who's that young man, Sally?' she asked. Sally blushed again. 'His name's Lawrence Ward,' she said. 'He's come to lodge with Mrs Malloy next door.'

'Oh, so your father knows him then?'

'Yes,' lied Sally, wondering how much of their conversation Mrs Gregson had overheard.

'That's all right then, but don't encourage him to come here, distracting you from your work.' Sally said nothing, but Mrs Gregson would have been amazed if she had known the emotions concealed beneath her meek exterior.

She hurried home, cradling her flowers, but she had only time to walk through to the back kitchen with them, when she heard her father lift the doorlatch.

'I'm – I'm only just in, Da,' she said, looking flustered.

'That's all right, girl. No hurry,' he said, sitting down to unlace his boots. Sally took the dish of tripe and onions from the oven, and he went into the back kitchen to wash his hands.

'Yer brought some flowers from the market, then,' he said, standing in the doorway to dry his hands.

'No, one of Mrs Mal's lodgers gave them to me,' she said, keeping her head lowered over the dish.

'But I thought they worked on the building,' he was beginning, when his glance fell on his newspaper which Sally, in her agitation, had knocked on to the fender.

'Watch what yer doing, girl!' he exclaimed. 'Yer could've had the paper in the fire.'

Sally was too nervous and excited to eat. As soon as her father finished his meal, she began to gather the dishes together. There was a tap on the door, and her face flamed as she rushed to open it. Lawrie stood there smiling at her, and she felt a rush of pride as she looked at him. Surely her da *must* like him.

'Da, this is Lawrence Ward,' she said. 'He lodges with Mrs Malloy.' It was hard to keep a note of pride from her voice, but her father seemed unaware of it.

Matthew looked puzzled as he took Lawrie's outstretched hand.

'Yer'll be well suited there, I reckon,' he said.

'Oh, yes,' Lawrie agreed eagerly. 'I've been very lucky.' He glanced at Sally, but she snatched up the dishes and escaped into the back kitchen. Lawrie cleared his throat nervously, then went on.

'I've come to ask you, Mr Palin, if you'll let Sally walk out with me. I've only been working ashore a few months, so I don't know many people, but the man at the Seaman's Mission could speak for me. I've no family, only an aunt in Anfield, but she'll vouch for me that I'm respectable.'

Matthew's mouth had fallen open, and he held up his hand as though to ward off the flow of words.

'Hold on, hold on,' he said. 'Good God Almighty, what is all this? Our Sally's only a child.'

'I'm eighteen in August,' Sally said, suddenly appearing in the doorway to the back kitchen.

'Oh, ye're there, are yer?' Matthew said grimly.'Come out here. What do you know about all this?'

Lawrie tried to speak, 'I asked Sally –' he said, but Matthew waved him down.

'Lawrie came to the market to ask me if he could ask you, Da,' Sally said.

Light seemed to break on Matthew. 'Oh, yes,' he said. 'So he's the flower feller. So yer know him from the market?'

'No, Da, he only came to the market with the flowers,' Sally said.

Her father shook his head, looking dazed. 'I'm going out of me mind,' he said. 'If yer don't know him from the market, where the hell *do* yer know him from?'

'He lodges with Mrs Malloy,' Sally began, but she was interrupted by a tap on the door, and only Lawrie was surprised to see Mrs Malloy. Matthew groaned quietly, and muttered, 'Never a show without Punch,' as Mrs Malloy came in, smiling.

'Ye got yer tea over then, Matt,' she said. 'Didn't I warn the lad to give ye time to get yer tea in peace, before he tackled ye?'

'So you're in on this, too, Mrs Mal. What's going on here?'

Before she could speak, Lawrie said quickly, 'I met Sally last night, Mr Palin, coming out of Mrs Malloy's house. I wanted to ask her out, but I thought I should do things properly and ask you, because it's very important to me.'

Sally and Mrs Malloy were silent, and Matthew rose to his feet. The two tall men faced each other for a moment, then Matthew said quietly, 'So you want to take our Sally out, and you want my say so first? Is that what you're talking about, lad?'

'I'm talking about marriage really, Mr Palin,' Lawrie said. 'I knew the minute I saw Sally she was the girl I wanted to marry.'

There was a gasp from Sally, and a stunned silence until Mrs Malloy broke it.

'Jesus, Mary and Joseph,' she exclaimed, crossing herself. 'I can see well how ye took the Pier Head Jump, and sailed off in the clothes ye stood up in.'

Matthew turned to Sally. 'Finish them dishes, girl,' he ordered.

He turned back to Lawrie.

'Sit down, lad,' he said. 'While I get this straight. How do you know our Sally? Oh, I know ye lodge with Mrs Malloy, but ye're only there five minutes, so where did you get to know our Sally?'

Lawrie twisted his cap between his fingers, and cleared his throat nervously, but he looked steadily at Matthew as he answered.

'I only met Sally last night, Mr Palin. She had just reached Mrs Mal's door when we came out, and Mrs Mal told her who we were. I know it sounds daft, but I just knew right away she was the girl for me.'

'Ye're right, lad, it does sound daft,' Matthew said grimly. 'Ye know nothing about her, and what's more, we know nothing about you, only that yer've got no sense.'

Lawrie was about to protest, but Matthew leaned forward and pointed the stem of his pipe at him.

'Now you listen to me, lad. Yer came to ask me about going out with her, and fair do's, yer showed respect an' I would 'a let her go out with yer, but not now I've heard this wild talk.'

'But I was just being straight,' Lawrie protested. 'I suppose I shouldn't have come out with it like that, but I didn't stop to think.'

'Aye, I can see that, but I'm not having her head turned with daft talk of weddings and such. Our Sally's lived quiet and close to home. She's not like the hardfaced girls who wait fer seamen to come ashore, and don't you ferget it.'

Lawrie's face grew red.

'I never mixed with sailors' women,' he said. 'I'll admit I used to get drunk when we put into port, but I gave the women a wide berth. Something I saw on my first voyage put me off.' Matthew sucked at his empty pipe and stared at him, and Lawrie stared back, then he said quietly, 'I was brought up to respect women, Mr Palin. I wouldn't do or say anything to upset Sally, but I stand by what I said about wanting to marry her. Maybe I shouldn't have blurted it out, but it's true.'

Matthew lifted the poker and rattled it among the bars of the grate, then he got up and walked to the door to the back kitchen, where Sally and Mrs Malloy were busy with the dishes.

'D'yer want to walk out with this lad, Sally?' he asked.

'Oh, yes, Da,' Sally said eagerly, then she blushed and bent her head.

'I think he's a respectable class of lad, Matt,' Mrs Malloy whispered. 'I've been weighing him up and asking about his mam and dad.'

Matthew nodded and turned back to the kitchen. 'All right then,' he said to Lawrie, 'But I warn ye, no wild talk, and have her back here by half past ten.'

Lawrie jumped to his feet, smiling broadly, and Sally dashed upstairs, whipping off her apron, and coming down within minutes wearing a black cape and a black straw hat. Matthew had sat down in his chair and was cutting up thin twist with his clasp knife, and rolling it between his horny palms.

When Mrs Malloy seemed inclined to linger, he shook out his newspaper dismissively.

'Goodnight to ye, Mrs Mal,' he said. 'And, Sally, be back here by half past ten, remember.'

'Yes, Da,' Sally said joyfully, as she and Lawrie went out of the door. Mrs Malloy followed them and detained them for a moment.

'Didn't I tell ye all would be well if ye asked him at the right time. Sure all he needs is to be handled right.'

But Sally and Lawrie were oblivious, already lost to the world around them as they walked along with arms linked.

From the first they understood each other perfectly. Sally could talk freely to Lawrie about Emily, of all her hopes and fears for her, and of the misery of the months after her brothers' death when Emily was also lost to her, and life seemed not worth living. Lawrie talked of his mother, of her suffering and her courage, and her love for his happy-go-lucky father.

'My aunt condemned him because he planned to go to sea and leave me after my mother died, but I think he couldn't bear to be ashore without her. They had nothing really, Sal, only two rooms and a few sticks of furniture, but we always seemed to be laughing when he was home.'

The time flew past as they wandered along talking, unaware of their surroundings, and it was only when a church clock struck ten that they realised how far from home they had walked.

'Oh, Lawrie, we'll have to step out,' Sally said. 'Da means what he says. He won't let me come out again if we're late.'

The next moment Lawrie had hailed a cab and was handing her into it.

'Lawrie,' she gasped, 'are you mad?' But he settled beside her with a grin.

'It's all right, Sal,' he said. 'I got a good pay off from my last trip, and I've still got some left.'

'It won't last long like this,' Sally said, but she sat back and prepared to enjoy herself, wishing that people she knew could see her. Lawrie asked the cabbie to drop them in Shaw Street so that they could stroll down to Gell Street, and still be indoors by ten thirty. Before Sally went in, Lawrie bent his head and kissed her gently.

'I promised your da I wouldn't talk about marriage, Sal,' he said, 'but I meant what I said – you're the girl for me.'

Blushing and smiling, she opened the door and slipped into the house.

Matthew said nothing, although he looked quizzically at Sally's pink cheeks and shining eyes as she flitted about the kitchen, cutting up sandwiches and preparing the meal for the following day. She did all her jobs mechanically, her thoughts far away, and was still lost in a happy dream when she said goodnight to her father and went to bed.

Chapter Eleven

The following morning Sally sang as she moved about the stall, and Mrs Gregson watched her sardonically.

'Full of the joys of spring this morning, aren't you, Sally?' she said.

Sally laughed happily. 'Yes,' she said. 'You know the lad who brought me the flowers? He asked Da if I could go out with him, and we went for a walk.'

'And that's what you're so excited about? You're easy pleased,' Mrs Gregson sniffed, but Sally was too happy to be offended.

'We walked too far really, because Da said I had to be in by half past ten and we were miles away at ten o'clock, but Lawrie stopped a cab, so we were home in time.'

'Made of money, is he? Where does he work?' asked Mrs Gregson.

'On the building, labouring, but he's only just left the sea and he got a good pay off from his last trip. He was away two years,' Sally said.

'Well, he won't keep it long at that rate,' Mrs Gregson sneered. Before Sally could answer she turned away to a customer, but Sally was too elated to be hurt by the older woman's ill temper. She longed for the evening when she could confide in Agnes Cassidy, who would be sure to be warmly interested in all that had happened.

The stall was busier than it had been for some time, and when Agnes came Sally could only manage a few whispered words about Lawrie, but at closing time she was delighted to see his tall figure approaching the stall.

He smiled at the girls, and raised his cap and wished Mrs Gregson 'Good evening'. Sally proudly introduced him to Agnes, but when a rush of customers arrived, he said quietly, 'I'll wait outside, Sal,' smiling fondly at her before turning away.

'Oo, Sally, he's lovely,' Agnes exclaimed. 'It made me go all funny just to look at him.' Sally blushed with pleasure, and later Agnes offered to finish the clearing up alone if Mrs Gregson would let Sally leave as soon as the stall closed. She grudgingly agreed, and at closing time Sally was away, skimming like a swallow to where Lawrie waited outside the market. They walked slowly homewards, Lawrie's arm around Sally's waist and her head on his shoulder.

'I won't delay you tonight, Sal,' he said gently. 'I know you're tired after your long day, and you want to get a cup of tea and put your feet up, but do you think your da would let us go out for the day tomorrow?'

'Oh, yes,' Sally said. 'Da has strong views about Sunday although he doesn't go to church. He says it should be a day of rest for women as well as men, so we have cold meals, and I can go for a walk or do as I like.'

'He's an unusual man, your da, isn't he? Mrs Malloy's always singing his praises to us.'

'Mrs Hart admires him, too,' Sally said proudly. 'She says men like Da should be in Parliament instead of the knaves or fools who got there by using their wealth or influence.'

'I'd like to meet Mrs Hart,' Lawrie exclaimed. 'She seems to have the right ideas. No wonder you're clever, Sal, the people you mix with.'

'*I'm* not clever,' Sally said, blushing. 'I'm only repeating what people say.' Lawrie turned his head and kissed her forehead.

'So your da won't mind if we have a day out? I was thinking – we could go to Eastham Woods on the Ferry if it's a nice day.'

'I'd love that,' Sally exclaimed. 'D'you know, Lawrie, I've hardly ever been on the river, only to New Brighton when Mam was alive.'

They were nearing Gell Street, and before they reached the street lamp, Lawrie stopped by the angle of a wall and drew Sally gently into his arms. They kissed, softly at first then with increasing urgency. Strange feelings invaded Sally's body, and she found herself wanting to press closer to Lawrie and to kiss him more fiercely, but after a few moments Lawrie drew away, still cradling Sally in his arms but drawing her head on to his shoulder, and laying his cheek against her hair.

'We must get home, Sal,' he said in a thick voice, as they moved away.

'Your da will be out looking for you.'

They walked on, and Sally would have felt hurt and rejected if she had not realised that Lawrie was trembling, too, and the same strange feelings were moving in him as in herself. She also dimly realised that out of his greater experience, Lawrie was trying to protect her.

Matthew agreed to the day out, and Sunday dawned bright and warm. As soon as Sally had cleared away the breakfast dishes and washed up, she took a jug of hot water from the black kettle on the hob, and hastened upstairs. She washed rapidly and put on her Sunday dress, then braided her shining brown hair, puffing it out becomingly at the sides, and took her black straw hat from its bag, but then she hesitated. Dare she add the white flower which had lain so long in the drawer? The year of mourning for the boys would not end until July, but the unrelieved black of her clothes seems out of place on this sunny May day. Her father, she knew, would say nothing, even if she added white gloves, but would he be hurt? As she stood irresolute she heard Mrs Malloy's voice downstairs. Quickly she pinned the white flower to her hat, and picked up the white gloves. Mrs Malloy would not hesitate to give her opinion and Sally felt that she could gauge her father's reaction from that. There would still be time to take off the flower if he seemed annoyed.

Nervously she opened the door at the foot of the stairs, and her father and Mrs Malloy looked up.

'Well, ye look as pretty as a picture, Sally,' she exclaimed. 'Ye've a grand day for the trip, thank God.'

Sally's eyes met those of her father. 'You don't mind, Da,' she said, quietly and breathlessly. 'The flower, I mean.'

'Hah, I'm not worried about outward show, girl,' he said gruffly. 'Enjoy yerself. I've had a word with that lad.'

'I'll go and tell him ye're ready,' said Mrs Malloy. 'He's been like a hen on a griddle these hours.' She bustled out and Sally began to tell her father about the food she had left ready for him.

'There's potted herrings there, Da, and cheese and pickles, and a couple of cold spareribs.'

Matthew nodded impatiently. 'All right, all right, girl, don't be worrying. I won't starve. I'll maybe take a walk to Daly's for a gill later on. Go on, there he is knocking.'

Lawrie's eyes widened in appreciation when Sally opened the door.

'Why, Sal,' was all he said, but he looked at her with so much love and pride that her eyes filled with happy tears. Lawrie was wearing a braid-trimmed suit and a straw hat, and Sally felt proud as he took her hand and drew it through his arm. Mrs Malloy was at her door.

'Well, as God made ye he matched ye,' she exclaimed. 'Ye're the smartest pair ever stepped on these flags, God bless ye.'

'That's not saying much,' Sally said. 'When you think of the cut of some of them that walk down here.' And they walked on, laughing. Sally stole glances at Lawrie as they went along. He's the handsomest man in Liverpool – or anywhere, she thought joyfully.

Crowds of young people were waiting for the Ferry to Eastham, and as soon as they were all on board the boat left the Landing Stage, and the band began to play.

The sun sparkled on the waves, and a light breeze fluttered the girls' dresses and carried the music of the violin and accordion over the water. Sally felt as though she would burst with happiness.

'I can't believe this is happening,' she whispered to Lawrie. 'I feel as though I should pinch myself to make sure I'm not dreaming.' His arm tightened about her waist, and he kissed her gently.

'We're lucky, aren't we, Sal, to have found each other out of all the people in the world? It must be fate.'

Sally looked around at the young people thronging the deck.

'I wish I was pretty,' she said wistfully.

'But you *are* pretty,' he said, astonished.

She shook her head. 'I mean pretty like Mam and Emily,' she said. 'I take after Da, with brown hair and freckles.'

'I love brown hair and freckles,' Lawrie said, laughing and kissing where freckles were scattered on the bridge of her nose. 'And I love big blue eyes like yours, too.'

Sally leaned against him and sighed happily. He *must* love me, she thought, because I know very well I'm not pretty, but she looked at the couples around them with new confidence.

At Eastham they disembarked and strolled along the leafy lanes, and through the woods, until they found a fallen log and sat down to eat the sandwiches and drink the milk which Sally had brought. Afterwards Lawrie lay back and instantly fell asleep, and Sally wandered about, gathering a posy of bluebells, and other flowers which she could not identify.

She came back and sat down beside Lawrie, looking lovingly into his face. In sleep his unguarded features looked very young and vulnerable, and Sally longed to gather him into her arms. Suddenly he awoke, and sat up immediately.

'I'm sorry, love,' he said. 'I don't know what came over me.'

'You were just tired out,' Sally said. 'Your work's very hard, isn't it?'

'No heavier than on ship, just different,' Lawrie said. 'I'm well used to hard work, but it's just so quiet and peaceful here. I could stay here forever, couldn't you?'

Sally nodded. 'Do you miss the sea, Lol?' she asked, looking down at the flowers in her hand. 'You know, like when we saw all the shipping in the river today – did it make you want to sail off somewhere?'

Lawrie shook his head. 'Never,' he said emphatically. 'No, I never liked the sea, except sometimes at night with a calm sea and the quietness and stars very bright . . . but no, Sal, I'd never want to go back. I was sorry as soon as I'd signed on for that China run, and I swore if I lasted it out, I'd swallow the anchor as soon as we docked.'

'But you'd been going to sea for years, hadn't you?'

Lawrie laughed. 'Since I was twelve,' he admitted cheerfully, 'but you know how it is. After every voyage I'd be spent up in no time, then I'd sign on to get the advance note, and there I was. Money always burnt a hole in my pocket, Sal, but I'll be different from now on.'

Sally blushed but did not attempt to reply to his declaration.

'But why did you take the Pier Head jump in the first place?' she asked.

'Well, my mother had just died. My dad had missed his ship to stay with her, but when she died, he arranged for me to stay with his sister, and he signed on again. I carried his bag down to his ship, and after he went aboard, I saw a pal on a barque in Wapping Dock, and went to give him a hand. I was a big lad, and the overseer came and asked if I wanted to take a trip, so I jumped at the chance.'

'But he didn't know anything about you, did he? Your family might have been frantic.' Lawrie laughed.

'He was four hands short, and they wanted to catch the tide, so I suppose he thought I was better than nothing, and he'd soon lick me in to shape. I knew my aunt didn't really want me, so it was all right, except that I had no spare clothes. It was a South American run, but of course we had to round the Horn. The men were a good crowd, though, and they helped me out. That's enough about me, Sal. I want to know all about you.'

'Just tell me first,' Sally begged. 'What did your father say?' Lawrie's smile vanished.

'He never knew,' he said. 'His ship went down off Holyhead with all hands. I found out afterwards that it was a real coffin ship, badly found and over insured, so I suppose the owners were pleased. Still, never mind.'

'Let's talk about you,' he pressed her.

'But you know all about me,' Sally protested, and Lawrie squeezed her waist.

'All right,' he said teasingly. 'Let's talk about us.' Sally blushed and smiled, and Lawrie gently tipped her face up to look into her eyes.

'You're the girl for me, Sal,' he said quietly. 'As soon as I saw you I knew, and I'll never change, no matter what happens, even if you turn me down. Will you, love?'

Sally shook her head. Too naive and too honest to be flirtatious, she said immediately, 'I felt the same as soon as I met you. It seemed as if I'd always known you, Lawrie.'

He flung his arms around her and kissed her, then drew her head on to his shoulder and stroked her hair away from her face, looking earnestly at her.

'I'm going to be different from now on, Sally. I've always been a happy-go-lucky sort of feller, spending my money as I got it, but I'm going to be really steady. I won't say any more to your da about marriage but if he sees I'm steady, he might listen to me in a couple of months.'

Sally smiled shyly, and moved her face closer to his.

'Don't change too much, Lol,' she whispered.

Lawrie crushed her to him. 'Oh, God, Sal,' he cried. 'I wish we could get married now.'

She clung to him, trembling, but suddenly voices were heard, and a party of four young people came walking along the path. Sally and Lawrie broke apart, and she sat smoothing her hair and blushing, but Lawrie gave them a cheerful 'Good day'.

'Just making back for a cream tea,' one of the men called. 'We've got a nice day for the trip, haven't we?'

'Aye, we have that,' Lawrie replied. Sally had moved a little behind him, her head bent. As soon as the party had moved out of sight he slipped his arm round her again.

'Do you fancy a cream tea yet?' he asked.

She shook her head. 'I'd rather stay here for a while,' she said. 'It's so lovely and peaceful, isn't it?'

Lawrie looked about him, at the sunlight throwing dappled shadows beneath the fresh new green of the trees, the numerous wild flowers, and the green ferns uncurling like tiny catherine wheels. Over all lay silence and peace, only broken by birdsong or the rustle of a tiny creature moving through the previous year's leaves. He sighed.

'Hard to believe that there's so much misery and cruelty in the world, when you look around here, isn't it?'

She nodded, uncertain of his train of thought.

'Those poor kids,' he went on, 'running around hungry and half naked, and nobody cares a bent farthing about them. And aboard ship – my God! The Lascars like walking skeletons working in 110 degrees and more, and if you'd seen their quarters. . . . Ours were bad enough, God knows, but at least we used to crib about it. They just took it like beaten animals, and yet they were men same as us.'

'But there are people who care, Lol,' Sally said timidly. 'Major Lestor and Canon Nugent, and some nob in London, Da says.'

'Aye, more power to them,' Lawrie said. 'But they're only clearing up a mess that shouldn't be there in the first place. This is the wealthiest nation in the world, Sal. No one should be hungry or homeless.' He glanced at her and saw that she was looking sad. With a shake of his head he jumped to his feet, and held out his hand to her.

'Sorry, Sal. I'm spoiling our day ranting like this. Should we walk a bit further? I'm sure there's more to see before we reach the village.'

They strolled along, holding hands. Sally kept peeping at Lawrie's face. She had seen another side to the merry lad he seemed to be, and she was delighted. He's soft hearted, she thought, and deep thinking like Da. Wait until I tell Da, he'll be made up.

Lawrie turned to look at her and she said hastily, 'You know a lot of words, Lawrie – I mean, the right words to say – but you couldn't have been at school for long.'

'No. I left when I was twelve, but my mother loved books. She'd been a governess once, to the Houghtons. They had shops in Liverpool at one time – I don't know what happened to them. Mother was governess to the three daughters, and Mr Houghton let her borrow books from his library.'

'Even after she was married?' Sally said.

'Oh, no, but she got to know about books there, so whenever she had a penny to spare we used to go to the stalls in the Haymarket to buy books. We used to take turns reading aloud out of them, and I suppose it was better than any learning I'd have got in school.'

'Mrs Hart used to read to Emily and me,' Sally said. 'I'd be doing the grate or scrubbing, and Emily used to sit by her while she read Mr Dickens' books to us, and *The Daisy Chain*. Oh, that was a lovely book, Lawrie, I used to cry all the time she was reading it.'

Lawrie chuckled. 'Well, I never read that, or cried over it,' he said. 'Did you ever read Lord Tennyson's poems?' Sally shook her head.

'My mother loved them,' Lawrie continued. 'Even near the end she liked to hear them. She used to say, 'See if Merlin can work some magic for me, son?'

They walked for a while in silence, both of them deep in memories, until they came to the end of the wood. There was a glimpse of the river sparkling in the distance, and where the path dropped down, a little cottage in a flower-filled garden, with a board inscribed 'Cream Teas' propped by the gate.

A stout, motherly woman took them to a table by the corner window in the little parlour, and plates of cakes and scones, and dishes of jam and cream, appeared as though by magic.

'Now, tha'll like a cut of home cooked ham, and some bread and butter too, I reckon,' the woman said.

'Yes, please,' Lawrie said, laughing. 'The fresh air's given us an appetite.' The woman laughed, too, and Sally looked proudly at Lawrie. He's at home anywhere, she thought. There were people sitting at other tables in the room, and she looked about her nervously.

'They're all very posh,' she whispered to Lawrie. He shook his head.

'No different from us,' he whispered back, 'and you're the prettiest girl here. I feel as proud as Punch.'

Sally laughed. 'Oh, *Lawrie*,' was all she said, but she sat up straighter and looked about her with more confidence.

After tea they walked round the village, then strolled near the river, their arms about each other's waists. The sky became flushed with pink as the sun slowly sank, then the evening star appeared in the translucent, pale green sky. All too soon the ferry boat arrived, but on board the chattering couples of the morning were silent, lulled by the tranquillity of the night as twilight fell on the shipping lying quietly in the river. The moon rose, making a silver track across the gently moving water.

Presently the musicians began softly to play favourite ballads, and a boy began to sing 'Love's Old Sweet Song'. Others took up the refrain, and as the boat sailed towards Liverpool they sang 'Thora' and 'Beautiful Dreamer', quietly and dreamily.

In the friendly dark Sally lay in Lawrie's arms, filled with an overpowering feeling of love and happiness.

Throughout her long life the memory of that perfect day stayed with her like a jewel, never dulled or flawed by time or circumstance.

Chapter Twelve

Sally felt as though she was floating on a cloud of happiness during the following days, and it was hard for her to realise that her father's mood did not match her own. He seemed even more morose, saying little during the meal and immersing himself in his newspaper immediately afterwards. Although Sally longed to talk to him about Lawrie, his manner was too forbidding. She managed to have a short time with Lawrie most evenings, but was always warned to be home early. Sometimes she felt guilty because she was able to feel happy again, so soon after the tragedy of the previous year, but she had not forgotten Emily or the lads. Things she came across in the house, a snatch of tune, even a familiar smell, could bring her grief flooding back.

She complained to Lawrie once as they walked down the street after the usual gruff dismissal from Matthew.

'My da's very hard to live with these days. All this year he's been so moody and bad-tempered. I know he's got cause but he could try to be a bit more pleasant. He makes me feel guilty if I smile or look happy.'

'I'm sure your da doesn't want you to feel like that, Sal. I expect he's all right when he's at work, but when he comes home it hits him about the lads, and he can't help feeling downhearted.'

'I suppose so,' Sally said. 'I wish you'd known him when Mam was alive. He was a different man. He was just getting over that when we lost our John and Alfie, and Emily, and he got so moody. Sometimes now I'm almost afraid to speak to him.'

They had wandered to a secluded spot on Rupert Hill, and Lawrie's arm tightened round her.

'Oh, Sal, I hate to think of you being worried or afraid. If only we were married and I could take care of you.'

Sally blushed and snuggled against him. 'I wish we were too, so I could look after *you*,' she said. 'You know, cook all the things you like, and darn your socks, and everything.'

'I'll ask your da again,' Lawrie said. 'We know we won't change our minds, so what's the point of waiting?'

'Don't say anything yet, Lol,' Sally begged. 'Not while he has this moody spell on him. I don't want him to think I don't care, just because I've met you, and I'm happy.'

Lawrie kissed her again. 'I'm made up that you're happy, love,' he said, 'and just think, we'll be like this for the rest of our lives.'

Sally smiled gently at him. What a child he was in some ways, she thought, believing that they could always be happy. She knew well that there would be bad times as well as good – and yet, perhaps Lawrie was right. If they had each other they could be happy even during the bad times.

She stood up and they began to walk home, but a plan was forming in Sally's mind. She knew that she was always welcome in Mrs Malloy's house, but she felt that she could not leave her father alone every evening, even though he seemed unaware of her presence, but why shouldn't Lawrie sit in their house? It would give her father a chance to get to know him, and she and Lawrie could be together.

As soon as the meal was finished the following evening, and before Matthew could pick up his newspaper, Sally said quickly, 'Do you mind if Lawrie comes to sit in here, Da?'

Matthew looked up in surprise. 'What for? What's wrong with next door?'

'Just to sit with me while I do the mending,' Sally pleaded.

Her father snorted. 'Well, all right, if he's got nothing better to do with himself,' he said.

'Thanks, Da,' she said joyfully, rushing into the back kitchen with the dishes and washing them rapidly. She put out the mending basket and her father's shirt and socks beside it, and went next door to tell Lawrie.

'Da says you can sit in with me while I do the mending,' she said, as Lawrie jumped to his feet when he saw her. Belatedly she realised that Mrs Malloy and Paddy were also there, and stammered good evening to them.

'Ah, well, it'll be a bit of company for ye, for ye may as well sit with a dummy as your da when he has his head in the paper,' said Mrs Malloy. Paddy only took the pipe from his mouth and bobbed his head in greeting, but Lawrie was struck by a sudden thought. He picked up a jug.

'Can I take this, Mrs Mal?' he asked. As he and Sally went out of the door he said quietly, 'I won't be a minute, love. Paddy might have wanted to go for a drink, so I'll get a drop of porter for him and Mrs Malloy. Should I get some for your Da, too?'

Sally shook her head.

'No, he can be a bit funny. He might take it wrong.'

'See you in a minute then,' Lawrie said, squeezing her hand, and walking off, whistling. When he arrived at number nine a few minutes later, Matthew only lifted his head to nod then returned to his newspaper, but Lawrie felt that he was showing indifference rather than displeasure at his presence.

Lawrie sat beside Sally on the sofa, gazing at her fondly as she threaded her needle and picked up Matthew's shirt.

'Mrs Mal says you're a clever needlewoman, Sal,' he whispered.

'I like sewing,' she said, pleased. 'I make all our clothes.' A shadow fell over her face as she remembered that now there was only herself and her father for whom to sew, and she glanced fearfully at him. He seemed oblivious to them, but they said little more, afraid to disturb him, and content to sit companionably together. The fire sank low, and Matthew leaned forward to put coal on it.

'Were you ever in the American South, lad?' he asked.

'In my early days, Mr Palin,' Lawrie said. 'I remember when we should have had a five week voyage from New Orleans with a cargo of cotton, but the weather was against us all the way, and we were over eight weeks at sea. I was glad to sight the Old Head of Kinsale lighthouse, I can tell you. I switched to steam after that.'

'Did yer see many niggers in New Orleans?' asked Matthew.

'I never left port, but there were a lot of them on the quayside humping bales. Big brawny fellows, most of them, but those weights must have damaged them. I suppose the way the overseers saw it, there were plenty more to take their place.'

'That's what I'm getting at, lad. Ye say these were big, strong men, and from what I read they're no better off than when they were slaves, so why do they put up with it? Seems to be more of them than white men there.'

'I wish I knew, Mr Palin,' Lawrie said bitterly. 'The same goes for here. Look at this country. Rich men with more money than they know what to do with, and the rest of the people very near starving, but we do nothing about it. The wealthiest country in the world, and swarming with poor kids who've never known a full stomach.'

'Aye, you're right, lad. Mind you, there's fellas working to change it. This fella, Will Thorne now, in London. He got a union going in the Gas Works there, and already they've got eight-hour shifts, just by sticking together, but a union hasn't got a chance in most places.'

'The men themselves are often their worst enemy,' Lawrie said. 'Tradesmen who won't let others into their union, because they haven't served an apprenticeship.'

Matthew nodded. 'That's where Thorne has got it right. He formed a union for craftsmen and labourers alike, and the subscription is only twopence a week, so everyone can manage it.'

'It's the only hope for the likes of us,' Lawrie said. 'We'll only get justice by sticking together. On our own we can just be trodden down.'

The fire had begun to burn brightly, and Matthew moved the black kettle over the fire, and stood up to take a bottle of rum from the cupboard.

'D'yer fancy a toddy, lad?' he asked. Lawrie agreed eagerly, and Sally jumped up to get two mugs and the bowl of sugar. Lawrie moved to sit at the table by Matthew, and Sally gathered her mending and took it upstairs, smiling in delight at the success of her plan. When she came down Lawrie was saying, 'But I always feel about the Chinks, though, that even when they bow and scrape to us, really they sort of look down on us. Why wouldn't they anyhow, with thousands of years of civilization behind them?'

He looked up and smiled at Sally as she opened the door at the foot of the stairs, then he turned to Matthew. 'D'yer mind if we go out for a breath of air, Mr Palin?' he asked.

'No, no, go ahead, lad,' Matthew replied. Sally hugged Lawrie's arm as they walked down the street.

'I'm made up to hear you and Da talking like that. He was just like he used to be.'

'I enjoyed the talk,' Lawrie said. 'Pity there aren't more men like him. We'd all be better off.'

Sally leaned against him, smiling happily, and feeling that her cup of joy was full, yet that evening they had their first quarrel.

Sally was always proud when she walked down the street with Lawrie, and the neighbours gossiping at their doors smiled approvingly at them, but she was less pleased by the glances Lawrie received from the girls they met. She always tried to avoid Brunswick Road, which was known locally as the Parade, because of the groups of girls and boys who passed and repassed each other, eyeing one another flirtatiously. That evening she and Lawrie wandered along Shaw Street, near to Brunswick Road, and a group of three girls with linked arms approached them. They all looked at Lawrie and the boldest of them said loudly, 'Ay, lad, does yer mother know ye're out?'

Lawrie laughed. 'No. Does yours?' he said cheerfully.

They walked away, screaming with laughter, and Sally's face became grim, but before she could speak, one of the girls ran back to them. Evidently dared by her companions, she said impudently, 'D'yer feel like a change, lad?'

'No, thanks, I'm suited,' Lawrie said, but he tipped his hat before walking away with Sally. She snatched her arm away from him.

'*Well*, I've never been so insulted in my life!' she exclaimed. 'And you never said a word to her.'

'I did.' Lawrie protested. 'I told her I was suited, and I am.'

'People wouldn't think so, to see you talking to those scrags,' Sally said furiously.

'Hold on now. I only passed a word with them. What did you expect me to do? Aren't I allowed to speak to anyone else?'

'Not to the likes of them,' Sally said, nearly in tears with anger and mortification. 'Not while you're with me anyhow. Making little of me.'

'I didn't hear anyone insulting you. They only made a joke – no harm in that, for God's sake.'

'They could see you were with me. Would you like it if I started talking to another fellow that way?'

'That's different –' began Lawrie, but Sally interrupted him.

'Oh no it's not! How is it different? It's all right for you to do it, but not me, I suppose. Anyhow, you must have been giving those girls the eye for them to come after you like that.'

'Well, by God. Talk about something and nothing. All right, that second girl was hardfaced – but it was only meant for a laugh. You were laughing yourself.'

'Only to show that I didn't care,' Sally said, with a sob. Lawrie's arms went round her.

'Sally, love,' he said. 'Here we are arguing over nothing. I won't talk to anyone in future if that's what you want. Come on, love, dry your eyes. We're wasting our time together.'

They strolled towards home, both quiet and thoughtful. Lawrie was deciding to be less exuberant and to consider Sally's feelings more carefully, and Sally was recognizing a demon of jealousy in herself which she knew she should curb. It was dark when they reached the house, and Lawrie drew Sally into his arms.

'I'm sorry, love,' he whispered, but at the same moment she said, 'It was my fault. I'm sorry, Lol.'

Lawrie kissed her cheek, then her mouth, and they clung together, both shaken by their brief quarrel. Suddenly Lawrie's lips pressed down hard on hers, almost bruising them, and his arms tightened round her until they hurt her. Sally clung to him, her arms around his neck, the tide of passion rising in her to meet his, but suddenly Lawrie raised his head.

'Oh, God, Sally,' he said thickly, before turning away and striding rapidly away down the street. Sally waited for a moment before she opened the door, and was thankful that her father had his back turned to her as he wound the tin clock, so that she could go through to the back kitchen. She filled a cup with water and drank it rapidly, then splashed her face with cold water, before venturing into the kitchen.

'That's a good lad,' her father observed. 'Plenty of feeling for others, and weighs things up.'

Sally felt unable to answer coherently, so she snatched up her father's empty cocoa mug and retreated again to the back kitchen. She was still there when he called goodnight and went upstairs, and after waiting a few minutes she turned out the lamp, and gently opened the door. A row in number thirty-eight had spilled out on to the pavement, and a drunken man was weaving his way up the street on the other side, but there was no sign of Lawrie. She closed and bolted the door and crept up to bed, but she lay awake until she heard Lawrie's footsteps returning up the street. If only he was coming in here to me, she thought longingly.

The next night was Sally's breadmaking night so she was too busy to invite Lawrie into the house, and they had time for only a short time together when the bread was out of the oven.

As soon as they left the house, Lawrie said quietly, 'I'm sorry about rushing away like that last night, love. Sal, I love you so much! Can't I talk to your da again about us getting married?'

'I wish we could,' Sally said. 'I was so worried last night. I was glad when I heard you come back, but I wished you were coming into our house instead of Mrs Malloy's.'

To her surprise Lawrie stopped dead, and turned to look at her. 'Sally,' he said, 'you'll think I'm cracked. I never thought about where we'd live – I just thought about us getting married and being together. I'm a fool.'

'But we'd have to live with Da, so I could look after him,' Sally said. They walked on for a while without speaking.

Finally Lawrie said soberly, 'I feel a bit more awkward-like now, about asking your da. If we just got rooms near, to start off with, you could still look after him, and he might like the idea better. I don't want to crowd in on him, Sal.'

'It's no use me saying what I think Da would like, Lawrie, because I never know these days. D'you think we should ask Mrs Malloy what she thinks?'

'Good idea,' Lawrie exclaimed. 'We'll do it now.'

Sally shook her head. 'We haven't time. I have to be back in a few minutes, but you could talk to her if you like.'

Lawrie lost no time in asking Mrs Malloy's advice. Paddy had gone to bed, and they were able to speak freely, but Mrs Malloy, for once, was unable to give a definite opinion. The only thing she would say was that it was unlikely that any decision need be made for some time.

'Matthew's not a man to be rushed, lad,' she said. 'I doubt he'll let ye marry inside a twelvemonth, but it'll give ye a chance to save up.'

'Oh, we can't wait that long, Mrs Mal,' Lawrie exclaimed. 'Surely when he sees that we know our own minds he'll agree to us getting married soon? It's just about where we'll live. I don't want him to think I'm just looking for a berth, but Sally doesn't like the idea of leaving him.'

'If ye like lad, I'll sound him out, but I'm not saying ye've much chance. Ye've nothing behind ye, and the building's a chancy job at best, what with the weather an' all.'

'I might get a job in a grain warehouse – I've got a mate who works there, and he's keeping his eyes open for me,' said Lawrie.

'Ah, well, I tell you what, lad. I'll see what I can do with Matthew, and you get settled with a better job before ye speak to him. Believe me, that's yer best chance.'

Lawrie reluctantly agreed, but he decided that he would see his friend as soon as possible and impress on him the urgency of his task.

Chapter Thirteen

Sally agreed with Mrs Malloy that her father would be more likely to let them marry if Lawrie had a settled job, but she suggested to him that it might be better if he remained on the building job for the remaining summer months.

'You could earn more with the overtime that's going now and we could save up. You could still try for the warehouse before the winter,' she said.

Lawrie agreed ruefully that what she said made sense, but he was dismayed to realise that Sally did not feel the same urgency for marriage as himself. Although he said nothing, Sally was quick to sense his feelings, and she said gently, 'I *am* anxious to get married, Lol, but I'd like some time for courting first, so I'm not just thinking about saving up. Y'see, when we're married we'll have all sorts of things to worry about. I'd like a sort of lighthearted time first.'

She felt that she had not explained properly how she felt, so she was surprised when Lawrie nodded.

'Aye, I see what you mean. I know you've had your share of worries in the past, but once we're married, Sal, I'll do the worrying for both of us, and you can sign off.'

They laughed and hugged each other, and Sally said, 'I can't believe it's only a fortnight since you came. You haven't even met Mrs Hart yet, or seen our Emily.'

'I suppose it's too late tonight for Mrs Hart,' Lawrie said. 'What about tomorrow, Sal?'

'Yes, tomorrow we'll go,' Sally said. 'She hasn't been – very well – but she's better now.' Even to Lawrie she was reluctant to talk of Mrs Hart's drunkenness, but the following evening asked her neighbour's permission to take Lawrie to meet her.

Later, when they called, Sally felt proud of Lawrie's appearance and manners, which seemed to impress Mrs Hart, and the time passed pleasantly as they discussed books and Lawrie's voyages to foreign lands. By the end of the evening she was sure that Mrs Hart, at least, approved of Lawrie as her husband, and that Lawrie was equally impressed by Mrs Hart.

'Now what about Emily?' asked Lawrie. 'Could we go there one evening?'

'Oh, *no*,' said Sally. 'It's a long way off.' Lawrie threw back his head and laughed.

'Ormesdale, Sal? I've just come back from China.'

She smiled. 'I'll write and ask if we can go one Sunday,' she said. She wrote to Hester immediately, but it was several weeks before a reply came, suggesting a date in August. Sally was surprised, she'd expected Hester to be anxious to view Lawrie as soon as possible, but she was even more surprised when the time came for the visit.

Matthew had intended to travel with them, but on the Saturday he arrived home from work looking grey and ill.

He refused food, and after drinking a glass of rum and hot water he went to bed. As usual, Sally went to Mrs Malloy for advice, but she advised her not to worry.

'If he rests his stomach and keeps warm he'll be grand,' she said. 'Lucky he has Sunday to get over it.'

'But we were supposed to go to Ormesdale,' Sally said in dismay.

'Well, yourself and the lad can still go, but your da will be better in his bed. I'll look after him. Don't fret, girlie.' After a night's sleep Matthew looked a little better, but he seemed thankful to stay in bed.

Sally and Lawrie set off in high spirits, and Walter met them at the station, but this time Emily was sitting beside him. She scrambled down and flung herself into Sally's arms, while Lawrie greeted Walter and admired the trap.

'Ah bowt it from Sir Ralph at t'Hall,' he said complacently. He turned to Sally. 'Thou'rt looking well, lass, but wheer's tha feyther?'

'He's not well, Uncle Walter, so he's having the day in bed,' Sally said. She looked at Lawrie, a worried frown on her face. 'I hope I did right to leave him, Lol.'

'Of course you did, love. He only needed rest, and Mrs Malloy's looking after him.'

'Eh, little 'un ud be reet upset if tha' hadn't coom. She's talked of nowt else,' said Walter. Emily had retreated behind Sally when Lawrie turned to her, but he bent his knees so that his eyes were level with Emily's, and took her hand.

'I've thought of nothing else since I heard that I was going to meet you, Emily. I've never had a sister-in-law before.' Sally laughed and blushed, and Emily looked from one to the other with a puzzled expression.

'I believe you've got your own garden. Will you show it to me, love?' asked Lawrie, and Emily nodded, and smiled at him.

They climbed into the trap, but this time Sally took little notice of the beauty of the countryside. She sat with her eyes darting between Lawrie and Emily. The child had lost her shyness and chattered away to him, about her garden, and about the baking that had been done in preparation for their visit.

Hester was standing in front of the open front door of the farm-house, and she scrutinized Lawrie from head to foot as they stepped down from the trap. Sally grew warm with indignation, but Lawrie seem unperturbed. He held out his hand and smiled at Hester, and in spite of herself she smiled back at him.

'Wheer's Matthew then?' she demanded.

'He's not well, Aunt, so he's having the day in bed,' Sally said. Hester sniffed.

'Proper unhealthy place, is that,' she said.

They went into the house by the front door, and Sally was amazed at the changes in the short time since their last visit. Walter had pointed out the extra fields he had acquired, and some sheds and pigsties at the side of the house had been cleared away, but she was unprepared for the opulence inside the house.

Emily was told to take Sally upstairs to leave her hat and jacket, but this time when they came downstairs, Emily led the way into the parlour, evidently on Hester's instructions. Hester was dispensing glasses of parsnip wine, and fingers of fruit cake. The weather was warm and sultry and Sally would have preferred the lemonade offered on her previous visit, but she had to follow Hester's example and sip genteely at the wine.

The room was stuffy and overcrowded with furniture. On Sally's right there was a small table on which a statue of a goddess holding a cornucopia reclined under a glass shade, and on her left a huge vase of bulrushes stood on a bamboo plant stand. She felt suffocated and was relieved when Walter put down his glass and took Lawrie out to see the farm.

As soon as they left, Hester began to bombard Sally with questions about Lawrie. She seemed especially interested in his aunt in Anfield. Did she own or rent her house? What did her husband work at before his death? Was she fond of Lawrie? Sally was bewildered.

'I don't know much about her,' she said. 'Only that she was supposed to look after Lawrie when his mother died, but he went to sea instead. He's been to see her when he's been ashore but he didn't stay with her. He says she's very houseproud – the house should be under a glass case.'

'Tha should *both* go,' Hester said. 'If he's all as she's got, he should keep up wi' her. Blood's thicker than water, tha knows, and he doesn't want what she's got left away from him.'

Emily came into the parlour, and Sally was glad to escape into the garden with her. As they passed the open kitchen door, she noticed a buxom girl working at the sink.

'Who's that, love?' she said, thinking that she, too, could ask questions.

'It's Ada,' said Emily. 'Aunt Hester's training her, but, eh – it's uphill work.' Sally laughed aloud, wondering whether her aunt and uncle realised that they had such a faithful mimic under their roof. Emily looked puzzled, and Sally began to ask her about the garden and the animals. They wandered round to where Lawrie stood talking to the farmhand, Billy Snell, and Emily ran up and took Billy's hand.

'Walter's been called away,' Lawrie said, and Billy Snell looked closely at Sally.

'So, thou'rt her sister. Tha'd do well to tek her whoam outa this. Theer's trouble brewing here, or ah'm a Dutchman.' He patted Emily's head fondly then stumped away, and Sally and Lawrie walked on with the child between them. As soon as Emily ran ahead, Sally said breathlessly, 'What did he mean, Lawrie? What's wrong?'

'Don't worry,' he said easily, 'Billy's annoyed because he thinks Walter's overreaching himself, buying more land, and it seems he's been speculating, too. "Nowt but gambling," Billy called it, but it seems to be successful by what Walter told me of his plans.'

A few moments later they were summoned to their meal. The table was laid in the parlour, and Walter carved a sirloin while Ada carried round the dishes of vegetables, breathing heavily as she paused by each person.

'Don't pant so, Ada,' Hester said, and Ada glared at her sullenly.

'Leave lass alone. She's doing her best,' Walter said, and Sally was surprised to see how meekly Hester accepted the rebuke. Lawrie praised the food, and plainly enjoyed it.

Hester said approvingly, 'Eh, I like to see a good appetite. Tha puts it in a good skin too, lad. I wish Walter showed more for t'good food as he eats.'

Again Sally was surprised by the venom in Walter's glance at Hester, but she seemed unaware of it.

After Ada had cleared away the meal, Walter went out, and Emily took Lawrie to see the hens. Sally's offer to do the dishes was brusquely refused by Hester.

'Girl does them,' she said, moving over to the sofa and patting the place beside her for Sally to sit down. She expected another barrage of questions, but Hester was silent for a moment. Then she said suddenly, 'Eh, Emily's the image of tha mam at that age, i' looks and allus singing and chattering same as she did. She sailed through, did Julie, nowt ever bothered her.'

'Mrs Malloy says that,' said Sally. 'She says she was as blithe as a bird.'

Hester sighed. 'Aye, well, she'd plenty to be blithe about. She'd a reet happy life, for all it were cut short.'

Sally was amazed, but suddenly Mrs Malloy's words after her mother's death came back to her.

'Hester was always black jealous of yer mam.' She sat looking at the luxury around her, uncertain what to say.

Emily and Lawrie returned, and Hester went out to check on Ada.

'I don't know what to make of my aunt,' Sally whispered to Lawrie. 'She doesn't seem happy about the improvements. Maybe Billy Snell's right.'

'No, he just doesn't like change, and maybe your aunt is the same, but I'm sure she'll come round to it. It's going to be a lovely house when they build out at the side.'

'Is that why they cleared the sheds and pigsties? Don't say too much to Da about it, Lawrie. He gets vexed with Uncle Walter.' They had another stroll with Emily, listening with delight to her tales of school and her sewing, and soon Hester called them for tea, again served in the parlour.

When it was time to go Lawrie shook hands with Hester and said firmly, 'Thanks for the hospitality. Next time we see you might be at our wedding. I'm hoping to persuade Mr Palin to let us get married soon.'

'Nay, you've nobbut known each other five minutes!' Hester exclaimed. ' "Marry in haste, repent at leisure" – that's i' the Bible.'

Lawrie only laughed. 'No fear of that,' he said. 'I've no doubts, and I hope Sally hasn't.'

Sally blushed and kissed Aunt Hester, then climbed into the trap. Emily came to the station with them, but Sally was less distressed at parting with her than on her last visit.

'I'll see you again soon, love,' she whispered as she kissed the child, and Emily clung to her.

'Will you bring our Lawrie?' she asked. Sally glanced at Lawrie and he put his arms round them both, and kissed Emily.

'Of course she will,' he said. 'I'm nearly your brother-in-law.'

Emily giggled, and Walter drew her back from the carriage door.

'Think on now, Sally, tell tha feyther about all t'changes. I hope as he's mended when tha gets whoam.'

'Thank you for a lovely day, Uncle Walter,' Sally said, determined not to give her promise. The train drew away, with Emily looking back and waving, and Walter strutting away.

'I'm not going to say anything to Da,' Sally said. 'Uncle Walter's changed. He hardly used to speak.'

'He's a rising man,' said Lawrie. 'He runs that farm well, and he dotes on Emily, doesn't he?'

Sally lost interest in Walter immediately. 'What did you think of her?' she asked eagerly.

'I thought she was a right little charmer. I can see why you were so upset at losing her, Sal, and I don't think it was right, but she seems to have settled down there now, doesn't she?' The carriage was empty of other people, so he had slipped his arm around Sally and she leaned against him.

'Yes, I suppose so,' Sally said, 'but I still think she would have been better at home. There's something – I don't know, something wrong there. Even Billy Snell seemed to see it.'

'I think there's change in the air,' Lawrie said. 'Is that what you mean, Sal?'

'No, even when we went last time, I was worried. Mrs Hart understood. She could see that I was afraid they would teach Emily the wrong things, but she told me not to worry. "As the twig is bent, so the tree will grow", she said.'

Lawrie bent his head and kissed her. 'You're lucky in your neighbours, love, Mrs Malloy and Mrs Hart. Don't worry about Emily. She's a sensible little girl, and we'll see her often.'

Sally smiled, and they sat in contented silence until the train reached Liverpool, then walked home arm in arm.

Matthew was sitting by a small fire, looking much better.

'I'll be all right for work tomerrer,' he said. 'How did yer get on?' Sally eagerly told him about Emily, that she had grown taller, and that she had made a complete set of dolls' clothes by herself.

'She seems really settled there, Da,' she said, stifling a sigh.

'Aye, well, there's good air there, and room to turn round,' Matthew said. He turned to Lawrie. 'What did yer make of Walter?' he asked.

Lawrie pondered for a moment. 'I couldn't quite weigh him up,' he said. 'He seems very quiet, but then he says something that makes you think he's deeper than he seems, but maybe I'm talking out of turn.'

'No, no, lad, I just wondered how he struck you. What about the farm?'

Lawrie glanced at Sally.

'It's certainly well run,' he said cautiously. Matthew nodded.

'He knows the job all right, and he could always make the money,' he said, 'but I wondered if things were going extra well. I seen him coming out of the Stork one day – he didn't see me – and he was dressed up to dolrags, and gabbing away to the fellow with him, another tailor's dummy. Didn't look like the same man, but it was him all right.'

'I didn't know him before so I couldn't say,' Lawrie said diplomatically, 'I thought Emily was a lovely little girl. Beautiful eyes, and lovely thick hair.'

'Aye, she's the model of her mother,' Matthew said with a sigh, but his mind seemed to have been successfully turned away from Walter. Lawrie rose to his feet.

'I'd better get next door,' he said. 'Mrs Mal will be waiting to hear the news.'

Matthew laughed. 'Yer've got the measure of things in there, lad,' he said. 'Mind you, she's been very good to me today, so I shouldn't call her.'

Sally went to the door with Lawrie.

'Thanks, love. You managed that well,' she whispered, as they parted with a hasty kiss. She hummed happily to herself as she prepared for the next day. How good and how clever Lawrie was, she thought. With him to look after her she need never worry about anything ever again.

Chapter Fourteen

The weeks went by, and Sally found that with two regular wages, and only herself and her father to keep, she could save regularly. Lawrie worked as much overtime as possible, even though it meant that he could see Sally only briefly, and each payday he gave Sally some of his wages to save. The money that Sally put in the old teapot grew steadily, but the money that Lawrie had left after he had paid Mrs Malloy seemed to run through his hands.

He frequently bought small gifts for Sally, and the ragged children of the area soon realised that he could never resist their pleas for coppers. When he was with Sally the street Arabs rarely approached him, but Sally knew that he was waylaid by them every day on his way home from work.

She realised that Lawrie was more horrified by the swarms of hungry, barefoot children than she was because she had been accustomed all her life to seeing them, but when she found that he was penniless halfway through the week she protested.

'I can't help it,' Lawrie said. 'I can't see a starving kid begging for a penny for something to eat, and walk away with money in my pocket, Sal.'

'But there's plenty of people with more than you who ignore them. I've seen lads begging to carry a case or run a message for toffs coming off a ship, and they've been chased away as though they were muck, even though they were desperate with hunger. People who wouldn't miss a pound, never mind a penny.'

'I know,' said Lawrie, 'but two wrongs don't make a right, Sal.'

'Yes, but what you can give is only a drop in the ocean. There's so many of them, and yet it leaves you without a farthing.' He only smiled ruefully and shrugged his shoulders, and she said no more, afraid of being thought heartless or mean.

One evening in late August, Lawrie's friend called to see him, and later Lawrie went to see Sally, smiling broadly.

'I'm fixed up, Sal,' he said. 'Jerry has spoken for me and I'm to start on Monday at the warehouse, if I suit.'

Matthew looked up. 'Yer've been laid off the building, then?'

'No, but this is a steady job, Mr Palin. You know how it is with the building trade in the winter.' He glanced at Sally who had moved behind her father's chair, and was signalling to him not to mention marriage.

'Has yer mate worked there long?' asked Matthew.

'A few years. He's an old shipmate, and he's worked there since he came ashore. He reckons the work's hard, but it's steady and the boss is all right.'

'Any steady job's worth having nowadays,' Matthew said, turning back to his newspaper.

Later, when Lawrie and Sally went out for a walk, he asked curiously, 'How did you know I was going to ask your da about us getting married?'

'I know you,' she said, laughing. 'Speak first, think later, as Mrs Malloy would say. You're not even sure of the job yet.'

'Don't worry, I'll make sure I suit,' Lawrie declared. 'How soon should I ask your da, then?'

'Perhaps when you've worked a month?' Sally suggested.

'Two weeks,' said Lawrie.

'Three weeks,' she laughed.

'Done,' he said, lifting her off her feet to kiss her, to the amusement of passers-by.

The following night he came to the market to meet her.

'We're going to celebrate tonight, Sal,' he said cheerfully. 'Your da's home and I've asked him. We're going to the theatre.'

'Oh, Lawrie, where?' Sally asked in great excitement.

'The Rossmadden. I've got a box.'

'The – the Rossi,' Sally stammered, trying to hide her dismay. Lawrie looked anxious.

'Why? Is there something wrong? I used to go there with my mam and dad when I was a kid.'

'No. So you've got a box. I'll have to dress up,' Sally said. The Rossmadden had been a good theatre at one time, but she had heard that it had gone down rapidly, and had a reputation for roughness. She consoled herself with the thought that they would be all right in a box. She had recently made herself a grey skirt and coat, and she decided to wear that with a white blouse, and hat and gloves. Lawrie wore a braided suit and a curly brimmed bowler, and Mrs Malloy surveyed them with pride.

'Royalty isn't better dressed than the pair of yiz,' she said. Sally was afraid that they might be too well-dressed for the Rossi, and her worst fears were realised when they arrived there.

The manager, in a frock coat green with age, and paper collar and cuffs, showed them to the box with a flourish. All the seats below were full and the noise was deafening. The box looked magnificent, but when Sally rested her hands on the plush-covered ledge, she withdrew them hastily when she realised that her white gloves were becoming filthy. As she drew back she brushed against the velvet drapes, and released a shower of dust which set her and Lawrie sneezing. This attracted the attention of the audience down below.

'Look at the nobs,' someone shouted, and immediately Sally and Lawrie were pelted with peanuts and orange peel. Lawrie seized her hand and they beat a hasty retreat, followed by the manager, frantically waving his arms, with the paper false front bursting from his coat and disclosing his lack of shirt.

'I'm sorry, Sal. God, what a fool I am,' Lawrie muttered as they rushed out, but when they reached the open air and looked at each other, they simultaneously burst into peals of laughter. There was a black streak across Lawrie's nose, and an even larger smear of dirt on Sally's face. They stumbled down the hill, helpless with laughter, until they reached a low stone wall and collapsed upon it.

'The nobs,' Sally began.

'The manager,' Lawrie gasped.

Every time they tried to speak they were overcome with laughter, but when they had calmed down Lawrie found a horse trough and they rinsed their hands, and used Sally's handkerchief dipped in the water to clean the dirt from their faces.

'I haven't laughed so much for ages,' Sally said. 'It was better than any show, Lawrie.'

'You're a girl in a thousand to take it like that,' he declared. 'Honest to God, I need my head examined, taking you to a place like that. Your da would have my life if he knew.'

'He'd be glad I had a good laugh.' Sally said. She stood looking down between the roofs of the town to where the sky was flushed with pink above the shipping crowded in the river. Then she said softly, 'Twelve months ago, Lol, I thought I'd never laugh again. I'd have been glad to die, I was so miserable, and now I love waking up in the morning and remembering about you.'

She turned her face against his chest, and Lawrie held her tightly, too full of emotion to do more than say, 'Oh, Sally, Sally love,' in a choked voice.

They strolled about for a while, happy just to be together, then made their way homeward, deciding to tell no one of their experiences in the Rossmadden.

On Monday morning Lawrie started in the new job. He arrived home at night exhausted, and covered in dust from the grain. After he had washed, and sat down to a meal which he seemed too tired to eat, Sally came in and sat with him, but she quickly realised how tired he was.

'I think you should go to bed right away, love,' she said. 'I've got my washing to do, and I'll see you tomorrow. Perhaps it'll be easier for you now you've got the first day over.'

'I'm sorry, Sal,' he said. 'It's just until I get used to carrying the sacks. It looks like a good job anyway, and I seem to suit.'

'That's good,' Sally said, kissing him gently and going out, leaving Lawrie to stumble thankfully up the stairs to bed. As the days passed, the lifting and carrying of the heavy sacks became easier for him, and for the first gruelling week, the thought that it was bringing his marriage nearer sustained him. At the end of the week he was relieved to be told that the boss considered him satisfactory.

When three weeks had passed he said to Sally, on the Friday night, 'I finish early tomorrow love, and so does your da, so it might be the best time for me to speak to him.'

'But I'll be at work,' she protested.

'I know, Sal, but it might be better if we talk man to man. I'll come to the market to tell you what he says.'

The following day Lawrie washed himself thoroughly and changed into his best suit before going in to see Matthew. The older man was lying back in his chair, his face grey and beads of sweat on his forehead. Lawrie forgot his carefully prepared speech.

'What's up, Mr Palin,' he asked anxiously. 'Do you feel bad?'

'Aye, I do, lad,' Matthew said. 'It's my guts again. Like a hand gripping me. I haven't been right since I had that do a few weeks ago.'

'Should I help you to bed? Would you like a drop of brandy?' Lawrie said, but Matthew shook his head.

'No. There's a bottle of rum in that cupboard. Boil up some hot water,' he said. Lawrie emptied some water from the big black kettle before putting the kettle on the fire, and the remaining drop of water boiled quickly. He mixed some rum and hot water and a spoonful of sugar, and some colour came back to Matthew's face as he sipped it then burped loudly.

'Eh, that's better,' he said. 'Well, you wanted to talk to me, lad.'

Lawrie looked undecided. 'I don't think I should bother you now,' he said.

Matthew waved his hand. 'Carry on, carry on,' he said.

'It's about me and Sally, Mr Palin. I know I rushed at it too much at first, but I felt as certain then as I do now. We've been going out together for four months nearly, and that's more like other people courting a year because we see each other so often.'

Matthew closed his eyes. 'Don't beat about the bush so much,' he said wearily. 'Out with it.'

'We want to get married as soon as possible, if you're agreeable. This job is steady. I won't get "rained off" in the winter, and I saved a bit out of my overtime.'

Matthew sipped at the rum and water.

'I'll tell you the truth, lad,' he said. 'The way I've been lately, I'll be glad to see things fixed up so our Sally will be looked after.'

'Don't say that, Mr Palin!' Lawrie exclaimed. 'Something's upset your stomach and it's taking time for you to get right again. I'm sure if you could have a few days in bed you'd feel as right as rain.'

Matthew sighed. 'Maybe so,' he said. He held a lighted spill to his pipe and puffed at it, staring into the fire. Lawrie wondered how he could re-open the subject of marriage, but Matthew suddenly said, 'Mrs Mal speaks well of yer, lad. Did yer know she was in here the other night banging me ear about you two?'

'No, she didn't say anything to me.'

'Aye well, women! She thinks I'm throwing temptation in yer way not letting ye get married, then the next breath she's saying ye're a decent lad, well brought up, only reckless with money, but our Sally's a good manager.'

'Sally's safe with me, Mr Palin,' Lawrie said, 'Only I admit, it's not easy. As regards money, I'm no hand at managing it but Sally'll be all the ballast I need, I promise you.'

Matthew leaned back, smiling at Lawrie's indignant face. 'Will ye live here?' he said.

'It's up to you,' Lawrie said. 'It's what Sally wants, I know.' His face grew red. 'But I'm not just looking for a berth, you know. I'd get somewhere decent for Sally even if it was only a couple of rooms to start with.'

'No need for that. Ye're welcome here,' Matthew said.

'So we can fix the date then?' Lawrie said eagerly.

'Suit yerself, lad,' Matthew said. 'I won't stand in your way. God knows I've not made such a good hand of me own life, to be telling ye how to live yours.'

'You've just been unlucky. Mrs Mal says you were a good husband and a good father. No one can do anything about death. It's just fate or God's will.'

'Aye,' Matthew said with a sneer. 'God comes in handy as a scapegoat.' He looked so grey and tired that Lawrie was alarmed.

'Should I ask Mrs Mal to come in?' he asked nervously.

'God's truth, lad, that'd finish me altogether.' Matthew said. 'I'll tell you what: if ye'll put the oven shelf in the bed for me, I'll go up in a minute.'

Lawrie was glad to obey and to mix another tumbler of rum and hot water for Matthew, before hurrying off to tell Sally the good news. First, though, he told Mrs Malloy that Matthew was ill and wanted to be left undisturbed, although he seemed to be in a bad way. To his surprise she took the news calmly.

'Ah, sure if Matty's finger ached he'd think he had gangrene,' she said. 'I've never met such a feller as him for looking on the black side.'

'He seems very depressed,' Lawrie said. 'Worrying about Sally, if anything happened to him, and even saying he'd made a mess of his life.'

Mrs Malloy nodded. 'The black dog's on him then. Never mind, lad, don't be worrying. It's just his way.'

Sally had found it hard to concentrate on her work that day. When Agnes came in she confided to her in a whisper that Lawrie was to ask her da about the wedding, and one look at his smiling face as he approached the stall told them that the news was good. Agnes gave a squeal of pleasure then tactfully withdrew, while Lawrie held Sally's hand and told her that her father had said that they could marry when they pleased, and live with him.

'Oh, Lawrie,' was all she could say, as they held hands and looked into each other's eyes. Mrs Gregson bore down on them like a ship in full sail.

'What's all this,' she demanded. 'What do you think you're playing at, Sally?'

They turned to her. 'Da says we can get married as soon as we like,' Sally said.

Mrs Gregson looked at their radiant faces, and a smile softened her grim features. 'Well, I'll get no more good of you tonight, I can see. Ye'd best get off home, Sally. Me and Agnes'll manage, and yer can make it up some other time.'

The September air felt crisp and fresh as they emerged from the Market, and began to walk down towards the river.

'We might as well have a blow. Your da won't expect us yet, and anyway he was going to bed.'

'Why, is he ill?' she asked in alarm, but Lawrie reassured her.

'He only needs warmth and rest,' he said. 'He can always knock for

Mrs Mal, but he'll be asleep by now, I'll bet. We've got things to arrange, love.' Sally agreed, smiling happily.

They strolled along the Landing Stage, arm in arm, too blissfully excited to make any serious plans, but within the next few days all the arrangements were made. Matthew was reluctant to take part in religious ritual and would have preferred a civil ceremony, but Sally and Lawrie wished for a blessing on their marriage and Hester would have been horrified at Matthew's plan. Mrs Malloy, for once, took no part in the discussion as she was a Catholic, except to say wistfully, 'I wish ye could be properly married, girl, in St. Francis Xavier's.'

Finally it was arranged that they would be married in the chapel of a young clergyman whom Lawrie admired because he had organized a group of young men to help the destitute people of the neighbourhood.

Sally and Lawrie were to have the bedroom which Sally had shared with Emily, and they bought a chest of drawers and a new mirror for the room. Sally made new window curtains, and Lawrie freshly white-washed the walls and painted the door and window frame. They were as pleased and proud with the result as any young couple with a new mansion. Sally made herself a blue coat and skirt, and a white broderie anglaise blouse, and bought new white gloves and a new hat. For Agnes Cassidy, who was to be her bridesmaid, she made a fawn coat and skirt, and their preparations were almost complete. They had only to wait impatiently for the day to arrive.

Chapter Fifteen

The days before the wedding were stormy, but when Sally woke on her wedding morning it was a beautiful October day, with only a few small white clouds floating in a clear blue sky. She went downstairs and cooked her father's breakfast, then took a kettle full of hot water upstairs to wash. She was brushing her hair when Agnes Cassidy arrived, and came up to the bedroom.

'Your room's beautiful, Sal,' she exclaimed. Then looking at Sally she added, 'And you are, too.'

Sally was standing with her arms upraised as she wound her shining hair into a neat bun on the nape of her neck, and Agnes marvelled at the change in her since she had met Lawrie. The tense, angular girl with a worried expresion had vanished, and been replaced by a tall, slim young woman with a softly rounded figure, and a face glowing with happiness. Tendrils of shining hair curled on her brow, and her clear blue eyes were fringed with dark lashes. Her cheeks were flushed now, and her full lips curved in a smile. Agnes gazed at her in wonder.

'Oh, Agnes, I wish I was.' Sally said shyly.

'You *are*,' Agnes insisted. 'Look in the glass.' Sally turned to look in the mirror. She was surprised and delighted at her reflection, and said impulsively, 'I'm glad, Agnes, for Lawrie's sake.'

'Oh, Lawrie, he'd think you were perfect no matter what!' Agnes exclaimed. 'I'll bet when you're really old, he'll think you look the same as today.'

Sally looked out of the window, her face tender as she thought of Lawrie. 'I'm so lucky, Ag,' she said.

'You are,' Agnes agreed. 'He's a true man.'

'I wish you could meet someone like him,' Sally said.

'So do I,' Agnes said wistfully, then with a return to her normal manner she added, 'so keep your eyes open for one for me.' They both laughed and the emotional moment passed. It was only when Sally had dressed in her blue suit, and carefully arranged the little white hat to frame her face, that Agnes said, 'Mrs Malloy told me ma you had a bloom on you, and I can see what she meant.'

'A bloom,' Sally echoed. 'She's a case, isn't she?'

At that moment they heard the voices of Mrs Malloy and Aunt Hester downstairs, and went down to greet them. The two women were loud in their praises of the girls' appearance, and Emily shyly produced the flowers she had brought. There were late white roses for the men's buttonholes, and a corsage for Agnes, and Emily had arranged a pretty posy of flowers for Sally.

'A proper knack she has,' Hester said fondly. Walter had brought in a large basket of provisions, and Matthew and Lawrie had earlier rearranged the room, with extra chairs brought in from Mrs Malloy's house, and a small table placed beside their kitchen table, over which Mrs Malloy had spread a crisp white cloth to make them seem as one.

In the back kitchen Lawrie had set up a small cask of ale, and several bottles of whisky, rum and gin, so all the preparations were well in hand.

'Are yiz ready?' Mrs Malloy asked. 'The lads are long gone to the chapel, and I want to get this table laid.'

'We've hired a carriage, Sally,' Hester said proudly. 'He'll take me and Walter and Emily, and come back for you and Agnes, and your da.'

'Can I go with you, and wait for Sally at the church?' Agnes asked. She knew that Sally and her father would like a few minutes alone together on their way to Sally's marriage.

The neighbours had gathered outside to see the wedding party leave, and there were Oohs and Ahs of admiration as Hester swept out in rustling maroon silk, followed by Emily in brown velvet and a chip bonnet trimmed with pansies, and Walter so smartly dressed that Sally had been afraid of some comment from her father as he surveyed him. He contented himself with a muttered 'Tailor's dummy.' Matthew himself looked unusually smart in a dark suit and bowler hat, and the wing collar that Sally had bought him. She felt proud when the carriage returned, and she went out to it arm in arm with her father.

Sally remembered little of the wedding service except Lawrie's smiling face turned to her as she walked down the aisle, and the sunshine which shone through the window as the minister pronounced them man and wife, and fell across their clasped hands like a benediction.

After the brief ceremony they returned to the house, where Mrs Malloy had laid the table with the bread and cakes which she had helped Sally to bake, and the ham and tongue and pickles provided by Hester. The tiny room was crowded with Mrs Hart, Mrs Dolan and Maggie Connolly, and the best man, Jerry, and Paddy Ryan. Lawrie's aunt, a thin, severe-looking woman, and Aunt Hester were established on the sofa and soon deep in conversation, while Agnes and Mrs Malloy filled plates and passed them round, and Lawrie and Jerry brought round the drinks. The neighbours all exclaimed about the change in Emily, and Walter stood smirking on the hearthrug, his thumbs in the armholes of his waistcoat. Sally and Lawrie exchanged loving glances as they moved about attending to their guests. The same thought was in both their minds – they would never be parted again.

As the time passed Sally watched Mrs Hart anxiously as she frequently held out her glass to be refilled, but she showed no sign of drunkenness, sitting bolt upright and smiling faintly, until the best man raised his glass and said, 'I wish Sally and Lawrie long life and happiness, and may they never want.'

'May they never want,' echoed Aunt Hester. 'Eh, love flies out t'winda when want comes in t'door.'

Mrs Hart rose to her feet, swaying slightly.

'I must disagree with you,' she said with dignity, 'As it says in the

Bible, "Better is a dinner of herbs, where love is, than a stalled ox and hatred therewith".'

Hester tossed her head, but before she could speak Lawrie said quickly, 'How about a song? Come on, Jerry, strike up. You know plenty of songs.' The best man stood looking bashfully at the floor for a moment, then he began to sing in a clear, tenor voice, 'When you and I were young, Maggie', followed by 'Beautiful Dreamer'. Sally and Lawrie smiled at each other, both thinking of the boy singing on the ferry boat returning from Eastham.

Emily was nearly asleep, sitting within Sally's encircling arm, and when a few more songs had been sung, Hester and Walter decided to leave. After they had gone, the rest of the party soon dispersed. Mrs Malloy and Sally cleared away, helped by Lawrie, then Mrs Malloy went home.

Matthew had sat down in his Windsor armchair, and Sally knelt on the rag rug beside him.

'We're going now, Da,' she said. 'Will you be all right?'

'Of course. I'm not helpless, girl,' he said gruffly, but he took her face between his hands and kissed her.

'God bless ye, Sal,' he said. 'Yer've been a good daughter to me.' He looked up at Lawrie. 'See yer look after her,' he said fiercely. Then, as though ashamed of his emotion, he turned away and took out his pipe.

Lawrie held out his hand. 'Thanks for everything, Mr Palin.' he said. 'I'll take good care of Sally, never fear.'

Matthew snorted. 'Yer'll be back tomorrer, for God's sake,' he said. 'That's if yer haven't already missed the boat.'

Sally and Lawrie laughed, and set off lightheartedly to walk to the Landing Stage, to catch the ferry boat to Eastham. Lawrie had arranged for them to spend the night in a cottage in Eastham Village. Sally felt proud and happy as she sat on the deck of the ferry boat with Lawrie's arm around her. She felt as though her life had taken on a new dimension, and all her senses seemed more acute.

Even though she felt drugged with love and weariness after the long day, she was aware of every part of the evening scene: the moonlight glinting on the brass plate on a bulkhead, the rattle of a cable and the voices of men calling to each other on a dredger, and the fussy hooting of tugs escorting a majestic liner down to the Bar. Sally sat in contented silence, her head resting on Lawrie's shoulder, as the dark bulk of Eastham Woods drew ever closer.

Chapter Sixteen

Less than twenty-four hours later she was again on the ferry boat, sitting quietly beside Lawrie as the boat sailed back to Liverpool. It seemed to her that in some ways the previous night's journey had happened only five minutes earlier, and in other ways as though a thousand years had passed. She turned her wedding ring round and round on her finger, thinking of all that had happened in the bedroom of the little cottage where they had spent the night.

She had gone upstairs first, to undress and climb into the soft feather bed between lavender-scented sheets. A little later Lawrie had followed her upstairs, undressed and blown out the candle, then slipped into bed and taken her in his arms.

Sally had only a vague idea of what to expect on her wedding night, and she was completely unprepared for the storm of emotion which Lawrie's lovemaking had aroused in her. She had responded fiercely, borne on a tide of feeling which was glorious, wonderful, but afterwards she had buried her face in Lawrie's shoulder, weeping bitterly.

He had held her close, stroking her hair, and asking anxiously, 'What is it, love? What's wrong?'

'I feel ashamed,' she sobbed. 'Behaving like that. You'll think I'm a loose woman.'

Lawrie had not laughed or blustered, just kissed her gently.

'Don't fret, love,' he said. 'It wasn't just natural for you to feel like that – it was right. That's how things should be between man and wife, Sal, but we're very lucky. Some people never manage it in all their lives together.'

Sally was comforted, and later they made love again, quietly and tenderly. She felt that all her life had led up to these hours in the little bedroom, scented with lavender and drenched in the moonlight pouring through the window. She had wondered fearfully if such happiness could last, but strong in Lawrie's love, she had pushed her fears away and drifted off to sleep in his arms.

Now she stole a glance at him as he lay back in the seat with his face tilted to catch the last of the sunlight. How handsome he was, she thought, her eyes lingering on his tanned face and firm chin, and how good and sensible. Well, sensible in many ways, she amended, just a bit reckless with money, but then he had never had to consider anyone but himself. He would be different as a married man. How thoughtful of him, too, to arrange for them to spend the first night of their married life in the cottage, instead of under her father's roof.

Lawrie opened his eyes and smiled at her, then lifted the hand which wore her wedding ring, and kissed it gently.

'Happy, Mrs Ward?' he asked softly.

'Oh, *yes*,' Sally said. 'And you?'

'Never happier, Sal, and just think, love, this is only the start. We'll never be parted again.'

Sally smiled, offering a silent prayer that he was right, then she said suddenly, 'If anything happened to you, Lawrie, I wouldn't want to go on living.'

'Don't say that!' he exclaimed. 'Don't even think it.' He tipped her face, and kissed the end of her nose. 'Now smile, Sally,' he commanded. 'Remember, I love you from the crown of your head to your little toenail. You're mine now, and I look after my own.'

'Oh, Lawrie,' she said, laughing as he meant her to do. The boat drew alongside the Landing Stage, and they disembarked and walked up the sloping roadway arm in arm, lost in their happy dream and oblivious to the crowds milling about them.

Matthew was sitting in his chair as usual, and Sally greeted him shyly, then began to bustle about, preparing a meal. Lawrie sat down opposite Matthew.

'It's a lovely evening, Mr Palin,' he said. 'Mild and pleasant yet there's a nice fresh breeze off the river. Just right for a walk.'

'I'll take your word for it, lad,' Matthew said drily. 'I get enough fresh air in the shipyard to last me.'

'There's crowds on the Landing Stage tonight,' Lawrie said. 'Do you never go down there, apart from going to work?'

Matthew shook his head. 'No. I did in my young days. I was always down on The Sticks, but there was something to see in them days. The river was full of sail – no stinking steamships.'

'But they're fast,' Lawrie said. 'And at least you don't lie becalmed.'

In a moment the two men were deep in discussion of the merits of sail versus steam, and Sally smiled fondly at them. It will be good for Da, she thought, to have another man to talk to. I hope he never draws back in to himself, the way he's been for the last few years.

The following weeks were very happy ones for Sally, as they all settled down to a new routine. Mrs Gregson had engaged another girl in her place on the market stall, so Sally was at home all day for a few weeks after the wedding, but in November she returned to work part-time to help with the Christmas rush. Her wages had risen to seven shillings before she left, so Mrs Gregson agreed to pay her four shillings a week for the part-time work. She managed to save all of this, and with two men's wages each week she also managed to save from the housekeeping, even though she provided good meals and even small luxuries. Her ambition was to have a nest egg saved in the old teapot for a 'rainy day', and shortly before Christmas her savings were unexpectedly increased.

She had made and bought small gifts and toys for Emily, and made socks for Walter and a set of antimacassars for her aunt. Although Sally had written three times to Hester, she had had only one short reply and assumed that her aunt was busy with the improvements to the house. There was no visit from Walter as on the previous year, but shortly before Christmas a parcel was delivered by carrier. It contained crystallized fruit, a box of figs, two bottles of rum, and a net purse containing five sovereigns.

'Send that money back,' Matthew ordered. 'We don't want their charity.'

But for once Sally defied him. 'It was a present to me, Da,' she said. 'They wouldn't send money to you in a purse, and I'm going to keep it. It's not charity, it's a Christmas gift.'

'Christmas gift,' Matthew snorted. 'It's that little bantam cock preening himself and showing off.' Sally's face set stubbornly.

'I don't care,' she said. 'I feel different now about Emily being there. I've seen that she's happy and they think the world of her.'

'What's that got to do with the money, for God's sake?' Matthew shouted.

'Well, I didn't want anything off them last Christmas. I thought they were trying to pay for Emily. I cooked the eggs and the sausages for you, but I only had fried bread.'

They were interrupted by a shout of laughter from Lawrie.

'Fried bread,' he exclaimed. 'Hey, Matt, she didn't mind dipping in your sausage fat for her fried butty! There's women for you.' The tension went out of the atmosphere and Matthew smiled faintly.

'Aye, lad, yer'd need a lifetime to fathom them,' he agreed, taking out his pouch and filling his pipe.

Sally said nothing. Occasionally she had been irritated by the masculine solidarity of Lawrie and her father, who seemed to have become very close, especially since Lawrie now addressed him as 'Matt' instead of the formal 'Mr Palin', but now she was grateful for Lawrie's intervention. She realised that she and her father were so stubborn that there could have been a serious clash of wills about the money without Lawrie's ready laughter.

On Christmas Day Mrs Malloy and Paddy were invited for dinner, and they all had a hilarious time afterwards. Frequent glasses of rum loosened Paddy's tongue, and he began to tell jokes and talk of incidents on the building site with a dry wit which had them all convulsed with laughter.

Later Lawrie persuaded Paddy to play the fiddle which lay in his bedroom, rarely used, and he played jigs and reels, and then the haunting airs of sorrow and parting of the years of Irish emigration. Tears ran down Mrs Malloy's cheeks, and she wiped them away with her apron.

'Ah, ye make it sing, Paddy lad,' she said. 'I was just thinking of last Christmas, and John and James. I wonder now how they're doing and if all goes well for them.'

'I'm sure it does,' Sally said. 'They were so happy to be going home, to their family and the farms.'

'Well, God knows they deserved it. They were grand lads.'

'Do *you* ever hanker to go back, Paddy?' asked Lawrie, but Paddy shook his head.

'No. What did I ever know there but hunger and cold and hard work. Striving to get a living for nine of us, on a bit of poor ground that wouldn't feed two.'

93

'Aye, you're right there, lad,' said Mrs Malloy. 'Wasn't I the same? I mind my poor mother, Lord rest her, singing those songs to try to help us along. Walking weary miles to the town to sell a few eggs or a creel of turf, and yet, God knows, it still draws me, Paddy, for all the years I'm living here.'

He laid the fiddle across his knees and shook his head.

'I've no wish to go back. All belonging to me there are long gone to their rest, or off to America. There's many a one of the lads in the same boat for all they cry over the songs, and them fuddled.'

'The ones that have the most to say are the ones born here in England,' observed Lawrie, and Paddy agreed.

'Indeed and you're right, Lawrie,' he said. 'Two of the lads on the job were born beyond in Heyworth Street, and begod, they're never done talking about the 'Ould Dart', and crying down this country. Sure they're more Irish than lads who crossed only last week.' They all laughed and Lawrie filled up the glasses.

'I'll drink to the Duggans,' he said, raising his glass. 'May they always prosper, for they did me the best turn anyone could. They went away and let me come here and meet Sally.'

'I doubt if that was why they went,' Matthew said drily, 'but I'll drink to that, lad. It was a good day's work when you two met.'

After Christmas trade fell away in the Market, and Sally's part-time job finished. She had been at home for a few weeks when one morning in February she felt queasy as soon as she stepped out of bed, only just managing to dress and go downstairs. When she lifted the lid of the jar of dripping a wave of nausea made her hurriedly replace it, and dash down the yard to the privy. She returned a few moments later, white-faced and trembling, to find the two men waiting anxiously in the kitchen.

'Sit down, love,' Lawrie said, rubbing her cold hands, while Matthew held up a newspaper to the fire to make it burn up more quickly, for tea for Sally.

'I'm all right now,' she said faintly. 'I must have eaten something that disagreed with me. Can you get your own breakfasts?'

'I'll have to go in a minute,' Matthew said, crumpling the paper and thrusting it into the fire. 'That kettle should soon boil, Lawrie.' He cut some slices of bread and spread them with dripping, then wrapped them up.

'I'll eat these with my coffee,' he said. 'Don't forget now, girl. Get Mrs Mal to come in if yer feel bad.' Lawrie left about half an hour later, but by that time Sally felt much better.

'I'm all right, she assured Lawrie. 'I'll get a stomach powder if I need it, but honestly, it's passed off now. Go on now, love, before you're late.'

A little later she was sipping a cup of tea when there was a tap at the door and Mrs Malloy came in.

'In the name of God, girl, are ye not well?' she exclaimed when she saw Sally's pale face.

'I've been sick, Mrs Mal. I must have eaten something that upset me.'

Mrs Malloy looked at her intently. 'What about your monthlies? When did ye last see them?'

Sally blushed. 'Just before Christmas. I missed last month, but I'd caught a cold that week.'

'Ye've caught more than a cold, girlie. I thought ye had a pinched look about yer nose. It's a baby coming, Sally.'

She was stunned. She and Lawrie had talked of the family they hoped to have, but it had seemed a nebulous idea, something that would happen in the future, and suddenly here it was, an accomplished fact.

'Oh, Mrs Mal, are you sure?' she gasped.

'Sure enough,' said Mrs Malloy. 'Are ye not pleased?'

'Oh, I *am*,' Sally assured her. 'It's just so unexpected.'

'I don't know why. If ye put yer finger in the fire, ye'd expect to get burned, wouldn't ye?' Mrs Malloy said robustly.

Sally bent her head. 'I feel as though I'd like to stop it for a little while, until I get used to the idea,' she murmured.

'Well, stop it ye can't, girl, and that's a fact, but sure ye've nine months to get used to the idea, or near enough. Let's see now –' she counted on her fingers – 'September, the end of September, ye'll fall due.'

'September! Honestly, Mrs Mal, I do want the baby, it was just that I didn't realise it was happening now. Lawrie'll be made up.'

'Aye, ye're luckier than most. Ye don't have to worry where the next meal's coming from, and ye've a good husband *and* a good father behind ye.'

Sally made a fresh pot of tea, and they settled down for a talk, and by the time the older woman got up to leave, Sally was accustomed to the idea of the baby, and full of plans.

'I'm glad I've got you to turn to, Mrs Mal,' Sally said as she opened the door for her. 'There's so much that I don't know.'

'Aye, ye miss yer poor mam, Lord ha' mercy on her. I wish she'd lived to see this day, girlie, but I'll try to watch over ye the same as she would have done.'

Sally went back into the house, thinking of her dead mother, lying so still and white, and Emily as a tiny baby unaware of her loss, making small happy sounds as she lay in her cradle beside her. Could that happen to me? she thought in sudden panic, but then she remembered Mrs Malloy's calm words.

'Ye're young and strong, Sally. Don't stretch and don't lift anything heavy, and ye'll be as right as ninepence.'

She waited impatiently for Lawrie's return, and as soon as he opened the door she rushed into his arms.

'Are ye all right, love?' he asked, before she could speak. 'I've been worried sick about you all day.'

'As right as ninepence,' she laughed. 'Oh, Lawrie, guess what? We're going to have a baby. Mrs Mal told me.'

'A baby,' he echoed, then lifted her off her feet and jigged about the kitchen. 'A baby. Us with a baby.'

Suddenly he stopped and set her down gently.

'I shouldn't be doing that, should I?' he said. 'D'you know, Sal, I never thought of a baby, but I'm made up, aren't you? Your da will be pleased too.'

Sally twisted her apron strings between her fingers, looking embarrassed. 'Will you tell him, Lol? I don't like to.'

'Yes, of course, love,' he said gently. 'Do you know when?'

'September,' she said. 'About the end of September, Mrs Mal said it would be.' She heard her father's footstep outside, and as he lifted the latch she fled into the back kitchen, but the next moment he appeared at the back kitchen door.

'Are you all right, girl?' he asked, and she nodded.

'Yes, Da,' she said quietly, keeping her head bent.

'Yer look a better colour, anyhow. Yer put the fear of God in me this morning, the white face on yer.' He went into the kitchen and sat down, and she heard a quiet rumble of voices as Lawrie told him the news. A few minutes later Lawrie came into the back kitchen.

'Come on in, Sal,' he said. 'I'll bring these plates and give you a hand.' He bent his head and whispered, 'Your da's made up.'

They went together into the kitchen and Matthew looked up. 'That's good news I hear, Sal,' he said. 'Yer'll have to look after yourself now, and listen to what Mrs Mal tells yer.'

'I will, Da,' Sally said, smiling shyly. Nothing more was said about the baby until the meal was finished, and Matthew rose to his feet.

'I'm taking a walk down to the Volunteer,' he said. 'I want to have a yap with Jim Priestly. I'll be a couple 'a hours, Sally.' He went out and Sally turned to Lawrie, her eyes shining.

'Isn't that thoughtful of Da? He knew we'd want to talk. He's just like his old self since you came, Lawrie.'

'Aye, it is, love. He'll make a good grandfather, won't he?' Quickly they cleared away, then sat on the sofa, their arms around each other.

'I can't get over it,' Lawrie said. 'Last night it seemed something far away – the thought of having a baby – and now here we are and it doesn't seem strange at all, does it?'

Sally nodded. 'I suppose people would think we were soft in the head if they knew how surprised we were, because married people always have babies, but I've only just got used to being married.'

Lawrie kissed her. 'I'll never get used to being married to you, Sal. God, I'm a lucky feller.'

She laughed and blushed. 'In the shops sometimes I don't realise people are speaking to me when they say "Mrs Ward".'

'What shall we call it?' Lawrie said. 'Sarah, if it's a girl?'

'No,' Sally said emphatically. 'And not Lawrence if it's a boy. I hate people saying Big Tom and Little Tom, and half the time Little Tom is a lot taller than his father. What about our two mam's names for a girl?'

'Mary Julia, or Julia Mary. Yes, I like that,' said Lawrie.

'And for a boy, John Matthew. That'd be better than Matthew John, seeing as my da's living with us.'

'We're living with him,' Lawrie reminded her. 'I'd like to get a better house and take your da with us, but I can't do it yet.'

'We're all right here for now,' Sally said. 'We've got our own tap and privy, and Mrs Mal's here to help us.'

'That's true,' Lawrie agreed. 'And we'll be glad of her advice, but someday, Sal, you see, you'll have a grand mansion and ride in your own carriage.'

'Behind matched greys,' Sally laughed. She pulled his head down to her and kissed him. 'Don't worry, lad, I'm perfectly happy as I am. I couldn't be happier if I was Queen of England.' Lawrie kissed her and held her close.

'I'll work my fingers to the bone for you, love,' he whispered.

The time passed rapidly as they talked and planned, and when Matthew lifted the doorlatch they were surprised to find that he had been out more than two hours.

Chapter Seventeen

Sally continued to suffer from morning sickness for a few weeks, and she was glad that her part-time job had finished, especially as the weather was so bad. The first payday after they knew of the baby, Lawrie came home with an elaborate rattle, tied with pink and blue ribbons.

'It will do for either a boy or a girl,' he said, and he said the same thing the following week when he bought a bone teething ring and a set of celluloid ducks. Sally admired the toys but as soon as the opportunity arose, she pointed out to Lawrie that they would have to be careful with money. She would be unable to work, and there were baby clothes to be bought, and eventually another mouth to feed. He agreed with her, and for a while he made no more extravagant buys, but Sally felt uneasily that she was changing him, and worried in case he thought her hard and mean.

In spite of this she was very happy, lovingly making tiny clothes with much elaborate stitching and embroidery, and hemming napkins made from an old sheet given to her by Mrs Malloy. Lawrie and her father were tender and considerate towards her, doing all they could to make her life easy, and she felt that she was very fortunate. She was touched by the kindness shown to her by everyone. Mrs Hart lined a basket with pretty sprigged cotton, and filled it with pins and a bottle of olive oil, and a jar of castor oil and zinc cream, and even a box of dusting powder and a swansdown powder puff, which Sally guessed must have been a treasured souvenir of her girlhood.

Emily's old cradle had been lent out to various neighbours and Lawrie decided to make a new one for the baby. He and Matthew spent many happy hours conferring over it.

Hester did not reply immediately to Sally's excited letter, and when she did it was on heavy quality notepaper with the address printed on it.

'Greenlands,' Matthew read out. 'Good God, what's wrong with Greenlands Farm same as it was before?'

Lawrie laughed. 'It might be Greenlands Manor before long,' he said.

'Aye, there's many a true word spoken in jest, lad,' said Matthew. 'That little runt is fairly jumping out of his latitude.'

'She doesn't seem pleased about the baby either,' Sally said indignantly. 'As much as says we're foolish.'

'Sour grapes, girl,' Matthew said. 'Take no notice.'

'If it wasn't for Emily I wouldn't bother with her,' Sally said. 'Maybe if I write to Emily herself she'll be able to write back. She's getting on well with her reading and writing, Aunt Hester says.'

Lawrie looked doubtful. 'Your aunt might take that as a snub,' he said. 'You don't want to fall out with her altogether, do you?'

'The lad's right,' Matthew said. 'Yer don't want to cut yerself off, girl.'

'How about going there again? It might be the best chance for a while,' Lawrie said.

'True enough,' Matthew agreed, 'but I don't fancy going there. Ask them to come here, Sally.'

She again wrote to Hester, inviting them to visit Gell Street, and this time the reply came promptly.

Sally was glad that she was alone when she received it, and after some thought decided to conceal it from her father and even from Lawrie.

> *Dear Sally and all,*
> *I hope this finds you well as it leaves us at present. Although Walter allowed us to go to Liverpool for the wedding, he is right against Emily being taken back there. He has engaged a govern-ess for her, and she is teaching Emily how to speak and behave. She is very pleased with the improvement in Emily even in three months.*
>
> *I am sorry for you, Sally, bringing a child into the world in that place, and I hope it won't be the death of you the same as your poor Mother, R.I.P. I hope your husband will make more shape than your father did, and stir himself to get you out of it. You will have your hands full at present so I won't expect to see you for a while.*
> *Your affect. Aunt,*
> *Hester.*

Sally shed angry tears every time she read the letter, and when Mrs Malloy called in she could not resist showing her it and reading it to her, although she swore Mrs Malloy to secrecy first.

'Bad luck to the wicked ould faggot!' Mrs Malloy exclaimed. 'Didn't I tell ye she was always black jealous of you and yours, Sally? I seen a difference in him when they were here, but I declare to God "Walter allowed", that's putting it strong.'

'He *has* changed, Mrs Mal. He seemed to be giving the orders there – well, some of the time anyway – and he seems to be coining money.'

'Aye, so she's taking out her spite on you. Read me out the letter again, girl.' Sally read the letter aloud, and Mrs Malloy nodded her head thoughtfully.

'It isn't the child only taking the lessons, Sal. Either the woman has Hester tutored or she wrote the letter for Hester to copy, and the quare one added her own spiteful bit at the end. Ye should be sorry for her, girlie, for the bitterness that's in her.'

Angry tears filled Sally's eyes. 'I'm not sorry for her, Mrs Mal. I'm worried about Emily being with someone who could write a letter like that, and yet I can't show it to Da and upset him.'

'It's yerself that shouldn't be getting upset, and harming the child ye're carrying, Sally. Don't be worrying about Emily – sure, she'll see a different side of yer aunt – and don't be thinking that yer da will ever bring her back, for that he *won't* do. Quiet yerself now, girl, and drink the tea.'

Mindful of Mrs Mal's warning about the baby, Sally resolutely put the letter out of her mind as much as possible but Lawrie, ever sensitive to her mood, looked searchingly at her several times, and after the meal was over, he suggested a walk.

'What's up, Sal?' he asked, as soon as they left the house. Sally was determined that he should not know the remarks about the baby, but she could not conceal her feelings.

'I had a letter from Aunt Hester,' she said. 'Saying that Walter won't let Emily come here because she's got a governess now. I suppose he thinks we're not good enough.'

Lawrie whistled. 'A governess. By God, he must be doing well.'

'I burnt the letter,' Sally said. 'I didn't want Da to see it.'

'Quite right, love. Did she say anything about us going there?'

Sally began to cry. 'She said I'd have my hands too full, but that's only an excuse. She doesn't want Emily to have anything to do with us.'

Lawrie drew her into a shop doorway, and wiped her eyes tenderly.

'Don't cry, Sal. Think about our baby. You don't want to upset him, do you?'

Sally tried to compose herself and they walked on in silence for a while, then Lawrie said thoughtfully, 'I wouldn't worry too much about Emily, Sal. She struck me as a very sensible little girl, and very fond of you and your da. Nothing can alter that, and even if they try to keep her away, she'll soon find a way to see you. Don't forget, they're both very fond of her, and I'll bet she'll get her own way, even if she has to play one against the other.'

'But a governess,' Sally said. 'She might change her.'

'Not a chance,' Lawrie said cheerfully. 'Don't forget what Mrs Hart said: "As the twig is bent, so the tree will grow." '

Much comforted, Sally walked home smiling, and whenever she remembered the letter, she thought of Lawrie's consoling words. The weeks of morning sickness had passed, and for the rest of her pregnancy Sally felt well and happy, and looked forward eagerly to the birth of her baby.

On a bright crisp morning in late September she woke feeling especially energetic. As soon as the men had left she turned out the bedrooms, and scrubbed the floors of both, and then down the stairs. Next she blackleaded the grate, and scrubbed out the kitchen and back kitchen. She was swilling the tiny yard, singing as she brushed vigorously, when Mrs Malloy's head appeared over the wall.

'Ah, cleaning out the nest, are ye, Sal?' she said knowingly.

'I felt like work and it's such a lovely day,' Sally said.

'Isn't that always a sign? Yer pains will be on ye before night, girlie.'

'But you said next week,' Sally protested.

'I said maybe then, but sure they come when they're ready, girl, early or late.'

Sally finished the yard, then shutting herself in the back kitchen she

101

washed herself from top to toe, and put on clean underclothes. She washed out her other clothes and put them on the rack suspended from the ceiling, and then, mindful of Mrs Malloy's warning, she got out the binders, napkins and nightdress she had made for the baby, and hung them to air on a string over the fire. She also put the mattress from the cradle to air then, suddenly exhausted, sat down with a cup of tea.

Her labour did not start that night, although she felt a throbbing in her groin, but the following morning after the men had left for work, she bent to poke the fire and was gripped by a fierce pain low down in her back. She banged wildly on the back of the grate to summon Mrs Malloy but the older woman only smiled at her agitation.

'Don't be worrying now, child,' she said. 'Ye've a long road to travel yet, and ye're only at the start.'

The pains came regularly throughout the day but in the evening they died away, then at nine o'clock they returned with force. Mrs Malloy ordered Matthew and Lawrie to go for a walk.

'She won't cry out to ease herself if yiz hang around,' she said, but they were too uneasy to go far, and paced up and down the street, avoiding a drunken woman lying against the wall.

'I'll have to get somewhere better for Sally and the baby to live,' Lawrie burst out, too agitated to be tactful.

'I wish yer luck, lad,' Matthew said drily. 'I took this house as a stopgap and I'm here over twenty years.'

Before Lawrie could answer, a loud cry from the bedroom followed by an infant's wail halted them. They made a concerted rush for the door. Lawrie bounded up the stairs, but Mrs Malloy called sharply, 'Wait now till I call yiz. A lovely little girl.'

'But Sally?' Lawrie called.

'She's grand, thank God. Don't bother me now.'

Lawrie retreated down the stairs, and he and Matthew moved restlessly round the kitchen, too anxious to sit down.

A little later Mrs Malloy came downstairs, the black kettle in her hand and a beaming smile on her face.

'Go up now, lad,' she said to Lawrie, then handed the kettle to Matthew and sank into a chair. Lawrie hurried up to the bedroom where Sally was sitting in bed, propped up by pillows, her hair in plaits over her shoulders and the baby cradled in her arms.

'Oh, Sal,' he said, cupping her face in his hands and kissing her tenderly. 'Are you all right, love?'

Sally's face was white, with dark shadows under her eyes, but she smiled happily.

'I'm fine,' she said. 'Isn't she beautiful?' drawing aside the shawl from the baby's face.

'Beautiful,' Lawrie agreed, gently touching his daughter's face with his finger. The baby was red and wrinkled, with a fuzz of red hair on her tiny head, but they gazed at her adoringly. There was a heavy footstep on the stairs and Matthew came into the bedroom, closely followed by Mrs Malloy, carrying tea for herself and Sally. Matthew bent over Sally and kissed her, then looked at the baby.

'So yer've got it all over, girl, and a fine healthy baby, Mrs Malloy says.'

Sally smiled at him, and Mrs Malloy broke in, 'Indeed and a good pair of lungs on her, too, thank God. Now will ye bring up the cradle, Lawrie, while I lay the child in it, and Sally can drink this tea.'

Lawrie brought the cradle upstairs then took the baby from Sally's arms, kissing the tiny face before laying the child in the cradle.

The two men bent over the cradle in awe and admiration.

'Look at her hands,' Lawrie whispered, slipping his finger into the baby's tiny palm. 'Everything perfect, even her finger nails, and she's gripping my finger. It's a miracle.'

'A good job over and all well, thanks be to God,' said Mrs Malloy, smiling as she sipped her tea. Lawrie turned eagerly to her.

'I don't know how to thank you, Mrs Mal, for all you've done.'

'Aye,' Matthew said. 'Yer've been a good friend and neighbour to us, in good times and bad. We'd be lost without yer.'

A pleased smile spread over Mrs Malloy's face, but she shook her head dismissively. 'Indeed and what are neighbours for, if it isn't to help each other? Drink up yer tea, girlie. I'll do a bowl of gruel for ye and then ye can get yer rest.' She took Sally's cup and went downstairs, followed by Matthew.

'I'll leave them two in peace,' he said. 'Let them enjoy this time. God knows it won't be long before they have troubles on them one way or another.'

'As long as they're spared to face them together,' Mrs Malloy said. 'Ye know well, Matt, troubles lay aisy on you while Julie was spared to ye.'

'I wish she'd lived to see this day, Mrs Mal.'

Mrs Malloy stirred the gruel. 'Eh, she'd be made up to see Sally with a baby and a good husband behind her the same as she had, but don't be worrying yerself about them. They're young and healthy, and maybe different times altogether are coming for them.'

'D'yer know what Lawrie's up to now? He's down at the Mission two nights a week helping that minister? They're down at the docks gathering up street Arabs and taking them to the Mission for the night, to save them from these foreign sailors who take the kids on board for their own dirty tricks. The kids go for something to eat.'

'He'll need to watch himself. Them Lascars are handy with a knife.'

'Seems there's Lawrie and another fellow from Scotland Road, used to be a fireman on the Cunard ships. Of course he would be in a different fo'castle than the A.B.s like Lawrie, but between the two of them they know the worst ships for this caper.'

'Glory be to God, our ships?'

'No, under foreign flags, but the talk gets round. Lawrie says the minister's from Oxford University but he gets stuck in like a good 'un.'

Mrs Malloy sniffed disapprovingly. 'Charity begins at home. Lawrie's needed here now. I'll drop him a hint.'

She went upstairs and Matthew groaned silently. I should have kept me mouth shut, he told himself. He tried to avoid intefering between

Sally and Lawrie, and he wondered what form Mrs Malloy's 'hint' would take. They were usually delivered with all the finesse of a blow from a sledgehammer.

Later that night Lawrie lowered himself carefully on to the extreme edge of the bed, as far as possible from Sally, who had fallen into an exhausted sleep. He lay for a short time marvelling at the miracle which had happened so recently in the little room, before he too fell asleep.

Chapter Eighteen

Matthew approved of the names chosen for the baby, Mary Julia.

'Mrs Mal's name is Mary so yer'll be killing two birds with one stone,' he said. 'She might think it's named for her.'

The skills which Sally had acquired when rearing Emily soon returned to her, but she found Mary a very different baby to the placid Emily. Mary's face always seemed to be red with rage as she fought against being dressed or undressed, or screamed when she was placed in the cradle. She was always hungry, seizing greedily on Sally's nipple when held to the breast, and even immediately after being fed, nuzzling frantically at Lawrie's or Matthew's clothes when they held her.

The house seemed suddenly dominated by the baby's feeding, her washing, and her screams of rage, and Sally looked harassed and exhausted. Lawrie was quick and deft like most sailors and he did a great deal to help Sally with housework and cooking while she attended to Mary, and he tried to cheer Sally by telling her that Mary would soon settle down, but sometimes she felt quite desperate.

'I had an aunt with red hair like that, and a temper to match,' Matthew observed one day, to Sally's dismay.

'So you don't think she'll grow out of it,' she said.

'Yer'll just have to get the upper hand while she's young,' he said. 'The aunt had them all ruled with her tantrums.'

Mary was two months old, and showing no sign of improvement when Mrs Malloy watched one day when Sally was trying to feed the child.

'Good God, I never saw the like,' she exclaimed. 'Sure, she's like a dog tearing at a lump of meat. Maybe she's not getting enough. I'll make her some pobs.' She broke some bread into a saucer and scattered sugar on it, then warmed some milk and poured it over the bread.

'Isn't she too young?' Sally asked fearfully, but Mrs Malloy shook her head.

'That one's been here before,' she said. 'Just watch her.' She cautiously took a little of the bread and milk on a small spoon, and held it to Mary's mouth. Within minutes the dish was empty, and as Mrs Malloy gently rocked her, the baby fell into a sound sleep.

'Thank God for five minutes' peace!' Sally exclaimed. 'Oh, that sounds awful. It's just that she never lets up, but perhaps she was hungry.'

'She made short work of the pobs, true enough. Ye'll know what to do with her now. Mother of God, I thought she was going to ate ye alive.'

'Perhaps I'll be able to get something done if she'll only sleep,' Sally said. 'Near the end of November and nothing done for Christmas.'

'I'm making me bunloaves on Thursday, girl, and I'll do yours if ye like.'

'Thanks, Mrs Mal. I'll see how I go on.' She opened the cupboard and took out a music box, painted with woodland scenes.

'Lawrie bought this for Emily,' she said, lifting the lid so that a Viennese waltz played. 'It's German.'

'It's beautiful, so it is, but he paid a pretty penny for that all the same. How much was it?'

'I don't know,' Sally said quietly. 'I didn't ask Lawrie because he bought it out of his own spends.'

'Tch, tch,' Mrs Malloy tutted. 'And he'll be walking home every night after his day's work, because there isn't a penny in his pocket. Ye should talk sense in to him, Sally.' She made no reply, but her mouth was set as she rose and returned the box to the cupboard. Mrs Malloy stole a glance at her face, and said placatingly, 'Still, isn't it always on someone else he spends his money, never on himself, and sure, it's better to be openhanded than mean.'

'Indeed it is,' Sally said shortly. Not for worlds would she admit to Mrs Malloy how often she was dismayed by Lawrie's extravagance. Only the previous week he had paid a shilling for a hammer, when she could have got a good one at the pawnshop for twopence. He had looked abashed when she pointed this out, and said, 'But this is a good strong one, Sal. It should last.'

'The one in Solly's would be better still, only second hand,' she had said angrily, and strangely enough it was Matthew who had acted as peacemaker.

'Keep it well out of Sally's way, lad,' he had joked. 'There's no knowing what our Mary might drive her to, she's got her that distracted.'

Mary still slept, and Sally moved the kettle over the fire to make tea.

'Ye didn't hear any more from the aunt,' Mrs Malloy said. Sally shook her head.

'No, I didn't tell Da about that letter saying Walter wouldn't let Emily come here, and he just thinks that she hasn't written yet. I told Lawrie part of it, but not the bit about having Mary here, because I wouldn't let him be hurt by it. I just burnt the letter.'

'Bad luck to her. Didn't I tell ye, Sally, she was eaten up with jealousy, the same one.' Sally's face grew red as she thought of the letter.

'Do you remember what she said, about the governess teaching Emily how to speak and behave? She knew better than either of them how to speak and behave before she ever went there! I go mad every time I think about that letter.'

'Then don't think about it, girlie. I shouldn't have brought it up.'

'No, I shouldn't have burdened you with it, but I had to tell someone. You won't breathe a word to Da, will you?'

'Not at all, ye know I keep a still tongue in me head, but what are you going to do with the box if ye don't write again?'

'Well, I wasn't going to have any more to do with them, I was so mad, but I talked it over with Lawrie and he said he thought I should write, just talking about the baby and not mentioning seeing them, otherwise I might cut myself right off from Emily.'

'True for him, Sal. There's sense in that.'

Sally nodded. 'He says they'll come to their senses soon. The money's just gone to their heads.'

'Put a beggar on horseback and he'll ride to hell,' Mrs Malloy said. 'But sure I don't know how he's making the money out of a bit of a farm, especially these days.'

'He's speculating, the fellow who works there told us, but he must be doing well out of it. Anyhow, I'll just send the gifts as usual for Christmas, and say nothing.'

The bread and milk twice a day seemed to settle Mary and Sally was able to get some work done during the day, and a few hours of undisturbed sleep at night. The baby was gaining weight, but she still had bouts of screaming when she was put in the cradle, her face red and her arms and legs thrashing about in temper.

Sally managed to make her bunloaves and mincemeat, and a Christmas pudding.

'I feel really well off,' she said, proudly displaying the contents of the cupboard to Lawrie. She also made a set of frilled satin cushion covers for Hester, and the usual socks for Walter, which she parcelled up with the music box and a selection of small toys for Emily, and sent off in early December.

She asked Mrs Malloy to bring Paddy Ryan with her for Christmas dinner, but Mrs Malloy refused.

'No, girlie, you're a family now,' she said. 'Me and Paddy will be grand on our own.' Mrs Malloy had not taken another lodger to replace Lawrie. She told Sally that she could manage on Paddy's money, with the small pension she received from the firm of sugar boilers her husband had worked for until his death in an accident.

A reply to Sally's letter to Hester came within a week, and to Sally's delight, a letter from Emily was enclosed with it. The letter from Hester was brief, and only expressed hopes that they were all well and that the baby was thriving, but Emily's letter was full of excitement about the baby. At the end of the letter there was a large X and Emily had written beneath it: *A kiss from Aunt Emily to Mary Julia*.

A few days before Christmas Sally had been to the shops in Brunswick Road, carrying Mary in her mother's shawl, and as she reached home a carrier's cart drew up beside her.

'Mrs. Ward?' the man asked. 'Ee are, love, parcels for yer.'

He carried in two large parcels. Sally put Mary in the cradle, ignoring her shrieks of protest, and tore eagerly at the wrappings. One parcel contained a length of white flannel and one of white lawn, and a bundle of spotted muslin as well as ribbon and skeins of white wool. In the other parcel there were two bottles of rum, crystallized fruits and figs, a purse containing five gold sovereigns and a folded paper, on which was written *Mary Julia*, which contained another two sovereigns.

'Oh, Mary,' Sally said, bending over the cradle, 'look what they've sent you.' She wondered if the money for the baby came from Emily, but when she lifted the material, she found another parcel beneath it. It contained an apron for herself, sewn and embroidered by Emily, handkerchiefs for Matthew and Lawrie, carefully hemmed and embroidered with their initials, and a doll, beautifully dressed, for the baby. Sally was too excited to stand still, and danced a jig in the kitchen, watched unblinkingly by Mary.

Sometimes Sally felt a superstitious fear that her happiness was too good to last. She was so lucky. Matthew was a changed man nowadays, enjoying a discussion with Lawrie and often going out to meet friends for a drink. Sally realised that this was to give her and Lawrie time on their own, and she was deeply grateful to her father. Lawrie's cheerfulness had made an immediate change in the atmosphere of the home, and now the baby was a source of joy to all of them. Matthew's newspaper was put aside as he nursed her, singing the old lullabies that Sally remembered hearing him sing to Alfred and Emily. The baby's hair was growing, still bright red, but her eyebrows and eyelashes were dark, and Lawrie never tired of looking at her.

'She's going to be a real beauty, Sal,' he would say, 'Look at her red gold hair, and dark eyelashes, and just look at that dimple.'

Everything about the baby was wonderful to them: her first smile, the way she held her rattle or a proffered finger, and when she began to focus her eyes on her own hand held before her face. They were convinced that there had never been such a clever and beautiful child, and as her tantrums grew fewer, the early traumatic days were forgotten.

Sally was happy for other reasons, too. Lawrie was a loving and considerate husband, holding Sally tenderly in his arms every night, but keeping steadfastly to his resolve to abstain from intercourse until Mary was three months old. He still did all the heavy work for her as he had done during her pregnancy, and brought tea in bed to her on Sunday mornings.

On Christmas Day Lawrie looked after the baby, and basted the leg of pork in the oven, while Matthew and Sally made their customary visit to the cemetery. They laid their flowers on the grave, and stood for a while thinking of those who slept quietly there, but Sally felt that her father's thoughts were less bitter than in previous years. Time and the advent of the baby had done their work.

Dinner was nearly ready when they arrived home, and Lawrie was rocking the cradle with his foot as he poked up the fire under the pans.

'I'm getting a dab hand at this,' he said cheerfully. 'I think I'll stay at home and send you to the warehouse, Sal.'

Mrs Malloy and Paddy came in after dinner, and Mrs Hart joined them as her husband was working on the tugs. The men were drinking ale and rum, but Sally was relieved that Mrs Hart drank only tea, like Mrs Malloy and herself. At teatime she brought out sandwiches and mince pies and bunloaf, and later Paddy produced his violin and played for them. It was a pleasant party, but at ten o'clock Mrs Malloy rose to her feet.

'We'll leave ye to get yer rest, girl,' she said. 'Ye might as well sleep while the quare one does. There'll be no sleep for ye once she's awake.'

The baby slept soundly as Lawrie and Sally crept about undressing, and she was still asleep when they climbed into bed. Lawrie took Sally in his arms.

'Over three months now, love,' he whispered. 'I've been longing for you. Are you all right, Sal?'

She said nothing, but she snuggled closer into his arms. Gently he began to caress her, then he stopped.

'I'd like more children, Sal, but not yet. I think it's too soon, but are you worried about it?'

Sally held him closely. 'Mrs Mal says it's all right while I'm breast feeding,' she said. Moonlight slanted through the little window, and in its light she could see his face as he raised his head and smiled down at her. Suddenly a wave of feeling swept over her, and she felt weak with love for him. Gently, then with increasing urgency, they caressed each other until their bodies seemed to melt together.

'Oh, Sally, Sally,' Lawrie whispered as they lay back exhausted. 'I keep thinking I can't get any happier, then I do.' They slipped into sleep for a few hours, then woke to make love again.

The baby was still asleep, and the grey light of the December morning was filtering into the room when Sally woke again. Lawrie was cradled in her arms, and although her breasts, now full and hard with milk, were aching, she lay still, unwilling to disturb him. She gazed at him adoringly, thinking that she must be the luckiest girl alive. Once again the cold finger of fear touched her. Could it last? What lay ahead of them? I don't care, she thought, unconsciously tightening her arm around Lawrie. As long as we have each other, I don't care about anything.

Lawrie's eyes opened and he smiled at her, He kissed her breast, then her lips, and looked in surprise at the window.

'Morning already. Hasn't she wakened at all?'

Sally shook her head and giggled.

'It must have been the butty dipped in gravy that you gave her,' she said.

'No. I had a word with her. I said, "Your dada's hoping for a very happy night, and don't you wake up and spoil it." See how obedient she is.' As though on cue the baby woke and howled loudly, and Lawrie jumped out of bed and picked her up.

'Don't wake your Granda,' he said. 'Let him have a lie in.'

He handed the baby to Sally, and she changed her and began to feed her. Lawrie lifted the hair at the nape of Sally's neck and kissed her neck.

'Whatever she does in the future, Sal, I'll always bless her for last night – and you,' he said.

Sally blushed. Although she always responded eagerly to Lawrie's lovemaking, she never liked to speak of it during the day. He said no more, but went downstairs to make tea.

Mrs Malloy's advice seemed to be sound, and for the next few months, although Sally and her husband often made love, there was no sign of another pregnancy. Mary continued to be a difficult baby, soon bored, and given to fits of screaming when she was thwarted in any way, but she grew ever more interesting to her besotted family.

In April, when Mary was seven months old, she was having pobs and gruel as well as breast milk, and Sally was alarmed to find that her milk was dwindling away. She consulted Mrs Malloy who advised her to drink plenty of water, and a glass of stout every night.

She found the bitter stout unpalatable but she persevered, with Lawrie beside her whispering, 'All in a good cause, Sal.'

She worried about Lawrie, knowing how the misery and destitution he saw daily grieved him, and knowing, too, that he gave away at least half of his 'carry out', and often his car fare, so that he walked home after his hard day's work. Sometimes she slipped coppers into his lunch tin, so that he could ride home, but she suspected that they were given away, too. She could never protest because he was the only one who suffered by his generosity. The money in the teapot still grew steadily, and the thought of it was a great comfort to her.

One sunny day in April she walked up to Shaw Street with Mary, and sat down by the small quarry. A few minutes later she was joined by a young woman and two children. The children ran off to scramble round the rocks, and the woman sat down near Sally.

'Lovely day, isn't it?' said Sally. 'The wind has blown all the smoke away too.'

'Yeh, I shouldn't be 'ere be rights,' the woman said, 'But I got that fed up with the boxes, I said, "Sod it, I'm takin' the kids out!" '

'The boxes?' Sally said.

'Yeh, matchboxes. It's ony tuppence ha'penny a gross, see, so we 'ave ter keep at it night an' day. Our Jinny's a good 'elp though.' She nodded at the puny little girl.

'How old is she?' asked Sally.

'Seven, and 'e's three. 'E was born three months after my feller died. I'd 'ad three miscarriages after our Jinny, and I'd 'ad such a time when I was carryin' Benny. Me feller dyin' of the cholera, an' bein' put out of me room, an' days when I never broke me fast, yet our Benny lived. Funny, wassen it?' She leaned over and looked at Mary, who had fallen asleep in Sally's arms.

' 'Ealthy lookin', isn' she?' she said without envy.

Sally felt ashamed as she looked at the emaciated woman and the ill nourished children. All three were barefoot and ragged, and Sally felt that she had never properly appreciated her own good fortune. Although her food had always been the cheapest available, and clothes, boots and coal were only obtained by careful budgeting, she had never been barefoot or hungry.

She took the two shilling piece she had brought out for her shopping from her pocket and handed it to the woman.

'Will you take this?' she asked diffidently. 'I've had a bit of luck – got some money from my uncle.' She was anxious to spare the woman any embarrassment, but she was too hungry and needy to care about any social niceties.

'Jinny, Benny,' she screeched, snatching the coin, 'Come ed, we're gonna 'ave sump'n to eat.' In a moment they were gone.

When Sally and Lawrie were alone that evening, she told him about the incident.

'Tuppence ha'penny a gross, Lol, that's terrible, isn't it? How can they make enough to live?'

'It's a bloody disgrace,' Lawrie said. 'And that's not all. It makes my blood boil to see kids standing barefoot in freezing weather, trying to sell matches in those same boxes, and the girls who work in the factories are paid starvation wages. More power to Annie Besant who organized a strike among them, and won.'

'Who's Annie Besant?' asked Sally. 'I never heard of women striking. I know there's lots of strikes – the seamen and the gas workers – but I don't understand it.'

'Listen, Sal,' Lawrie said eagerly, 'people like us have got to stick together and fight for our rights. It's the only way we'll change the terrible conditions.' He picked up a bundle of wood which was drying in the hob, and stood it on the fender. 'See the way those sticks stand up because there's a string round them holding them together? Now if I undo that and try to stand one stick up it falls over. It's the same with a union. If we all band together we'll get something done, but one man on his own is helpless. The upper classes are too strong.'

Sally looked doubtful. 'But things are being done. The Mission, and the hotpots for poor kids at Christmas, and things like that.'

'No, no,' Lawrie said impatiently. 'That's only scratching at the surface. We need to alter things so there are *no* starving children.'

He took Sally's hand. 'I'm glad you did that today, Sal. I feel as though you're with me. I've sometimes wondered if you thought I was soft going on about the poor kids, but I get so angry about it all. It's so unnecessary in a rich country like this.'

'Oh, no, I do agree with you, Lol. I don't think you're soft, but you don't think I'm mean, do you?'

'Mean? How could I think that, love?'

'Well, because I'm always trying to save. I know we're all right now, but I worry in case something goes wrong. Mrs Mal said once we were all walking on the edge of a pit, and I feel safer with something behind us.'

Lawrie kissed her. 'I think you're a wonderful manager, Sal, and I'm proud of you. I'm made up that you agree with me about the unions too. We'll show 'em, Sal.'

Sally longed to warn him to be careful, but she looked fondly at his eager face and held her tongue. While she had him beside her, she felt that nothing else mattered.

Chapter Nineteen

Sally wrote to thank her aunt and uncle for their gifts, and enclosed a letter to Emily. In Emily's reply there were references to the building men, and the new maid, so Sally realised that they must still be prospering, although Hester gave no details in her short letter.

The gift of material had unexpected results for Sally. She made dresses and petticoats for Mary, and with some of the spotted muslin she made herself a pretty blouse. She was wearing it when she took the baby to visit Mrs Gregson in the market, and some of the other women gathered round to look at the baby, and admired her blouse.

One stallholder lingered when the others had gone, and said to Sally, 'Our Josie'd like a blouse like that, Sal. Will you make her one?'

'Of course,' Sally said, but Mrs Gregson broke in swiftly.

'If you're going to do dressmaking, Sally, you'd better fix a price. Say a shilling for making the blouse, seeing it's for Josie, and she can bring you the material and thread.'

'Oh, she'll pay for it, never fear. Just tell me what to get, Sally. I'll see you before you go,' the woman said huffily.

She went back to her stall and Mrs Gregson looked at Sally's flushed face.

'You needn't look so flustered,' she said. 'You'd have done that sewing for nothing, and she'd have let you, but that girl earns good money in the tobacco works. Don't be a fool to yourself, Sally.'

A few days later Josie came with a friend to see Sally.

'There's some lovely material in a shop in London Road,' she said. 'Me mam said you'd tell me how much to get, and the cotton and that. Gertie'd like a blouse too,' indicating her friend.

'Don't bother about the sewing thread,' Sally said. 'Just bring me a yard and a half of material.' The blouses were ready by the end of the week, and the girls were delighted with them. On the following Monday three girls from Ogden's, the tobacco works, came to order blouses, and within a month Sally found it worthwhile to invest in a second-hand sewing machine from Solly, the pawnbroker, paid for weekly out of her sewing money.

The money in the teapot grew steadily, especially when her first client, Josie, ordered a suit, and again many of the girls followed her example. Mrs Malloy was always willing to look after Mary, and Sally spent happy hours, doing work that she liked, and knowing that her nest egg was growing.

In addition to the sewing for Ogden's girls, she also made some print dresses for a girl who was going into service, and a large order for mourning clothes. She disliked making the mourning clothes, not only because of the sadness of her clients, but also because she found the black material a strain on her eyes, especially as the nights were drawing in and some of her sewing was done by lamplight. Lawrie worried that she was doing too much, and tried to persuade her to cut down on the sewing, but it was Matthew who made her do less.

He had always drawn the lamp close to his elbow, so that the light fell on his newspaper, but now Sally either drew the lamp away a little, or sat very close to him to get the light for the fine stitching of her hand sewing.

Suddenly one night he turned on her. Lawrie was out at the Mission, and Sally was treadling furiously at the sewing machine, trying to finish a skirt before Lawrie came home.

'Stop that bloody machine,' Matthew roared. 'There's no peace in the place with yer. If yer not at that, yer nearly knocking the paper out've me hand, crowding in on me fer the light.' Sally stopped treadling.

'I'm working to make a few shillings extra,' she said indignantly. 'Nothing wrong with that, is there?'

'Why?' Matthew demanded. 'Yer've got two men's wages coming in, but much wants more. There's many a one 'ud give their right arm for a home like you've got, and the money ye handle.'

'I've got the chance to make some money, and I'm ready to work hard to better myself. I can't see anything wrong in that.'

'Better yerself! D'yer call it bettering yerself to neglect yer child, and have the place like a madhouse when we want a bit er peace at night? Yer getting a right grabber, Sally.'

Tears sprang to her eyes.

'I'm not neglecting Mary,' she shouted. 'I'm doing this for *her*, to get her out of this place.'

'Oho, "this place". It's coming out now, is it? Yer home isn't good enough for yer. Well, you can get out any time you like.'

He picked up the poker and rattled it furiously among the bars of the grate, looking over his shoulder at Sally.

'I'll tell you this, madam. This is my house, and while you're in it ye'll keep a civil tongue in yer head, and I'll have some peace here after me day's work.'

Sally stood with angry tears pouring down her face, and at that moment they heard Lawrie's footsteps. He lifted the latch and looked from one to the other in amazement, but neither Sally nor her father spoke.

'Well, it looks as if I've walked in on a row,' he said. 'Is it anything to do with me, Sally?'

She shook her head. 'Not really,' she said.

'Yes, it is,' Matthew broke in. 'I've been tellin' yer wife that she's neglecting her duties, grabbing for money.'

'Ah, come on now, Matt, that's coming it a bit strong isn't it?' Lawrie protested. Sally went to him and he put his arm around her.

'Don't cry, love,' he said. 'Looks to me as if something's been said, and one word's borrowed another. What's it all about?'

'Because I'm sewing at night,' Sally said. 'Da says I'm neglecting

114

Mary.' She broke into fresh angry tears, and Matthew flung himself back in his chair with an impatient exclamation.

'I think the best thing we can do is have a cup of tea,' Lawrie said. 'And let the argument rest for the time being.'

'I'll have me cocoa,' Matthew said gruffly, but it seemed an indication that he was willing to let the matter rest.

Sally made the supper, and Lawrie talked about affairs at the Mission, and told anecdotes of the lads they were trying to reclaim from the streets, until Matthew said goodnight. Then Sally sat on Lawrie's knee and whispered the details of the row to him, and he said thoughtfullly, 'I'm not taking your da's side, Sal, and I know why you're doing as much as you can while you've got the chance, but I do think you should slow down on the sewing.'

'But fancy him saying I was neglecting Mary,' Sally said.

Lawrie nodded, but he said gently, 'We know you're thinking about Mary's future, and you're seeing to her food and clothes now, but she is an awful lot with Mrs Mal, you know. You don't want her thinking Mrs Mal's her mother, do you?'

Sally was horrified. 'Indeed I don't!' she exclaimed. 'But she did cling to Mrs Mal the other day when I went to take her . . . I'll have to keep her at home more.'

Lawrie nodded, well satisfied, and they discussed how Sally could fit in some of the sewing. She decided she would use the machine in the afternoon, when Mary had been with her in the morning, and would probably sleep while Mrs Molloy looked after her, and Lawrie suggested buying another lamp, so that Sally could sew at night without annoying Matthew.

Letters still passed between the family at Ormesdale and Sally, but nothing was said about a meeting and she was too busy to brood about it. She always included a note for Emily in her letter to Hester, and Hester always included a reply from the child. '*I wish I could see Mary*', she often wrote, or, '*Does Mary know I'm her aunt?*'

Mary was eighteen months old when in March '94, an invitation arrived at last from Ormesdale. Sally's feelings were mixed as they boarded the train. She longed to see Emily and to show off the baby, and she was proud that they were all so well dressed, but she was worried about the grim set of her father's mouth.

'I hope Da doesn't let Walter annoy him,' she whispered to Lawrie, but he squeezed her hand and whispered back, 'Don't worry, love, I'll keep the peace.'

At the station in Ormesdale they looked about for Walter, but a man came forward, lifting his cap.

'Mr Hesketh has sent his carriage for you, sir,' he said to Matthew. Lawrie's eyes were twinkling, but Matthew's face was a study as they stepped into the carriage. Lawrie leaned forward towards Matthew.

'Sithee, sit up straight, lad,' he said. ' 'art among the nobs now, tha knows.'

In spite of himself Matthew laughed, and Mary held out her arms to him, and covered his face with wet kisses, shouting, 'Granda, Granda.'

115

There was a strong bond between Mary and Matthew, and often he could soothe her when others had failed, so now Sally was pleased that the baby distracted her grandfather from the pretensions which annoyed him.

They were amazed when the carriage turned off before they reached the farm, and drove between stone gates engraved *Greenlands*.

'So it isn't a different name for the farm, it's a different house!' Sally exclaimed. 'And the size of it.'

The house was large and very ugly, with numerous turrets and a flight of steps to the front door. No one waited outside for them now, but when they had been admitted and their coats were being taken by a maid, Emily burst from one of the rooms off the hall, and rushed up to Sally.

'Is this our Mary?' she said, standing on tiptoe to draw back the shawl from the baby's face. 'Mary, Mary, I'm your Aunt Emily.'

Hester appeared at the door of the room. 'Now, Emily,' she said, 'Uncle Walter said you must wait in here.' They all moved towards her and she retreated into the room, casting nervous glances at Walter, who stood on the hearthrug, frowning.

'Emily, I told you to wait here until Rose had announced the visitors,' he said, enunciating his words carefully.

'Save yer play acting fer yer friends, Walter,' Matthew said roughly. 'We're family, remember.' Spots of red appeared in Walter's sallow cheeks, but he said no more. Hester took the baby, and sat down with Emily beside her, to remove Mary's shawl and bonnet.

'Eh, she favours your family, Matt,' she said. 'The image of your Aunt Dora.'

'That was the bad-tempered one, wasn't it?' Walter said maliciously. 'Even Julie couldn't get on with *her*.'

Sally flushed. 'Mary's not bad-tempered, and she's not spoiled,' she said. 'Da said everyone gave in to his aunt's tantrums.'

Mary looked about her with bright eyes, then used one of her few words. 'Man,' she said, pointing at Walter.

Matthew snorted and Lawrie said quickly, 'I don't mind her saying "man" to every man she sees, but we passed a dirty old tramp the other day, and she pointed at him and said "Dada".'

They all laughed, and Emily said eagerly, 'She's lovely. Can I hold her, Uncle Walter?'

Sally and the men were amazed that Emily asked Walter's permission, and even more amazed by his calm assumption of authority.

'Yes,' he said. 'You can, but be careful.'

'Is that all right with you, Sally? She's your child,' Matthew said angrily, and Sally agreed quickly.

'Yes, yes, Da. Sit well back in the chair, Emily love, and I'll put her on your knee.'

The maid appeared with glasses of wine and biscuits for the adults, and Hester said timidly, 'Wilt tha bring milk for Emily?'

The girl looked at Walter, and flounced out when he nodded. A few moments later she came back.

'Mr Hanson to see you, sir,' she said to Walter.

'Show him into the study,' he said importantly, then turned to Matthew. 'I shall have leave thee. Business.'

Matthew sat back and folded his arms, scowling at the floor, and Hester began to question Sally eagerly about the baby's food and her teeth.

Sally answered all her questions then said, 'I didn't know you'd moved, Aunt Hester. I thought it was a different name for the farm.'

'Walter sold the farm. He's in business now in Liverpool with another man,' Hester said.

'What's his business?' Lawrie said idly, but Hester seemed flustered and glanced nervously at the door as she said in a low voice, 'Importing things and export, summat like that.'

Lawrie dropped the subject, and said to Matthew, 'Didn't you meet someone in Maybury's who knew Hester years ago?'

'Aye, a feller called Andrews, Johnny Andrews. He married a girl was in service with ye, Jessie Bamber.'

'Jessie Bamber!' Hester exclaimed. 'I remember her well. Only the size of sixpenn'orth of copper, and she ruled that big Johnny.'

'She still does, be all accounts,' Matthew said. 'He told me he was asleep in the chair one night, and she took the boots off his feet, and soled and heeled them before he woke up.'

Hester laughed heartily. 'Eh, that were Jessie all reet. A fine stirring little body, did twice the work of them big strong wenches worked wi' us.'

For a while there was a happy atmosphere in the room as Hester and Matthew recalled old acquaintances, and Emily crooned over the baby, but a blight seemed to fall on them when Walter returned. Hester spoke more slowly and carefully and Matthew sat in grim silence. They were relieved when the maid announced that luncheon was served and they moved into the dining room, but conversation was still difficult.

Lawrie spoke about the fresh controversy about the Maybrick case, but Walter ignored him and drew Matthew's attention to the cutlery and silver on the table, and the massive sideboard loaded with silver. Matthew was taciturn and Hester seemed to look at Walter before venturing any remark. Sally became more and more agitated, unable to speak or to swallow, and when Mary woke and began to cry, she thankfully excused herself and took the baby into the garden.

A little later she was joined by Hester and Emily, but when Emily saw a young woman walking up the drive, she darted away to meet her.

Hester said fondly, 'Eh, she has come on, has Emily. She didn't like t'fust governess, but this one she's reet fond of, and Miss Blake's fond of Emily. She's a vicar's daughter, tha knows.'

'Do you think Emily's happy?' Sally said. 'It's such a change from the farm.'

'She's tekken to it like a duck to water, and this girl's got a reet nice way of doing things. She's learning me to speak different and how to do things now we're mixing with different folk.' She drew herself up and looked about her proudly.

'Your Uncle Walter's a coming man, Sally. He's nobbut only just started.'

Emily came back with a tall girl who smiled in a friendly way when she was introduced to Sally.

'I've heard a great deal about you,' she said. 'And about the baby. Emily's very proud of her status as an aunt.'

Sally smiled and they chatted for a few minutes. Later when tea was served, Miss Blake was present. Sally noticed how unobtrusively she guided Hester in dispensing the tiny sandwiches and cakes, and her calm indifference to Walter's show of temper when a cup of tea was spilled. She felt happy to know that Emily was in the care of this gentle girl.

Shortly afterwards Sally made the move to leave, pleading the baby's bedtime as an excuse. Emily stood with her arm around Matthew's neck, watching Sally dress the baby in her shawl and bonnet.

'I'll be able to picture our Mary now when I think of her,' she said. 'I didn't know she was so pretty or that she had red hair.'

'Titian, Emily,' Miss Blake said with a smile. 'Titian was a famous painter who always painted ladies with hair like Emily's.' Sally smiled at Miss Blake, carefully storing the information in her mind for the future, in case Mary was ever called 'Carrots' by her schoolmates.

As the carriage drew away Matthew sat in silence for a few minutes, then he turned to Lawrie.

'What d'yer think that little runt's up to? No one ever made money as fast as that without dirtying his hands.'

'Hard to say, Matt,' Lawrie said, with a shrug. 'Hester seemed a bit uneasy about it, but he's probably just sailing a bit close to the wind.'

'He was wanting me to praise him and his tackle, but by God, he'll wait a long time for that! I'm only waiting for him to get what's coming to him.'

Sally looked alarmed.

'Oh, Da, do you think there's going to be trouble? What about Emily?'

'Don't worry, love,' Lawrie said. 'He's pretty crafty, and if anything did happen, Emily's always got us to fall back on.'

On the train Matthew took Mary in his arms and showed her the cows in the fields as they rattled along.

Lawrie said suddenly, 'I bet Walter'd gladly change places with you this minute, Matt.'

Sally lay back in her seat, closing her eyes to relieve the headache which made her temples throb. When they entered their own house she burst out, 'Oh, thank God to be home.'

'Aye, that's an uneasy place to be while they're all watching their tongues and learning their manners,' Lawrie said. 'Still, Emily's young enough not to worry, and the governess seems a nice girl.'

The fire had not been lit, so Lawrie went in to Mrs Malloy with the teapot, while Sally attended to the baby.

'That's a good lad, Sally,' Matthew said suddenly. 'He has a knack for saying the right word.'

She blushed with pleasure and smiled fondly at Lawrie when he came back a few minutes later with a teapot full of hot tea, and some warm milk for Mary.

'I've told Mrs Mal you'll tell her all about the visit tomorrow, Sal, otherwise I'd have been there for hours,' he said with a grin.

'As long as I don't have to talk to her tonight,' Sally said. 'All I want is my bed.'

She drank the hot tea gratefully, gradually unwinding after the strain of the day. Like Emily, she felt that she had a clearer picture now than the letters had given her.

Chapter Twenty

A few weeks later Sally and Lawrie were out for a walk with Mary when they met Mrs Hart and her husband, a quiet, gentle man. They stopped to chat and to admire the baby, and as they moved away Sally said remorsefully, 'I feel awful about seeing so little of Mrs Hart these days, but I never seem to have a minute, with the baby and the sewing.'

'Well, Tom's home oftener now that his shift has been changed,' Lawrie said. 'It's funny, she seems a different woman when he's home, doesn't she?'

'Well, yes,' Sally said doubtfully. 'And yet, I wonder sometimes, Lawrie. She seems so happy with Tom, yet she used to say things that made me wonder if she was sorry she married him. Things about the charm of difference and all that.'

'Too much time to brood,' Lawrie said. 'She seems to have no friends. A lonely life. Pity she doesn't hit it off with Mrs Mal.'

Sally shrugged. 'Oh, well, you now what Mrs Mal's like. I think she asked too many questions and Mrs Hart snubbed her, but it's a shame, really.'

'All the same, the Harts made a lot of sacrifices to be together. We were lucky, Sal, it was all plain sailing for us.'

Life did indeed flow smoothly for them at this time, and Sally bloomed with happiness, although she was still easily alarmed.

Following a few foggy days in late September Mary developed a hoarse, racking cough, and Sally slept little, rising at intervals to rub the baby's chest with goosegrease or dose her with Mrs Malloy's cough mixture, which was renowned locally as a sure cure.

Whether because of Mrs Malloy's medicine, or her own resilience, Mary recovered rapidly. She was now two years old, a happy lively child, but still given to tantrums if she was thwarted in any way. Matthew indulged her far more than he had his own children, and often interfered when Sally tried to check her.

One day when Mary had danced and screamed in temper Sally smacked her, and she immediately ran to her grandfather.

'There then, love,' he said, cuddling her, and glaring at Sally.

'You've no call to do that,' he said. 'She's only a baby.'

'It's for her own good,' Sally said angrily. 'You were the one who said your aunt grew up a tyrant because she was never checked.'

'Aye, well, mebbe it's not Dora the child gets her temper from. Ye're very free with yer hands and yer tongue yerself these days, madam.'

Sally compressed her lips and walked into the back kitchen without replying. What hope have I got of bringing her up properly, she

121

thought angrily, with Da butting in, and spoiling her, and Lawrie refusing to put his foot down? Anything for a quiet life, that's Lawrie. Unable to find an outlet in a row with her father, her anger turned upon her husband.

When he came home after working late, he was amazed when she turned her cheek away from his kiss, and banged his dinner down on the table.

'What's up?' he asked.

'Nothing's up,' Sally snapped. 'What could be up? Everything's always perfect according to you.' She bounced into the back kitchen and began to bang pans about, and Lawrie ate his dinner slowly, waiting for enlightenment but carefully avoiding Matthew's eye. When Sally reappeared in the living room, he ignored her angry look and only asked quietly, 'Where's Mary?'

'In bed. The best place for her.'

Lawrie stood up. 'I'll go up and see her,' he said, opening the door at the foot of the stairs.

'Don't go waking her up,' Sally warned. 'I've had enough of her today.'

Matthew snorted loudly, and Lawrie crept upstairs. He bent over the truckle bed where Mary lay asleep, shielding the candle with his hand. She lay with one hand beneath her cheek, looking angelic and vulnerable, and Lawrie bent and kissed her gently. When he came back dowstairs he smiled at Sally, and she smiled back, feeling ashamed of her ill temper.

'Yer look tired, lad,' Matthew said. 'Yer late tonight, aren't yer?'

Lawrie yawned and sighed. 'Aye, it's this new boss. I'll be glad when old Leather comes back. This feller must have been boss of a cotton plantation before, the way he carries on.'

He stretched out on the sofa and soon fell asleep, while Matthew sat reading and smoking, and Sally embroidered the neck of a satin blouse. Gertie, one of her first customers from Ogden's, had acquired a very generous 'gentleman friend' who readily paid for more elaborate clothes for her, and Sally reaped the benefit.

In bed that night she slipped her arms about Lawrie's neck and kissed him.

'I'm sorry I was so bad-tempered, Lol,' she said. 'I don't know how you put up with me.'

'I know you've got a lot on your plate, love, with the sewing on top of looking after us, and then training Mary and keeping the peace with your da.'

'He drives me mad, Lawrie. He's ruining her, kissing and cuddling her when I've scolded her or smacked her. He wasn't as soft with us, I can tell you.'

'Well, Mary's a kind of second chance for him. I suppose all grandparents are like that. They think they've been too strict with their own kids, and of course they've got more time to play with their grandchildren.'

'And they don't have to deal with the results,' Sally said grimly. 'I wish you'd say something to him, Lawrie.'

122

'She's only a baby yet, Sal. She'll grow out of these tantrums, I'm sure.'

'I hope you're right,' Sally said. 'But I doubt it.' It's no use, she thought, Lawrie won't see trouble until it gets up and hits him, but I'll never change him. And I don't want to, she told herself, as Lawrie held her in his arms and kissed her passionately.

As time went on Mary's tantrums grew fewer, but she was still self-willed and disobedient at times, although usually she was a happy and charming little girl. She had a quick mind, and to her parents and grandfather she was the cleverest and most entertaining child ever created, although she and Sally often had a clash of wills. Sally knew that it was wrong, but occasionally she found herself mentally comparing Mary with Emily, who had been such an affectionate and well-behaved child. She felt that a brother or sister would make a difference to Mary, but she began to fear that she would never have another child. Twice she missed a period, and thought that she was pregnant, but each time she suffered severe abdominal pain the following month and lost a great deal of blood.

'It looks as if ye start a baby then lose it,' Mrs Malloy said. 'Still, never mind, girlie, it'll give ye a spell.' But Sally worried in case this was to be the pattern, and Mary would be an only child.

Emily had never played in the street, but Mary was so restless and full of energy that Sally was forced to let her play out, watched over by one of the Dolan girls. Kate Dolan was ten years old, so Mary was often with older girls instead of the three year olds like herself, and she began to acquire some of their mannerisms and tricks of speech.

'Yer want ter keep her off the street,' Matthew said disapprovingly. 'She's gettin' real rough, and she came out with a word just before yer'd only hear from a docker.'

'What can I do, Da?' Sally said. 'I can't be out with her the whole time, and she won't settle in the house. She's got too much energy.'

The following Saturday Lawrie came in grinning.

'Our Mary's in good form,' he said. 'One of the big girls took her top just now, and the next minute Mary laid into her, fists flying, and the big girl turned and ran.'

Matthew laughed and Lawrie turned to him. 'No sooner a word than a blow with her,' he said.

Sally was not amused.

'Why didn't you bring her in?' she demanded, opening the door and calling to Mary, who was sitting on the kerb opposite with other children. She scowled at Sally but made no move and Sally went over and jerked her to her feet. Maggie Connolly, now an enormously fat woman, was sitting with her huge bottom propped on her window sill. She called to Sally.

'That's a bad-tempered little faggot yer've got there, Sally. Yer'll 'ave yer own share with her before long.'

Sally said nothing. She knew that she should feel grateful to Maggie who had breast fed Emily so willingly, but Maggie had become a bitter and surly woman after the death of her little Susan. Even before Susan died of the fever at the same time as Sally's two brothers, Maggie had resented the fact that Emily was healthy and pretty, while Susan was a sickly child with a bad squint.

'She'd be the better of a bloody good hiding,' Maggie shouted as Sally reached her front door with Mary.

'She gets many a smack,' Sally said, hustling Mary into the house. Perversely, her anger with Mary vanished when she heard her criticized by someone else, but she resolved to find a better environment for her as soon as possible.

Sally and Lawrie still went for a walk every Sunday, now with Mary trotting between them. During the summer months they usually went down to the Landing Stage, or to Kensington Fields, but as the days grew shorter and colder they confined themselves to the streets stretching up the hill towards Everton Road. The streets were wider and the houses larger than Gell Street, and there was one street which Sally particularly admired. The bay-windowed houses were all neat and well cared for, and one day when she walked there with Mary, she got into conversation with a woman who was brushing her step.

She learned that the houses had three bedrooms, and downstairs a parlour, kitchen and back kitchen. They had their own water supply and lavatory, and even gas lighting, yet the houses were only four shillings a week dearer than Gell Street. She had redoubled her efforts to save, often getting up to do washing and ironing before the men left for work so that she would have more time to sew, and the teapot now held nearly one hundred pounds.

She said nothing to Lawrie or her father about the houses but the following day she went to see the landlord, a small dark Welshman named Mr Jones.

'You don't come from round here, do you?' he asked, when he had taken particulars from Sally. 'You don't speak like them.'

She blushed with pleasure. 'I was born in Gell Street,' she said. 'But my mam came from the country.'

'Now I've got good tenants, see,' said Mr Jones. 'They look after my houses and they always have the rent ready for me. I see your rent book's clear from Gell Street, but are you sure you can manage the extra for my house?'

'Yes,' Sally said proudly. 'We've got savings, and my husband and my father are in steady work. I do sewing and I make good money, too.'

'I see. Now people don't often flit from here, but as it happens I have a house coming empty. An old lady gone to live with her son, and he's clearing the house next week, so I'll give you first option on the key. Come and see me next week.'

Sally went home, greatly excited, but she waited until Lawrie and her father had eaten their meal before she said, 'You know those houses in Egremont Street we looked at, Lawrie? They're only four shillings a week more than these.'

'*Only* four shillings,' Matthew said. 'Four shillings can take some finding, girl.'

'We could afford it, Da.'

'Too much to go in for. Yer won't alwis be on the crest of the wave, Sally,' he said.

'Do you know Egremont Street, Matt?' Lawrie asked. 'We've walked up there sometimes on a Sunday.'

'I might have passed it, lad, if it's near Everton Road. I've been up there to the Necropolis, or to the pub on the corner of Cresswell Street, but I usually strike down the other way, y'know.'

'It's a nice street, Da, and good solid houses. Their own water and lavatory, and *gaslight*,' Sally said.

'And how do yer know all this?' asked Matthew.

'I got talking to a woman brushing her step there, and she told me the landlord's name. I went to see him, and he said people don't often flit from there, but an old lady from one house has gone to live with her son, and he'll give me first option on the key,' Sally said breathlessly. The two men looked at each other.

'Well, yer don't let the grass grow under yer feet, girl, that's for sure,' said Matthew. 'Wharrabout leaving good neighbours like Mrs Mal and Mrs Hart?'

'We'll only be ten minutes' walk away, Da. I can still see them.' Matthew shook his head.

'It's not the same as having a good neighour the other side of the wall. Yer won't find many like Mrs Mal, either.' Sally said nothing, and he added irritably, 'It'd made a difference to me and Lawrie, too. Another ten minutes drag up the hill after the day's work.'

Sally looked at Lawrie for support, but he made no response. He's as anxious as me to move but he won't push it, she thought angrily, just because Da's against it and he doesn't want to be two on to one.

Aloud she said, 'It would be healthier for Mary.' She felt a pang of remorse when she saw the shadow which crossed Matthew's face, but she stifled it quickly. *Someone's* got to fight our battles, she told herself. She stood up and gathered the dishes, and Lawrie followed her into the back kitchen.

'You've sprung this too suddenly on your da, Sal,' he whispered. 'Give him time to think about it.'

'We can afford it, and I've got money saved for furniture,' she said sullenly. 'What does he think I've been working for? Anyhow, I thought you were the one who couldn't wait to move.'

'Yes, and I was the one who jumped into things, and you were the cautious one,' he said with a smile. 'We seem to have changed places. Let it rest tonight, Sal. Let him think about it.'

Fortunately, Mrs Malloy came in when they went back into the kitchen, and the conversation was general. When she left Matthew stood up and took his cap from behind the door.

'I'm walking down for a gill,' he said gruffly. He did not suggest that Lawrie went with him, and Lawrie said nothing, but while he was out Sally and Lawrie discussed the pros and cons of the move. Lawrie was adamant that Matthew should not be pressed to move.

'He's been very good to us, Sal, giving us a home, and being tactful going out and leaving us on our own, very often when he didn't feel like going out, I know.'

'But the house might go,' Sally argued.

'There'll be other houses, but if we push him into this and he's

125

miserable, we'll always be sorry. It'd spoil the house for us.'

Sally was not convinced. She had been so sure that there was no obstacle to the move, and she felt that she would be justified in forcing the issue with her father for Mary's sake, but when Matthew came home he solved the problem for her.

'Yer can do what yer like about that house, Sally,' he said.

'Oh, Da, are you sure? We'd just decided we wouldn't say any more about it, but it would be better for Mary.'

'Aye, yer'll have a better class of neighbours. This street's going down the nick. I seen two women fighting across the street, and a couple of drunks, so she'll be better away from it. The air's better up there too.' He sat down and began to unlace his boots. Lawrie drew his chair nearer to Matthew's.

'Listen, Matt,' he said. 'Don't think we've been plotting this. Sally just saw the landlord on an impulse, and he just happened to have the house coming empty.'

'It's all right, lad. I could see yer were as thunderstruck as me when she came out with it, but it's time to move. He must be a good landlord an' all, if he's got people waitin' for his houses. God knows, they're in and out of these houses like bloody fireflies.'

'Another thing, Matt,' Lawrie said diffidently, 'don't take Mary's health into the reckoning, if you don't really want to move.'

Matthew took out his pipe. 'I don't get yer, lad,' he said.

'I know you think about your lads – that it's not healthy round here – but there were plenty of others, barefoot and half starved, who took the fever and got over it. Your lads had good food and clothes and a good home, yet they didn't. It's the way things go.'

Matthew was lighting his pipe with a spill, and he sat still for a moment until the spill burned down and touched his fingers. He threw it in the fire and turned to Lawrie.

'D'yer know, that never struck me,' he said. 'I alwis blamed meself that I didn't do better for me family, but like you say, there were plenty worse off than us who got over the fever.' He sat puffing at his pipe for a moment, then he said firmly, 'Still an' all, the child should have her chanst. I'm just like an owld snail in me shell. Go and see that feller, Sally, and tell him yer'll take the house.'

'Yes, Da,' Sally said joyfully, folding up her sewing. She felt too excited to do any more, while so many plans were milling about in her mind.

Chapter Twenty-One

Sally went several times to see Mr Jones, and two weeks later he gave her the key to number forty, Egremont Street. Mrs Malloy advised waiting until they were in the house to buy furniture, but Sally was anxious to make a good impression on the new neighbours.

She decided to put the shabby iron bedstead which she and Lawrie slept on in the third bedroom, and together they chose a brass bedstead and a new feather mattress and bolster.

'I'll never get up in the morning out of this,' Lawrie laughed. From Solly's pawnshop they bought a mahogany wardrobe and chest of drawers, but Sally decided that their washstand, though rickety, would serve for the present.

As soon as she got the key she went to inspect the house. It was cold and dirty, with the atmosphere of a house unlived in for weeks, and showing signs of only minimum care for a long time, but Sally was delighted with it.

There was a long narrow passage from the front door, with stairs rising steeply at the end. On the left a door led to the parlour, a small bright room with a bay window, and a door beside the stairs led to the kitchen, with the back kitchen opening off it. Straw and bits of newspaper littered the floor, and the grimy walls showed lighter patches where pictures had been taken down. The black grate was rusty, but in the back kitchen there was a stone sink with a tap over it, and a brick boiler, with shelves running round the walls and a cupboard in the corner.

Sally glanced round rapidly, then went upstairs. The stairs were well lit by a skylight in the ceiling, and Sally was pleased to see that the middle bedroom was as large as the front bedroom which she earmarked for her father. The new bed and furniture would fit in the middle bedroom and still leave room for Mary's truckle bed. They had decided that Mary should still sleep in their room at first, in case she was nervous in the new house, but eventually she would be able to have her own bedroom.

We're getting on, Sally thought exultantly. Our Mary with her own bedroom!

She could not delay as she had left Mary with Mrs Malloy, but she offered to mind Mary again the next day, while Sally cleaned the house.

'She's been as good as gold,' she declared. 'Ye can take a snack with ye, and have a full day at the place tomorrow.'

After Lawrie had eaten his meal, he and Sally walked up to the house. Under the cover of darkness they carried a bucket and scrubbing brush, an old pan, a sweeping brush and shovel, and some candles and gas mantles.

As soon as they arrived they lit the candles and Lawrie removed the broken mantles and fitted new ones, then he located the gas meter and put a penny in the slot. In the bedrooms there were gas brackets from the wall, but downstairs the fittings were in the centre of the ceiling, operated by chains hanging on either side. When the gas was lit Sally and Lawrie looked at each other in amazement.

'Why, it's as good as daylight,' Sally exclaimed. 'I'll be able to sew until all hours.'

'It'll be good and bright for your da to read his paper, too,' Lawrie observed.

Lawrie was as pleased with the house as Sally, when they took a candle and explored it. He held the candle close to the bedroom wall.

'No sign of bugs here, Sal,' he said. 'No sign of vermin anywhere except a few mouse droppings, but I'll soon deal with them.'

'We could get a cat. Mary'd like that, wouldn't she?' Sally said. They looked round all the bedrooms, and Lawrie decided that he would whitewash all the walls at the weekend.

'Your Da will give me a hand,' he said, 'and we'll paper the kitchen. The parlour can wait for a while.'

Downstairs he gathered up the straw and bits of newspaper and started a fire in the grate, while Sally measured the windows for curtains, then he fitted new gas mantles in the parlour and the bedrooms.

The following morning Sally carried a parcel of bread and cheese for her lunch, and a bag of coal and firewood to the house. She lit the fire and had just finished blackleading the rusty grate when there was a knock on the door, and she found a skinny girl of about twelve years old standing there.

'Me mam said would you like some hot water to scrub out?' the child said. 'She seen you bringing a bucket in last night.'

So much for coming in the dark, thought Sally, but aloud she said, 'I'd be very glad of it. I was going to heat water in a pan on the fire, but it's not burning up yet.' The child vanished and reappeared a few minutes later with a bucket full of hot water in one hand, and a floor cloth and scrubbing brush in the other.

'I'll give you a hand,' she announced, 'we can put half this water in your bucket and fill up with cold.' She offered to scrub the kitchen floor, so Sally started on the back kitchen. The draining board was filthy and engrained with dirt in the deep cracks. She wrinkled her nose in disgust. I'm not putting my dishes on *that*, she thought, taking it off and deciding to ask Lawrie to make a new one.

She scrubbed the sink, then stood on a backless chair which had been left, and scrubbed the shelves. By this time the pan of water on the fire was hot, so she threw out the filthy water in her bucket and replaced it from the pan. She had planned to help the little girl with the kitchen floor, but to her surprise it was finished, so she scrubbed the stone-flagged back kitchen instead.

The girl, whose name she told Sally was Susan Kilgannon, had brought an invitation from her mother for Sally to go in for a cup of tea. Sally demurred, because she felt so dirty, but before she knew what was happening, Susan had swept her next door and sat her down in a chair opposite her mother. The room was spotlessly clean and very cosy, with a bright fire, and a red cloth edged with bobbles on the table. Mrs Kilgannon was a tall, bony woman with grizzled hair and a whining voice.

'Susan's me last one,' she said plaintively. 'All the others have got married and left me.'

Susan was bustling about, and she soon produced cups of tea, and a plate of buttered fruit loaf.

'You've taken something on with that place next door,' Mrs Kilgannon said. 'There hasn't been a hand's turn done there for years.'

'Mrs Williams was very old, Mam,' Susan said. 'She couldn't do much.'

'She never tried,' her mother whined. 'I don't like Welsh people, do you, Mrs –?'

'Mrs Ward's my name,' Sally said. 'I like some Welsh people and I don't like others, the same as English or Irish people. Mr Jones seems a good landlord.'

'Yes, he is,' Mrs Kilgannon admitted. 'He'll do repairs but he's very keen on the rent.' To Sally's amazement she brought out a clay pipe and filled it, and Susan lit it for her.

'My only comfort,' Mrs Kilgannon said with a sigh. Sally was not sure whether she was referring to Susan or to the pipe, so she said nothing. A little later she thanked them for the tea and left.

Later she told Mrs Malloy about her new neighbour.

'I didn't take to her much,' she admitted. 'Although it was kind of her to ask me in for the tea, and send the girl with the hot water.' She sighed. 'I'm going to miss having you next door, Mrs Mal,'

'Aye, and I'll miss you, girlie, but sure, you're not moving to China, as yer aunt would say.'

'Fancy you remembering that,' Sally said, smiling. 'I think I'll be wearing a track up and down to see you.'

'Now don't be getting faint hearted, girl. Haven't we the scum of the earth moving into these houses? Ye'll be well out of it, if it's only for the child's sake.'

'I hope Da will be all right,' Sally said. 'Lawrie's a bit worried about uprooting him, to suit ourselves.'

'Ah, he'll be grand. Be the time ye've been there a month he'll feel he's always lived there.'

The preparations for the move went ahead briskly, but before it happened Sally's happiness was clouded by a tragedy. She was anxious to leave the Gell Street house spotless, and was outside cleaning the window when two men approached her.

'Does Mrs Hart live around here, missis?' one asked.

'Yes, next door, number eleven,' Sally said. The men stood looking at each other and twisting their caps in their hands, and a cold feeling touched Sally.

'Is something wrong?' she said.

'It's Tom Hart, missis. He was lost overboard this morning.'

'He must of caught his foot in a hawser,' the other man said. 'We couldn't do nothing. There was a strong tide running.'

Sally had dropped her washcloth, and was steadying herself on the windowsill. 'Is there no hope? Couldn't he be picked up – another ship?' The men shook their heads, shuffling their feet awkwardly and glancing at each other.

'We were thinkin', missis, if you're her neighbour . . .' said one.

'It'd come better from another woman,' the other man said.

'Yes, yes,' Sally murmured. 'Oh, poor Mrs Hart, whatever will she do?' Tears ran down her face, and the men cleared their throats.

' 'E was a good mate. We're very sorry, missis.'

'Aye, he was a good mate,' the other man echoed. 'Everybody liked Tom Hart. Tell her we're sorry, missis. Ta ra.'

Thankfully they escaped, and Sally went indoors to compose herself.

She was glad that Mary was playing with Kate in the Dolans' house, and made a pot of tea and drank a cupful quickly before covering the teapot and leaving a cup ready beside it, then going next door.

Mrs Hart was reading, but she looked up with a welcoming smile when Sally tapped at the door and opened it.

'Come in, Sally, and sit down,' she said, then something in Sally's sorrowful expression seemed to strike her.

'Oh, Sally, what is it, dear? Has something happened?'

Sally sat down and took her hand. 'Yes, but not to me. Oh, Mrs Hart, it's Tom.'

'Tom. What is it, Sally? Tell me quickly.'

'Two men came. They said he fell overboard this morning.'

'Dead?' she said, her hand suddenly gripping Sally's.

'They think so. There was a strong tide running and they couldn't reach him.' Tears began to run down Sally's face, but Mrs Hart sat as though turned to stone. Sally stroked her hand.

'The men were very sorry, Mrs Hart,' she said gently. 'They said he was a good mate. They were upset.'

'Yes, yes, thank you, Sally,' Mrs Hart said almost absently. Sally withdrew her hand.

'I'll go and get a cup of tea for you,' she said. She went home and poured the tea, and when she returned Mrs Hart was still sitting motionless, with her hands lying in her lap. Sally put the teacup in her hand and guided it to her lips, and she sipped mechanically.

Sally said quietly, 'It must have been quick, Mrs Hart. He couldn't have suffered.'

'Yes, quite, quite,' Mrs Hart murmured. She seemed to waken from her reverie, and handed the cup to Sally.

'My poor Tom,' she said, wringing her hands. 'I ruined his life, Sally.'

'Don't say that, Mrs Hart. He was happy.'

Mrs Hart gave a shuddering sigh, rocking herself from side to side.

'No. He was a born gardener and he had to leave all that. I was always a source of worry to him, too. I couldn't adapt, you see. It was the smells, Sally. I could bear everything else but not the smells.' She fell silent for a moment.

'I wanted so much to be a good wife, but nothing went right. Even our child died. I was an inadequate mother, Sally, as I was an inadequate wife.' Sally made a movement of protest, and Mrs Hart took her hand again.

'You are a kind girl, Sally,' she said.

She had never spoken of her early life, but hoping to distract her, Sally said tentatively, 'How old were you when you got married, Mrs Hart?'

'I was twenty-two, Sally, but I had always been treated as a child. My mother said I was delicate but that was only an excuse for keeping me with her. Dominating me as completely as Queen Victoria dominates her children. Everyone was crushed. The servants crept about, and no voices were ever raised, except my mother's.' She sat staring into the fire for a moment, then turned to Sally with a smile lighting up her haggard face.

'He seemed so free, Tom – so alive. He was working on a flower bed and when he looked up and saw me, he smiled. Such a happy, carefree smile. I'd never seen anyone like him.'

'Did you leave right away?' asked Sally.

'Oh, no. We used to meet whenever we could. I'd led such a dull life and it was so exciting, meeting in odd corners of the garden, or hearing him whistling "Speak to me, Thora". My name is Thora, you see.'

'It was like that with me and Lawrie,' Sally said shyly, 'As soon as we saw each other we knew we would get married.'

'I don't know how my mother discovered, but she was furious, and Tom was so brave. He told her that I was over the legal age, and that we were going to be married, and she couldn't stop us. I defied her for the first time in my life and said I was going with Tom.'

'You were brave too, then,' Sally said. Mrs Hart smiled vaguely, staring into the fire.

'She was so angry. She said if I went she would close the gates, and they would only be opened when her coffin was carried through them. It was very melodramatic, but from people like my mother that was considered acceptable.'

'It was very romantic,' Sally said.

Mrs Hart smiled sadly. 'No, I see now that we were silly. We should have been more discreet and made careful plans, but we were young and very much in love. We ran away with no plan and scarcely any money, just sufficient to take us to Liverpool, where Tom had a brother.'

'Did you live with his brother at first?' asked Sally, hoping to keep her talking to help her over the first shock of the news.

'No, we found a room near Rodney Street. I wore a cheap wedding ring, and poor Tom slept on the floor.'

'But why didn't you stay with his brother?' asked Sally.

Mrs Hart smiled sadly. 'He was more sensible than we were, and he refused to be involved. He saw, as we did not, that as we were within thirty miles of my home we were within reach of my mother's spite. Tom could not find work in the public parks without references, and a job on any large estate was out of the question.'

'Why?' asked Sally.

'Because, Sally, Society is like a loosely woven web, all threads connected. A little pull on one affects all the others. A servant who offends one of the set soon realises its ramifications and power to exclude. Tom and I had not realised that my mother's power extended so far in the business world of Liverpool.'

'Surely Mr Hart was not dealing with business men, though,' said Sally.

'Oh, no, he was beneath their notice personally,' Mrs Hart said bitterly. 'But they had only to tell their employees that he must not be taken on in any capacity.'

'Why didn't you move on, Mrs Hart?'

The older woman sighed and shrugged. 'Who knows, Sally? Perhaps our small store of courage and money was spent, and then Tom found this house, and your mother was kind to me. Also he found a job on the tugs – perhaps my mother's brief did not run to the river.'

'Your mother was sorry later, though, wasn't she? Mrs Malloy told me that she sent you money regularly.'

'My mother! No indeed. She would never have sent it, nor would I have accepted it. The money is from the estate of my godmother who died in America shortly after my marriage.'

Sally stood up to look out of the window, as she heard Mary screaming in the street.

'I'll have to go to Mary, Mrs Hart,' she said. 'I'll be back very soon. Is there anything I can do before I go? Should I ask Mrs Malloy to sit with you?'

'No, thank you, Sally. You've been most kind and tactful, but please, I would like to be alone for a little now.'

It was nearly an hour later before Sally was free to go again to next door, but she found the door bolted and there was no answer to her timid knock.

'I seen her goin' in with a straw bag full a bottles,' a girl playing nearby volunteered. Sally worried all day about Mrs Hart, listening anxiously for the usual sound of drunken singing which these orgies of drinking produced, but there was no sound, except for a few crashes. She went to see Mrs Malloy and told her of Tom Hart's death.

'God help her,' Mrs Malloy exclaimed. 'What has she left at all?'

'I'm so sorry for her, Mrs Mal,' wept Sally. 'She's had such a tragic life, and I'm wondering what's happening to her now.'

'Everyone has their own way of dealing with trouble, child, and if the drink is a help to her and she has the money for it, she may as well have it.'

'It wasn't her mother who sent the money, Mrs Mal, it was her godmother.'

'Aye well, she comes from moneyed people right enough, but still, girl, ye had what she never had, a good mother. Don't be fretting yerself now. The drink will drown her trouble for a while.'

Sally found it impossible to refrain from worrying, and when Lawrie came in she asked him to climb the wall dividing the back yards to look for a light. He could see none, and he went and knocked loudly at the front door, and called Mrs Hart, but there was no answer. Lawrie and her father both advised Sally to stop worrying until Mrs Hart's drunken spree was over, and then to help her as much as possible, but Sally was filled with foreboding. Before she went to bed she went again to the house, and when she tapped at the door, it opened at her touch.

She went back for Lawrie and a candle, and together they went into the house. It was dark, but full of the smell of oil from an overturned lamp, mingled with the smell from bottles rolling about the floor. The fire had long gone out and several chairs were overturned, but there was no sign of Mrs Hart. Lawrie searched through the house, then he persuaded Sally to go home while he looked around the surrounding streets, but his search was hopeless.

The following morning a watchman on the riverfront told him that a woman had fallen in the river at about nine thirty the previous night. He could only say that it was a dark figure carried rapidly downstream with her long hair streaming behind her, but Sally and Lawrie were sure that it was Mrs Hart. Mrs Malloy, as always, supplied comfort and commonsense.

'Ye did all ye could for her, girlie,' she said. 'Yer were a real good neighbour, but sure, ye couldn't help her with troubles of her own making.'

'Oh, Mrs Mal, it wasn't her fault that her mother was so spiteful, or that she lost Tom like that.'

'Aye, she had her troubles, but Sally, she should never had married out of the class she was born to. What good did it do for herself or Tom? Still, Lord ha' mercy on her, she paid for her mistakes, and God stiffen that unnatural mother she had. She'll be paid out in this world or the next for the way she treated her child.'

It was a long time before Sally slept that night, as she lay thinking of all that Mrs Hart's example had meant to her and to Emily.

Chapter Twenty-Two

Sally grieved sincerely for Mrs Hart, but the excitement of the move helped her to overcome her sorrow. Lawrie and Matthew had worked hard, whitewashing the bedrooms and papering the kitchen, then laying linoleum on the floors, and Agnes Cassidy helped Sally to clean and polish, and to hang curtains.

Agnes was unselfishly delighted at Sally's 'step up in the world' as she called it. She was courting now, but there seemed little prospect of marriage for some years. Her young man, James, was employed in a large drapery establishment where he lived in, and he was determined that they must save for at least two years before they married.

'It suits me,' Agnes confided to Sally. 'Me mam needs me money. Our Liam and our Dan are working now, but they only get buttons – not as much between them as our Tom used to turn up to me mam.'

'Your mam must miss Tom's money,' Sally said.

'Aye, he offered to give her a few shillings a week, but me mam wouldn't take it.'

'If Tom could afford it –' began Sally, but Agnes broke in.

'It's her – his wife. Me mam said she would begrudge it, and she wouldn't cause trouble between her and our Tom. She didn't want nothing begrudged either.'

'Doesn't your mam like his wife then?'

'She can't stand her, and neither can I,' said Agnes frankly. 'Plate face, me mam calls her, but it's no worse than her real name – Magdalen.'

'Couldn't you get married and live with your mam?' asked Sally, but Agnes shook her head.

'No, it wouldn't work. Me mam is always on her best behaviour when James is there, but she couldn't keep it up all the time. You know her, Sal, she's always so lively, and James is so quiet. Could you see them living together?'

'No, not really,' Sally admitted. She disliked the prim, censorious James, and could imagine his reaction if Mrs Cassidy lifted her skirts and danced to Liam's mouth organ, as she often did.

Sally had written to her aunt to tell her of the move, and she was surprised to receive a prompt reply, in which Hester said that Walter would be in Liverpool on that day, and he would leave her and Emily to help in the move. Sally was almost as excited about this as about her new house, and so was Mrs Malloy, who looked forward to seeing Emily again.

The move was planned for a Saturday, and as soon as the men had left for work, Sally stripped the beds, and tied the bedding in sheets.

135

Lawrie and Matthew had made several trips the previous night, with small items on a handcart, so only the large furniture remained. Mary was with Mrs Malloy, and Sally hastened to Egremont Street with a basket containing the remaining dishes and a small stock of food, and a straw bag containing the kettle.

Susan Kilgannon had been in to light the fire, and Sally felt that with her own kettle on the hob, and her own rag rug on the new lino, the kitchen felt like home already. Lawrie and Matthew had both asked for a short day at work and soon they arrived with the furniture loaded on a cart.

The table and chairs and the sofa were carried into the kitchen, and the driver helped the men to carry the beds and the new furniture upstairs. Sally hoped that her neighbours were watching, especially when Walter's carriage stopped at the door, and Hester and Emily descended from it. The coachman handed Hester a large basket, and Sally went out to welcome them, and to greet Walter, who remained in the carriage.

Hester put the basket on the table and unpacked it.

'Now, Sally,' she said, 'I'll bet as tha's etten nowt wi' all the excitement, so fust thing we'll do is have summat to eat.' She unpacked a large boiled ham, sausages, eggs, pickles, and bread, cheese and fruit cake.

'Us'll have the ham and that later,' she said. 'Now I'll fry up some sausages and eggs, because the men must be clemmed, too.'

She tied a large white apron over her silk frock, and began to cook, while Sally buttered bread and Emily flew about exploring, and talking to Lawrie and her father. The men were tramping about upstairs setting up the beds, and there were shouts of laughter from them. Hester turned to Sally.

'Eh, that lad of yours has made a difference to Matthew. He was allus glum like, was your da, but he seems properly livened up now.'

'Da's had a lot of trouble,' Sally said defensively, 'but he does enjoy Lawrie's company, and we often have a laugh together.' The food was ready so Sally went upstairs to call the men, and was delighted to see the beds up and the furniture in place.

She asked if they were ready for something to eat. Savoury smells were drifting upstairs as Hester fried the eggs and sausages, and the men clattered downstairs and set to eagerly. Hester bustled about, piling their plates, while Sally cut more bread and butter, and made a pot of tea.

'By God, that was good, Hester,' Matthew said, pushing his plate away. 'Yer haven't lost yer touch, girl.' Lawrie and the driver echoed his thanks, then the three men went out to the yard, as the carter had offered to take the rubbish away.

'I suppose you don't do much cooking now, Aunt Hester,' Sally said.

She sighed. 'Nay, I don't lass,' she said. 'And I were allus a notable cook, tha knows, but now – eh, I'm nobbut a stranger in me own house, Sally.'

'It's just getting used to different ways, Aunt,' Sally said, hoping to cheer her. 'Mrs Malloy says there's nothing wrong in getting on.'

'Aye for a man mebbe, he's not at whoam all day, but a woman's house is all her world. Now I can do nowt wi'out someone tekkin' huff, the woman i' kitchen or one o' them impident young lasses. Still, I shall get used, I suppose.'

'I'm sure you will, and it must be nice to have servants, in some ways, and then you've got your own carriage, too.'

'Aye, lass, thy Uncle Walter has properly getten on,' Hester said, brightening and starting to cook for Sally, Emily and herself. They had just finished eating when Mrs Malloy arrived with Mary. She exclaimed in amazement when she saw Emily.

'Glory be to God, child, I'd never have known ye, if it wasn't for yer mam's eyes and her curls ye have.' She lifted the corner of her apron and wiped her eyes, and Emily smiled briefly at her, and turned eagerly to Mary.

'I'm your Aunt Emily,' she announced, taking Mary's hand. Sally brought out a ball, and sent the two little girls to play in the empty parlour, while she poured tea for Mrs Malloy, and Hester urged her to have ham and pickles or a piece of cake.

Later Sally showed them over the house, and Mrs Malloy was loud in her praises of it.

'Indeed and ye could have been here weeks, the way everything is settled,' she said. 'Ye've something to show for all the hard work, all of yiz.'

Between them they made up the beds with fresh bedding, and Sally brought up a shovelful of hot coals to put in the tiny grates to air the rooms.

'Fireplaces everywhere!' Mrs Malloy exclaimed. 'Sure, ye've moved in to the quality now, girlie.'

Hester said nothing but Sally thought she looked wistful as Lawrie joined them, and he and Sally excitedly demonstrated how the gas was lit. There was an air of happiness and hope for the future as they proudly showed off their new house and furniture which made Hester look pensive, but she came into her own again when later she prepared a lavish tea.

Mrs Malloy was happy, sitting with Mary on her knee and Emily sitting beside her, telling her about her lessons with Miss Blake. Sally watched Emily lovingly.

'She's a real little charmer, isn't she?' she whispered.

'Aye, she can do owt wi' Walter. It were her made him bring us.'

The tin clock was on the mantelpiece with the tea caddy and Sally's prized vases. Hester looked at it and sighed.

'Us'll have to be getten ready, Emily love,' she said, taking off her large white apron. Emily put her arms round Mary and hugged her, and Mary clung to her until Sally drew her away. Hester looked anxious as Sally helped Emily with her coat and bonnet.

'Nay, Emily, hurry tha self, do. T'carriage 'ull be here in a minute.'

Emily kissed Mrs Malloy, then her father and Lawrie, but when Sally bent to kiss her, she slipped a little parcel of dolls' clothes into the child's hand.

137

'Dress your dolly when you get home, love,' she said. 'And give my regards to Miss Blake.' The two children kissed again and Sally turned to Hester.

'Thank you for the food and everything, Aunt,' she said. 'I wish I had something ready to give you.'

'Eh, tha's given me a reet happy day, lass,' Hester said. 'I don't know when –' She turned away, her face working, but Emily created a diversion by pulling at Sally's sleeve.

'Can I stay in your other bedroom if Uncle Walter will let me, Sal, or can Mary come and stay with me?'

'We'll see,' Sally said mechanically, feeling upset by Hester's distress, but the next moment the carriage could be heard, and Hester drew herself up. She patted the satin bow under her chin, and looked about her, as though daring them to notice her earlier agitation. Even her voice altered, to Sally's amazement.

This time Walter came into the house, looking around and saying patronizingly to Lawrie, 'You've done very well.'

Lawrie's eyes twinkled. 'Dost think so?' he enquired, but Sally drove her elbow into his ribs, and he said no more.

They all crowded to the front door to see the visitors off, with Emily running back to kiss Mary, and to whisper, 'Don't forget, Sal.'

Mary cried loudly as the carriage drew away, but when Sally hustled her indoors and followed the others to the kitchen, she was amazed to find them laughing.

'Did ye ever see the like of the mannikin!' Mrs Malloy exclaimed, and Matthew broke in, '*Spats,* fer God's sake. Did yer see the spats? And then when this fella started takin' a rise –' he indicated Lawrie, and leaned back in his chair, laughing loudly.

'Aye, until Sally winded me,' Lawrie grinned.

'You shouldn't laugh at him. You've eaten his food,' Sally protested, smiling in spite of herself. Suddenly, the cloud which Hester's distress had thrown over her happiness disappeared.

'I'll make a fresh cup of tea,' she said, but her father took out the rum bottle.

'Me and Lawrie'll have this,' he said. 'What about you, Mrs Mal? I know our Sally won't touch it, but you'll have a drop to hansel the house, won't yer?'

'I'll have it both ways, Matty lad. I'll have a drop in me cup of tea,' Mrs Malloy laughed. Matthew raised his glass.

'Good health and happiness to all in this house,' he said.

They all raised their cups or glasses, and Mrs Malloy gave Mary a sip from her cup.

'Please God, it'll be a good move for yiz and a happy home. Haven't ye all the makings of it here,' she said.

'Only one thing wrong with it,' Lawrie said, 'you're not next door. But we'll hope to see as much of you, Mrs Mal.'

Mary's eyes were closing as she sat on Mrs Malloy's knee, and Sally took her and undressed her gently, slipping on the nightgown which had been warming on the fireguard.

'I'll take her up,' Lawrie said. For a moment they all stood looking at the child sleeping peacefully in his arms.

'God bless her,' Mrs Malloy said. 'Sure, she has it all before her, but she's getting a grand start in life, thank God.'

That night as Sally lay in Lawrie's arms she felt that her own cup of happiness was full. They made love passionately and without restraint, and Sally was not surprised when soon she found that she was pregnant again. This time everything went smoothly, and she was not even troubled by the morning sickness which she had suffered before Mary's birth.

Mary had started school, and Sally's fears that she would cause scenes were unfounded. She stood mutinously by the gate of the schoolyard the first morning, her lip out-thrust and a scowl on her face, refusing to go any further.

Fortunately a bigger girl who entered the gates touched Mary's hair, which Sally had curled in ringlets and tied with a satin bow, and said admiringly, 'Yer 'air's luvely.'

Mary rewarded her with a beaming smile and consented to stand with the other new entrants.

Matthew had taught her to count to ten, and how to write her name, and she came out of school on the first morning full of importance.

'I'm the cleverest in the class,' she announced. Sally felt that she should check such boastfulness, but she was too thankful that Mary liked her school and her teacher to interfere.

Sally had never been happier, and she sang as she washed, and polished, and planned ways to beautify the house. She still had some savings in the teapot, so she felt free to use the money she made from sewing to buy items for the house.

A plant stand and an aspidistra now stood in the parlour window, flanked by Nottingham lace curtains, tied back with broad yellow satin bows. Gradually she managed to buy an overmantel, and some small ornaments to stand on the shelves beside the mirror, and a brown velvet cover for the mantelpiece beneath it, edged with bobbles. A small table was covered by a matching brown velvet cloth edged with bobbles. Sally swelled with pride whenever she looked round the room.

Until she could afford more furniture she had her sewing machine in the parlour, and she was able to take customers in there for fittings, and leave the men undisturbed instead of banishing them to the back kitchen, or taking her customers up to the icy bedrooms as she had done in Gell Street. The gaslight made her tasks easier, but as spring and summer came she needed neither light nor heat in the parlour. Her only problem was her increasing bulk, which made it difficult for her to use the sewing machine as June approached. Her customers from Ogden's tobacco works were still faithful, and several of her new neighbours asked her to make clothes for special events.

Chapter Twenty-Three

Matthew had settled very happily in the new house, and any regrets he had were dispersed when he visited Mrs Malloy in Gell Street. The Dolan family had done a 'moonlight flit', owing months of rent and money to some of the small shops, and Matthew was disgusted by the people who had taken the Dolans' house.

'A fight every night,' he told Sally. 'And half naked children thrown out in the street, afraid to go in.'

'What about Mrs Mal?' Sally said anxiously. 'She didn't say anything when I was there the other day, and it all seemed quiet then.'

'She tells me she's not worried about what goes on outside her own front door, as long as it's closed and she's inside, but Maggie Connolly told me Mrs Mal took the kids in one night, and the so-called father came roaring at her, rotten drunk. She gave him the length of her tongue, and he scarpered.'

'The people in our house seem all right, but the one's in Mrs Hart's house are real rough,' said Sally.

'Aye, we're well out of it, girl, with the child to think of, and another one coming. I'm glad Paddy's there with Mrs Mal, though.'

'Are you happy here, Da? Lawrie thinks we rushed you into it, I know.'

'I am, girl. I'm very comfortable, and I've got a few good mates in Maybury's pub, fellers I can talk to. And Lawrie's good company, so tell him not to worry about me.'

'He'll be glad, Da. It's the only fly in the ointment here, he said, feeling you weren't happy.'

'I tell you what, Sally, I think he should watch his step with that new boss. Talk to him, girl.'

Sally frowned. 'I will, Da,' she said. Her father's words reinforced her own worry about affairs at the warehouse. Mr Leather had died and the new boss was a bully, anxious to show that he could get more work from the men than Leather had done. One of the men, Jack Turner, wanted to start a union, but most of the men hung back, afraid of the consequences, and only Lawrie backed him wholeheartedly. Inevitably the day came when Jack spoke up for one of the men, a frail consumptive who was trying to carry weights far beyond his strength, and Jack was immediately dismissed.

'I felt ashamed,' Lawrie told Sally. 'We should all have backed Jack, but he had warned me beforehand, not to get involved. You can't afford to risk the sack,' he said, 'but I've given no hostages to fortune!'

'What did he mean?' asked Sally.

'*I* asked him that, and he said he meant he had no wife or kids to consider, only himself. He's a real clever chap, Sal. God, I'd have given anything to walk out alongside him.'

She said nothing, keeping her head bent over the sewing, but presently a tear splashed down on her hand.

'What's up, love?' Lawrie said in dismay, trying to lift her chin.

'You're sorry you got married,' she sobbed.

'Not a bit of it,' Lawrie said. 'You've got me wrong, Sal. I wouldn't be without you and Mary – and our son when he comes – for anything. I suppose I want to have my cake and eat it.'

He put his arm round Sally, and wiped her eyes, and she gave him a watery smile.

'And I'm a bit moody with the baby coming and that,' she said. 'But I do worry in case you get into trouble, Lawrie.'

'I shouldn't talk about it and worry you. I'll watch that in future, Sal.'

'No. I don't want you to keep things to yourself. I'd rather you talked to me – I don't want us to have secrets from each other, Lol, and anyway I know you can't talk to Da about unions.'

'I can't understand him. He seemed to be all for men standing up for fair deals, but now he takes the other side.'

Sally sat looking into the fire, pondering Lawrie's words, then she sighed and shrugged her shoulders. 'You know what it is, Lol. Da reads about things and gets annoyed about people being put on, so he talks about putting things right, but he won't take any chances. You know the way Mrs Malloy says "ye've got to hold a candle to the divil" – he said that once when I said they should say something when their wages were cut.'

'He's not the only one like that, Sal, more's the pity. Still, one of these days we'll get something done. Let's forget it now, though. Would you like a cup of tea?'

A few days later, a warm and pleasant June day, Sally felt the first warning pains, and sent Susan Kilgannon for Mrs Malloy. In a short time Susan was back to help Sally to prepare her bed and fill the black kettle, and then to air the tiny baby clothes.

Mrs Malloy soon arrived with a clean apron in her basket, to take charge.

'Your mam said she'd take Mary. Will you look after her, Sue? She's always good with you,' Sally said, and Susan readily agreed.

'That's a good girl,' Mrs Malloy observed as she clattered away.

'I think she's put on,' Sally said. 'As far as I can see her mother never lifts a finger, but Susan keeps the house spotless and waits on her hand and foot.'

'Is she ill?' asked Mrs Malloy. Sally was about to reply when she was suddenly gripped by a fierce pain. Others followed at rapid intervals, and within an hour a tiny girl was born. She was unmarked by her easy passage into the world, with a fuzz of dark hair on her head, and her tiny features were perfect. As soon as she had tidied the bedroom, Mrs Malloy knocked on the back of the grate to let Susan know that she could bring Mary in. Susan was enchanted with the baby, but Mary was more interested in the gingerbread man that Mrs Malloy had brought her.

Lawrie and Matthew were delighted when they arrived home from work, and found Sally and the new baby asleep upstairs and Mrs Malloy bustling about the kitchen.

'Are you disappointed she's not a boy?' Sally asked Lawrie anxiously when she woke.

'Not a bit of it,' he said, smiling down at the sleeping baby. 'She'll be company for Mary. They'll be able to go to dances together until they start courting.'

Sally laughed aloud as she looked at the tiny baby, and the next moment Matthew came into the room.

'That was good to hear, girl,' he said. 'A real belly laugh so soon. It hasn't taken much out of yer this time.'

'No, Da. Very quick and easy, and Mrs Mal was great. She never alters, does she?'

Later when Matthew thanked Mrs Malloy for her help, she smiled and shook her head.

'Ah well, lad, aren't we all put on the earth to help each other? Many a thing has Sally done for me, and her mam before was the same. The young woman in yer ould house – she'll be needing me soon, I'm thinking.'

She jerked her head meaningly towards Mary, but the little girl piped up, 'Is she going to have a baby, too?'

'Don't get too sharp, girl, or yer'll cut yerself,' Matthew said. 'What do yer think of yer little sister, eh?'

'She's stupid,' Mary said, tossing back her long auburn curls. 'I wanted one to play with.'

'She'll do that soon as she's a bit bigger,' Lawrie said. 'You'll have to be a good girl now and help Mama.'

Catherine Emily was the name chosen for the baby, much to Emily's delight, although the baby was four months old before she saw her. Walter dropped her and Hester at the house as he travelled to Liverpool in his carriage.

Catherine was even more fascinating to Emily, because she was a tiny replica of herself, with brown eyes and a curly fuzz of dark curls, although the baby's hair had been rubbed away at the back of her head by the pillow. Emily worried about this until Sally explained that this always happened, and that the hair would grow again.

Mary was less interested in the baby, and when Sally had checked her sharply, once for trying to lift the baby from the cradle, and once when she was forcing a piece of bread and jam in Catherine's mouth, she lost interest completely in her.

Mary was as wild as ever, often emerging from the schoolyard dishevelled and scratched after a fight with other girls, but she was still quick and eager to learn. At the end of the term the headmistress sent for Sally and told her that Mary would be moved up to the second class after Christmas.

'She is well advanced, and she seems to be restless and fidgety because she already knows the work that the infant class is doing,' the headmistress said. 'Of course if she doesn't keep up she will be moved back.'

Sally felt proud and pleased. She always ensured that Mary attended school regularly and punctually, neatly dressed and clean, hoping that this would mean that she was separated from the rougher children. Now she felt vaguely that the harder school work, and the fact that she was with older girls, would make Mary quieter and less aggressive. She was still Matthew's favourite, and Lawrie made an extra fuss of her since Catherine's birth, in case she felt overshadowed by the baby, but Sally worried about her.

Catherine was a good baby, healthy and placid, sleeping soundly at night, and during the day lying happily in her cot, playing with the rattle handed down from Mary, or gurgling as she watched the shadows thrown by the leaping flames of the fire.

Her brown eyes and dark hair were like Emily's and also Lawrie's, and Sally could see that the baby was very similar to him in temperament. Life was much easier for Sally, with Mary at school and Catherine needing so little attention, and she was able to spend hours at her sewing machine. Being able to leave her sewing spread about in the parlour made a difference, too, and the gaslight made life easier for everyone.

As she worked she thought of the family at Ormesdale, and of Hester's distress on the day of the move, and wondered at her aunt. Surely it must be wonderful to have risen so far? To have servants to do the work, and sit in a silk dress giving orders. There was the rub, she thought. Hester did not give the orders, only Walter did that, and Sally wondered afresh how this had happened. How did the small, meek Walter suddenly become so important, and her voluble, bustling aunt so insignificant? As usual, Sally talked of this to Lawrie.

'She doesn't feel needed, Sal,' he said. 'She did so much on the farm as well as running the house, but now those sorts of talent aren't needed.'

'But Walter likes the new life. He seems to have swelled up while Hester seems to have shrunk.'

'Aye, but Walter's deep. I always thought there was a lot more to him than met the eye, you know. He sat there quietly while Hester talked and seemed to give the orders, but he only did what he wanted to do. Hester knew it, too; she knew how far she could go with him.'

'Well, I never saw that. I always thought she was the boss.'

'Yes, but remember, Sal, I came fresh to it so I could see things more clearly.'

'I'm sure there's more to it than that, Lawrie. There's some mystery there. Every time I see Hester she looks smaller and quieter. I know she seemed more like her old self on the day we moved, but even then there was something wrong.'

'Don't worry about it, love. You'll soon hear if she's ill, and there's nothing wrong with Emily, is there? She looks a picture of health.'

'She does. D'you know, Lawrie, I never realised that Emily was so like you until Mrs Mal spoke about it? I was saying that Catherine was like Emily, and she said she was, but then Emily was like you in colouring.' Sally giggled. 'I had to laugh at Mrs Mal.' She said, 'All three of them with the same aisy ways, and you and your da, God help ye, cast in the same mould.' She evidently doesn't think much of me and Da!'

Sally missed Mrs Malloy as a neighbour and a friend next door, especially as she found Mrs Kilgannon hard to understand. One day she would be cheerful and friendly, and the next day she would pass Sally with barely a nod. She was often very miserable, too, but Susan explained that to Sally.

'It's me mam's dying duck act,' she said. 'She always puts it on when the lads come to see her, so that they'll mug her to a drink or an ounce of tobacco. She tried it on with our Nelly, but she said me mam should be mugging her with all she's got coming in.'

Sally could sympathise with Nelly. Mrs Kilgannon had let her parlour and back bedroom to her cousin, and the middle bedroom to her nephews, twin brothers who went to sea and wanted a room in which to keep their possessions and to come home to.

Mrs Kilgannon confided to Sally that she had borne eleven children, but only six survived. Three boys and one girl were married, another girl was in service, and Susan was still at home.

'I might as well 'ave lost the six I reared for all the good they are to me,' Mrs Kilgannon lamented to Sally, but Sally thought that she did very well. Two of the sons were dockers, and one worked at the abattoir. Mrs Kilgannon always seemed to be well supplied with fruit and other goods which arrived in Liverpool by sea, and meat from the abattoir. The 'dying duck act' derided by Susan usually produced a few shillings from each in turn, by playing skilfully on their sympathy. Susan did all the work of the house, because her mother went out cleaning every morning in a large house in Fitzclarence Street, and came home, as she said, 'Worn to the bone'.

Susan was a great help to Sally. Mary adored her and never threw a tantrum while she was in Susan's care, and she was also always ready to watch over the baby or shop for Sally. She had none of her mother's avarice, and protested when Sally gave her sixpence for her help.

'Mr Ward give me tuppence last night,' she said. Sally sighed, and spoke about it to Lawrie when he came in.

'But she's such a good kid,' he said. 'I only told her to get some sweets for herself.'

'But there's no need. I give her the odd sixpence, and I'm making her a dress. You can trust me to see to her, Lawrie.'

Later, as Sally ironed she wondered. Did Lawrie think I wouldn't pay Susan? Does he think I'm mean? *Am* I mean to bother about tuppence?

She banged down the iron. No, I'm not mean, she thought, I'm careful, and I believe the old saying: 'Look after the pence and the pounds will take care of themselves.' I only wish Lawrie believed it, too.

She expected her father to be shocked when she told him about Mrs Kilgannon's booty from her sons, but he only laughed.

'Good luck to them,' he said. 'I hope they don't get caught, that's all.'

'But, Da, it's stealing,' Sally said.

'And aren't *they* stealing from the likes of us, girl?' he demanded. 'The masters, I mean. Why do yer think they call us hands? Because that's all we are to them, hands to work, and strength to use 'til it runs out.' He got up and strode over to the window and back again, then rattled the poker in the bars of the fire.

'It's a war, Sally. Them an' us. We're just tools to them, to be used and thrown away when we're wore out. Hands! But we're not just hands, we're bloody men like themselves, with wives and children ter keep, and they'll find it out.'

'Don't get excited, Da,' Sally pleaded, alarmed by his red face and rapid breathing. 'I'm sorry I spoke.'

'No, it's all right, girl,' Matthew said more quietly. 'I'm just made up them lads are getting their own back any way they can. God knows, the dockers go through the mill.'

Sally went on darning socks without answering. I'd better keep my mouth shut in future, she thought, and let him and Lawrie argue the toss. I don't know what they're getting annoyed at half the time.

Sally decided to say nothing to Lawrie about her father's outburst. She had noticed that when the two men argued about injustice at work, Matthew always played the part of peacemaker, trying to calm Lawrie when he grew fiery. Lawrie went twice a week to meetings aimed at starting unions, and Matthew often said it was a pity that this had replaced Lawrie's evenings at the Mission, but he was disillusioned about the Mission work.

He had quickly fallen foul of the man who had replaced Mr Hunter.

'He keeps the kids standing there, dripping wet very often, and always cold and hungry, while he makes them sing hymns or pray before they get the soup,' he said. 'I told him Mr Hunter did it the other way round, and do you know what he said, Sal? "Don't be impertinent, Ward. Mr Hunter encouraged you, but don't put yourself on a level with your betters." '

'The cheek of him!' Sally exclaimed.

'Aye, but I told him,' Lawrie said gleefully. 'I said, "I put myself on the level of a carpenter's son, born in a stable, and so should you if you mean what you preach." '

'Oh, Lawrie, what did he say?'

'Nothing. Just stood there with his mouth open like a stranded fish. I was made up, Sal. I usually think of those sorts of answers hours afterwards when I'm in bed.'

Pleased though Lawrie was with his repartee, it meant that he was not now welcome at the Mission. Sally worried less about this than she might have done if she had not been so busy with the children, and the house to run, as well as ever increasing orders for sewing.

Chapter Twenty-Four

Sally still kept to the same high standard in her sewing, although she was now so busy, and she was rewarded when one of her customers from Ogden's showed a blouse that Sally had made to her aunt, who worked for an exclusive Bold Street dress shop. It was arranged that Sally would be employed as an outworker, for rush orders or when they were exceptionally busy. The standard demanded was high and the work had to be done rapidly in the short time allowed, but it was well paid. She was thankful that Susan was always willing to look after the children, so that she could concentrate on the sewing.

Sally saved most of the money, and she was glad that she had when Lawrie arrived home in the middle of the afternoon of a day in May 1897. He had been in high spirits during the earlier part of the week, because a meeting of the men at work had been addressed by Thomas Mann, and they had decided to form a union branch. Lawrie and a man named Jim Baty had been elected shop stwards.

Sally was sewing in the parlour when he arrived home, and was instantly alarmed by his white face and grim expression.

'Whatever's wrong, love? Are you poorly?' she said.

Lawrie laid a handful of coins of the table, and sank into a chair. 'No. I've got the sack, Sal. I'm sorry, love.'

'But why? What happened?' Sally said.

'What I should have known would happen,' Lawrie said bitterly. 'The excuse was a burst sack, but anything would have done.'

'How could he sack you for a burst bag?' she asked.

'The bag was only an excuse, Sal. He sacked Jim Baty as well, and he was nowhere near the bag. No, it's because of the Union. I'm a fool, love. I should have thought of you and the children.' Sally could not bear to see him so upset, and she put her arm round his neck and bent to kiss him.

'Don't be daft,' she said stoutly. '*Someone* had to make a stand, and we're better off than most of the lads. Anyway, you'll soon find something else.'

Some colour had returned to Lawrie's face, and he hugged her and picked up his cap.

'I will, Sal,' he said. 'I'll go right away before the word gets round.'

'Wait for a cup of tea,' Sally said. 'Five minutes won't make any difference, and I've got something to show you.' She poked the fire and pushed the kettle closer to it, then she took down the old handleless teapot from the mantelpiece, and tipped out the contents on to the table.

'Forty-eight pounds, three and six,' she said proudly. 'I've been saving my sewing money. I used a lot for the house but I've built it up again.'

'Good God,' Lawrie said, staring at the coins in disbelief. 'Forty-eight pounds – how? – I mean, it's only shillings, isn't it?'

'Sometimes, but I charge half a crown for a costume, and the Bold Street money has made it mount up.'

'Well, you're a dark horse and no mistake,' Lawrie said, putting his arm about her waist and squeezing her. 'I'd no idea.'

'You don't think I've been sly, do you, Lol?' Sally said anxiously. 'I just wanted to surprise you.'

'Well, you've done that all right. Looks as if we'd be better off if you were the breadwinner, Sal.'

She realised too late that it had been tactless to display the money when Lawrie was already feeling inadequate, and hastened to try to cheer him.

'That money's not all from the sewing. God, I'd have to sew day and night to make that! It's what I've been able to save from the two wages coming in, as well. It doesn't cost much more to feed us than when it was just me and Da, and the girls cost hardly anything to keep up to now.'

Lawrie smiled. 'You're a great little manager. It's a good job I've got a sensible wife, because I can't keep a penny in my pocket. I don't know how you do it.'

'It's because of what I saw in our street, Lol,' Sally said soberly. 'Like when Mr Henderson was killed. People help for a while with coppers or a bit of food, and Mrs Henderson tried to do some step scrubbing, but she was a sick woman herself, and she had to give up and go in the workhouse in the end. Maggie Thompson and the Kales were the same. The kids earning a few coppers and the mother struggling on, but it's no use because they've nothing to fall back on. That's why I tried to save.'

'Aye, I know,' Lawrie agreed. 'But most people have no option, Sal. It's got to be hand to mouth, that's why Jack's fighting for a widow's pension, and a few bob when people are too sick to work.'

'Oh, Lawrie, that's just a dream. Where will the money come from? Anyhow, you don't need to worry about losing your job while we've got this, and I think you did right to try to make things better.'

Lawrie stood up and flung his arms round Sally, then kissed her.

'You're one in a thousand, love. The way you've taken this, and the saving and everything. I'm going to make sure you're never sorry you married me, Sal. I'm off to ask around.'

'Wait until morning,' Sally urged, but Lawrie was adamant.

'No, I might just miss a chance. Ta ra, love. I feel like a new man.' He picked up his cap and went down the yard, whistling.

Sally called after him, 'Nothing wrong with the old one.'

He turned to laugh and wave as he opened the back gate, and Sally heard him stepping jauntily down the entry. Left alone, she swept the money back into the teapot, and took the teacups to the sink, looking

148

thoughtful. She would have to be careful not to hurt Lawrie's pride, she thought. Although always cheerful, and apparently happy-go-lucky, Lawrie was very sensitive, as he showed by his awareness of other people's feelings.

She quickly finished the ironing, and when Catherine woke, she picked her up, and threw her mother's shawl around them both, while she went to meet Mary from school, and do some shopping. She was determined to buy something tasty for tea.

At the school gate, Mary's face fell when she saw her mother waiting for her.

'Wharra yer wearing that ole shawl for?' she muttered.

Sally resisted an impulse to shake her, and said quietly, 'Don't be impudent, Mary. It's your grandma's shawl, and I'm not ashamed to wear it.'

She tried to take Mary's hand but the child pulled away, her lip out-thrust.

'Take my hand,' Sally hissed. 'Another word and I'll smack your face.'

She grabbed Mary's hand and hauled her along, with the child scuffling her boots along the ground.

'Stop scraping your boot caps,' Sally snapped. 'Are you *trying* to annoy me, Mary?'

Mary looked up at her mother and seemed to realise how agitated she was, for she gave no more trouble, but Sally found that her hands were trembling as she selected bacon ribs and cabbage. Lawrie's news must have been more of a shock than she realised at the time, she thought.

They had just reached home, and Sally was putting the ribs in a pan, when Lawrie came whistling up the yard. He threw his cap in the air as he came in the back door, and gripped Sally round the waist, waltzing her round and round the kitchen.

'I've got a job, I've got a job,' he chanted jubilantly. The children stared at them, open-mouthed, and Sally pulled away, laughing and tucking up strands of hair which had fallen about her face.

'Where? What is it?' she asked breathlessly.

'A warehouse in Leeds Street. Second man on a wagon. I helped to load it and asked if there was anything going, and I got taken on.' His beaming smile vanished for a moment. 'The only thing is, the usual feller has broken his leg – that's how I got the job.'

'Oh, Lawrie, that's not your fault. If you hadn't taken the job someone else would.'

'True enough,' he agreed. 'But I'll have to keep my eyes open for something else, because he'll want his job back when he's fit.' He began to grin again.

'It's better money, Sal. Twenty-four shillings a week, so you'll be able to put a bit more in your old teapot.' He picked up Cathy, and flung her up in the air.

'Your dada's got a job,' he said, and the child chuckled gleefully, then he had to do the same with Mary, who laughed even louder.

Matthew pursed his lips, and looked solemn when Sally told him of the events of the afternoon.

149

'Yer'll have to watch yer step, lad,' he said to Lawrie. 'Yer got away with it this time, but yer won't always be so lucky.'

'Well, I was more than pleased to get the job, Matt, although I'm sorry for the lad who broke his leg,' Lawrie said. Matthew shook his head.

'Yer'll find that's a luxury yer can't afford, lad: pity. Same as yer can't afford to be the one to speak out, not when yer've got a family ter think of.'

Lawrie said no more, but later in bed he said to Sally, 'I can understand why your da thinks like that, Sal but I can't agree it should be every man for himself. We'll never get anywhere if we don't stick together and fight for our rights.'

'Oh, Lawrie, don't get mixed up with that stuff in this job, for God's sake! You've done your bit. Promise me, Lol.'

'All right, love,' he said, gently stroking the hair from her face. 'I'm sorry I gave you such a shock. I'm not making much shape at the coach and horses I promised you, am I?'

'I don't care, love,' she said, clinging to him. 'I don't want anything like that, as long as I've got you, and we can get by.'

He kissed her gently, then with increasing passion, and as ever her passion rose to meet his. Later when they lay exhausted, Lawrie's arms around Sally and her head on his shoulder, he said tenderly, 'This is another way I'm lucky, Sal. It's always been perfect for us, right from the start, and there's not many fellers can say that.'

She turned her head and kissed his chin. 'Maybe that's the fault of the other fellers,' she said with a giggle.

Lawrie laughed and held her more closely. 'I keep thinking this can't get better, then it does. You're a wife in a thousand, love.'

A moment later Sally drew away from him. 'You'd better get some sleep, Lawrie. You can't be tired on your first day.'

'What do you think they'd say if I told them why?' he whispered, and she turned away, stuffing the sheet in her mouth to stifle her giggles. Lawrie kissed her neck.

'When I think of the way I felt walking home today, Sal, I never thought I'd end the day laughing. Thanks, love.'

'Goodnight and God bless, Lol,' Sally whispered.

'Goodnight and God bless, my little love,' he said. In a few moments they had both slipped into sleep.

Lawrie enjoyed his new job, and found the driver he worked with very fair and pleasant. An air of excitement filled the town, as preparations were made to celebrate Queen Victoria's Diamond Jubilee, with flags and bunting everywhere. On June 20th, Lawrie went alone to a church parade at Wavertree Playground, to hear Monsignor Nugent preach to a large crowd. He had always respected Monsignor Nugent because of his work for destitute children, and he hoped that his sermon would touch the hearts of the wealthy people in the crowd.

On the day itself, June 22nd, 1897, Lawrie was given the day off, and he and Sally took the children to watch the procession of Trades and Friendly Societies, led by bands and carrying banners, marching through the city. Everyone seemed to be dressed in their best, and there was an air of festivity, heightened by the display of flags and the decorated shops. Sally was delighted to see an old neighbour from Gell Street, who had fallen on hard times when her husband was injured, making her way with her children to Saint George's Hall, where a dinner had been provided for one thousand poor people.

Later she and Lawrie found a vantage point on Rupert Hill, to watch a display of electric lights and fireworks from the ships in the river. Catherine slept in Sally's arms most of the time, but Mary sat on Lawrie's shoulders, screaming with delight at the spectacle.

It was a happy time for the whole family, and the beginning of a very happy period in Sally's life. She realised now how worried she had been while Lawrie worked at the grain warehouse, and why she had been so anxious to save because of her fear of the future. Now everything seemed set fair for them, and Sally decided to spend less time on the sewing, and more with Lawrie and the children.

He was enthusiastic at her plan to take the children out more often, and Matthew said gruffly, 'Ye're learning sense, girl. These years soon pass.'

Sometimes they went on the ferry boat to Seacombe, or on the horse tram to Woolton Woods, and sometimes they just walked up to Shaw Street Park to see the new drinking fountain.

Mary greeted every experience with exuberant delight, and people turned to look at the daintily dressed little girl, with her long auburn curls and pretty face, screaming with excitement. Sally was proud of her, but she knew that Mary's mood could soon change and turn to tears and tantrums, and she was happier to see Catherine's quieter pleasure.

One Sunday Matthew and Susan Kilgannon joined them for a trip to New Brighton. It was a bright sunny day with a light breeze, and the children's excitement had been mounting while they watched Sally cutting thick sandwiches of cheese and boiled bacon, and wedges of ginger cake. Bread and butter and a dish of pickled herrings went in the basket, too, with a can of tea and a can of milk. Lawrie had bought buckets and spades for the children, and Susan proudly carried these on to the boat.

The river was crowded with shipping, sail and steam, and Lawrie pointed out various ships on which he had sailed, or in which he knew some of the crew. When he pointed out the *Akbar* and the *Clarence*, reformatory ships for delinquent boys, Mary made them laugh.

'Are there any ships for bad girls, Dada?' she asked apprehensively.

'No,' Matthew cut in, 'but there are homes for bad girls where they have to wear a little hat and have their ears pinned back.'

Mary was quiet for a moment, then she was off racing along the deck, with Susan in pursuit. The children squealed with delight when the boat reached New Brighton, and they saw the crowded golden sands and the pools left by the ebbing tide. They all settled on a vacant patch of sand, and the two little girls began to make sand pies, helped by Lawrie and Susan.

'I don't know who's enjoying the digging most, youse two or the two little ones,' Matthew observed, and Susan raised her radiant face to Sally.

'Oo, isn't it luvely?' she said. 'I've never been here before y'know, Mrs Ward.' Sally smiled at her, happy to see the child enjoying herself, free of the drudgery which was her usual lot.

Soon everyone was hungry and the contents of the basket disappeared as though by magic. Sally lay back, turning her face up to the sun and sipping the last drop of tea from the lid of the can. Lawrie said suddenly, 'The tide's turned. How about a paddle?' Sally took off the little ones' boots and stockings, and tucked their frocks in their knickers, and Lawrie took off his boots and socks, and rolled up the legs of his trousers.

'Come on, Mr Palin,' Susan said, excitedly flinging off her boots and stockings. 'Roll up yer trousers like Mr Ward.'

'No, lass, my paddling days are over,' Matthew said with a smile. He turned to Sally.

'You go, girl. I'll mind the clothes.' Sally needed no second bidding. She took off her boots, but left her stockings on to paddle, happily ignoring disapproving glances from some of the nearby matrons.

When they returned to Matthew he pulled some coins from his pocket.

'Ee are,' he said. 'Susan, you and Mary and Catherine can have a go on the donkeys.' While the children had their donkey ride, the adults replaced their boots and shook the sand from their clothes then picked up the basket and prepared to move off. Susan carried Catherine to meet them, but Mary refused to be parted from the donkey, clutching it round the neck and screaming when the man tried to lift her down. Lawrie and Matthew were about to try to drag her from the donkey and scold her, but Sally shook her head at them.

'Come on then,' she said. 'If Mary wants to stay, we'll go and get something to eat before we get the boat home.' She began to walk away, followed nervously by Lawrie and Matthew, but in a flash Mary was off the donkey, and running after them.

'Mama, Mama,' she screamed, but Sally only said sharply, 'Get hold of the other side of this basket and don't let go of it. Any more tantrums out of you, my lady, and I really *will* leave you behind.' Mary was subdued for a short time, but as usual quickly recovered.

They walked along the 'Ham and Egg Parade', then when Sally had tidied up the children, they all went to a photographer's booth, and had their picture taken. What happy memories that blurred old photograph brought back in later years!

At teatime Sally and Susan went up Victoria Road and bought a loaf and butter, a pint of pickled shrimps, and sponge cakes and 'wet nellas'. While Sally cut and buttered the bread, Susan went to a stall for a big brown teapot of tea.

At seven o'clock they returned home, sunburned and windblown. Catherine and Mary were asleep in the arms of their parents, and Susan carried the basket and the buckets and spades. She looked up at Sally when they reached home.

'I'll never forget today, never,' she said, her eyes shining.

'Neither will I, love,' Sally said, bending to kiss her. 'You've been a good help to us today, and a good example to Mary.'

As Susan left, Lawrie was gently lowering Mary on to the couch. Still asleep she shouted loudly, 'No, no.' Sally sighed. It's going to need more than a good example for that madam, she thought.

Chapter Twenty-Five

Sally still wrote regularly to Hester and Emily, but Hester's replies were brief, and Emily's letters contained only questions about Mary and Cathy, and details of her lessons with Miss Blake. Although Sally asked several times for Hester and Emily to visit them again, or offered to visit Greenlands, her requests were ignored. She became more than ever convinced that there was some mystery at Greenlands, but Lawrie comforted her.

'Probably something quite simple, love,' he said, 'and whatever it is, it's not affecting Emily. She seems happy enough, so don't worry.'

Sally tried to take his advice, but her thoughts often wandered to the family at Ormesdale. She was concerned about Susan Kilgannon, too. She was becoming very restless and unhappy at home, and Sally felt that she would soon be away. She was now fourteen years old, and she told Sally that she wanted to go into service.

'I'd like to work in a shop, but I'd never gerra job like that, and I'm not gonna be me mam's handrag no longer.'

'Does your mam know you want to go in to service?' Sally said. 'It can be a very hard life, Sue.'

'No harder than wor I've got now, Mrs Ward. Yer know I always done all the housework because me mam said she was wore out cleaning? Well, I found out she doesn't do no cleaning hardly – only two mornings for some old one in Fitzclarence Street what's half blind and cracked as well.'

'But your mam goes out cleaning every day. She told me so,' Sally said.

'Aye, she told me an' all, *and* all the others,' Susan said grimly. 'She does two half days, and the other days she sits with an old crony in Plumpton Street drinking fender ale. Our Joe's wife looked down the area and seen her in a basement kitchen, and after that she kep' watch because she was mad about me mam gettin' money off our Joe.'

'But don't turn against your mam, Susan,' Sally urged. 'Perhaps Cissie exaggerated, and after all, your mam is entitled to some pleasure.'

'Oh, I'm not worried about Cissie. If the lads are soft it's their own lookout, but the day Cissie told me, me mam had got me a job cleaning a public house in Great Homer Street. I'd heard of daily cleaning in two posh houses but me mam said I had to take the job in the public 'cos that way I could be back in time to see to our place,' Susan said breathlessly. Her cheeks were flushed and tears were welling up in her eyes. Sally put her arm around her.

'Don't get upset, love,' she said gently. 'Perhaps you *would* be better off in good service. Could your Nelly speak for you?'

155

'She wants to, but me mam says she can't do without me here, yet she wants me to be earning as well,' Susan gulped.

Sally was silent, uncertain what to say. She was indignant on Susan's behalf, but afraid to make matters worse by interfering while Susan was still under her mother's control. She took Susan's hand and smiled at her encouragingly.

'Whoever you work for will be lucky, Sue. You've been a great help to me, love. Try not to worry but just wait and see.'

To Lawrie and Matthew Sally was more forthright. 'That woman's a selfish, lazy bitch,' she said angrily. 'Fancy sending that child to clean a public house of all places, just so that she can still run round after her.'

'Them lads must be daft,' Matthew said. 'She looks more like a man than many a man, yet they fall for that tale about her being delicate. It's to be hoped they do something about young Susan, because *you* can't do nothing, girl.'

Sally agreed, and tried not to worry about Susan, but two weeks later she was delighted to hear that Susan was going to work in a house in Sefton Park, as a kitchenmaid, living in.

'It's a big posh house,' Susan told her. 'Only the master and mistress and seven servants, no children. I'll be with the cook mostly and she seems awful nice. Our Nelly spoke for me because the cook is cousin to the cook in her place.'

'And your mam's agreed?' Sally said.

Susan laughed. 'She's goin' mad,' she said. 'But our Nelly got the lads to come round with her on her day off, an' they all told me mam off and made her let me go.'

Sally learned that Susan had her working uniforms, so she made her a brown woollen dress, trimmed with velvet, for her day off, and Matthew and Lawrie bought her a brown hat.

'I'll miss her,' Sally sighed. 'Not just for the way she helped me with the children, but for her company as well. I hope she's happy in her place, and not put on because she's so willing.'

'She'll be fine,' Lawrie said. 'She was anxious to go, and the work will seem easy to her after the way she's worked here. She was made up with her new dress and hat, wasn't she?'

Sally agreed, smiling, and thinking that it was good that she had tried to avoid worrying about Susan, as things had turned out so well in the end. Perhaps it was a sign that she should not worry about the family at Ormesdale, but simply hope for the best.

She resolved not to let anything spoil her present happiness. The man who had broken his leg was still off work, and she wondered sometimes how Lawrie would fare when he returned, but with her newfound confidence she felt sure that Lawrie would soon find another job.

Her optimism was rewarded just before Christmas 1897 when the man returned to work, limping badly, with one leg shorter than the other, and was given a job in the checking office. Lawrie's job as second man on the wagon was made permanent, and their happiness seemed complete. Sometimes in the evening as she sat sewing and her father and Lawrie amicably discussed some item of news, or smoked in companionable silence, Sally looked about her at her comfortable, well-lit room, and her heart was filled with thankfulness at their good fortune.

Even though Sally was doing less sewing she missed Susan's willing help, and Mrs Kilgannon had taken to dropping in, usually to complain of the way her children treated her. At first Sally found it difficult to concentrate on her work with the whining voice as an accompaniment but she learned to let the words wash over her, and murmur noncommittally from time to time. Catherine gave her little trouble, sitting quietly on the hearth rug tipping pegs in and out of an old pan, or dressing and undressing her doll.

She was a placid, gentle child but Mary found that she had a temper, too, one day when she stamped on the face of Cathy's doll. Cathy flew at her like a fury, her fat little arms flailing, and her curly head butting into Mary's stomach.

Sally dragged them apart, and smacked their bottoms soundly.

'Say you're sorry to each other,' she ordered. 'I never saw the like. Sisters fighting like fishwives.' Mary muttered 'Sorry', managing to give the doll a sly kick while her mother was looking at Cathy, but her sister said loudly, 'No, no, not sorry.'

Sally gave her another slap, and the child's eyes filled with tears, but she kept her lips obstinately closed.

Fortunately at that moment Mrs Kilgannon's head appeared above the dividing wall in the backyard.

' 'Ave yer gorra drop of milk ter spare, Mrs Ward?' she asked, and when Sally took the milk to her Mary disappeared into the Kilgannon house. She was fond of Mrs Kilgannon's cat, and of 'Killey', as Mrs Kilgannon had told her to call her. Sally took Cathy into the house, and told her sorrowfully how upset she was to see her two little girls fighting. The soft approach had much more effect on Cathy, and she cried and clung to her mother, promising not to hit Mary again.

Sally went back to her mangle, marvelling that her children were so different in temperament. She could talk until she was blue in the face to Mary, she thought, and it would have no effect, but Cathy's obstinacy was more easily dealt with by kind words than by a slap. Still, she consoled herself, they rarely quarrelled, and perhaps it was better that they were different.

Sally was very happy in the Egremont Street house, not only because of the many advantages to it but also because the neighbours, although they had little time or money to spend on appearances, prided themselves on their respectability. In the afternoon, the sacking aprons they wore for the hard and dirty housework were replaced by clean starched white ones, and they felt free to stand at their doors for a gossip, or to visit each other, with freshly washed faces and neat hair.

Sally was generally regarded as a good neighbour, always friendly and pleasant, ready to lend small amounts of food, or to help in other ways. She helped without charge with the sewing for girls departing for service, and supplied the neighbours when necessary with scraps of material for mourning bands, from small pieces left from her mourning work.

There was a custom there when deaths occurred which infuriated Matthew. Deaths were frequent, and the many infant deaths aroused only pity, but when an adult died two of the neighbours collected for a wreath.

The first time that they came to Sally, it was for a girl of nineteen who had died of consumption. The collecters spoke their formula.

'We're collecting for poor Eileen Hughes. A lovely girl. She'll be a sad loss to her poor mam.'

'Yes, indeed,' said Sally, immediately producing her purse. 'But it must console her mother to know she did all she could to make Eileen happy while she lived.' The remark was repeated and approved at all the other houses, as well as to Mrs Hughes, and did much to make Sally popular.

'A real clever girl, but with a feeling heart,' was the verdict.

'Ridiculous,' Matthew fumed, especially when the collection was made on the death of a man. 'Flowers, begod, and they'll be looking for food before long.'

'But it's only ha'pennies and pennies, Da,' Sally protested. 'And it's a comfort to people to know that neighbours care about their loss. It's respect to the dead, too.'

'Pah,' Matthew snorted. 'It's just an excuse for them nosy women to go round gossiping.'

Sally was right in her judgement of the feelings of the bereaved women. A funeral oration in Ancient Rome or a panegyric preached on the death of a bishop could not have meant more or been such a source of comfort as the few simple words spoken by neighbours as they handed over their coins, which were repeated to the bereaved when the wreath was given.

None of the neighbours were jealous of the smart appearance of Sally and her family, or her ability to make money with her needle. They were proud of her and boasted to relatives of the 'superior dressmaker' who lived in the street, although many of them prophesied a bad end for Mary, when their children arrived home scarred from battle with her. Sally was always watched approvingly when she walked down the street with her quick light step, her slim erect figure always smartly turned out, and Cathy, neatly dressed, trotting beside her.

Often Sally was going to Bold Street with completed work, because more and more she was being called on to help with rush orders.

She usually broke her journey to leave Cathy with Mrs Malloy, then continued alone to Bold Street, returning later to collect Cathy and to have a cup of tea with her old neighbour.

One June day soon after Cathy's third birthday, Mrs Malloy was waiting at her door with Cathy when Sally returned from Bold Street.

'Ye look a picture, so ye do,' the old lady exclaimed as Sally reached them. 'Aren't ye looking better every time I see ye.'

Sally was wearing a blue coat and skirt, and a high-collared white blouse, with a large flower-trimmed hat pinned to her shining hair.

She smiled at Mrs Malloy. 'I just feel better able to deal with that woman at Libby's if I'm dressed up,' she said. 'She's always so smart herself and I believe she can be a tartar, although she's always all right with me.'

'And why wouldn't she be?' demanded Mrs Malloy, as she poured water into the teapot. 'She could find no fault with *your* work, girlie.'

'Happiness suits yer, child,' she added softly, looking fondly at Sally's fresh complexion and bright eyes.

'I *am* happy, Mrs Mal,' Sally said. 'Everything's going so well for us. Sometimes it worries me. I think it can't possibly last.'

'God between us and all harm,' Mrs Malloy said, crossing herself. 'But don't be always looking for trouble, child. Sure your da's a changed man these days, and ye've the best of husbands and these two little darlin's.'

She smiled at Cathy and stroked her hair. 'Cathy has been a grand help to me,' she said. 'Getting the cloth from the table drawer, without telling, and fetching the spoons.' Cathy smiled up at Mrs Malloy and took her hand. There was a strong bond between the old lady and the quiet little girl.

'I wish it was always sunny like today,' Sally said. 'Da's fine in this weather but as soon as the fogs start, he starts coughing. He never got rid of his cough all last winter.'

'Ah, well, there's months yet before ye need worry about fogs. Is that more work ye have there, girl?'

'Yes, mourning work,' Sally said, glancing at the parcel beside her. 'A mother and four daughters, and I've got two of the dresses for jet beads and embroidery. They're wanted by tomorrow night and there's a lot of work on them, so I'd better get home and make a start.'

'Not much grief there be the sound of it,' Mrs Malloy commented, as she helped Cathy with her coat.

A few weeks later Sally realised that she was pregnant again. Her first feeling was of dismay because she had so much sewing to do, but she quickly stifled the feeling.

'I don't want ever to feel that a child is not welcome, Lol,' she said. 'I'd feel guilty when I looked at it afterwards, especially when there's a good home for it to come to.'

She was glad that she had been prepared to welcome the baby when early in September she was gripped by a familiar pain, and within hours had miscarried. Although she regained her strength fairly quickly, she felt sad and dispirited for many months afterwards.

Lawrie did all he could to cheer her, bringing titbits home and coaxing her to eat, and being patient with her outbursts of ill temper. He did extra work at the yard, which earned him a few shillings, which he spent on small luxuries for Sally: a pot of calf's foot jelly, a few new laid eggs from a farm he passed on the wagon, and once a tiny bottle of scent.

She thanked him for these gifts, but without enthusiasm. She felt that he was wasting money which she could have spent more wisely, but Lawrie was unaware of her feeling and put her irritability down to her weakness. She was just as ungrateful when her father tried to persuade her to drink mead.

'It's very strengthening, girl,' he said, but Sally screwed up her face in disgust.

'I suppose it is, Da,' she said pettishly, 'but I just can't drink it.'

It was Mary who finally roused Sally from her despondency. She had been making a noise and when Sally snapped at her, the child planted herself in front of her mother.

'Why are you always bad-tempered now?' she said.

'I am not!' Sally exclaimed. 'Don't be so hardfaced, Mary.'

'Killey says you are,' Mary insisted. 'She says you don't know you're born, always whingeing and everyone running after you.'

'*Well*, I never,' Sally gasped, jumping to her feet, but Mary skipped nimbly out of her way.

'That's that,' Sally shouted. 'It's the last time you go in there, madam.' But Mary had slipped through the door and was out of earshot.

Always whingeing, Sally fumed, as she peeled potatoes for the meal. Fancy her talking to a child like that – and that impudent little faggot repeating it to me! she thought. But as her anger cooled she began to see that there was some truth in Mrs Kilgannon's remarks. She said nothing to Lawrie or her father, but she made an effort to throw off her depression and very soon recovered her usual spirits. She tried, without much success, to stop Mary from visiting next door, and she was cool to Mrs Kilgannon when she met her, but she realised that her neighbour was too self-engrossed to notice. She's a fine one to talk about whingeing, Sally thought.

One result of Sally's illness was that Matthew and Lawrie stopped arguing about whether or not Great Britain should be at war with the Boers, and later they were united in dismay, as news began to arrive of the garrisons at Mafeking, Ladysmith and Kimberley being besieged by the Boers.

Lawrie had told Sally that he had seen the Gordon Highlanders marching along the Dock Road, to board the *Cheshire* and sail to Capetown, and Sally thought often of those young men sailing off to war. She was convinced that the baby she had lost was a boy, and thought of the mothers of the soldiers and wondered how she would feel in their place.

She had little time to brood as sewing orders flowed in to her, and in spite of her intention to spend more time with the children, she was kept fully occupied.

Susan Kilgannon's servant's uniform had been worn by her predecessor, a much fatter girl, and Susan brought the dresses home to show Sally. She put one on.

'Just luk ar' it, Mrs Ward,' she said with disgust, 'It'd fit two of me. I told the cook ir' ony fit where it touched and she said I should be glad to gerrit for nothing.'

'Let me see, Sue,' Sally said. She pinned some of the seams and turned up the hem, and before Susan returned to Princes Park, Sally had skilfully altered the dresses.

The following day Susan's employer noticed the improvement in her appearance, and after questioning her, told Susan to ask her neighbour to come to the house in Princes Park.

'I may be able to give her some work,' she said graciously.

160

Sally went to see Susan's employer, Miss Haygarth, but she firmly refused when she was asked to attend daily to do the household mending, and any other sewing required.

'I'm sorry, Miss Haygarth, I can only work from home,' she said. 'I'm employed by Libby's for rush orders and I have to be available for them.'

Miss Haygarth seemed impressed. 'Libby's, you sew for Libby's?' she said.

'Only what their own workroom can't manage, embroidery and trimming mostly, and sometimes mourning wear.'

'I see. My brother has authorized me to supply the maids with new print dresses and I would like you to make them. What do you charge?'

'Three shillings and sixpence, Miss Haygarth,' Sally said boldly.

'Very well. I will arrange to have the material sent to you.' She pulled the bell rope beside the fire.

'Take Mrs Ward to the kitchen, and tell Emma, Jane and Susan they are to be measured – and yourself, of course.'

'Yes, Miss. Thank you, Miss,' the maid said, smiling at the visitor, and Miss Haygarth nodded her head as Sally rose.

'Cook will give you tea, Mrs Ward,' she said graciously.

Sally enjoyed the work, sewing the fresh clean print material, and knowing that the young maids would be pleased with their dresses. The money she earned made a useful addition to the money in the teapot, and Miss Haygarth often employed her later, to alter her dresses or to make small items for the bazaars she often held.

Chapter Twenty-Six

Sally was so busy that the new century, so eagerly awaited, seemed to arrive quite suddenly. On New Year's Eve 1899 she sat with her father, and the two little girls who had been allowed to stay up for the occasion, waiting for Lawrie to let in the New Year.

When midnight struck he rapped on the door, and came in carrying bread, salt, and coal.

'Happy New Century, Sal,' he exclaimed, flinging his arm around her and kissing her, and as the children clamoured to be kissed, Sally turned to her father.

'Happy New Century, Da,' she said, kissing him.

He nodded, 'Let's hope it's better than the last one,' he said.

'Bound to be,' Lawrie said cheerfully. 'Working men with the vote! We'll change the world.'

'Oh, Lawrie, no, not politics,' Sally said, clapping her hands over her ears. 'Not now.'

Lawrie laughed. 'Come on, get your coat, Sal,' he said. 'We'll have a walk round. There's all sorts on.'

They dressed the children warmly, then all set out. The noise from the sirens of the ships crowding the river was deafening, and a band was playing further down the street. Everywhere people were dancing and singing. Someone was banging a drum outside a house, and a barrel organ was being played in one of the courts. Cathy clung to Sally's hand, alarmed by the unfamiliar darkness and the noise, but Mary was in her element, dancing ahead and shouting with glee.

In Langsdale Street crowds were gathered outside St Francis Xavier's where a Midnight Mass was being celebrated, and glorious music poured out from the large congregation and the trained choir.

'Let's go and see Mrs Mal,' Lawrie said, and they all trooped down to Gell Street. Mrs Malloy and Paddy were sitting either side of the fire drinking glasses of porter, and were delighted to see the family.

'Isn't this grand?' Mrs Malloy exclaimed, while Paddy poured drinks for the men, and she made cocoa for Sally and the children. 'Paddy let in the New Year and we were just sitting here like a pair of ould Marley horses, wondering what to do with ourselves.'

'The new *century*, Mrs Mal,' Mary piped up, and Mrs Malloy laughed and patted her head.

'Aye, it's your turn now, child,' she said, then looked at Sally and Lawrie.

'Sure, there's grand times ahead for all of yiz, please God. Weren't we born at the wrong time altogether, Matt, with all that's in store for these young ones?'

Paddy raised his glass. 'Long life and good health to yiz all,' he said in his quiet voice.

'And to you, Paddy,' said Lawrie. 'We'll see changes now, but all to the good, I'm sure.' He lifted his glass and smiled across at Sally.

'May all our dreams come true,' he said.

Most of the revelry had died down as they walked home, the two men carrying the sleeping children, but Sally still felt too excited and happy to be tired.

The new century promised well. In the spring the news of the relief of Mafeking brought great happiness to the nation, and in Liverpool the increased trade through the port gave an air of prosperity and hope for the future. Sally's life continued to sweep smoothly along.

As far as possible she avoided sewing on Sundays, and spent her time with the family. In later years when Cathy looked back on her childhood it was the Sundays she chiefly remembered: the outings in fine weather, and perhaps even more enjoyable the winter afternoons when they all gathered round the fire, after the Sunday dinner had been cleared away and the dishes washed.

Soon they would hear the barrel organ being played, right outside the door, because the man knew that the two little girls would be sent out with a penny each from their father to give to him. The man who sold crumpets and lightcakes followed him, and Mary and Cathy took turns apiece with the toastfork, to toast the crumpets and lightcakes before the fire.

Cathy usually managed to toast them fairly evenly, but Mary was too impatient to cook them properly. Either she would tear them off the fork before they were ready, or she would thrust the fork so close to the fire that black lines would be burnt on them from the bars of the grate. They were all delicious though, eaten hot and running with butter.

Cathy loved Sunday tea, too. It was always cold meat from the joint and pickles, and a hot savoury dish, potted herrings or cheese and onion pie, or sometimes potted shrimps, spread on the crusty bread her mother had baked the previous day.

Apple pies stuck with cloves would follow, or jam turnovers and an open jam tart criss-crossed with pastry, with a pastry letter C and a letter M on the portions for herself and Mary.

Sometimes Mrs Malloy and Paddy came to tea, and sometimes Agnes Cassidy with her fiancé, James Horton. The children liked it best when Agnes came alone, so that Mama was not so insistent on polite behaviour as when James watched them disapprovingly.

One Sunday early in February 1900 Agnes came alone, and they all had an enjoyable day, finishing with Agnes playing the piano in the parlour while they all sang.

'I'll bet old Miss Hagerty didn't teach *you*,' Mary said scowling.

'Don't speak like that of someone older than yourself, Mary,' Sally said sharply. 'You're very lucky that Miss Hagerty has agreed to teach you.'

'You're very lucky to have a pianner, let alone lessons,' Matthew said.

'I never had piano lessons,' Agnes said. 'I always used to play on the pianos outside shops and run away when the men came out.'

'But you can play now, so why do I have to take lessons?' Mary asked.

'Agnes has a natural ear for music, that's why,' Sally said. She believed in answering the children's questions as far as possible, although she knew that her father thought that she allowed them too much latitude.

'Children should be seen and not heard,' Matthew growled now, and Mary tossed her head.

'I've got two ears so I should be twice as good,' she said pertly. Lawrie stood up.

'Come on, girls, bedtime,' he said. He turned to Sally. 'I'll see to them while you have a gas with Agnes.' He ushered the children into the kitchen. Their nightdresses were warming on the fireguard, and he left them to undress and went into the back kitchen where a gas ring had been installed, and made cocoa for them. Matthew had followed them and, left alone, Agnes and Sally sat down by the parlour fire.

'I *have* enjoyed today, Sal,' Agnes said. 'Mary's a case, isn't she?'

Sally smiled. 'I've got to laugh at her sometimes, but she's getting to be a hardfaced little faggot. My da makes her worse, too. Sometimes he can't see a fault in her, and he interferes when I shout at her, yet other times he says she's too impudent. Lawrie should be more strict with her, but you know him, anything for a quiet life.'

'He gets on well with your da, though, doesn't he?'

'Until they get on to politics,' Sally said with a sigh. 'You know, Da used to believe Gladstone would help the poor, and Lawrie said we needed men in Parliament like Keir Hardie, but Da's turned right against Gladstone since the War, yet he skits at Lawrie when he talks about Thomas Mann and the Labour Representation Committee. He says they're all out for what they can get, and Lawrie goes mad.'

'It's the same in our house,' Agnes said. 'Our Liam calls himself a Socialist and he's always ranting. I think they're all nuts, Sal. What can the like of us do to alter things?'

'That's what my da says now. He says things gradually get better anyway. He's always talking about some fellows who got penal servitude for forming a union, and an old woman he knew when he was a child whose father was transported for it. At least Lawrie's only risking his job, but that's bad enough.'

'Oh, it is, Sal. He was lucky to get another job so quick. They usually blacklist fellers, our Liam says.'

'I know. My da says Lawrie's done his share and he's got us to think about. His first duty is to his wife and children.'

'It's true though, isn't it, Sal?'

'Yes, but mind you, Ag, these meetings are all talk. Daydreams. You know what Lawrie told me they were saying? Old people and widows should get a pension and Parliament should pay for it. Can you imagine it?' They both laughed, and Sally leaned forward and poked the fire. Then keeping her eyes on the flames, she said quietly, 'Any plans yet, love?'

Agnes shook her head. 'No. James wants us to have a house and all the furniture first.'

'You've been courting a long time now, Ag,' Sally said gently.

Agnes nodded, staring into the fire, her eyes bright with tears. 'Seven years last November,' she said. 'It's nearly five years since our engagement. I'll be twenty-five in March, Sal, and no further on.'

Sally was silent for a moment, then keeping her eyes lowered she said quietly, 'Are you quite sure he's what you want, love? You're an attractive girl and so lively. You could have anyone.'

'But not a gentleman like James,' Agnes said quickly. 'Oh, I know he's a bit – a bit slow, but he's a gentleman from a posh home, and he asked me out, and he stuck to me even when he saw where I lived.'

'But he couldn't blame you for that. He must know your mam did well to keep the home going at all when she lost your da.'

Agnes flushed. 'I know, and I'm not moaning about me mam, you know that, Sally. I'm not moaning about waiting to get all our stuff either. It's the way James's class of people do things, and it's sensible really.'

Fortunately at that moment there was a diversion. Lawrie knocked at the door, and ushered in the two little girls to say goodnight. Agnes kissed them tenderly, and Sally stood up but Lawrie said easily, 'You're all right, Sal. I'll take them up. Say goodnight to Mama.'

The children kissed Sally and went out with their father, and as the door closed behind them, Agnes turned to Sally and sighed.

'God, Sally, Lawrie's one in a million, isn't he? D'yer realise how lucky you are?'

'I do, Ag, and I'm sorry I said all that about him before. He only gets mixed up with the politics and union stuff because he's so worried about other people, but he's promised me he won't take any office with them.'

'I don't understand any of it,' Agnes said frankly. 'But fellers are all the same. The man next door to us is always moaning. He's a docker and he's lucky if he gets half a week on, although he's out down to the pen every morning at five o'clock.'

'Lawrie says it's degrading for the dockers to have to stand in the pen and be picked out like cattle by the ganger. My da says they have to give backhanders or buy drinks to get picked.'

'I know they're always skint next door, and she's got a club foot so she can't do much. Your sewing must make a difference here, Sal.'

'It does. I'm getting a lot of work from Libby's in Bold Street, and some from where Susan works. I don't get much from the Ogden's girls now, because the craze is for made up blouses from some shop in London Road. Why don't you try taking in sewing, Agnes?'

'I'm no good at it, Sal. I hate the tailoring really, but it's all I know, and I'm all right machining trousers.'

'It's been a godsend to us,' Sally said. 'It means that bit extra for food and clothes and bits for the house, and I've furnished this parlour with it.'

'It's lovely too,' Agnes said, looking round her. The talk turned to the Market and Mrs Gregson, and Sally was careful not to mention James again.

When Agnes had gone and they were in bed, Lawrie stroked Sally's hair back from her face.

'What's up, Sal?' he asked gently. 'What's worrying you?'

'How do you know I'm worrying?' she said.

'I always know, love. What is it? Mary?'

'No, she's been better lately. It's Agnes, Lol. That James doesn't love her, I'm sure, or he'd be more anxious to get married.'

'Well, I can't say I'm struck on him myself,' said Lawrie. 'But he must be what Agnes wants.'

'She's making a mistake, I'm sure she is. She thinks he's a gentleman because he wears posh clothes, and works in that shop. She thinks he's doing her a favour going out with her, too, but *I* think the boot's on the other foot.'

'How does she get on with his family?' asked Lawrie.

'I don't know. I think she's only seen his father once in all these years – his mother's dead, and I don't think he often goes to the Cassidys'.'

'That's not too good, but everyone's different you know, Sal, and probably James loves Agnes in his own way.'

'I think she's worth better than that prig. She's such a lovely girl.'

'They've been goin' together for a long time though, love, and either of them could have ended it any time if they wanted to.'

'I'm sure Agnes isn't happy,' Sally persisted, but Lawrie held her tightly and kissed her.

'Stop worrying, love,' he said. 'She probably had a little moan to you because you're old friends, but I'll bet she wouldn't change James and he wouldn't change her. He doesn't suit us, but that doesn't mean he doesn't suit Agnes.'

Sally said no more, uneasily conscious of her own 'little moan', but she was not convinced. Away from James, Agnes was the lively girl Sally had always known, but in his presence she was subdued and unsure of herself. Sally feared that marriage to him might change her completely.

She realised that her own marriage had changed her in some ways. As a child she had grown up with misery and destitution around her, and accepted it as normal. Her own circumstances of respectable poverty only gave her a feeling of superiority until she met Lawrie, but now she felt the same compassion for the starving ragged children as he did.

'Sometimes I'm sorry I ever met you!' she exclaimed to Lawrie one day, when she had distributed coppers to barefoot, hungry children, crying with cold and hunger outside a public house. 'That money was hard earned. Sewing beads on a dress for hours, and it's only a drop in the bucket, anyway.'

'I know, Sal, although those kids were very glad to get the coppers, but don't you see, that's why I want to work to get things changed for poor people, with the unions, and working men in Parliament.'

'But that's crazy, Lawrie. How can men go to Parliament while they've got to work to keep their families?'

'Ah, now you've hit the nail on the head, love. I say the Liberals should have arranged for M.P.s to be paid when they had the power, between '92 and '95. They would have done if they were really fighting for justice. That Lib Lab fellow in Yorkshire said that money was the golden key that opened the door to Parliament, and he was right.'

'Don't get so excited, Lol,' Sally said. 'You're rushing me off my feet.' In his agitation Lawrie was walking so quickly that she could not keep up with him.

'Sorry, love,' he said, slowing down and squeezing her arm.

'I wish you wouldn't argue with Da, Lawrie. All that about Home Rule and Chamberlain, and Gladstone and Keir Hardie, the other night. I thought you were both going to have apoplexy!'

Lawrie laughed. 'You should hear us at the meetings,' he said cheerfully.

'Don't forget,' Sally warned him, 'you promised not to get mixed up in anything and risk your job. It's a good job and you're well treated there, you know.'

'I know, I know,' he said.

'So I don't see why you should be joining up with grumblers. Anyway you've got your own family to think of. I wish you were still at the Mission.'

Lawrie made an impatient movement but said nothing, and after they had walked in silence for a while, Sally said timidly, 'What's up, Lol?'

He shrugged his shoulders without replying, but as they drew near the house he said quietly, 'Don't worry yourself, Sally, I won't take any office, at least until the children are older, but I'll go to the meetings and support those who *can* fight for us.'

For the following few days there was a feeling of constraint between them, and Lawrie was unusually quiet. He said nothing when her father read provocative items aloud from his newspaper, or commented on something political said at work.

It was a relief to Sally when Lawrie told her about a scheme started to repair broken boots for the boys who sold newspapers or carried bags in the streets.

A single lady, the wealthy sister of a well-known philanthropist, had offered to supply the leather, and Lawrie was one of the men who would do the cobbling. He worked enthusiastically, pleased to have something constructive to do, but Matthew was cynical about it.

'They'll only pawn them boots, you see,' he said. 'There's no way yer'll stop them.'

'What if they do?' Lawrie retorted. 'Boots are important to the lads in the winter, so if they need food or shelter more than them it'll be a good thing they've got them to pop.'

Sally said nothing. She was thankful that Lawrie had found a way of easing his conscience by helping the boys, and she felt less guilty about being so adamant against his involvement with unions and politics.

Matthew had an attack of bronchitis immediately after Christmas, so the New Year was passed very quietly by the family. He insisted on returning to work after ten days, although his breathing was so bad that Sally had to meet him in Shaw Street every evening, to help him up the hill. His temper was so short that she was afraid to argue with him, and she took care to have the children in bed before he came home, in spite of their protests. She longed for the spring as she had never longed before.

Chapter Twenty-Seven

On the evening of January 22nd 1901 church bells began to toll and Sally went to the front door. Mrs Kilgannon was talking to two other women, and she turned and shouted to Sally, 'The Widder of Windsor has snuffed it! That's what them bells are for.'

'Oo, Mrs Killey,' one of the other women said. 'Ye're proper disrespectful. She never done you no harm.'

'She never done me no bloody good, either,' Mrs Kilgannon said. 'And the new feller won't be no better. Too busy running after his women.'

'It's the end of something that's lasted a long time,' Sally said. 'Poor Queen Victoria. Somehow she seemed as though she'd last forever.'

'Bloody nearly did,' Mrs Kilgannon cackled.

Sally was surprised by the seriousness with which her father and Lawrie treated the Queen's death.

'What do you think, lad?' Matthew asked. 'Might be changes now.'

'Bound to be,' Lawrie said. 'He's been wanting to have a go at ruling, and he's not had the chance. He'll stir things up, I think. Get us more mixed up with France and that.'

'Aye. Their morals suit his kind,' Matthew said, glancing at Sally. She turned away to hide a smile. Da thinks I know nothing, she thought.

'All these lads coming home from South Africa, too. They'll stir things up a bit,' Lawrie said. 'They've seen a bit of the world.'

'Aye, but there's changes around already – electric trams and all the building that's going on. The old lady lasted a bit too long, I reckon.'

'Oh, Da, she couldn't help living so long,' Sally said reproachfully. 'I don't suppose she wanted to die any more than anyone else.'

Mrs Malloy seemed to be the only one Sally knew who felt genuine sorrow and sympathy for Queen Victoria.

'Lord ha' mercy on her,' she said. 'Didn't she have her own share of troubles, and if she made mistakes the badness was in the people around her, putting the ideas in her head. Sure, she was only a bit of a girl when they made her Queen.'

Lawrie took the two little girls to the Town Hall at noon on January 25th to hear the Lord Mayor reading the proclamation of the accession of King Edward VII.

'So that you can tell your grandchildren that you heard it,' he told them, but this produced such a barrage of questions about the grandchildren that he began to regret taking them.

On February 2nd an elaborate memorial service was held in St Peter's Church, with all the city notables present, but Sally felt little interest in it.

A far more exciting event was a visit from Emily. Miss Blake had business in Liverpool and it was arranged that she should bring Emily to Sally's house, and call for her in the evening when she was returning home.

All the family were amazed to see how tall Emily had grown, and how much older she looked. She wore a long black skirt heavily braided, and a jacket trimmed with astrakhan, and she carried an astrakhan muff.

Her hair was tied back with a large black bow, and a small black hat framed her glowing face. Miss Blake only stepped from the cab long enough to hand Emily over to Sally, and to arrange to call back for her at six o'clock, before being driven away.

Sally had completed her sewing orders by staying up late every night so she could devote all her time to Emily, and they spent a happy day. Sally was interested in everything Emily could tell her about her life in Ormesdale, and Emily sat cuddling Cathy and talking, or listening as Sally told her about Mary, Lawrie and her father.

At four o'clock they walked up to meet Mary at school. Sally had dressed herself and Cathy carefully, and she was filled with pride as she waited with Emily and Cathy outside the school, and saw the admiring glances they drew from the people who passed.

Mary was one of the last to appear, and she was closely followed by the headmistress, Miss Carrington.

'I cudden find me 'at,' Mary announced. Sally had bent over her, straightening the hat and reproving Mary for her speech, when she realised that Miss Carrington had paused beside them.

'Good afternoon, Mrs Ward,' she said. Sally straightened up, looking flustered.

'Good afternoon, Miss – Miss Carrington,' she said. She realised that the teacher's eyes were on Emily, and said proudly, 'This is my sister, Emily, Miss.' Emily smiled, and Miss Carrington's eyes swept over her.

'You did not attend our school, Emily,' she said.

'No, Miss Carrington, I live with my uncle and aunt in Ormesdale, and I have a governess,' Emily said. She had lost her Lancashire accent now, and spoke in the cultured tones taught by Miss Blake. Miss Carrington was clearly impressed.

'Indeed,' she said. 'You are very fortunate.' She turned to Sally. 'How old is this child, Mrs Ward?' she asked. 'What is her name?'

'Catherine Emily,' Sally answered. 'She'll be ready for school after the holidays.'

'I will be pleased to have her as a pupil,' Miss Carrington said graciously. 'Mary is industrious and attentive, her teacher tells me, and her marks are good.'

'Thank you. I'm very glad,' Sally said. Miss Carrington inclined her head and moved away. Fortunately she did not see Mary sticking out her tongue at her retreating back, and Sally was too happy preening herself to notice.

'That was good to hear, Mary,' Emily said, 'Do you like school, love?'

'Yes, I do. I like Miss Baldwin,' Mary said.

'It sounds as though you're very clever,' Emily said. 'Doesn't it, Sal?'

'Yes. You must be good in class, Mary, so if only you'd stop fighting and try to speak better you'd do very well,' Sally said.

During the day she had tried to probe delicately about affairs at Ormesdale but Emily's answers were vague. She seemed to spend most of her time with Miss Blake.

'Auntie sits in the drawing room, or in her bedroom,' she said when Sally asked about Hester. 'She nets purses.'

'Do you have visitors? Are there any other children for you to play with?' asked Sally.

'I play with Jamie sometimes. His father is the under gardener.'

'*Under* gardener!' exclaimed Sally. 'Dear God, how many people work for Uncle Walter?'

'Three in the garden and two in the stables, and some other men who come to do things to the house,' Emily said. 'And in the house, Rose and Susan and Jean, and Cook and Mary Ellen.'

'No wonder Aunt Hester doesn't have time to write,' Sally said. 'She must have plenty to do with all that lot to look after.'

Emily agreed doubtfully, then she said, 'Only the Vicar's wife comes to call, but men come to see Uncle Walter. Sometimes I sing a song for them or recite my poetry.'

'And are you happy, love?' Sally asked earnestly.

'Oh, *yes*. I love Blakey,' Emily replied, and Sally's worries were eased.

Emily had only a brief time with her father and Lawrie before Miss Blake returned for her, but both men were delighted with her.

'See what a nice young lady Emily's grown,' Matthew said to Mary and Cathy when she had gone. 'Just by doing what she's told. Youse want to take her as a model.'

Lawrie opened his mouth to protest that Sally should be their model, but she realised what he was about to say and shook her head warningly, afraid to provoke her father.

A few weeks later Mary brought home a note from Miss Carrington, asking Sally to call to see her. As usual Sally feared the worst, and cross-examined Mary about her behaviour.

'I haven't done nothing,' Mary said indignantly, and Sally tried yet again to correct her speech. The following day she dressed carefully before presenting herself at the headmistress's room.

'Ah, come in, Mrs. Ward. Sit down. I'll come right to the point. I believe you sew for Libby's of Bold Street, and also you make all the clothes necessary for yourself and your children. Is that right?'

'Yes, Miss Carrington,' Sally said. 'I like sewing,' she added nervously.

'Good, good. Now I belong to a Ladies' Sewing Circle, and I have suggested that you join us. We meet at my house every Tuesday evening from eight o'clock until ten, to make garments for the heathen. Are you free to join us?'

'Oh, *yes*,' said Sally, pink with delight. Miss Carrington inclined her head.

'This is my address,' she said, handing Sally a piece of paper. 'My mother kindly supplies the material, and we contribute one shilling each week for sewing thread and other items required.'

Sally rose to her feet, clutching the piece of paper.

'Should I just go to the house next Tuesday then?' she asked.

'Yes. Eight o'clock. We have a pleasant evening in addition to supporting a worthy cause,' Miss Carrington said. 'Good afternoon, Mrs Ward.'

Sally walked home as though walking on air. A sewing circle with Miss Carrington and the other ladies, and in St Domingo Vale! She could have crowed with pride and pleasure. Lawrie was sincerely pleased to hear her news, knowing how much it meant to Sally, but Matthew was unimpressed.

'Sewing for heathens, begod,' he said. 'Aren't there enough heathens running around Liverpool, barefoot and half naked?'

Sally's face flushed with anger. He spoils everything, she thought, but managed to say nothing.

Matthew had again become morose and ill-tempered, constantly carping, especially at Lawrie. Sally feared that sooner or later there would be trouble between them. She knew that Lawrie made allowances for Matthew, because he was a sick man, and also because he was her father, but like many easygoing people, Lawrie's temper when roused was fierce, and Sally dreaded the day when Matthew drove him too far.

On the Tuesday evening Lawrie walked with Sally to St Domingo Vale, and waited across the road until he saw her admitted to the front door of the house. Sally enjoyed her evening. At first she was unsure of herself, and the ladies were inclined to patronize her, but her skill was quickly recognized, and her work was much admired.

Lawrie was waiting, hidden by bushes, when Sally came out of the house at ten o'clock, but when he saw that she was with two of the ladies, he withdrew unobtrusively. He had been afraid that the ladies might have snubbed her or been unkind, and he wanted to be at hand to comfort her if she was upset, but he could see that his fears had been groundless.

He reached home before Sally, and she was bubbling with excitement when she arrived.

'Oh, Lawrie!' she said. 'You should see that house. Miss Carrington's father was a soldier, and he brought lovely things home from India. Brassware and ivory, and even a carpet. The fireplace was lovely, too. Marble, with garlands of carved flowers, and plaster garlands on the ceiling, too.'

'What were the other women like?' asked Lawrie.

'Very nice. A bit stiff at first, but then they started asking me about embroidery stitches and things like that.'

'Embroidery stitches? Don't tell me they embroider the shifts for the heathen,' he said, laughing.

'Lawrie, you know they don't,' Sally giggled. 'One of the ladies had a collar she was embroidering in her handbag, so I showed her some stitches, and the others tried them out on scraps of material.'

'So you were a success, love,' Lawrie said, giving her a hug. 'I'm glad you've had a bit of pleasure. God knows, you work hard enough.'

Sally became even more vigilant about ladylike behaviour, and mealtimes became a constant lesson on good manners for the two little girls.

'Sit up straight. Take your elbows off the table. Don't speak with your mouth full,' Sally enjoined them, and she corrected Mary's speech so often that Matthew protested.

'That girl'll be afraid to open her mouth before you're finished,' he said. 'For God's sake give it a rest.'

Sally tossed her head without replying, and the training continued.

She was even more busy with her sewing. Agnes Cassidy now worked for a firm of clerical tailors, and she was able to arrange for Sally to make some of the heavily embroidered vestments supplied by the firm. Sally found the work an exciting challenge, and it was comparatively well paid. It also increased her standing enormously in the Ladies' Sewing Circle.

In late April, 1901 Agnes came to see Sally with the news that she and James were to be married in July. His firm was opening a branch in Brunswick Road, and James was to be the manager, with living accommodation provided over the shop. Sally heard the news with mixed feelings. She was glad that Agnes seemed happy, and that she would be living quite nearby, but she wondered what the future held for her lively, warm-hearted friend, spending all her waking hours with the prim, disapproving James.

The wedding took place on a chilly July morning in St Francis Xavier's. Only James's cousin, who was best man, was present from his family, and Mrs Cassidy was there with several of her daughters. Tom and Liam Cassidy had made the excuse of having to work on the day, but the real reason was their bitter opposition to the wedding.

'The lads are heartbroken,' Mrs Cassidy had mourned to Sally a few weeks earlier. 'Sure, we were all hoping she'd get fed up and give the little runt his marching orders. Me poor girl, whatever way will he treat her, Sally?'

'I'm sure he'll look after her,' Sally tried to console Mrs Cassidy. 'As Lawrie says, she must see something in him that we don't.'

'Yes, his bloody airs and graces,' Mrs Cassidy said. 'He has her dazzled, the way he goes on like Gentleman Joe.'

'Agnes will soon cure him, once they're married,' Sally said. 'She'll liven him up.'

'Never,' sobbed Mrs Cassidy. 'It's him that will crush her down. Our Liam says he'll break his back if he doesn't treat her right, but who's to know? She'll never let on, will she, Sally?'

'Don't cry,' Sally said. 'Let's just hope for the best. Nobody knows how it will turn out, and Agnes is well able to stand up for herself.'

Mrs Cassidy refused to be comforted. 'D'ye know that he won't have a wedding breakfast? My house is not good enough for him, and he won't have it over the shop. He's afraid he might be asked to put down his hand for the drinks. What class of a man would behave like that, Sally? He'd skin a flea for its hide, so he would.'

'He knows you haven't got much room, Mrs Cassidy. D'you think they would agree to the breakfast in our house? You and I could see to the food, and Lawrie'd see to the drinks as a wedding present for them.'

Mrs Cassidy dried her eyes. 'You've a heart of gold, Sally,' she declared. 'Sure, I'd feel she'd gone off more decent like if we had a meal and a bit of a drink.'

'I'll ask them then,' Sally said, 'but I won't let on that I know anything about it. I'll just say we'd like to do it as a wedding present for them.'

James agreed to the wedding breakfast in Sally's house. 'If you wish,' he said stiffly, when she asked him. 'But it must be understood that I'm not willing to incur further expense.'

'Mrs Cassidy and I will arrange for the food,' Sally said quietly, 'and Lawrie will see to the drinks. It will be our pleasure – for Agnes,' she could not resist adding.

During the wedding service Sally knelt at the back of the church with Mrs Malloy, looking at the soaring columns of stone, and the beauty of the stained glass windows, and remembering the days when she sat there with Emily on her knee, hoping that the child would absorb the beauty around her.

Her heart was heavy for her friend, who seemed to be making such a tragic mistake, and she knew that her feelings were shared by others. As the words were pronounced which would bind Agnes irrevocably to James, Kathleen, the sister who was bridesmaid, began to sob loudly. She was gently reproved by the priest, and Sally and Mrs Malloy slipped away to prepare for the wedding party.

'Put a good face on it, girl,' Mrs Malloy advised. 'What's done is done, and ye'd better make the best of it.'

Either because they took their cue from Sally and Mrs Malloy, or because the rest of the guests had reached the same conclusion, they were in a cheerful mood, and it developed into a merry party. Lawrie helped by keeping all the glasses well filled, and James had the grace to thank Mrs Cassidy and 'Agnes's friends' for their efforts, in his speech.

Sally thought of her own wedding party in the tiny kitchen in Gell Street. She and Lawrie had had so little with which to start life together, in material things, but they had a happiness which was missing today.

She remembered Mrs Hart quoting from the Bible, 'Better a dinner of herbs where love is, than a stalled ox and hatred therewith', and hoped that Agnes would not find the truth of the proverb.

Agnes and James were to go straight to the shop, to prepare for the opening a few days later, and Sally hugged her friend as she prepared to go.

'Every happiness, love,' she whispered. 'Don't forget, I'm here any time you want me.' Agnes smiled and kissed her, then after a clammy handshake for Sally from James, the Cassidys bade them an emotional farewell.

As they left, Mrs Kilgannon appeared on her doorstep, and showered them generously with rice.

'Yer'll be wantin' that fer a rice pudden tomorrer,' one of the Cassidys called cheerfully, as the rice descended like hail. James pursed his thin lips but said nothing.

In September 1901 Cathy started school. Sally was surprised to find how much she missed the quiet little girl. She had helped her mother in many small ways, always singing cheerfully to herself as she stood on a stool to wash dishes, or picked up threads and pins, but she was still a shy, timid child, and Sally worried about how she would fare at school.

'She'll be all right,' Lawrie consoled her. 'Mary's there to look after her and fight her battles at first, and she'll soon learn to stand on her own feet.'

Cathy's first battle was with Mary! Sally took them to school and met them to come home on the first day, but on the second day Cathy was sent off in Mary's care.

Sally always provided Mary with a jam sandwich or a piece of cake for the eleven o'clock break, so both children were clutching small parcels of ginger cake as they set off.

'Hold Mary's hand, Cathy, and be careful crossing the road,' Sally said. As soon as they were safely round the corner out of sight, Mary dropped Cathy's hand, and tried to snatch her parcel of cake, but Cathy hung on to it grimly. When it seemed that Mary was succeeding, Cathy buried her teeth in Mary's hand.

'Ow,' Mary screamed, letting go of the parcel, 'you wait till I tell Mama.'

Cathy realised that it was an empty threat because her mother would want to know all the facts, but she expected Mary to take revenge, and was relieved when Mary abandoned her to run after a fat girl, shouting, 'Yah, yah, pianner legs.'

Cathy quietly attached herself to a group of children walking in front of her, and arrived safely at the school. At four o'clock Mary waited for Cathy at the corner of Egremont Street, and gripping her hand tightly, dragged her home. Sally was pleased.

'That's a good girl, Mary, looking after your little sister like that,' she said. It was only as the children undressed for bed that she noticed the teeth marks on Mary's hand.

'Who did that?' she demanded. For a moment Mary hesitated, looking at Cathy and looking away, but finally she muttered, 'Some girl.'

'*A* girl, Mary,' Sally said. 'Why? What were you doing?'

'Nothing,' Mary said, and Sally clicked her tongue in vexation.

Later she said to Lawrie, 'Mary was fighting again today. She had teeth marks on her hand. I wonder if we should move them from that school?'

'Where to?'

'Well, Miss Edwards from the Sewing Circle said her niece goes to a private school in Mill Road. It's run by two sisters, and they're strict about behaviour and good manners.'

'But what about ordinary lessons?' Lawrie asked. 'Our Mary's good at her lessons, and I think she's getting good teaching there.'

Matthew took his pipe from his mouth. 'What'll it cost?' he said.

'Two shillings a week,'

'Each!' exclaimed Matthew. 'Talk sense, girl. Where are you going to find that kind of money? I've heard about these places – money for this and money for that. It's all right for them that have got plenty.'

'I can afford it,' Sally said angrily. 'I'm working hard at the sewing to give the girls a chance.'

'A chance!' Matthew exclaimed before Lawrie could speak, 'A chance to be miserable, that's all. Yer've got Mary nagged to death as it is, and it hasn't made a ha'porth of difference to her. Yer can't make a silk purse out of a sow's ear.'

'Hold on, Matt. That's a bit strong,' Lawrie said. 'She's only a bit wild, but she seems to behave all right when she's learning. I wouldn't want her to miss that and be unhappy.' Sally's eyes had filled with angry tears at her father's words, and Lawrie put his hand on hers. 'We'll have to think about it more, Sal,' he consoled her. 'Find out more about it.'

Sally looked sulky, but she shrugged and said, 'All right, but I want to do something before Cathy gets settled in school.' She was more willing to postpone the idea because she suspected that she was pregnant, and if so she would have less time for sewing. When she made enquiries about The Cedars, as the school was called, she found it was more expensive than she expected, and money would be required for many extras.

She said no more on the subject to Matthew and Lawrie, but one evening when Lawrie was out, her father suddenly attacked her.

'Ye're gettin' too big for yer boots, girl. Going round with yer nose in the air, thinkin' yer better than anyone else. It's them women in Domingo Vale, putting ideas in yer head.'

Sally was thunderstruck.

'I don't know what you mean by that,' she said.

'Don't yer? Strutting round like Lady Muck, and trying to make the girls as stuck up as what you are. They'll finish up neither flesh nor fowl,' he said.

'I only want them to be ladies,' Sally flashed. 'Nothing wrong with that, is there?'

'Wasn't yer mam a lady? She didn't have none of yer fancy ideas, but I'll tell yer this – she was a better wife and mother than you'll ever be. She didn't go calling her husband to the neighbours either.'

'I don't call Lawrie,' Sally exclaimed.

'Don't yer? Wharrabout talking to that one over the road?' He spoke in a mincing voice. ' "Lawrie's hopeless with money." I know yer think ye're keeping the bloody house with yer sewing money, but that lad never fails to turn up his wages to yer.'

'I know he does. I was talking about his own spends,' Sally said.

'Aye, but does she know that? She probably thinks he spends his own wages and your bloody sewing money an' all! Ye're that busy showing how clever yer are, making out ye're better than anyone else, yer don't stop ter think.'

Sally stood speechless with shock and mortification, and Matthew said more quietly, 'I'm telling yer fer yer own good, girl. I don't want to sit here watching yer jumping out of yer latitude, that full of yerself that yer make a mess of yer life, for want of a word.'

Sally went into the back kitchen and began to put clothes in soak, her tears dropping into the water as she worked, but when she was calmer she began to wonder uneasily if there was some truth in her father's words.

As the days passed she became certain that she was pregnant, and tried to forget his criticism. She felt well, and confident that the pregnancy would go smoothly, and although she was busier than ever she was perfectly happy. She and Lawrie looked forward eagerly to the new baby, hoping that it would be a son, and the ladies of the Sewing Circle fussed gently over her, putting a footstool for her feet and warning her not to overtire herself. Matthew was gentle with her, too, perhaps regretting his bitter words.

It was well that Sally had this happy time, for it helped to fortify her for the dark days so soon to come.

Chapter Twenty-Eight

In November 1901 the fogs on the river were so bad that there was a ceaseless clamour from the foghorns of the ships crowding the Mersey, and in the streets of Liverpool people groped their way, women with shawls, and men with mufflers held over their mouths.

Illness and death was everywhere. In the clammy bedrooms sufferers from asthma and bronchitis fought a losing battle for breath, and the many invalids with consumption were speeded on their painful journey to the grave.

Matthew's bronchitis was worse than it had ever been before, and Sally used every remedy she could find to try to relieve him. In the other bedroom Cathy lay in bed, shivering and burning in turn, and complaining that it hurt her to cough. Matthew's health improved but Cathy grew steadily worse, and Sally watched with terror as the child tossed sleeplessly, her cheeks burning and her lips dry and cracked.

Lawrie heard that Mrs Malloy was ill in bed, and Sally felt grieved that she could do nothing to help the old lady who had done so much for her in the past, but all her thoughts and fears were concentrated on her suffering child.

Mrs Kilgannon often came in to see Sally, and she dreaded the visits. Always there was some bad news which Mrs Kilgannon seemed to announce with pleasure. Sometimes it was to tell of a ship which had been lost on its homeward journey, or of others which had collided in the fog.

'Lost with all hands,' she would annouce, or, 'Must be hundreds drownded.' More often it was to tell Sally of deaths in the neighbourhood, very often a child, 'Just about your Cathy's age', or a man 'Getting on in years like yer da. No fight left in 'im.'

Lawrie came home one night to find Sally in tears, after Mrs Kilgannon had called to tell her of four children who had died of diphtheria. He dashed out and hammered on the Kilgannons' door. He was even more annoyed, when he was admitted, to see Mary sitting on the fender.

'Go home,' he said, his voice and his appearance so fierce that she scuttled away without a word.

'What's up?' Mrs Kilgannon quavered.

'I'll tell you what's up,' Lawrie said furiously. 'Going in there upsetting Sally, telling her about every death you hear about! Don't you think she's got enough on her plate without you making things worse? Have you got no sense, or do you just enjoy upsetting people?'

'I didn't mean no harm. I was just telling her what was going on because she hadn't been out,' Mrs Kilgannon whined.

181

'Well, for God's sake don't tell her about any more deaths. You'd be better not going in at all if that's all you can talk about. And send Mary home if she comes here, will you? Her mam needs her.'

'Orl right,' Mrs Kilgannon muttered, but as he turned to go she said, 'I never done it on purpose, yer know. I think the world of her.'

'I'm sure you do, Mrs Killey,' he said more calmly.

Sally looked apprehensive when he returned home, but he smiled at her.

'It's all right, love,' he said. 'We didn't fall out. She said she was trying to bring you the news because you can't get out – and, d'you know, I believed her. She's just thick enough for it to be true.'

'I'm glad you didn't fall out with her,' Sally said. 'Mary came in here as if Spring Heeled Jack was after her. I thought you must be having a row.'

'Where is she now?' asked Lawrie.

'Upstairs. I sent her to sit with Cathy. Oh, Lawrie, I'm so worried about her! She hasn't slept and she's like a little furnace and she's had nothing to eat. All she wants is cold water all the time.'

Lawrie went upstairs and found Mary gently wiping Cathy's face with a cold flannel.

'That's a good girl,' he said, taking the cloth and bending over the sick child.

'How do you feel, sweetheart?' he asked, but for once Cathy's ready smile was absent as she lay there, her cracked lips parted, and her chest heaving as she laboured for breath. Lawrie took her burning hand but it lay limply in his. He looked up to see that Sally had followed him and was standing, her arm around Mary, both of them staring at him with frightened eyes. He forced a smile.

'Mary had the right idea,' he said. 'Bathing her face.' He handed the cloth to Sally. 'Wring that out in cold water, love, and we'll bathe her face and hands, and we'll take one of these blankets off her as well.'

'But she might get fresh cold,' Sally protested.

'No, it'll do her good, Sal, honestly. It'll bring the fever down.' Cathy seemed more comfortable when her hands and face had been sponged, and her pillow turned, and she took a little milk from the cup held to her mouth.

'I'll sit with her,' Lawrie said. 'Mary, you make a cup of tea for your mam.'

'I'd better look at Da first,' Sally said, going into the other room, while Mary went downstairs. She found her father exhausted by a bout of coughing, but concerned about Cathy.

'I wish I'd taken more notice to her,' he said, 'but she was always that quiet, and all the attention went on the other one.'

'Oh, Da, don't talk like that,' Sally begged. 'She's going to get better soon.' He looked at her tear-filled eyes.

'I'm sure she is, girl,' he said gently. 'Look out for yerself an' all. We don't want you going sick on us.'

Sally went downstairs and lifted a jar of beef tea from the oven. Mary had made tea and cut hunks of bread which she was spreading with jam, and Sally sat down wearily by the fire and sipped the hot tea. Mary took a mug of tea and a plateful of bread and jam to Lawrie.

'Has your mam had anything to eat?' he asked.

'No, Dad, but she's got a cup of tea and I've made some butties for her,' Mary said.

'That's a good girl. Try to get her to eat,' he said, but Sally could eat nothing.

She came upstairs a few moments later with beef tea in a feeding cup for Matthew, then went in to Cathy.

'I wonder will she take some beef tea, Lawrie?' she said, but he shook his head.

'I wouldn't bother her with it, love,' he said. 'She's just had a little drink of water.' They stood looking down at the child, now tossing about and muttering in delirium, and Sally's tears fell fast.

'She seems to be getting worse all the time. I'm so frightened, Lol,' she said. Mary came upstairs and Sally sent her in to her grandfather, but she came back a moment later to say that he was asleep.

'That's good,' Lawrie said. 'You go into our bed now, Mary. Why don't you go with her, Sal? Just lie down for an hour and I'll call you.'

Sally shook her head. 'No, I'm not leaving her. You know what it is, don't you? The ninth night.'

They looked at each other in silent anguish. The ninth night of pneumonia – when the crisis of the illness was reached, and pneumonia sufferers either sank under the fever or came safely in to calm waters.

Mary went off to bed and Sally and Lawrie knelt side by side beside Cathy, stroking her forehead and her hands, moistening her lips with water, and praying desperately for relief for the suffering child.

Eventually Lawrie persuaded Sally to lie down on the side of the bed where Mary usually slept beside Cathy, so that she could rest yet still touch and see Cathy, and he was relieved when Nature took her toll, and Sally fell into a troubled sleep.

He knelt on, oblivious to the sounds outside the house of clattering horses' hooves and wheels, and ships' sirens on the river, hearing only his child's agonized breathing.

About midnight Cathy's voice grew louder as she sang or muttered in delirium, and her tossing grew wilder. She turned her head from side to side on her damp pillow, and Sally woke and leaned over her.

'Oh, Lawrie, what can we do?' she sobbed, trying to gather Cathy into her arms. 'She's going! Oh, Cathy, Cathy.'

Gently Lawrie wiped the child's face with a cool cloth, and turned her pillow.

'Lay her down, love,' he whispered. 'Try to keep her cool.' Cathy looked up at them, her eyes feverishly bright, and her terrified parents hung over her, until gradually her frenzied muttering died away, and her tossing body became quiet. She lay still, her eyes still open, then her eyelids drooped and her breathing became more regular. Sally and Lawrie looked at each other with wild hope. Could this be normal sleep? They were almost afraid to hope, but Cathy lay quietly now, breathing without effort, and her head seemed cooler.

Sally clung to Lawrie, and they wept together, the relief that they felt a measure of the fear that had filled them. Suddenly Lawrie looked up, to see Mary watching them with terrified eyes.

'It's all right, love, it's all right,' he said. 'She's turned the corner.'

'Thank God,' Matthew called, and they realised that he had been lying awake, and sharing their fear.

From then Cathy grew stronger each day, and Matthew soon recovered enough to return to work. Sally was plagued by a persistent pain in her back, and shooting pains in her groin and womb, but was too relieved and happy at Cathy's deliverance to be upset by her own discomfort.

Lawrie was as considerate and loving as ever with Sally and the children, but he had grown very subdued and thoughtful. Often when the girls were in bed, he would sit staring into the fire, his thoughts seemingly far away.

'That lad's got something on his mind,' Matthew said one evening when Lawrie had gone out to a meeting, but Sally dismissed the idea.

'Probably some of these fancy plans they talk about down there,' she said, and Matthew said no more.

Although Matthew managed to get to work each day, he was still not strong. He would sit gasping for breath when he arrived home, while Sally fussed around him, mixing a mug of rum and hot water, and Mary pulled off his boots and put slippers on his feet. This had been Cathy's job, and Mary did it very unwillingly.

One wet Monday a few weeks later everything seemed to go wrong for Sally. She woke with a headache and a dragging pain in her back, then twice the fire under the washboiler went out. Later as she pushed a pan on to the fire, it suddenly overbalanced, and water spilled from it to douse the glowing coal, and send a cloud of steam into Sally's face. Her tongue felt rough and sore from the scalding steam, and as she jumped back from the fire she crashed into Cathy, who started to cry, more from shock than pain.

'Oh, Cathy, get out of the way,' Sally snapped, snatching up the pan and dashing into the back kitchen. She came back with the shovel, and lifted off the wet coal with tongs, replacing it with dry coal from the bucket, then she held a newspaper over the fire to make it burn up. Only then did she notice Cathy's tear-streaked face as she huddled miserably on the sofa, but before she could speak, Cathy suddenly laughed.

'Oh, Mam, your face is all black,' she giggled, and after a moment Sally laughed, too.

'You'll have no luck, laughing at your mam,' she said, but the cheerfulness did not last.

She heard a sound from the parlour and went in, to find that the line she had stretched across the room had broken and the wet sheets were lying on the floor. By the time she had washed and mangled the sheets again, Mary was home from school. She had lost her hair ribbon, and the toes of her boots were badly scuffed.

'You've been climbing again, haven't you?' Sally said, and although Mary protested her innocence, her mother felt that she was telling lies.

The washing was still spread about the kitchen to dry when Matthew came home, and he grumbled about it.

'Where else can I put it, Da?' Sally said. 'I've already got some over the banister and some in the parlour. I've got to get it dry somehow.'

'Better get *her* up to bed out of it,' he growled, nodding at Cathy. 'This is no place for a bad chest.' Sally knew that this was an oblique reminder of his own bad chest, but she said nothing.

She had already narrowly averted a row when Mary made sounds of disgust as she pulled off her grandfather's boots. Sally had dragged her into the back kitchen and Mary had said sulkily, 'They smell, Mam,' but after threats and warnings from her mother, she went back and finished her task without further protest.

After their meal Sally hustled her up to bed with Cathy.

'You can tell each other stories,' she said, but Mary was annoyed.

'It's not fair,' she said. 'Me dad's not even home yet.'

'He's late,' Sally said. 'Now I'll leave the nightlight and I don't want to hear another word, Mary.' She kissed the children and went downstairs.

'I'll have me cocoa and I'll go up meself,' Matthew said. 'The quare feller's late, isn't he? It's ter be hoped he hasn't give his car fare away and walked home, a night like this.' Sally took Lawrie's meal from the oven and put it on the hob, and sat down to her sewing.

Rain was flung against the window by the wind, and Sally grew more and more worried and angry as the time passed. It was nearly an hour later when Lawrie walked wearily up the yard, and stood in the back kitchen with rain running from his clothes on to the floor.

'Good God,' Sally said, glaring at him. 'I suppose you gave your fare to some scrounger and walked home on a night like this.'

'No, I didn't. I had to take an extra load to the Dingle. Came in late and he couldn't afford to turn it away.'

All the frustrations of the day added to Sally's anger that she had wrongly accused Lawrie, because of her father's words.

'Your dinner's dried up,' she said, poking furiously at the fire. Lawrie said nothing as he took off his soaking cap and jacket, and took down the towel to dry himself.

'You'd better get those trousers off, too,' Sally snapped. 'Would have to be you taking the extra load. I suppose you offered.'

'No, I didn't. Poor old Bluebell was tired before we even started,' he said.

'*Bluebell*!' Sally rolled her eyes. 'The horse you worry about. Nothing about me worried to death here, and everything going wrong.'

Alarm leaped in Lawrie's eyes. 'Wrong? What? Cathy?'

'No,' Sally said impatiently. 'The washing and the fire, and Mary's boots, and then Da had a cob on because of the washing hanging about.'

'God, don't say things like that, Sally! Enough to frighten the life out of me after what we've been through.'

He took off his trousers then hung them over the back of the wooden chair and went upstairs. Sally laid the corner of the table for his meal, feeling ashamed of herself. Only a few weeks ago nothing mattered against the fact that Cathy had been spared to them, and already she was taking it for granted and worrying about unimportant things. Still, I've got a lot on my mind, keeping everything running smoothly here, she told herself.

Lawrie ate the dried up fish and potatoes without comment but his manner was stiff and withdrawn, and soon after the meal he decided to go to bed. Sally had noticed how he huddled over the fire, and she took the oven shelf upstairs and put it in to warm the bed.

Several times during the night she woke to find him drenched in sweat yet shivering.

'It's all right, Sal, I'm sweating it out,' he told her. 'Go to sleep. I'll be all right.' Later she woke to find him missing from the bed and crept downstairs after him. He was huddled over the fire, which he had revived with wood, sipping a hot drink.

'I pinched that lemon – made a drink with it,' he said hoarsely.

'You'd better go back to bed,' Sally said. 'But lie on my side of the bed, yours is damp. I'm staying up now.'

She built up the fire and brought her clothes downstairs to dress before it, then she folded the clothes which had dried, and hung Lawrie's still damp trousers and jacket on the fireguard to dry. As she worked she wondered uneasily whether he would be fit to go to work. If he had to stay off it would be the last straw, she felt. Already the money in the teapot had been depleted by the weeks without Matthew's wages, and the sewing money she had lost while Cathy and Matthew were ill.

At six o'clock Lawrie came downstairs for his clothes. 'Are they dry?' he asked.

'Just about,' Sally said, 'but are you fit to go, Lol?'

'Aye, I'll be all right,' he said. 'At least today's dry.'

Sally made his sandwiches and filled his tea can while he sat by the fire to eat his breakfast, but he looked drawn and haggard and she said impulsively, 'I don't think you're fit, Lol. Have the day off and get yourself right.'

She felt guilty about her sharp words of the previous night, but Lawrie smiled at her and shook his head.

'No, I'd better not,' he said. 'It'd be a bad time to do it.' He stood up and picked up his 'carry out' and took his cap from where it was drying on the oven, and the next moment he was gone, leaving Sally puzzled by his words, but too busy to dwell on them for long.

Chapter Twenty-Nine

Sally was so busy, catching up with neglected household tasks and sewing orders, that it was a shock to her to realise that Christmas was only a week away. All thought of the relatives at Ormesdale had been crowded out of her mind, but now she wrote to Emily, explaining why she had not written to them. There was no answer from Ormesdale, and the usual Christmas parcel did not arrive, but Sally's mind was filled with matters nearer home.

She had managed to visit Mrs Malloy for a few hours, and found her recovering from an attack of rheumatism.

'It's just me legs, girlie,' she said. 'Otherwise I'm grand, thank God, but I can't manage the broo up to your house yet.'

Sally was relieved to find her so cheerful, and before she left she arranged that Lawrie would call on Christmas morning, and he and Paddy could help Mrs Malloy up to Egremont Street for the Christmas dinner.

Cathy had grown taller and thinner, but her health was improving steadily. Sally watched her anxiously, often thinking of Matthew's words about Cathy being pushed into the background by Mary's demands for attention, but Cathy seemed quite happy, curled up in Matthew's chair reading, or being taught to knit socks by Sally.

Lawrie seemed happier too. There was a rush of orders at the yard, and he often worked late, and earned extra money. On Christmas Eve he came in with an enormous goose.

'Good God, Lawrie, we're not feeding the five thousand,' Sally exclaimed, but he only laughed.

'The goosegrease will be good for Cathy's chest,' he said, 'And it should last us for a few meals, so it's a saving really.'

On Christmas morning Lawrie went to Gell Street, and returned with Mrs Malloy, supported by himself and Paddy. The goose was a magnificent sight, on a huge plate in the centre of the table, surrounded by roast potatoes.

'God bless us, I never saw the like of it,' Mrs Malloy gasped, and there was much hilarity when Lawrie stood to carve it.

'I don't know whether to cut it or fight it,' he said, but with some help from Matthew it was successfully carved.

After dinner Mrs Malloy was given a place of honour by the fire, with a blanket round her knees, and the children pressed her to tell them of her early days in England, when she had worked as a nursery maid in a wealthy family.

'Sure, the mistress was kindness itself to me,' she said, 'when I was a poor homesick girl, grieving for me mammy and the people back home, but I made it up to her. Pressed down and running over, she said.'

'Why, Mrs Mal? What did you do?'

'Well now, they had four beautiful girls, and just the one son, and he was small and sickly. The mistress was ever about the nursery, not like some of them grand ladies that never see their children, and she worried herself to death about Master John.'

'Was that the little boy's name?' asked Cathy.

'It was, child. One night the master and the mistress went out to dinner, and they were no sooner gone than the little lad started with the croup. Now the nurse had a weakness for the drink, and she'd been at the gin bottle on the sly all day, and I was demented trying to rouse her, but she was pelatic drunk.'

Cathy leaned against Mrs Malloy's knees, her eyes round. 'Were you frightened, Mrs Mal?' she asked.

'I was indeed, child, but I ran down and asked the cook for a kettle of hot water, and I draped a sheet over the cot, and let the kettle steam inside it, the way it would ease the child, and him fighting for his breath, God love him. I got the ipec wine and I dosed him with it, too. The cook had sent off for the master and mistress, and they came in with a doctor that had been visiting at the same house. The child was choking with something and I'd just taken him on me knee and put me fingers down his throat. He was terrible sick all over meself and the floor, but it gave him ease, thank God.'

Lawrie poured a drink for Mrs Malloy, but the children waited impatiently while she drank it.

'How did you know what to do?' asked Mary.

'I didn't. I hadn't a notion, girl, only what I'd heard in bits of talk. God must have guided me, but the poor mistress – she couldn't say enough in praise of me. The master was quieter like, but when I left to get married, didn't he put a purse in me hand with twenty gold sovereigns it.'

'Did the little boy get better then?' asked Cathy.

'Oh, he did indeed, and a fine big lad he grew, too. The master sent me to the station in a carriage, the day I left, and Master John and Miss Isabel ran all down the drive after me, crying on me to go back. Ah, my heart was sore leaving them.'

'Then why did you go?' Mary said.

Mrs Malloy smiled. 'Well now, if ye were a bit older, girlie, ye wouldn't be asking me that,' she said. 'Hadn't I only seen Jimmy Malloy half a dozen times, but when he asked me to marry him and move up to Liverpool, sure I couldn't wait to do it.'

The adults all laughed, and Mrs Malloy looked across at Sally.

'Do ye remember your wedding day, girl?' she said. 'Poor Mrs Hart, Lord ha' mercy on her, the advice she was after giving ye, and yer aunt swelling up like a turkey cock. Did ye hear nothing from them, Sally?'

'No. It's the first time they've let Christmas pass, but maybe they're vexed because I haven't written.'

'But you wrote just before Christmas,' Lawrie said. 'Perhaps there's been sickness there too.'

'God knows it's everywhere lately,' said Mrs Malloy. 'But Cathy is grand, the way she's thrown it off.' They all looked at Cathy, and found she was falling asleep, leaning against Mrs Malloy. Sally hustled the girls off to bed, but Cathy's sleepiness vanished when she lay in bed beside Mary.

'Wasn't that lovely,' she said, 'Mrs Mal being able to save that little boy's life? I think I'll be a nursery maid when I grow up.'

'That's if Mam will let you,' Mary said. 'She said she wants me to work in a shop, but I want to be a parlourmaid like Susan Kilgannon.'

'I thought Sue worked in the kitchen,' Cathy said.

'She did at first but she's changed her job twice since then, and she managed to get this place as an under parlourmaid.'

'What does she have to do?' asked Cathy.

'Oh, all sorts of things, but she lights fires, because she told me that she was lighting the fire one day when the young master came in. He'd been out *all night* at a dance, Cathy, and he said a lot of poetry to Susan. That's why she likes being a parlourmaid because when she was in the kitchen she only saw the cook.'

'The only thing is, we'd have to live in, wouldn't we, Mary, and only see Mama and Dada once a week?'

'I wouldn't care,' Mary said. 'It'd only be for a little while, then I'd marry a rich young man, and live in a big house. You could come and see me,' she added graciously.

'Is Susan going to marry that man?' Cathy said.

'She might or she might marry one of the others,' Mary said, but Cathy's eyes were closing, and soon Mary too was asleep.

Shortly after Christmas a letter came from Emily, evidently written hurriedly and blotted as though with tears. She wrote that Miss Blake had quarrelled with Uncle Walter, and with Rose, and she had gone to a post in the Lake District. Emily was not going to have a new governess. She was going to a boarding school in Brussels, and the Vicar's wife would take her there. She promised to write to Sally from Brussels.

Sally was torn between distress that Emily had been parted from Miss Blake, and pride that she was to be educated abroad. The visits to Miss Carrington's home had been discontinued when Cathy and Matthew were ill, but Sally told the headmistress of Emily's move at the first opportunity. Miss Carrington seemed impressed.

'A finishing school,' she said. 'Excellent. It will give her more poise, and improve her grasp of languages.'

Sally basked in Emily's reflected glory, but at the same time she worried about the row which seemed to have provoked the decision. She wrote to Hester asking for more information, but there was no reply, so she realised that she would have to wait for Emily's next letter to learn what had happened.

She was very busy with orders from Bold Street at this time, and often she sat up after midnight doing the intricate embroidery and other work she could do without disturbing the household with the sound of the sewing machine.

Often she had a dragging pain in her back, but otherwise the pregnancy went smoothly, although the child did not seem very active

189

in her womb. Secretly she worried that she might be carrying twins, because she had grown so large and unwieldy, but she said nothing of this fear to anyone else.

A letter came from Emily in early March, but it was short and stilted. She wrote that the journey to Brussels was very interesting, the lessons were very interesting, she was well and she hoped that they were all well.

'It doesn't tell us anything,' Sally said. 'It doesn't even sound like Emily. Oh, Lawrie, I wonder what's wrong?'

'Nothing's wrong, love,' Lawrie said. 'They probably check the girls' letters for spelling mistakes and all that, so Emily might feel strange knowing that they'll read it.'

Sally agreed that that might be the reason, and hoped that the next letter would be better.

Sally was hoping that Matthew would escape further illness as the winter was so nearly over, but he suddenly developed bronchitis again. It was the worst attack he had suffered, and he was so ill that Sally sent to the Dispensary for a doctor. By an unlucky chance it was the same man who had attended Alfred and John in 1890. He was thinner and greyer, and much less pompous in manner, but Matthew recognized him immediately, and answered his questions in surly monosyllables.

When Sally returned to the bedroom after showing the doctor out, Matthew was scowling.

'What's the good of bringing *him* here?' he snapped. 'He done no good to me lads, and he'll do none fer me.'

'Oh, Da, this is different,' Sally protested. 'No one could have saved the lads, but he's given me pills and cough mixture for you, and he's told me how to relieve your breathing.'

'The miracle man,' Matthew sneered, but a bout of coughing made him clutch the sheets as he tried to gulp air into his lungs.

The doctor's remedies gave him some relief and he fell into an exhausted sleep, disturbed at intervals by bouts of coughing. He insisted on having a bottle of laudanum beside his bed, and as soon as the worst of the bronchitis was over, he took large doses of it every night. When Sally protested he said roughly, 'Mind yer own business, girl. I've got ter get me sleep and get back ter werk.'

He returned to work after three weeks off, but he still looked grey-faced and shaky.

'Are you sure you're well enough for work, Da?' Sally asked timidly, when she saw how he collapsed into his chair, gasping for breath, when he returned from work.

'I'm orl right. The lads are carrying me till I get me strength back. I've done the same fer them,' he replied. His temper was so short that Sally was afraid to ask any more questions. Even Lawrie, usually so forbearing with Matthew, had several rows with him, but Lawrie himself had been edgy for some time, and one night matters came to a head.

The two little girls were playing with a doll while the men read and Sally sewed, and suddenly a quarrel broke out. Before Sally could speak, Lawrie had jumped to his feet, smacked both children and

190

bundled them off to bed, threatening to put the doll in the bin. Cathy's sobs and Mary's screams seemed only to infuriate him more, and he dashed into the lobby, shouting threats up the stairs. Sally was aghast.

'Lawrie,' she began as he came back into the kitchen, but before she could say any more he shouted, 'Don't *you* start!' He snatched up his cap. 'I'm going for a drink,' he said, flinging out of the room.

Before he reached the front door, Matthew said loudly, 'More fool you, girl, ruinin' yer eyes sewing fer him ter drink the money.'

The only reply from Lawrie was a loud bang of the front door, but Sally threw down her work and burst into tears.

'Don't sit there whingeing,' Matthew said. 'Leave off the sewing and let him see he can't have everything his own way. Why should you be werking yerself in ter the ground, making the money? He'll let yer while yer'll do it.'

Sally raised her head, anger damming her tears.

'You know that's not true,' she said furiously. 'Money's the last thing Lawrie thinks about, and he's the one who's always trying to make me do less.' As usual when Lawrie was criticized she leapt to his defence, forgetting her own anger with him.

She did not resume sewing, but when Matthew had taken his rum and hot water and gone off to bed in a huff, she crouched miserably over the fire, feeling ill used and sorry for herself. I suppose Da will say he's narky because he's ill, and Lawrie will blame it on the worry we've had, she thought, but haven't I been worried too, and more ill than they know, but I'm supposed to just carry on. Her tears flowed, and when Lawrie had still not returned at ten o'clock, she made herself a cup of tea and went to bed. She heard him come in and move about, banking up the fire and locking up, but when he came upstairs she kept her back resentfully turned against him.

The following morning when the men had gone to work and the children to school, she quickly tidied up and then sat down to complete the sewing she had left undone the previous night. She still felt angry and unhappy and often the stitches were blurred by tears in her eyes, but shortly after midday there was a knock at the door, and she was delighted to find Mrs Malloy standing on the step.

'What a lovely surprise, Mrs Mal,' she exclaimed, smiling as she ushered Mrs Malloy in to the kitchen.

'Aye, I'm not often up this road,' Mrs Malloy said, 'but I thought I'd try out me legs, girlie, and thank God I'm moving grand.'

'I'm so glad to see you, Mrs Mal. I was feeling so downhearted,' Sally said. She stirred the fire and put the kettle on for tea, and Mrs Malloy looked at her shrewdly.

'What's troubling ye, child?' she asked.

'Oh, all sorts of things. I'm just fed up with everybody and everything, especially Lawrie and my da,' said Sally.

'Is your da gone to his work then? I heard he was bad again.'

'Yes, he had a terrible dose this time, but he's gone back to work – too soon, I think, but I daren't say. He's so narky nothing suits, and he's picking on everyone.'

'Poor Matt. He was ever a bad patient, and ye've had yer own share with him this winter, girlie.'

'And Lawrie,' Sally said, growing ever more indignant as she thought of her wrongs. 'He's started flying off the handle, too. Da says he's got something on his mind, but what about me? I've got plenty to worry about, but they think they can have moods and take it out on me, and I'm not supposed to have feelings.' She began to cry, and Mrs Malloy clicked her tongue sympathetically.

'Put up yer feet on this stool,' she said. 'Ye've been working too hard altogether with the way ye are. Ye're very big, girlie.'

'Yes, that's another thing I'm worried about,' Sally sobbed. 'What if it's twins?'

Mrs Malloy shook her head. 'No, I don't think so, child. You look more like ye're carrying a lot of water.' She looked at Sally's hands. 'Yes, yer hands are puffy, girl, and so is yer face. Ye'll have to rest yerself more, child.'

'There's so much from Libby's though, and they're so particular,' said Sally. 'I daren't take too long over them either.'

The kettle boiled, and Mrs Malloy jumped to her feet. 'I'll make the tea, girlie, while ye rest. Now when ye take in the dress ye're working on, why don't ye tell the old wan there that ye can't take any more for a while, because ye're due to be confined?'

'I don't want to offend her,' Sally said doubtfully, 'I need the work even more now with Da's wages being so chancy.'

'Now what kind of an unnatural creature would take offence at that, girlie? Anyhow, she'd be cutting off her nose to spite her face, the grand sewing ye do for her, and so cheap.'

Sally sipped the hot tea, feeling comforted. 'That's what I'll do, Mrs Mal,' she said. 'It *has* been getting me down lately, especially worrying about getting it just right.'

'And don't be worrying yerself about yer Da and Lawrie. Aren't they all the same, the men? There was a priest giving out from the pulpit the other Sunday – "Women are the weaker vessels" says he. I nearly laughed out loud, God forgive me. Sure where would they be without us, and haven't we got them bate in every way?'

Sally laughed. 'It's true, Mrs Mal, but they'd be very surprised to hear it all the same.'

'Isn't that all that saves them, that they're too thick to see how they're depending on us? Don't be worrying yerself about moods now, Sally. Just take care of yerself, and the little one yer carrying, and let the rest go hang.'

Sally looked with affection at the little woman, perched like a small, brown bird on the chair.

'Oh, I *wish* you still lived next door to us, Mrs Mal,' she said, realising afresh how much she missed Mrs Malloy's knowledge and love of the family, and her rock-like commonsense.

'I wish so, too, child, but I'm glad I tried out me legs today so I know I'll be able to get to you when yer time comes.'

'Thank God for that,' Sally said, with heartfelt relief.

'And the children now. Are they all right?'

Sally hesitated for a moment, then she said, quietly, 'I don't want to be burdening you with all my troubles, Mrs Mal, but I *am* worried about them and I can't talk to Lawrie these days.'

'No burden, girl. What's troublin' ye?'

'I don't know what to do with Mary. She's so disobedient and so – so sly. I tell her not to go out and she's gone as soon as I turn my back. She knows she'll get a smack when she comes in, but she doesn't care.'

'It's just wildness. Sure she can't help her nature,' the old lady said.

But Sally burst out, 'There's more. The gas penny – I always leave a penny handy on top of the meter. I think she's taken it but she denies it.'

'Ye couldn't have forgot, maybe,' suggested Mrs Mal.

'I tried to believe that, but when the second one went – I don't leave one there now. The worst is, I might have been doubting Cathy, only . . .'

She stopped, her lips trembling, and Mrs Malloy said gently, 'What else, girl? Get it all off yer chest now.'

'A while ago, I left one and six I got for making a skirt on the parlour table. Later on I couldn't find the sixpence, only the shilling, although I looked high and low, and that night Mary had red stains off sweets on her face and her pinny. She said Mrs Killey gave her three-pence.' Sally paused to wipe her eyes and Mrs Malloy said nothing.

'I was sure, *sure* then that she'd taken the sixpence but she brazened it out. Even said I could ask Mrs Killey, knowing very well I couldn't let people know she was a thief.'

'Well now, child, ye've got yerself too upset altogether over this. There's many a child goes through a spell like this. Don't be thinking now she'll end up in the Bridewell.'

'But I've always done my best for her. She's had more than most kids, and then to steal what I'd worked hard for!'

'She wouldn't see it like that. She's just that quick she'd have it whipped up and spent without a thought. But ye should tell Lawrie and get him to speak to her.'

'And Cathy – she's so picky over her food she's driving me mad. Won't eat this and won't eat that, when she *needs* it. There's many a hungry child in this town would be glad of it, but if I say a word to her, she sits there crying.'

Mrs Malloy stood up and poured another cup of tea for Sally.

'Drink that,' she said, 'and listen to me. Everything has got on top of ye, but stop and think, girl. Mary's very wild and thoughtless, but think how she was when Cathy was ill, so she has a feeling heart. And the moods: do ye not see where they come from when ye look at yer da? At least she's lively with them, and wouldn't ye rather have that than the way he is?'

'I never thought of that,' said Sally.

'Aye, and Cathy. She's picky and mardy because the weakness is on her yet, but remember, girl, ye could have been sitting here grieving for her, and her in her grave.'

'Oh, Mrs Mal, don't say that,' implored Sally, but Mrs Malloy said firmly, 'Aren't I only making ye see that these troubles ye have are not

193

the end. They'll pass over. Death is the only thing that can't be cured.'

They both sat in silence for a moment, as Sally pondered on Mrs Malloy's words and realised the truth of them. Then she said humbly, 'I'm sorry to have poured all that out on you, Mrs Mal, after you struggling up here to see me.'

'I'm glad ye did,' Mrs Malloy said emphatically. 'Aren't ye all as dear to me as me own flesh and blood, and you most of all, girl. I just want ye to see that too much has been on ye these months while ye haven't been able for it, that's all, but out of all ye told me, child, there's only one thing troubles me.'

'Mary's stealing,' said Sally.

'Not at all, not at all, sure that's only a child's naughtiness. No, it's when ye said ye can't talk to Lawrie these days. What's wrong at all?'

Sally sat looking into the fire, her face troubled.

'I don't know, Mrs Mal. I don't know how it started, but he just seems so far away all the time, and yet so touchy. Da says he has something on his mind, but you know what Da's like. He's always looking for faults, and he makes things worse.' Sally was unwilling to repeat Matthew's remarks about the sewing money, even to Mrs Malloy, so she went on, 'Lawrie turned on the children last night because they were fighting over a doll, and of course Da had to butt in, as if they don't have enough rows of their own. I'm fed up with the whole lot of them.'

'Well, ye surprise me, girl, and that's the truth. It's not like Lawrie at all, especially the way you are.'

'Oh, he still does a lot to help me,' Sally hastened to say. 'And it's the first time he's lost his temper with the girls. It's just this sort of barrier between us, and I don't know what it is.'

'Well, I'll tell ye now, it won't be anything bad, for he's too good a lad, Sally. The leopard doesn't change his spots, as they say, and he won't have changed his nature. Just let things take their course, and don't be worrying.'

Sally smiled. 'I'll try not to, Mrs Mal. I feel better already.'

'That's good. Let it all wash over ye, and do ye study just yerself and the child ye're carrying. The good weather will be on us soon, please God, and we'll all be the better of it.' She picked up her shawl.

'I'll have to be going, girl. Ye'll have the children in on top of ye, and the sewing half done. Don't forget what I told ye now.'

'I won't,' Sally promised. She bent impulsively and kissed Mrs Malloy, and when the older woman had gone, she went in and picked up her sewing, feeling happier than she had felt for a long time.

Chapter Thirty

Lawrie and Matthew said little during the evening meal, even when Sally told them of Mrs Malloy's visit. Later, when the girls had cleared away and washed up the dishes, Lawrie went into the back kitchen, and Sally could see him folding the pile of dry clothes, and the sheets, which she found awkward to deal with now, and putting them through the mangle to save ironing.

The girls said goodnight to him, and went up to bed. When he came back into the kitchen, Sally was about to tell him more about Mrs Malloy, but he suddenly picked up his cap from the dresser.

'I'm going to a meeting, Sally,' he said. 'Why don't you go to bed? I'll be back before ten.' She made no reply, and he bent and kissed her briefly before going out. She finished the dress for Libby's and folded it carefully in a piece of sheeting, then turned to her father.

'I'm going to bed, Da,' she said. 'Can I make your cocoa now?'

'No, leave it,' he growled. 'I've only just had me tea.' Sally took down the tin of cocoa and a mug, and placed them ready on the table, but he pushed them aside impatiently.

'Leave it, I said. Get ter bed. Yer've had yer orders from the boss ganger.'

Sally's face grew red with anger, but she went into the back kitchen, and drank a cup of water, while she composed herself. 'Let it wash over ye.' Mrs Malloy's words passed through her mind, and placing her hand reassuringly on the bulge which contained her child, she said goodnight quietly to her father, and went up to bed.

She fell asleep immediately, and slept heavily for a few hours, then woke to hear her father mounting the stairs, and Lawrie moving about, leaving things ready for the morning. She pretended to be asleep when he came up, but for the rest of the night she slept badly, troubled by strange dreams, and by pains in different parts of her body.

In the morning she dragged herself unwillingly downstairs. Lawrie always lit the fire, and it was burning brightly. She huddled over it, feeling too ill to do anything, but the girls had dressed and washed themselves ready for school.

'Mary, cut the bread,' Sally said, 'and you spread the dripping, Cathy.' The two little girls, alarmed by her white face, quickly made their breakfasts, and Cathy brought a cup of tea to her mother.

'Are you all right, Mam?' she asked anxiously. Sally tried to smile.

'I'll be all right in a minute, love,' she said. 'Come straight home at dinner time, both of you. I might need some messages.'

When they had gone she sat on by the fire, and it took an effort of will even to get up for another cup of tea. She was unable to eat anything, but gradually she began to feel a little better, and after a while she banked up the fire with slack, and got ready to walk to Bold Street.

She intended to take Mrs Malloy's advice and refuse further work, but the woman who dealt with her was in such a fury that she gave Sally no opportunity to speak.

'Here,' she said, snatching the dress from Sally and thrusting another one at her. 'You know the design. I want it tomorrow.'

She shook out the dress that Sally had finished.

'I warn you, this had better be right,' she said. 'I've had nothing but trouble today.' She flung away, and Sally found herself being handed her pay and hustled out by another woman before she could speak. She walked wearily down Bold Street, her headache seeming to grow worse with every step, until she felt as though her eyes were closing because of the weight pressing on her forehead. Even with her eyes closed, lights seemed to be flashing before them.

She reached the bottom of the road and stood leaning against a post by Central Station, until with sudden desperation she hailed a cab. It would take most of her pay, but she felt that she *must* get home.

Outside her house she thankfully paid off the cabman, and stumbled in, dropping the dress on the sofa and falling into a chair. Waves of pain washed over her, and she realised with terror that her labour was beginning.

I'll have to get help, she thought, but her limbs seemed weighted down, and the pain crushed her, leaving her unable to move. Suddenly she heard a noise in the yard, and saw Mrs Kilgannon's bony figure approaching. She wore a sacking apron and a man's cap was skewered to her grizzled hair, but an angel in shining robes could not have been more welcome to Sally.

Mrs Kilgannon seemed to take in Sally's situation at a glance.

'Ah, yer times on yer, luv,' she said. 'Grab holt of me neck and I'll get yer up the stairs.' She was surprisingly strong, and she had Sally upstairs in a moment.

With rough kindness, she helped Sally to undress and put on her nightdress, then she clattered downstairs to send for help. Sally lay back, thankful to have reached the haven of her bed, but soon waves of agony washed over her, until she felt as though she was drowning in a sea of pain. She was vaguely conscious of noise and movement of people in the room, and at one stage of Mrs Malloy bending over her saying, 'Push, girl, push. Ye'll have to do all the work. The child can do nothing to help itself.'

She tried to speak, to ask if the child was dead, but the words would not come. Some time later her pain seemed to reach a crescendo, then she heard a voice.

'Ah, God, an' a little lad, too! It's blue, so it is.'

She was conscious of nothing else, only a relief from struggle and a great weakness. Once she opened her eyes and saw a dark square of window, and figures moving about in the lamplight, then she closed them again.

The doctor bent over her. 'Mrs Ward, Mrs Ward, wake up. It's all over. Mrs Ward.'

She turned her head away pettishly. Leave me alone, she tried to say, although she made no sound.

It was so peaceful and pleasant, she felt, floating gently away to a world of brightness and warmth. 'She's going, she's going,' she heard dimly, then her shoulder was suddenly gripped and she was shaken.

'Sally,' Mrs Malloy said urgently, 'Sally, rouse yerself, girl. Cathy's taken a bad turn. What should we do?'

Sally's eyes flew open, and she was lifted forward by Mrs Malloy while pillows were thrust behind her. In a swift change she was back from her journey.

'Cathy,' she said. 'Cathy.'

'Yes, what should we do?' asked Mrs Malloy.

'Bathe her face,' Sally said mechanically, trying to push back the bedclothes and get up. Lawrie restrained her and dropped to his knees beside her, cradling her in his arms.

'She's all right, love,' he said. 'Cathy's all right.'

'I had to give ye a shock, child,' Mrs Malloy said. 'Sure ye were sliding away on us altogether.' They called Cathy, and she came into the bedroom, white and trembling.

'Mama's all right, love,' Lawrie said as Sally lay back on the pillows, trying to smile at her frightened child. 'She's just tired.'

Mrs Kilgannon swooped on Cathy. 'Ah, luk at 'er, her eyes like piss 'oles in snow,' she cried. 'Come on with Killey, luv, an' we'll make a cup of tea.'

They went out together, and Sally closed her eyes, drifting off again in her delightful dream. Lawrie's arms tightened round her.

'Oh, Sal, love, don't leave us,' he whispered, tears running down his face and wetting Sally's cheeks. Thoughts of Lawrie and her children, her father and Emily and Mrs Malloy, floated through Sally's bemused mind, and reluctantly she drew back against the flow of the pleasant stream.

Never again, though, did Sally fear death. In the years to come, although she valued life because she was happy with her family, death itself held no fear for her. She remembered the gentle floating, the sensation of warmth and brightness when she approached so near to death, and she knew that when her time came, she would feel no fear, only sadness at leaving those she loved.

She slept intermittently during the night, but whenever she awoke, Lawrie was awake, too, bending anxiously over her. Twice he went down to make her a drink, and on the second occasion she felt able to to say weakly, 'Is the baby dead, Lol?'

'Yes, love,' he said quietly. 'He'd been dead for a while, the doctor said. That's why it was so hard for you.'

'A little lad,' she murmured. He held her close.

'Yes, love, a little lad,' he said gently. She said no more and was asleep again when Lawrie and Matthew were getting ready for work, and Mrs Malloy came in.

'Ah now, sleep is a great healer,' she whispered. 'She'll be better

197

able to bear the loss when she gets a few days over her, and plenty of sleep.'

Everything seemed remote to Sally, and she lay passively while Mrs Malloy and Mrs Kilgannon tended her and ran the house. Mrs Kilgannon told of seeing Sally arriving home in a cab with a parcel, and going in to see what was happening. They found the parcel on the sofa, and Mrs Kilgannon volunteered to take it to Libby's and explain that Sally was ill. Sally took no interest in what they did but only lay quietly, often weeping silently for her dead baby, the tears trickling from her eyes, soaking the hair round her ears and the pillow beneath her head.

Mrs Kilgannon took the parcel to the shop and returned in great indignation.

'Bad luck to the bloody old cow,' she said. 'Snatched the dress off me, and said her customer would be very annoyed. "Mrs Ward's dying," I said, an' all she said was, it was "inconvenient". I gave her a mouthful, I can tell yer.'

Although Sally realised that she would probably be refused any more work from Libby's, especially when Mrs Kilgannon gave more details of her battle, she felt too ill to care.

Even when she was up and about again, she knew that the close eye-straining work would be more than her nerves could stand, yet she worried about the loss of the money involved. She did the minimum of housework, and sent the children for the shopping, but she felt constantly tired. Mary was now nearly ten years old, and Cathy six, but it was the younger child who was the greatest help in the house. Mary did exactly what she was told to do, then escaped, never offering any help not demanded by Sally or Lawrie, but she was an excellent shopper.

She refused to be fobbed off with faded cabbages or rancid bacon, unlike Cathy who was too timid to protest, and who wept when she was told to take things back.

'I'll take it back,' Mary would offer, ever ready to do battle. In the end, she did all the shopping, and Cathy helped her mother about the house. Sally and Cathy grew very close at this time.

Sally was delighted one day when Mary returned from school with a bottle of smelling salts, and a kind letter from Miss Carrington, assuring her that the ladies of the Sewing Circle were distressed to hear of her illness, and would pray for her recovery.

As the days lengthened, and the weather improved, Sally became stronger, and several times she ventured out for a walk, clutching Lawrie's arm.

As she held his arm she realised how thin he had become, and looked anxiously at his gaunt, haggard face.

'You don't look well, Lol,' she said, but he brushed her concern aside.

'I'm fine. It's yourself you've got to worry about,' he said. The doctor had warned him that Sally was not strong enough for another pregnancy, and at night he lay stiffly on his own side of the bed, well away from Sally. He still seemed unusually silent, although he

198

adopted a cheerful air if he thought he was being watched, but she tried to believe that it was because of the worry he had suffered.

One Saturday in late April Sally felt so much better that she decided to walk down to meet Lawrie returning from work. He had come home late on several nights, because he had been preparing the harness and making the decorations for the horses to wear for the May Day procession, but Sally thought that she could sit on a seat in Shaw Street Park to wait if he was delayed.

She had barely started down the hill when she saw Lawrie turn the corner, walking with a woman whose basket he was carrying. They were talking animatedly, and suddenly Lawrie's hearty laugh rang out, the laugh which she had not heard for months. Sally turned and fled back to the house.

So that was it! That was what he had on his mind. The shock was more severe because another woman was something she had never even considered. She sat in the chair, white-faced and shaking, too shocked even to cry. It was nearly half an hour later when Lawrie returned home, and Sally had partly recovered.

She was standing in the back kitchen, cutting up spring cabbage, when Lawrie walked up the yard. As he came behind her and bent to kiss her, she moved her head so that his lips touched only her hair. *Judas*, she thought bitterly, but she said nothing, and Lawrie walked through to the kitchen, seeming to notice nothing wrong.

'You should see old Bluebell,' he said. 'You'd think she knew we were getting ready for May Day. Trotting along like a two year old, she was.'

Sally felt constrained to speak and she said stiffly, 'Mrs Mal says there won't be so many floats in the procession this year, with trade so bad and so many firms going out of business.' From where she stood she could see Lawrie through the angle of the door, unobserved by him, and she was shocked by his reaction to her careless words. He collapsed into a chair as though he had been struck and put his head in his hands.

Impulsively Sally dropped the knife and rushed to him, her anger forgotten at the sight of his distress.

'What is it, Lol? What's wrong?' she exclaimed, cradling his head in her arms. He groaned.

'Oh, Sal, how does Mrs Mal know that?'

'A few of the women in Gell Street have lost cleaning jobs because of it, the bad trade I mean, and I think people at the church talk to her about firms going down, people like the Lightbodys. But why –?'

He drew her down on to his knee. 'I didn't want to say anything until I was sure, love,' he said, 'but I think you'd better be prepared. The firm's breaking up.'

'Breaking up,' Sally repeated. 'But why? I thought you were busy.'

'I don't know what's wrong, and that's the truth, Sal. Maybe the boss isn't able for some of these crafty business fellers, but God, he's fought hard to keep things going. We've all pulled with him, taking extra loads or anything, but it's no use. I think we'll go under.'

'But what about the Mayday?' Sally said.

'Aye, well, we've told him we'll put on a good show. Just let those swine who've undercut him see we're behind him, and who knows, Sal, it might turn the tide for him.'

'D'you think it might?' Sally said hopefully, but Lawrie shook his head.

'No, I don't really. I think it's too late, but at least we'll go down with all flags flying.'

Sally kissed him. 'Don't worry, love,' she said. 'You'll get something else. Look how quickly you got this job.'

Lawrie pressed his cheek against her hair. 'I've looked everywhere,' he said in a muffled voice. 'Nothing doing.' They clung together, both silent while Sally tried to absorb the shock of the news, and Lawrie struggled with conflicting feelings; relief because he had shared his worry, and guilt that he had upset Sally.

'How long have you known?' she asked presently.

'Months. We couldn't believe it at first, didn't want to, but then we got more and more sure.'

'Why didn't you tell me?' she said.

'How could I? God knows you had enough to bear, and then being so ill yourself as well.'

'I wish you'd told me,' Sally said. 'I knew there was something wrong, and I've been worrying about it.'

'That's what I wanted to avoid,' he said. 'At first I hoped it wouldn't happen, then I wanted to land something else before I told you, and now I've gone and blurted it all out.'

'Never mind,' Sally said. 'Something will turn up.' She spoke mechanically, because although she now knew what had been on Lawrie's mind during the past months, she still wondered about the scene she had witnessed, and waited for Lawrie to mention the woman, but he only talked, endlessly it seemed to Sally, about all that had happened at work.

It was when Matthew came in and Lawrie was chatting to him, that he spoke of her.

'D'you remember Billy Rooney, Matt? He was a shipmate of mine, and I think you knew his father.'

'Aye, old Clasher Rooney we used to call him.'

'That's the one. I met Billy Rooney's missis today, and she was telling me some of his antics. God, he was a great shipmate. Nothing daunted him, and he'd get a laugh out of nothing.'

'Old Clasher was just the same,' Matthew said. 'A right card he was.'

Lawrie laughed. 'I was telling Mrs Rooney about one time when we had this feller on our watch, proper Bible thumper, and Billy was always leading him on, pretending to be converted. One night after we'd been in port someone had pinched a woman's dress, and Billy put it on and lay in the other feller's bunk. When he went to get in, Billy held up his arms and the feller jumped back as though he'd been stung. Give him his due though, he laughed too. Billy took a lot of the starch out of him.'

'Aye, there's always a comedian in any gang,' Matthew said.

'Where did you meet Mrs Rooney?' Sally asked.

Lawrie said readily, 'Just coming up from Shaw Street. She had a basket that very near weighed a ton, so I gave her a lift with it. She's got four lads, and she says they all eat like horses, so I told her to get them to carry the grub home with her.'

A weight had rolled away from Sally in spite of the news about Lawrie's job, and she laughed when he told them about the monkey which Billy had brought home from his last trip, telling his family that an African Chief had given it to him for saving his life.

Sally and Lawrie decided to say nothing to Matthew about their worry, hoping that something would happen before he had to be told, and the following weeks were peaceful.

The firm still struggled on, and Sally regained some of her strength. She managed to get some plain sewing from two sisters who ran a small workshop in Salisbury Street, who employed her as Libby's had done, for rush orders, but the pay was much poorer than Libby's. The forewoman at Libby's had made it plain that Sally could expect no more work from them.

Mrs Malloy's health had improved also, and she often walked up to see Sally.

'Did ye ever hear from Emily?' she asked one day, and Sally took a letter from behind the clock.

'This is the last one,' she said, and began to read aloud. The letter was the usual formula. The weather was cold, her studies were interesting, she was happy, but at the end she had added that she was not returning home for the summer holidays. She was to have a holiday in Switzerland, with one of the mistresses and two girls whose families were in India.

'So she's not coming home!' Mrs Malloy exclaimed. 'That's a queer do altogether, Sally. Sure, ye'd think they'd be broken hearted sending her away, and longing to see a sight of her again.'

'I thought that,' Sally said. 'I wrote again to Aunt Hester, but she didn't answer. She never does. If I knew where Miss Blake had gone I'd write to her, but Emily doesn't seem to know.'

'Ah, well, at least the child doesn't seem to be worrying, and she's getting a grand sight of the world anyhow, and a fine easy life, too.' She sighed and shook her head. 'Isn't life a lot harder now for some? I was after meeting poor Mrs Cassidy yesterday, and she was heart-broken about her girl.'

'Why? What's happened?' Sally cried in alarm.

'It seems Agnes is expecting, and the quare feller is taking no care at all of her. Mrs Cassidy says he works Agnes like a skivvy. Won't let her serve in the shop, but has her dragging and pulling at heavy bales, and cleaning out the shop as well as the house. Her mam says she's half starved too, and she has to come home to get a decent feed.'

'But that's terrible!' Sally said. 'I must go and see her. It's so near, but I just haven't had time lately. It seems to take me so long to do everything.'

'Things will be better with ye soon, please God,' Mrs Malloy said as she got up to go. 'The bit of sunshine makes all the difference.' She went out, for once leaving Sally more depressed than when she arrived.

It was nearly a week later before Sally found time to go to James's shop. There was no sign of Agnes, but James grudgingly lifted a flap in the counter to allow Sally to go through to the house. Agnes was in a dusty stockroom, unpacking a bale of goods. She greeted Sally joyfully, and took her upstairs to the house part.

'How are you, love?' Sally asked, looking with dismay at Agnes. She had lost all her fresh colour, and her face looked grey and pinched.

'I'm all right, Sal,' she said. 'After all, having a baby isn't an illness, is it?' Sally thought this sounded like a quotation from James, so she said nothing. Agnes made tea, but while they were drinking it, a young girl came upstairs.

'Please, Mrs Horton,' she said. 'Mr Horton says, have you unpacked the collars?' Agnes lifted her chin.

'Not yet, tell him,' she said, and the girl withdrew, looking frightened. Sally felt that she might be causing trouble for Agnes, so she drank the tea quickly, and prepared to leave.

'Will you come and see us on Sunday, Ag?' she said. 'Come for tea, you and James, or you on your own, whichever suits you.'

'I'll – I'll see,' Agnes murmured.

'I'll ask James on my way out,' Sally said. He was deferentially ushering out a customer when she went through to the shop, and as soon as he was free, Sally said quickly, 'Will you come to tea on Sunday, James? You and Agnes.'

He pulled at his wispy beard. 'Er – Sunday. It's a very busy day,' he said.

Sally pretended to be shocked. '*Sunday*? Surely you don't work on *Sunday*, James.'

'No, no,' he said hurriedly. 'But Church, er, sacred reading.'

'No problem. I'd only expect you in the afternoon,' Sally said. 'I'll see you on Sunday then.' She turned away, thinking angrily, the creeping whited sepulchre!

On Sunday she prepared a lavish meal, and Agnes and James did full justice to it. Afterwards Lawrie kept James talking, and sent the girls out to wash up, so that Agnes and Sally had the opportunity for a quiet chat. Agnes did not complain, but it was clear that she was unhappy, and that she was bullied by James. Both Sally and Lawrie disliked him more every time they saw him, and Sally grieved for her friend.

After the visitors had gone, Sally and Lawrie walked up to Rupert Hill, to sit in quiet companionship in the dusk. As Sally sat with Lawrie's arms around her, and her head on his shoulder, she felt that she had never really appreciated how lucky she was to have him as a husband. With Lawrie beside her, she could face any trouble that came and deal with it, she thought.

Chapter Thirty-One

Sally's fortitude was tested sooner than she expected. At the end of August Lawrie's boss went bankrupt, and he was out of work.

'It's almost a relief,' he told Sally. 'It's been hanging over me for so long.' During the first week he managed to get three days loading wagons at a tobacco warehouse, and two half days on the docks, so his earnings were not much less than his usual wage. The next week he was less fortunate, and despite all his efforts, he was only able to earn ten shillings.

'That's the regular wage for farmhands,' Sally said cheerfully. 'We've just been spoiled.'

In spite of her brave words, she worried about the future. Her own earnings were so much less than previous years, and prices were rising, even though trade was so bad. Her father had already suffered a cut of two shillings a week in his wages, because of falling orders. Lawrie tried hard to obtain work, and often Sally woke at three thirty in the morning, to find that he had already gone from the bed, trying to find work on the docks, or in the markets.

She had always been skilful at making nourishing meals from cheap ingredients, and now she also cut back on all the small luxuries they had grown used to. One of her first economies was to return the piano.

'It's two shillings a week, and sixpence for the teacher, and Mary's not making any shape at all at it,' she told Lawrie.

'What about Cathy?' he asked doubtfully.

'Oh, she's too young. By the time she's ready we'll have got over this patch, and we can get another piano,' Sally said.

'Well, you know best, Sal,' he said, and Matthew agreed with the decision.

'You were flogging a dead horse, anyroad, girl,' he said. 'That one would rather be swinging round a lamp-post than playing a pianner.' Sally was relieved to see that Matthew was sympathetic towards Lawrie, and rarely criticised him now.

Since the Taff Vale judgement was given that unions could be sued for unlimited damages by employers, Matthew had ceased to argue with Lawrie about his political and union activities.

'Ye're in the right, lad,' he said once. 'The whole gang of them are lined up to tread the likes of us down. There's no justice fer werking men. The law is used *by* the rich and *for* the rich to keep us down. We do the werk and they get all the profit – and throw us off like old clothes when they've worn us out.'

Sally was relieved to see the harmony between the two men, although Lawrie rarely went to meetings now. He was too exhausted at night, and unwilling to spend even the few coppers it would cost.

Sally had told the piano firm that she would be unable to keep up payments on it, and the following week it was collected.

'I seen yer pianner going back,' Mrs. Kilgannon remarked at the first opportunity.

'Yes, Mary never practised,' Sally said. Mrs. Kilgannon looked sceptical.

'Yer could have kept it for furniture,' she said. 'It's nice to have a pianner in the parlour. Looks classy, I always say.'

'Do you?' Sally said sharply. 'Why? You haven't got a piano in yours, only a lodger.' Mrs Kilgannon flounced indoors and banged the door, and Sally went into her own house, feeling unrepentant. I'm in no mood for her nosing, she told herself. Lawrie was still struggling on, getting a few days of casual work each week, but unable to find a permanent job. In October he managed to get two full weeks in a timber yard, but when the order was filled, he was turned off.

Just before Christmas Mrs Malloy came with sad news. Agnes Cassidy had died in childbirth, after being in labour for two days and giving birth to a stillborn child. Mrs Malloy wept as she told Sally, and described Mrs Cassidy's grief.

'She's blaming herself, God help her, that she didn't bring Agnes home away from that feller. She says the girl was half starved and there was no strength in her.'

Sally stood dry-eyed, unable to comprehend the tragedy. 'I can't believe it,' she said. 'She was such a strong, healthy girl. How could she have gone down so quickly?'

'The midwife told Mrs Cassidy the cord was round the baby's neck, and he was only a poor little weakling anyhow. That's what killed him and gave her such trouble, and her mam swears it was all the lifting and dragging the poor girl had to do.'

'What about him, James?' Sally said, and Mrs Malloy made a sound of disgust.

'Bad luck to him. He didn't deserve such a good girl, and it's only her work he'll be missing, the miserable dog,' she said.

'I'll never forgive myself,' said Sally, starting to cry.

'I only went once to the shop to see her, and had them here once. I might have got her away from him.'

'Talk sense, girl. Like I told her mam, the law wouldn't let her leave him, no matter what went on, and ye may depend he'd have had the law on her if she tried, the same feller. Ah, well, she's out of all her trouble now, Lord ha' mercy on her.'

Sally grieved deeply for Agnes, and reproached herself for not doing more to help her, but soon other troubles drove the thought of Agnes from her mind. Cathy developed a hoarse, racking cough, and none of Sally's remedies seem to ease it. She watched anxiously as Cathy grew paler and thinner. The weather was bad, so she kept the child indoors, and sent a note to the headmistress by Mary.

'It doesn't matter her being off. She's a dunce anyway,' said Mary frankly. 'She's bottom of the class at arithmetic.'

'I like English and History,' Cathy said.

204

'Yes, but you can't do sums,' said Mary.

'All right, Miss Clever Clogs,' Sally said sharply. 'Just take the note and have less to say.'

When Mary had gone, Cathy said quietly, 'It's true, Mam. I can't do sums.'

Sally smiled at her. 'Never mind, we'll get Mary to help you, seeing she's so clever, and you can help her with English, because you're better than her at that.'

She slipped her arm about Cathy, and cuddled her, realising with anguish how thin and frail the child seemed. Often during the nights when Cathy's coughing sounded through the bedroom wall, Sally went in to bend over her and lift her to try to give her some ease, and went down to make her a soothing drink. It was in these hours that Sally's troubles seemed worst, yet they were only beginning.

Lawrie was still hunting for work, usually managing to find enough casual work to bring in ten to fifteen shillings a week, although one black week he only earned five shillings. Sally was still getting some sewing, although the embroidery work for the clerical tailors was now being done by a community of French nuns, but another firm of tailors supplied her with trousers to machine. The work was so badly paid that she had to work for many hours to make as much as she once had for the sewing of a dress, but at least the money was steady. Nobody seemed able to order dresses now, and Sally often looked back wistfully to the days when she had more work offered than she could handle, all well paid and pleasant work, too.

In February 1903 a crushing blow fell. Matthew's cough had been bad and his breathing laboured, but he continued to go to work. Sally went down to meet him every night to help him up the steep hill from Shaw Street, but one night there was a terrific gale. Ships in the river dragged their anchors, and several ships were sunk after collisions. On land, slates and chimney pots were hurled through the air, and people were blown over by strong gusts of wind. Sally met her father struggling along Shaw Street, his face purple with effort, and tried to help him along. They were making no headway until a burly man stopped and took Matthew's other arm.

'Come on, lad, I'll give yer an 'and,' he said, shielding Matthew from some of the wind with his body, and hurrying him up the hill.

When they arrived at Egremont Street he left them, waving away the thanks that Sally gasped.

She was alarmed by her father's congested face, and his struggle for breath. After he had rested for a few moments in his chair he decided to go to bed.

With Mary's help, she managed to get him upstairs, and she was relieved to hear Lawrie come in, in time to help her father to undress and get him into bed. She mixed rum and water and took it up, but her father refused it, and she and Lawrie watched in alarm as he fought for breath. Lawrie brought the bolster from their bed, and put it behind Matthew to lift him and help his breathing.

Finally he gasped out, 'I'm all right now, girl, I'm all right. Thank God I'm in me bed.'

205

'Should I get the doctor, Da?' Sally asked, but he waved her away.
'No I don't want nothing. Leave me alone.'

When she took the girls up to bed, she crept into her father's room, but he seemed to be asleep, lying back with closed eyes, and breath whistling through his parted lips. Later Lawrie went upstairs several times, but he seemed unchanged, so Sally went into the parlour and began to work on the trousers, treadling as quietly as possible in case she disturbed him.

The wind still howled around the house, shaking doors and windows, and bringing soot down the chimneys, but suddenly Sally heard a different sound. She dashed from the parlour into the lobby as Lawrie burst from the kitchen.

'It's your da,' he said, bounding upstairs ahead of Sally. When she reached the bedroom she found Lawrie bending over her father, who lay on the floor, breathing stertorously.

Together they managed to lift him into bed again, but Sally was alarmed to see that the left side of his face was twisted, and his left arm seemed useless.

'Oh, Lawrie, is it a seizure?' she said, but he shook his head warningly.

'You'll be all right now, Matt,' he said, bending over Matthew. 'You've had a bit of a fall.' Matthew tried to speak, but he could only make a guttural, unintelligible sound, and saliva dribbled from his twisted mouth.

'Yes, all right,' Lawrie said cheerfully, as though he understood the sounds. 'Try and get some sleep now, Matt.' They tucked the bed-clothes around him, and went downstairs.

As soon as they were in the kitchen out of earshot, Sally burst into tears.

'It *is* a seizure, Lol, I'm sure it is,' she sobbed.

'Yes, but it might come all right. It could just be the cold, or the struggle against the wind,' Lawrie said. 'Don't get upset now, Sal. It might pass off just as quick.'

'Do you think you should go to the Dispensary?' she said, but he shook his head.

'We'll have a job to get a doctor out in this, love. We'll see what a night's sleep does for your da.' Sally dried her eyes, only half convinced.

'I'll go and potter round up there and keep an eye on him,' Lawrie said. 'While you finish what you're doing. The sooner we get to bed the better, Sal, I think. We might have to be up in the night to see to him.'

She hurriedly finished her sewing, then after making cocoa for herself and Lawrie, she banked down the fire and went upstairs.

Lawrie was sitting by Matthew, who was mumbling incoherently, and urged Sally to get some sleep. He promised to waken her to take a turn at watching over her father. Sally woke at three o'clock, and sent Lawrie to get a few hours' sleep while she sat with Matthew. He mumbled constantly, and tried to get out of bed, using his good arm and leg as a lever. Sally was glad to see the darkness fading, and the dawn of a new day.

Lawrie went early to ask a doctor to call, but when he came, he could give them little comfort.

'His heart is very diseased,' he said. 'The paralysis may show some slight improvement, but he will almost certainly have another seizure which will probably prove fatal. Certainly he will never recover and he will always be bedridden.'

'There's no hope at all that he will get better, doctor?' asked Sally.

'None,' he said, closing his bag with a decisive click. 'He's more fortunate than many. A clean bed and a comfortable home, and a daughter to look after him.'

Sally showed him to the door, and went in to sit by the fire, trying to comprehend the blow which had so suddenly fallen upon them, and to foresee and accept the life which lay before her. Lawrie had gone out to get a few hours' work, clearing the debris of the storm, and even in that short time Sally was worn out when he came home, by her struggle to keep her father in bed. The doctor had left some medicine, which he said would help Matthew to sleep, but Sally had not managed to give it to him.

'It dribbles out of his mouth, and he won't keep still,' she told Lawrie tearfully when he came home.

'Have you tried giving it in the feeding cup?' asked Lawrie, and Sally shook her head. She was still too upset and confused to think clearly, but Lawrie's idea was a good one, and after Matthew had the medicine, he slept peacefully for a few hours. When Sally went downstairs again, she was pleased to find that Cathy had swept the floor, and washed the dishes. The fire was burning brightly, and Sally sat thankfully beside it while Lawrie made a pot of tea.

'You're a good girl, Cath,' she said, ruffling Cathy's curly hair as she crouched, carefully holding the toasting fork to the fire. 'Have you had anything to eat?'

'Me and Mary had dripping butties,' the child said. She was looking better, her cheeks less pale and her cough almost cured, but she was still too thin for Sally to stop worrying about her.

'We'll have to feed you up, love,' she said. 'You're missing a lot of lessons, off school for so long.'

Cathy's face fell. 'Don't you need me here, Mam?' she asked hopefully.

'You're a good help, love, but you should be at school really. You'll be sorry when you're older if you don't get the education.'

'What's that, Mam?' she asked, and Sally gave her a tired smile.

'You'd learn all about it at school,' she said, 'but you're not ready yet to go back.'

During the following weeks she often felt that she could not have managed without Cathy, who did many small tasks, and who could sit with Matthew, and call her mother if she was needed. This meant that Sally could snatch a few hours of sleep on the sofa, to make up for her broken nights.

Life became so difficult for Sally that often she looked back in amazement at the trivial worries of the past. Compared to the problems she faced now, all her previous tribulations shrank into insignificance.

Matthew was a difficult patient, resenting his dependence on Sally and Lawrie, yet demanding attention at all hours of the day and night. Lawrie was often in a quandary, needing to search for work, yet knowing that after an almost sleepless night, Sally was unfit to cope with the sick man. Matthew's left side was still useless, but the paralysis of his face had eased, so that now he could make himself understood. Sometimes this seemed to Sally a mixed blessing.

Ironically, the storm which seemed to have caused Matthew's seizure had created such havoc that Lawrie was able to get plenty of work on repairs. For several weeks he was able to earn almost a full week's wage, which was a great relief to Sally because as well as being without Matthew's wages, she found it almost impossible to do any sewing.

As the weeks went on Sally grew more and more tired. She had never really recovered from the birth of the stillborn child, emotionally or physically, and sometimes she wept from sheer exhaustion, seeing how much needed to be done, and knowing that she lacked the strength to do it. Even after Cathy returned to school she still tried to help her mother, but she was not yet seven years old, and could only help in small ways. She helped her most by sitting by her grandfather and talking to him, while her mother rested or worked in peace. Mary still did the shopping, but her visits to Matthew only seemed to agitate him, so Sally stopped forcing her to go to the sickroom.

Sally rarely saw Mrs Kilgannon now, partly because of the words about the piano, but chiefly because Sally was so harassed and Mrs Kilgannon was unwilling to help unless there was some drama involved, but one day Susan came when she was home on her day off. Now twenty years old, Susan was a tall, handsome girl, strengthened by years of good food and hard work, and she immediately took charge.

'Go and lay down,' she ordered Sally. 'I'll just go and change into me old clothes and I'll come and clean through for you. Go on, I'll call you if the old feller wants you.'

Sally was glad to obey, and she slept deeply for nearly two hours. She peeped into her father's room when she woke, but he had fallen asleep so she went downstairs. Everywhere was shining.

'Oh, Sue, how hard you've worked, and on your day off, too! I feel ashamed,' she said, but Susan only laughed.

'I enjoyed it,' she said. 'D'you want a cup of tea?'

'Yes, but I'll make it,' Sally said.

'No, you won't. Sit down,' Susan commanded. 'I made a drink for your ould feller, and I told him you were having a lay down, because you were tired out. He promised me he wouldn't make no noise.'

'He's asleep now,' Sally said.

Susan smiled knowingly. 'Aye, I thought he might be,' she said.

Sally was about to ask what Susan meant, but before she could speak, Susan began to tell her about life in the big house where she worked.

She said she had hated the work of a kitchenmaid, and in one of her many changes of employment, she had managed to train as a parlourmaid.

'I've got the looks for it, see,' she said proudly.

Sally had already heard some of Susan's adventures from Mary, who hung on Susan's words when she was at home on her day off, but she enjoyed sitting chatting with Susan and sipping tea, and was sorry when she had to go.

'I'm so grateful, Sue,' she said. 'You don't know what it means to me to have help like this. Everything was getting on top of me.'

'I'm glad to do it, Mrs Ward. You were good to me when I was a kid. Remember the day out at New Brighton? I was talking about it to the ould feller upstairs. He was good to me, too.'

The visit cheered Sally immensely, and Susan's cleaning gave her a fresh start with the housework. Matthew was surprisingly amiable when he woke.

'That's a good girl,' he mumbled. 'Strong. Lifted me like a feather.' He said nothing about Susan's lecture about Sally's need for rest, but she noticed that he was much less demanding that night.

Sally's savings in the teapot had been quickly used, to provide extra bedding and other items needed for Matthew's nursing, or to eke out Lawrie's wages in the weeks when he could only earn a few shillings. Sometimes Sally could earn a little by sewing, while Lawrie looked after Matthew, but lately that tiny amount had been needed immediately, to provide a meal for the family or some invalid dish for Matthew.

Gradually Sally realised that she would have to pawn or sell the contents of the parlour, which she had been so proud of. She knew that some of the neighbours pawned goods on Mondays and redeemed them on Saturdays, so she decided to go on a Tuesday, to avoid being seen.

She packed a pair of vases and a pair of candlesticks into her basket, and slipped furtively into the pawnshop, always known as 'Solly's'.

'I'd like to pawn these or sell them please, Mr Solomon,' she faltered.

'Vell, vich do you wish, little one, to pawn or to sell?' he asked, smiling at her.

'To – to sell, I think,' Sally said. 'I wouldn't be able to redeem them for a long time, I'm afraid.'

'But to sell – that vay they are lost. Better perhaps to pawn,' he said.

'I know, but I wouldn't want them back when they'd been here,' Sally said, then stopped, appalled, afraid that she had insulted the old man. He nodded understandingly.

'They vould remind you of the bad times, hein? Vell, goot times vill come again.' He took the goods to the back of the shop and returned a moment later with half a sovereign which he put on the counter.

'Oh, thank you,' Sally gasped, delighted to receive so much.

'Goot quality goods.' He shrugged. 'How is the fader?'

'No better,' Sally said sadly. 'The doctor says he won't get the use of his left side back ever.'

The old man wagged his head from side to side.

'But he has a blessink, yes? A goot daughter. Ve all should be so lucky.'

Sally left the shop, glad that the ordeal she had dreaded was over, and feeling comforted by the old man's words.

Chapter Thirty-Two

As the months passed, more and more of Sally's household goods found their way to Solly's. Lawrie was still desperately hunting for a permanent job, and trying to earn money in any way possible. Sometimes after standing for hours in the pen at the docks, hoping to be picked for work unloading ships, he would be turned away. Cold, wet and hungry, he would try to get work washing dishes in a hotel, rather than return home empty handed. He never grumbled to Sally, knowing that she already had enough to bear, but he looked ever more gaunt and haggard.

Sally too had grown thinner and paler, worn down by the constant worry about money, and the exhausting nursing, and it was hard to recognize in her the confident, cheerful housewife, queen of her little kingdom, that once she had been.

She refused to let Mrs Malloy help them with money. Paddy Ryan had fallen at work, and been taken to the Infirmary where, as quietly and unobtrusively as he had lived, he died in his sleep. Mrs Malloy was too old and ill to look after a strange lodger, so she needed all her own pittance to survive. Sally was grateful, though, for the hours Mrs Malloy spent sitting with Matthew, who always behaved better in her presence, and for the occasional gift of a freshly baked loaf, or some small delicacy for her father.

At this time in Sally's life she found kindness in unexpected places. She had been unable to pay the rent one week, and was greatly distressed when she faced Mr Jones, knowing of his reputation as a hard man, but he had been very understanding.

'Indeed, troubles neffer come singly, Mrs Ward,' he said. 'But you've been a good tenant, so pay me whateffer you can. We'll put the rest on the book for now.'

'Oh, thank you, Mr Jones,' Sally said. 'My husband is trying so hard for work. I'm sure he'll get something soon.'

'Well, times are bad, but I know you'll clear the book when you can. For now – chust what you can manage. Don't go hungry to find the rent.'

Sally's eyes filled with tears. 'You're very kind,' she said in a choked voice.

He shrugged. 'Better for me to keep a good tenant, see, than a bad payer doing a flit.'

The old pawnbroker, too, was kind and understanding. The day came when all the small items had been sold, and Sally approached him to ask him to buy the parlour furniture. He came in the evening to see it, and offered Sally a fair price. She was seeing him out of the front door when she realised that Mrs Kilgannon's door, which was beside hers, was ajar, and her neighbour was listening to their conversation. She realised that the old man had seen it, too, when he raised his voice.

'So my nephew vill bring a handcart, and ven he has loaded the furniture, he vill help to bring down the fader's bed. Better for you and the fader to have him downstairs.'

'Yes, *thank* you, Mr Solomon,' Sally said fervently. He placed his finger against his nose.

'The furniture – it vill be safely stored until you vant it, Mrs Ward,' he said, nodding and smiling as he left, and Mrs Kilgannon's door closed with a disappointed bang. Sally returned to the kitchen, smiling, and Lawrie looked up with surprise.

'I'm glad to see you smiling, love,' he said. 'I thought you'd be upset.' She told him of how cleverly old Solly had dealt with Mrs Kilgannon.

'One in the eye for her,' she added with satisfaction. 'She's watching us like a hawk to see signs of trouble, and I think she's pumping Mary, too.'

'God, some people are queer,' Lawrie said. 'Enjoying seeing others foundering. I can't make them out.' He stood up and stretched. 'I tell you what though, Sal, that's a good idea, having your da's bed downstairs. It'd be better all round.'

'Yes, if he'd agree,' Sally said doubtfully. Lately Matthew had grown so cantankerous that she knew that he would probably refuse to move, and he had turned against Lawrie so much that it was better for her to suggest it, yet she dreaded provoking a scene.

The following morning the solution presented itself. Mrs Malloy arrived soon after the girls had gone to school, and she was enthusiastic about the idea of moving Matthew downstairs, when she saw the empty room.

'Leave him to me, girlie,' she said. 'I know how to handle him.' Sally was apprehensive, especially when she heard her father's voice raised in anger, but Mrs Malloy was smiling broadly when she came downstairs.

'Yer da agrees with me, that he'd be better off downstairs, where ye'd be near at hand when he wanted ye. Sure, it'll be years before the girls are needin' the parlour for courtin',' she said loudly. She hustled Sally into the kitchen and closed the door, smiling at Sally's bewilderment.

'Ah, it's not only old Solly can be crafty, girl,' she said. 'I knew well he'd be against it, if it was to save yer legs, so I told him ye didn't want to give up the parlour, but I thought he'd be better off downstairs.'

Sally agreed, sadly aware that Mrs Malloy was right about her father's reaction to the move. Sometimes she wondered what had happened to the loving father she had once known.

The move was easily accomplished, and it made life a little easier for Sally. With the money for the furniture she was able to pay a small amount off the arrears of rent, and lay in a stock of coal for the winter. Coal was an ever present problem. Sally needed it to light the boiler for the sheets and nightshirts constantly in the wash because of her father's incontinence, and she needed a good fire in the parlour because he felt the cold so much. She now only lit the kitchen fire when she needed the oven, or to dry washing, and most of the cooking was done on the gas ring.

It meant that the family gathered in the parlour for warmth, but Lawrie tried to sit out of Matthew's line of vision, knowing of his irrational dislike of him. The sight of Mary also annoyed Matthew, and she used this as an excuse to escape from the house. Several times when Mary had been alone with her grandfather, Sally had heard a commotion and had rushed in to find Matthew striking out with his stick in his good hand, and shouting unintelligibly while Mary skipped about, just out of reach of the stick. Although Sally suspected that Mary deliberately provoked these scenes to gain more freedom, she was too worn out and harassed to deal with her firmly.

Sally worried about her, especially in the small hours of the morning when she had been awake to attend to Matthew, and was unable to go to sleep again. Mary had grown tall and graceful, with the quick light step which had been noticeable in Sally until recent years. Her striking red gold hair and pretty features attracted all the local boys.

'But she's only eleven,' Lawrie protested when Sally told him of her worries.

'Yes, but she's old for her age, and she's got a taste for low company. Those impudent girls she hangs around with – they're older than her and as rough as can be,' Sally said.

'I'll have a word with her,' Lawrie promised, but although Mary listened submissively, and promised to spend more time at home helping her mother, she still managed to have the last word.

'But you don't want me to tell Nelly and Josie I can't play with them because they're poor, do you, Dad?' she asked, opening her blue eyes wide. '*You* always used to like poor people.'

'It's because they're cheeky and dirty, not because they're poor,' Lawrie said. 'We're poor ourselves but we're clean and respectable.'

'But they're dirty *because* they're poor,' Mary said.

'Crafty little faggot,' Sally said later. 'She knows fine well why I don't want her hanging round with them.'

The following day was an exceptionally bad one for Sally. Lawrie had left the house before four o'clock in the morning to hunt for work, and although the fact that he had not returned must mean that he had found some, Sally longed for him to come home. The parlour chimney had smoked, and Matthew had complained about it all day. Sally's efforts to clear it only made it worse.

Matthew had knocked the dish from Sally's hand when she was trying to feed him, breaking it and spilling the food on the floor, and his bed had needed changing three times. Mrs Malloy had shown Sally how to roll up the wet sheet, and spread the dry one, then lift him from one to the other, but it was almost beyond her strength, and she was exhausted when she started the washing. Immediately Matthew began to bang his stick on the bedrail and shout for her. She went back to adjust his pillows, then a second time to give him a drink, but when the

213

shouting and banging started again, she dashed in and snatched the stick from him. She had never done that before, knowing how he valued having his stick to call for attention, but she felt that she could bear no more.

Later she returned the stick to him, but he glared at her as though he hated her.

'Where's the quare feller?' he said. 'Out boozing while you pull yer guts out – yer daft mare.'

'He's looking for work,' she said.

He gave his guttural laugh. 'Soft sis, yer'll believe anything,' he taunted. 'Couldn't wait to get his knees under me table, and no bloody wonder.'

Sally walked out of the room, weeping and trying to tell herself that it was not her father speaking, only the sick stranger he had become. He called after her that his bed was wet, with such satisfaction that she felt sure that he had done it deliberately.

When the girls came in from school she gave them their meal of boiled black pudding, then sent them to sit by the parlour fire, to get warm and to keep their grandfather company while she did the washing. Later when she went to get Mary to turn the mangle for her, she found Cathy alone with Matthew.

'Where's Mary? Where's she gone?' Sally demanded.

'I don't know, Mam,' Cathy said. 'She didn't say anything. She just went. I'll do the mangle.' Sally checked that her father had fallen asleep, then she and Cathy went out to deal with the washing.

They were still in the back kitchen when Lawrie came in. He looked pinched and grey with cold and fatigue, but he proudly handed four shillings to Sally.

'I've been carting all day,' he said. 'Feller brought a load into the market and I unloaded with him, then he took me round, picking up and delivering all day. His regular fellow was drunk and he couldn't rouse him, he said.' Sally looked up hopefully but he shook his head.

'No chance, love,' he said. 'It's his nephew and he said his sister would have his ear off if he sacked him.'

'Go in to the fire and I'll bring your tea in there,' Sally said. 'He's asleep, thank God.' Lawrie washed his hands at the sink while she heated the black puddings on the gas ring.

'Like that, is it?' he asked.

'Not half,' Sally said grimly. 'I've had enough of him to last me a week.'

Matthew was still asleep when they crept in, and Lawrie crouched over the fire, holding his plate on his knee.

'Where's Mary?' he whispered, and Sally shrugged her shoulders and nodded towards Mrs Kilgannon's. The peaceful interlude lasted only a short time, and Matthew woke as Sally carried a mug of tea in to Lawrie.

'Yer stupid get,' her father snarled. 'Wharrave I told ye? Running after his bloody arse.'

Lawrie stood up. 'All right, Matt,' he said loudly. 'That's enough. Don't use that language in front of Sally.'

Matthew tried to struggle up in the bed. 'Don't you talk to me like that, yer bloody upstart,' he panted. 'Me own daughter – say what I like. Stupid bloody cow. Yer knew what –'

'That's enough, Da. Shut up,' Sally shouted, fearful of what he would say next, but he lashed out at her with his stick.

'Don't tell me – shurrup. Bloody upstart, can't keep yer. Won't werk.'

Sally dashed crying from the room into the lobby, just as Mary slid in through the front door.

Sally seized her. 'Where have you been?' she demanded. 'I've told you about going in next door, haven't I?'

Mary pulled away. 'I hate it here,' she said sullenly, 'That room stinks with him. Why can't we have a fire in the kitchen?'

'Because we can't afford it, that's why,' Sally screamed.

'I'm sick of it,' Mary yelled back. 'Look at me boots. Look at this ole dress. It's not fair.'

Lawrie was in the doorway and Mary pointed at him. 'It's his fault, getting sacked. Killey said so.'

Sally leaped at her, seizing her hair and banging her head against the wall.

'Impudent bitch,' she screamed. 'I'll kill her, I'll kill her!'

Cathy ran from the kitchen, yelling in terror, and Lawrie shouted at Sally and tried to pull her away from Mary, but she seemed like someone demented as she clutched Mary's hair, screaming.

With Cathy's help he managed at last to pull her away, and gave Mary a push which threw her at the foot of the stairs.

'Sally, go and sit in the kitchen,' he panted. 'Cathy, get your mam a drink, and you –' he gripped Mary's arm and pulled her to her feet, thrusting his face close to hers – 'if you ever speak to your mam like that again, or ever set foot in that place next door, I'll kill you. D'you hear me, I'll kill you.'

'Yes, Dad,' she faltered, terrified by his white face, lips drawn back from his teeth in a snarl. He thrust her away.

'Get upstairs,' he said. 'And one word – one word.'

He went into the kitchen where Sally had collapsed sobbing into a chair. Cathy stood beside her, holding a cup of water. He crouched down, drawing Sally into his arms.

'Oh, Lawrie, Lawrie, I would have killed her,' she sobbed.

'Never mind, love, she just went too far this time, but by God, she won't again!'

'And my da? Is he all right?'

'To hell with your da. He's another one can stew in his own juice,' Lawrie said forcefully. 'We're in rough water, girl, yet there's two pulling against us. But by God they'll pull with us from now on or go overboard. Maybe he can't help himself, but the other one can and will.'

'Oh, Lawrie, you're trembling,' Sally said. She dried her eyes. 'I'm going to make us a hot drink, and we'll have a fire here, too. We're not sitting in there again tonight.' She went and put the kettle on the gas ring while Lawrie lit the fire, then she went and peeped into the parlour, but her father was asleep, evidently exhausted by his rage.

When the fire was burning, Sally drew Cathy down beside her and the three of them sat drinking the hot tea, not talking but drawing comfort from each other, and gradually growing calmer after the emotional storms of the previous hours.

Mary was very subdued during the following days, but Sally was gentle with her, feeling that she had been unlucky that her impudence had come right after the scene with Matthew, and also ashamed that she could have murdered her own child, if she had not been restrained. It was a chastening thought for Sally, that adversity had revealed traits in her character that she had been unaware of all her life. It made her more tolerant of failings in other people which she would once have been quick to condemn.

Matthew also was quieter, possibly because he had provoked a worse scene than he intended, or perhaps because Sally told Mary, in his hearing, that Lawrie had said that those who didn't pull with the family could go overboard.

Their hand to mouth existence dragged on, made more difficult by the bad weather. Lawrie tramped so far in search of work, and in such wet weather, that the second-hand boots he bought only lasted a few weeks. He was never again able to earn four shillings, as on that fateful day. Usually it was only one and sixpence or two shillings, sometimes nothing at all.

One day he called to see Mrs Malloy to ask her advice. She insisted that he sat close to the fire, and had a cup of tea and some hot soda bread before they talked. In her scullery she lifted the corner of her apron and wiped away a tear to see the contrast between the confident, happy-go-lucky young man Lawrie had been, and the haggard, shabby man who sat by her hearth now.

'Oh, lad, lad,' she whispered to herself. 'Oh, God help ye.' But she managed a cheerful smile as she returned to the kitchen.

'Now, lad, what's the problem?' she asked, stirring the fire to avoid looking at him directly.

'I don't know what to do for the best, Mrs Mal. I'm only getting a half day here and a few hours there, sometimes nothing at all, and there's nothing steady going because there's too many after every job. We can't go on like this, especially the way Matthew is, and I'm so heavy on boots. I'm thinking it would be better if I got a ship. At least Sally'd have something regular.'

'But how would she manage, lad? She's not able for all the lifting and cleaning of him on her own, and she needs ye to take the burden of the worry off her, too. And sleep – how would she get any sleep at all without ye spelled her, with the way he is?'

'I know, I know, Mrs Mal. I've thought about it all until I feel I'm going mad. What's worse for her, though – watching farthings, trying to scheme out the coal, very often having to wash sheets in cold water? The girls are getting old enough to help, and at least Sally'd have something coming in, without having to find my food and boots. What do you think?'

'Have ye said anything to Sally about this?' she asked.

216

He shook his head. 'No. It's driving *me* mad trying to decide. I don't want to worry Sally with it until I can see what's best.'

'Don't say anything,' the old lady counselled. 'Sure, she'd be heartbroken at the very thought, and it would maybe be the straw to break the camel's back.'

'You don't think I should sign on then?' said Lawrie.

'No, I don't. Ye're needed too much here. And don't worry, lad. Ye're keeping yer heads above water yet, and the tide will soon turn for ye, please God. If there's anything I can do –'

'No, no, Mrs Mal,' Lawrie said hurriedly, 'I just wanted your advice. I'm glad you don't think I should go. I'd have been worried to death all the time I was away.'

'Aye well, it's always darkest before the dawn, as they say. Tomorrow ye might land a real good job, who knows? At least the rest of ye are keeping well, apart from Mattie, thank God.'

'Yes, that's something to be thankful for. The sewing machine's gone back, you know. It was a worry to Sally, having to find the money for it every week, and sometimes she was only earning enough to cover the payment, so we let it go.'

'Ye did right. She has enough to do without the sewing, and no time for it anyhow. She's having her own share with Mattie, and indeed so are you, lad. All honour to both of yiz for the care ye give him. God will reward ye for it, one day.'

Lawrie glanced at the clock and stood up.

'I'll have to go, Mrs Mal. I want to try the hotel again,' he said. 'Thanks for the tea and the good advice.' He looked more like his old self than when he arrived, and Mrs Malloy was pleased to see his cheerful smile.

'Tell Sally I'll see her tomorrow. I'll bring up a newspaper if Jinny McBride gets one for me. She cleans offices, and the fellows are after throwing away their papers,' she explained.

'That's good. Cathy can read it to him, and give Sally a bit of peace,' he said. 'Thanks, Mrs Mal. I'll see you soon.'

He strode off, and Mrs Malloy stood watching him, grieving at her young friends' troubles, and offering a prayer that Lawrie would soon find a steady job.

Chapter Thirty-Three

Sally had not seen Mrs Kilgannon for a while, and Mary had not dared to go in next door, but one day Susan came in to see Sally. She looked very different from on her last visit, wan and frightened, her face streaked with tears. Sally jumped up and put her arm around her.

'Oh, Sue, love, what's wrong?' she asked.

Susan burst into tears. 'I'm in trouble, Mrs Ward,' she sobbed. 'I'm expecting. Didn't you hear me mam screaming before?'

Sally drew her to a chair, and sat down beside her, holding her hand. 'Don't cry, love,' she said gently, 'don't get upset. It's bad for the baby.'

Susan's sobs broke out afresh, and gradually she told Sally the whole story. Old and hackneyed as it was, the distress and disillusion were as keen every time, and Susan's suffering was plain to see.

A young nephew of her employer had been staying in the house after coming down from Oxford, and Susan believed that they had fallen in love. The stolen meetings in the garden, with the stars overhead and stocks and tobacco plants filling the air with perfume; the meaning glances and the touching of fingers unobserved by his aunt, had been the stuff of romance to her. As head parlourmaid she had her own room, and there he had crept every night, to sit cuddling her and talking of marrying by special licence, and living in a cottage in the country.

'He showed me a picture of the cottage,' sobbed Susan. From there it was but a small step to lying on her bed, their bodies fusing together in passion.

'I was so happy,' Susan wept, 'even when I missed me monthlies because I thought he'd say we'd get married right away, but he just went away. I told the missis but she said I was telling lies, and turned me off without a character. Me mam says I can't stay because of the neighbours, and she's sent for our Nelly and the lads.'

'Rubbish,' Sally said indignantly. She could see it all so clearly: the young man, bored and restless, embarking on a flirtation with the pretty parlourmaid to pass the time, and poor young Susan, believing every word he told her. She put her arm round the girl.

'Don't worry, Sue,' she said. 'You stay here and I'll go to see your mam.'

Nelly admitted her next door, her eyes swollen with weeping, and took her to where Mrs Kilgannon sat rocking, her apron thrown over her head. She moved it to say wildly, 'The disgrace, an' I've alwis kept meself respectable.'

Before she could say more, Nelly admitted her three brothers and they burst into the kitchen.

'Where is she?' shouted Joe. 'I'll bloody kill her!'

Mrs Kilgannon began to howl, throwing her apron over her head again and rocking to and fro. Sally had an uneasy feeling that she was enjoying the drama, especially when all three lads shouted together.

Sally brought her fist down on the table with a bang, and in the sudden silence said quietly, 'Susan's not to blame. The fellow took advantage of her, a young girl away from home, and the aunt knew he was to blame.'

Various emotions passed over Joe's face, then he turned to the others.

'She's right,' he said. 'We'll go and sort the both of them out, him and the old girl. Our Sue was took advantage of.'

Mrs Kilgannon started up in alarm. 'Don't, Joey!' she cried. 'She'll have the law on yer.'

The smallest of the brothers spoke up.

'Orl right, Mam, we'll leave it for now,' he said, nodding significantly at the other men, 'But wharrabout our Sue?'

'I'm not having her here,' Mrs Kilgannon said. 'I couldn't hold up me head.' She began to howl again.

'Orl right, orl right, don't rabbit on,' he said.

Sally said quietly, 'Sue's in my house now, and she's welcome to stay.'

'But the neighbours'll see her and it'll cause more talk,' Mrs Kilgannon objected.

'Then why don't you have her at home where she belongs?' Sally said. 'She could be having a little spell at home before she goes to a new place, for all anyone knows.'

'That's a good idea, Missis,' said Henry, the smallest brother. 'It'll give us time to fix something up, Mam.'

'But who's gonna keep her?' whined Mrs Kilgannon. All Sally's dislike of the woman came surging back, but the brothers only looked resignedly at each other, and reached into their pockets.

Nelly followed Sally down the lobby when she left.

'Good job you were here,' she whispered. 'To quieten the lads. Me mam only thinks about herself, she doesn't care about our poor Sue.'

'I'll just make her a cup of tea,' Sally whispered. 'Will you come in for her then?' Nelly agreed, and Sally went in to Susan.

'Your Nelly's coming in for you in a minute,' she told her. 'We'll go and sit by the parlour fire until she comes.' She gave Susan an edited version of what had happened, and told her that she was to stay at home until Henry made arrangements for her.

When Lawrie came in a little later, weary after hours of dishwashing after a Masonic dinner, Susan had gone home and Sally told him of the events of the day.

'Poor little Sue,' he said. 'Girls like her are easy game for some of these so called gentlemen.'

'I hope the brothers don't get themselves in trouble,' Sally said. 'I'd feel it was my fault.'

'Not a bit of it,' Lawrie said. 'They're used to sailing close to the wind.' He yawned widely. 'I think I'll go up, Sal,' he said. 'Anything needed?'

She shook her head. Matthew was still asleep, and she said quietly, 'No, everything's done. Go on up, love.'

He bent and kissed her goodnight, holding her close for a moment, then releasing her with a sigh, and climbing wearily upstairs. Sally now slept on the truckle bed in the parlour, to be on hand when her father woke during the night. She banked the fire and lay down, but tired though she was, sleep eluded her. Her mind was filled with the thought of Susan's suffering, and fears for her own girls. She worried about both of them, but her fears were mainly for Mary.

Cathy was sometimes in trouble in school for giggling in class, or daydreaming when she should have been writing or doing arithmetic, but at home she played in the street with her best friend, Katy Dawson, at jacks and ollies, or skipping or whatever was the fashion, and was always available when Sally needed her. In her cheerfulness and readiness to help, Sally could see a likeness to Lawrie which endeared the child to her even more, but much as she loved Mary, her eldest was a constant source of worry to her.

She had grown into a beautiful girl, looking and behaving like someone much older than her years, and spent as little time as possible in the house. At the first opportunity she was away to join a group of rough boys and girls, larking about at the street corner, and no amount of scolding or even chastising made her alter her ways. Sally knew that Mary bitterly resented having to wear a shabby dress and patched boots, and wondered uneasily if that was why she chose such rough friends. Shabby though she was, she was still better dressed than her companions, and Mary needed to shine in any group of which she was part. She had started her periods some months earlier, and had impatiently waved away Sally's attempts to explain things to her.

'I know, I know,' she said. 'Some girl told me all about it.'

What else was she being taught, Sally now wondered, and how could she instil better principles into her? Was it already too late? It was a long time before Sally slept.

A couple of days later Susan came to see her.

'Our Henry's made arrangements for me,' she said. 'The woman his wife works for, cleaning – well, she's got queer ideas, Sarah says. Thinks women should vote and do men's jobs, and kids should get free dinners and milk.'

'Nothing queer about those ideas,' Sally said. 'Lawrie thinks the same.'

'Aye well, this woman's on the Board of Guardians and when girls go before them in trouble, she says she wants to see the feller too, so our Sarah told her about me. I can work for her till the baby's born, she says, and then she'll help me to make arrangements.'

'She sounds a good woman, Sue,' Sally said. 'You will be all right there.'

Susan nodded. 'Our lads went to see *him*, y'know. They got some money off him, and our Henry took his watch. "That's for your son," he said, so Reginald knew who he was, but he didn't call out or nothing. Our Nelly heard that he said he got bashed up by about ten men. They was all talking about it when her missis had an At Home.

221

Saying the streets wasn't safe. Our Nelly was dying to laugh.'

'I'm glad they did it that way,' Sally said. 'I was worried in case they went to his aunt. That sort stick together and she might have turned nasty.'

Susan left two days later, before any of the neighbours asked questions about her being at home, but the next time Sally saw Mrs Kilgannon the older woman flounced past her, evidently resenting Sally's attempts to help her daughter.

'She doesn't like being under an obligation to you,' Lawrie said when Sally told him, but she had little time to waste worrying about her neighbour's moods.

Emily's letters had been arriving from Brussels every eight weeks for some time, always very stilted and written to a formula. In her replies Sally had said nothing of her troubles, only giving news of Mary's and Cathy's progress. Matthew had been bedridden for eighteen months when a letter arrived from Emily in July 1904.

It was written from Ormesdale, and Emily said that she would not be returning to Brussels. Aunt Hester was very ill, and Emily hoped that Sally would be able to come to see her. With great regret Sally wrote back that her father was too ill for her to leave at present, but she hoped that Aunt Hester would soon recover. Apart from the impossibility of leaving Matthew, Sally could not have afforded the fare, and her clothes and boots were too shabby for visiting, although she said nothing of that to Emily. A reply came quickly.

Emily wrote that she was very sorry to hear that her father was ill, and would love to see him, but Aunt Hester needed her so much at present that she could not leave her. A few days later a parcel arrived from Ormesdale, containing two jars of calves' foot jelly, a bottle of rum, a bottle of Madeira wine, and two dozen fresh eggs. Sally was overcome, especially when she read the enclosed letter.

'The Madeira wine is for you, Sal,' Emily had written. *'It will keep up your strength for the nursing. The other things, I hope, will help to build up Da. I hope soon to hear that he is better.'*

Sally had no scruples about using some of the eggs for the family. They had all made too many sacrifices for Matthew for her to feel that she was being unfair to him. He seemed to enjoy the calves' foot jelly, but when she told him that Emily had sent it, he said ungraciously, 'Why didn't she bring it herself? Too posh now, I suppose.'

Sally tried to hide her irritation. 'She can't leave Aunt Hester, Da. She's very ill.'

'Not as ill as what I am, I'll bet,' Matthew grumbled.

Sally gave him some rum and water in the feeding cup, but he became so flushed and breathless that she decided that it would be unwise to give him any more. He fell asleep after his meal, and when the girls came in from school Sally fried eggs and potatoes for their meal, and gave each of them a glass of wine and water. If it's good for me it should be good for them, she reasoned. The girls enjoyed their unusual treat, and Sally was happy to see their pleasure, but when Matthew woke he refused an egg beaten in milk, and demanded a kipper.

'A *kipper*, Da,' Sally said.

'Yes, a kipper. I fancy a kipper.'

He was beginning to show signs of distress, and Sally said hastily, 'All right, Da. I'll try to get you a kipper.' She went back to the kitchen, wondering what to do. There was not a penny in the house until Lawrie returned, but she had a sudden brainwave.

'Here, Mary,' she said. 'Take these two eggs to Daly's. Tell her they're new laid, and ask her for a pair of kippers.'

Mary returned in triumph with the kippers and one egg.

'I offered her one, and she took it,' she crowed. 'I told her it was laid this morning on me uncle's farm.'

Sally felt that she should check Mary's fantasies, but she was too thankful for her talent for striking a bargain, and unwilling to spoil her moment of triumph.

Lawrie returned cold, wet and dispirited, with only two shillings, but he cheered up when Sally showed him the parcel, and poured him a glass of rum and water.

'I'm not giving any more rum to Da,' she said. 'It seemed to take his breath. I'll try him with some wine tomorrow. You might as well drink the rum.'

'How is he?' asked Lawrie as she quickly fried the eggs and potatoes for his meal.

'Don't ask,' Sally said, rolling her eyes. 'He wanted a kipper, and Mary swopped an egg for a pair at Daly's. I was ages trying to get all the bones out before I gave it to him, then he said he didn't want it. He's driving me mad.'

She dished up the meal to Lawrie, smiling as he rubbed his hands in anticipation.

'Why don't you go and sit by the parlour fire with a glass of wine?' Lawrie said. 'I'll do Mary's boots before I come in.'

Sally went into the parlour, knowing that Lawrie was trying to give her some peace to drink the wine, staying in the kitchen so that Matthew would not start one of his tirades at the sight of him. It was a vain hope, because as soon as Lawrie began to mend Mary's boots, Matthew started to shout.

'That feller! Does what he likes in me house. Only banging ter disturb me. Scum of the earth.'

'That's enough,' Sally said sharply. 'He's got to patch Mary's shoes.' She was tempted to tell him that it was not his house, that Mary could have new boots if he was not there, but she rushed out of the room, slamming the door behind her, before the temptation was too much for her. She went to Lawrie and put her arm round his neck, kissing him lovingly to show that she appreciated his rueful grin as the only response to the insults.

The gifts from Emily cheered Sally when she needed it most, for their fortunes were now at their lowest ebb. Everything possible had been sold, and every day was a battle for survival. Their clothes were literally falling to pieces, and it took all Sally's skill and ingenuity in patching to keep them respectable.

Lawrie patched their boots with pieces cut from even more

223

dilapidated pairs, but the future filled Sally with terror. What would they do when clothes and boots were absolutely beyond patching? There was never the tiniest margin to buy more. Lawrie always pretended to think that a good job was sure to turn up and solve their problems, but Sally often saw the same fear in his eyes.

Soap, rent, pennies for the gas, as well as coal and food, all had to be found from the little Lawrie was able to earn, and Matthew's needs were a constant drain on their resources. Spirit to rub him with to prevent bedsores, oatmeal, milk and sugar for his gruel, laudanum to ease his pain and bicarbonate of soda for his indigestion were all necessities. Often Lawrie started his day with only a piece of bread and dripping, and took one more slice to sustain him through the day of tramping round seeking work, or doing heavy work when he was able to get it.

Often Sally wondered if he would ever get another steady job. When she remembered him, healthy and well-dressed, setting off at first to seek work yet not succeeding, she could see little hope for the gaunt, shabby man he had become. Would he even be strong enough now for steady work? It was little wonder that Sally lay awake at night, worrying about the arrears on the rent book, and wondering how they could survive the coming winter.

Sally was also worried about Mrs Malloy. She had sent Cathy to her with two of the eggs, and a small bottle of the wine, and Cathy had told her that the old lady's rheumatism was already bad.

'She said she could hardly get up from the chair, Mam, and it's only October, but she said the eggs and wine would cure it.'

'I hope they do,' Sally said. 'But I doubt it. I'll have to try to get down to see her.'

She knew how much pain her old friend suffered with the rheumatism, so she was sorry to hear that it was starting so early in the winter for that reason mainly, but she was also sorry on her own account. Matthew was so unreasonable now that he could not be left with either Lawrie or Mary, to give Sally some respite, and she worried that Cathy was too young to spend so much time minding her grandfather. Mrs Malloy's visits had given Sally a much needed break from the constant attendance on him. Sometimes Sally felt that she hated him, but she always tried to crush the thought quickly. He's my da, I must respect him, she told herself, but it increased the pressure on her.

One day she felt that she could bear no more from him. She had been disturbed by demands for a drink or his pillow turned several times during the night, and feeling ill and exhausted, was unable to cope with his constant demands and complaints during the day. Lawrie had come in soaking wet, and as soon as Sally started to make him a hot drink, Matthew began to shout.

'Never mind running after that feller, neglecting yer own father,' he said. 'Lift me up. Fix me sheet.' Sally went in, gritting her teeth, and lifted him.

'Now turn me piller,' he said. 'An' me hot water bottle's cold.'

'I've just filled it,' Sally said.

'Well, me feet are freezing, fill it again,' he shouted in his guttural tones. Sally snatched the bottle from the bed and went into the kitchen.

'I'm sick of him, sick,' she said to Lawrie, her face red and her chest heaving with anger.

'If he wasn't here, we'd be all right. I could get work. None of this scratching and scraping. I wish –'

Lawrie put his hand over her mouth. 'Don't say it, Sal. You'll be sorry tomorrow if you do.'

'But it's true, Lol. He's not even grateful. Never a thank you, only bad words about everyone.'

'I know, love, I know,' Lawrie soothed her. 'You're getting the rough end of it, but he can't help himself.' He put his arms around her and she leaned against him.

'You shouldn't have married me,' she sobbed. 'You never bargained for having him like this, did you?'

'Oh, Sally, it's the boot on the other foot. You never bargained for me being out of work, and dragging you down to the way we've been these last two years.'

She held him tight, kissing him passionately. 'Lawrie, you know that's not your fault. It's the way things are here now, but my da, he could stop it if he tried, the way he behaves I mean. If he doesn't, I swear I'll put him in the Infirmary.'

'*No,*' Lawrie said violently, 'we're a family. We sink or swim together. Matt was good to us, giving us a home, letting us get married. He can't help the way he is now. It's the illness.' Sally drew away from him, her face colouring with shame, and Lawrie said gently, 'I know it's easy for me to talk like that. I don't have to put up with him day and night like you, but his mind *is* warped, love, the same as his body.'

'I know,' Sally said with a sigh. During the following days she was more than usually patient and loving with her father, trying to atone for harsh words of which he knew nothing.

Matthew was slightly less bad-tempered, but his language was still foul, and Sally worried about the effect on the girls. She would have worried even more if she had realised the slow poison that was being dripped into their minds by her father's unreasonable hatred of Lawrie.

Chapter Thirty-Four

One evening Lawrie returned in triumph with four shillings and sixpence, having had half a day's work on the docks, and an afternoon's carting. Sally immediately sent Mary to the corner shop for bread, sugar and tea, and oatmeal for Matthew's gruel.

Lawrie sat down to take off his boots, then sat for a moment holding one and staring at the floor.

'Y'know, Sal, there was a little feller at the pen with a withered arm,' he said. 'The foreman picked him but when he saw the arm, he dropped him and I pushed in quick. The little feller was screaming: "I can still use me hook", like someone demented. I felt mean, grabbing the job off him.'

'Oh, for God's sake, Lawrie, if you hadn't done it, someone else would. It's every man for himself in the pen, from what I've heard. You're too soft altogether.'

'Maybe,' Lawrie said, putting his boots in the hearth.

'There's no one needs the money more than we do, that's for sure,' Sally said sharply. She was irritated by Lawrie's scruples, although she had long ago realised that his concern for others was one of the traits that made him the man she loved.

Mary took all their remarks at their face value, and knew nothing of Sally's thoughts. When she and Cathy were in bed she whispered, 'Did you hear Mam and Dad fighting? No wonder she gets fed up with him, he's so soft.'

'I don't know what you mean,' Cathy whispered.

'He doesn't try hard enough to get a job. That's why we have to go to school like this. Patches on our frocks, and these awful boots. It's Dad's fault – Grandad told me.'

'But he does try to get a job,' Cathy said. 'He goes out very early.'

'He shouldn't have lost his proper job. Grandad says it was because he was trying to play the big feller, and he only married Mam so he could live with her and Grandad, and she could make money sewing. It must be true because I asked Mrs Mal and she said Dad lodged with her – he didn't have a home.'

'I'll bet Mrs Mal didn't know why you were asking,' Cathy said shrewdly. 'Mam told me not to take any notice when Grandad says nasty things, because he's sick.'

'Well, she would, wouldn't she?' Mary said, with a toss of her head.

Cathy watched her father and mother apprehensively, alert to every sharp word by Sally, or impatient reply by Lawrie. A few weeks later her fears seemed to be realised.

227

Sally had been told by Mrs Kilgannon that Lawrie had given away his midday butty, and she taxed him with it as soon as he came home.

'Are you mad or something?' she demanded. 'We're only just keeping our heads above water, and you give food away.'

'The child was starving, just skin and bone,' Lawrie said. 'He hadn't eaten for two days.'

'And you'd had so much,' Sally jeered.

'I'd had bread and dripping this morning, and I had a home and something to eat to come home to,' Lawrie said angrily, 'Surely you don't begrudge a child a slice of bread?'

'What about our own children?' Sally said.

'They're not starving –'

'Not yet,' Sally interrupted.

Lawrie went on, 'I didn't take the bread from the girls anyway. It was my own carry out, and you'd have known nothing about it, only for that nosy cow next door. She never moves out of the house, but she can always find some way of causing trouble.'

Cathy was trembling, staring at her book without really seeing it and watching anxiously as Sally flounced about, and Lawrie doggedly ate his scanty meal, neither of them speaking. Soon the familiar banging of her grandfather's stick began, and Sally went in to him. After a few minutes had passed, Lawrie followed her.

'He's slipped right down,' Cathy heard her mother say, then she could hear her grandfather's guttural voice.

'Get off. Leave me alone. Took me girl from a good home. Scum of the earth.'

Cathy sat gripping her book, waiting for her father to shout back, but it was her mother who said sharply, 'That's enough, Da. Be thankful it's Lawrie you're living with. Any other man would have put you in the Workhouse Infirmary long ago.' They came back to the kitchen, her mother saying, 'Never mind shaking your head at me, Lawrie. He shouldn't say such things and he knows it.'

'Listen Sal, it's not your da speaking there. He might have been moody at times, but he was a decent man. He'd never have thought or said such things. I tell you, his mind is twisted as well as his body.'

Sally sighed. 'Aye, he's nothing like Da as he was, is he?'

'No. By God, Sal, I hope when my time comes I go off clean, no dragging my anchor for years, a burden to myself like your poor da.'

'Lawrie, you still surprise me,' Sally said. 'No wonder Mrs Mal said they threw away the mould when they made you.'

They smiled at each other, and Cathy felt that a great weight had rolled away from her. She would soon put Mary straight, she thought.

As the winter approached, Sally's courage began to fail. Through all their troubles, she and Lawrie had been able to cheer each other. When one was down, the other could find a reserve of hopefulness to support them. Lawrie had once said that they were like the couple in the clock, taking turns to appear on bad or good days. Now depression settled on Sally and would not lift. The long strain of nursing and penny pinching and the prospect of the long winter ahead, with no reserves, filled her with despair.

Their clothes had been patched and darned until it seemed that only the patches remained, and all their boots were in danger of disintegrating. Nothing remained in the house that could be pawned or sold, and Sally felt with terror that they had reached the end of the road.

She missed the comfort of Lawrie's arms around her as she lay sleepless on the truckle bed in the parlour, although in some ways it made it easier for both of them. For a long time he had been afraid to make love to her, with the doctor's warning in his mind, but sometimes their feelings betrayed them and they spent terrified days waiting for Sally's period to appear. The only way of contraception that they knew was withdrawal, but they both found this an intolerable strain, and Lawrie was reluctant to practise it. He told Sally that men at work had called it 'getting off at Rainhill', because there was a railway station and also a lunatic asylum at Rainhill, and withdrawal was thought to cause madness.

A black-edged envelope arrived one morning, containing news of Aunt Hester's death, but Sally could not lift the heavy cloud pressing on her sufficiently to feel any sorrow, or any concern for Emily. When a letter arrived from her asking if she could visit them, shame at their bitter poverty, and unwillingness to let Emily see her father as he now was, roused Sally enough to write back, asking her not to come.

The girls crept about, frightened by her remote air of quiet despair, and even Matthew was less troublesome than usual, seeming to feel intimidated as she did what was necessary for him, as though her mind was miles away.

Lawrie did his best to cheer her, but his own sufferings had gone on too long for him to have reserves of spirit to help her from her depths of depression. One night Cathy saw her father cry, for the first time, and the sight terrified her.

He sat on the broken-backed chair in the rear kitchen, holding his tattered boot, the tears running down his face. Cathy backed away from the door quickly before he saw her. She looked into the parlour, at her mother's stony expression as she fed her grandfather, and knew that there was no comfort there.

Silently Cathy slipped out of the door, as she had seen Mary do so often, and raced down to Gell Street.

'Come in, child, come in,' Mrs Malloy said. 'Sure ye look as though the devils of hell are after ye. What is it at all, queen?'

'It's Dad, Mrs Mal,' Cathy wept. 'He's crying and Mam's been funny for days. Mary says she might be going queer like Sadie Munrow.'

'Oh, Holy Mother of God, haven't they had too much to bear altogether!' Mrs Malloy exclaimed.

She drew Cathy to her, weeping with her, then she dried Cathy's eyes and her own on her apron.

'It's not much use, girlie, us to be weeping and wailing here. That's no help to them at all. We must put on our thinking caps.'

Cathy nodded, watching Mrs Malloy trustfully as she sat tapping her fingers on the arm of her chair. A few minutes later an idea seemed to strike Mrs Malloy.

229

'Did ye say yer dada was holding his boot, child?' she asked.

'Yes, the sole was hanging off, Mrs Mal.'

'Ah, well, we'll see about that. Do ye go upstairs, child, and in the back bedroom, open the cupboard. There's a pair of boots there, and a jacket and trousers on the peg. Bring them all down to me, girlie.'

When the child had gone upstairs, Mrs Malloy looked up at the old pipe on the end of the mantelpiece.

'Ye'd want me to do it, Paddy lad,' she whispered. 'Didn't ye always think the world of him. Why didn't I think of it before?'

Cathy came carefully down the narrow stairs, holding the jacket and trousers and a pair of strong boots.

'Now the jacket and trousers might be on the small side, but your mammy will fix them,' said Mrs Malloy. 'But Paddy ever bought a good size in boots, the way he could wear a couple of pairs of socks.' She sighed. 'He felt the cold in his feet always, God love him.' Tenderly she folded the clothes and put the boots on top of them.

'We'll parcel them up in a minute, child. Will ye move over the kettle be the fire, and make us a drop of tea now?'

Cathy obeyed, looking sympathetically at Mrs Malloy. 'Are your knees still bad, Mrs Mal?' she asked.

'They are indeed, child. I'm all right when once I get on me feet and moving around, but I have to keep going for a while when I'm up, to make it worth the struggle of getting out of me chair.' She smiled. 'Still an' all, I'm well in meself, thanks be to God, and me hands are grand. I'm just on the end of a pair of socks for your dada.' A thought seemed to strike her, and she picked up her knitting.

'Five minutes now and I'll have the second one done. I'll give them to ye and it'll be the excuse for sending up Paddy's things. Yer dad didn't know ye saw him, sure he didn't?'

'Oh, no, Mrs Mal, I just saw him from the door, and Mam was seeing to Grandad, so I ran down here.'

'Ye did right, child. Ye're a great comfort for yer poor mam in her troubles, and Mary will be too when she loses the wildness. God knows yer mam needs all the help ye can give her, both of yiz. There now, pour out the tea while I cast off.'

Later they parcelled up the clothes and socks, and Mrs Malloy told Cathy to say she'd been asked to run down for the socks that were ready for Lawrie.

When Cathy arrived home, breathless at carrying the large parcel, her father and mother were changing her grandfather's bed, and her father showed no sign of his earlier desperation.

'Where have you been?' Sally said as they came through to the kitchen. 'I needed you.'

'Mrs Malloy told me to go there tonight, because she had a pair of socks ready for Dad,' Cathy said.

'What's this?' Lawrie said in amazement when he opened the parcel. Sally had taken the bedding through to the back kitchen and she came back to look wonderingly first at the clothes and then at Cathy.

Cathy took a deep breath. 'Mrs Mal said when she was making the socks she thought of Paddy's things lying idle, and he'd have wanted you to have them,' the child recited. 'She said, the clothes might be small but Mam's clever with her needle, and Paddy bought big boots so he could wear extra socks 'cos he felt the cold.' She stopped, breathless but proud of the way she had remembered what Mrs Mal had told her to say, only to see her father and mother looking at each other with tears running down their faces.

'Oh, Dad, aren't you pleased?' she cried in dismay. Lawrie hugged her.

'Cathy, it's the best present I ever had. You'll never *know* how glad I am. God Bless Mrs Mal, and Paddy, and you, pet, for carrying them home.'

'It's an answer to prayer,' Sally said in a low voice.

'What is it? What's going on?' Matthew demanded fretfully, and Cathy went in to him.

'I've brought some clothes and boots from Mrs Mal, and some socks she made for Dad,' she said.

'Ah, time was when she made socks fer me,' he groaned.

'You've got some on now to keep your feet warm,' Cathy pointed out. He was surprised.

'Have I? I never see me feet.'

Cathy giggled. 'Good job, Grandad,' she said. 'Your big toes are horrible. They're much longer than your other toes.'

'Cheeky faggot,' he said, but fondly. 'Sign of cleverness, that is.'

'Is it? Mine are all the same size – I mean they all just slope evenly so I can't be clever.'

'No need fer a girl ter be clever,' he mumbled. 'Just be good.'

Sally and Lawrie were still in the kitchen, where Lawrie was trying on the boots.

'They're great, Sal,' he said excitedly. 'It's grand to feel a good pair of boots on my feet again.'

'Try the coat,' said Sally. She was examining the trousers. 'Plenty to let down here,' she said.

The jacket was tight and the sleeves were too short, but Sally got out her scissors and needle and thread and worked on them. The girls had gone to bed by the time she finished, and Lawrie tried on the coat and trousers, and the new socks and the boots. They were all a good fit, and he laughed aloud, his old hearty laugh which had been missing for so long.

'I tell you, Sal, King Eddie doesn't feel better dressed than I do! I'll go and see Mrs Mal and show her tomorrow,' he said. Sally was smiling too, her depression forgotten, and Lawrie said impulsively, 'Give the truckle bed a miss tonight, love. We'll hear him if he calls.'

Feeling only slightly guilty, Sally measured out a dose of laudanum for her father. He used to take it to make him sleep, she told herself, long before he had it just for the pain. As soon as he fell asleep she crept upstairs to Lawrie.

Their problems were still as great, and the future as bleak as a few hours earlier, but the gift had lifted their spirits and filled them with hope. Their love and desire, so long crushed down, drove them to make love with a fierce abandon which left them exhausted. They lay in each other's arms, happiness and relief washing over them like a tide.

Sally tightened her arms around Lawrie, and realised with a shock how thin he was. I can feel his ribs, she thought, horrified.

'Oh, Lol, you're so thin,' she said, lifting her hand and tracing his gaunt cheeks. He kissed her tenderly.

'And so are you, love, but never mind, this is the turn of the tide for us, Sal. I'm sure of it.'

'If only you're right. It's been – well, I've just felt desperate lately.'

Lawrie's hand gently stroked her body as he kissed her eyes her forehead, her ears.

'Oh, Sally love, I've missed you so much,' he whispered. His mouth fastened on hers, and passion rose in them as they made love again, but more gently.

'I thought we'd be too weak for this,' Sally whispered later.

'Weak? I could do anything,' he said. 'Climb mountains, fight tigers. But tomorrow – I'll go out and *make* someone give me a job.'

Sally smiled. 'D'you know, Lol, I don't feel a bit worried now. Isn't it strange?'

'Everything will go right for us from now on,' he said. 'Listen, even your Da has been quiet.'

'I gave him a dose of laudanum,' Sally admitted in a low voice. She could feel the laughter rising in Lawrie, and clapped her hand over his mouth. 'Don't. You'll waken the girls,' she said urgently.

The bed shook with his suppressed laughter, as he gasped, 'I won't waken Matt, that's for sure! You're a right fast and loose woman, Sally Ward.'

She smiled doubtfully. 'Do you think I did wrong?'

'Not a bit of it. I'm made up you thought of it.'

'What did you mean, a fast and loose woman?'

'It was just a joke in the dock canteen. An old feller said to me: "Keep away from dese fast and loose women, lad." The woman serving the cocoa had a face like a butcher's chopblock, and big bunions, but she just said, "Orl right, I've had me moments – more than what you've had, Grandad, be the look of yer." '

'Well, she was able for him anyhow,' Sally said indignantly. 'Poor woman.'

'It's all just a joke,' Lawrie said. 'They don't mean any harm.'

Sally sighed. 'I'd better go downstairs in case anyone wakes.'

Lawrie kissed her again. 'Mrs Mal would be shocked to know the effect her clothes had, wouldn't she?' he said.

'Not shocked. Surprised maybe, but she'd be made up if I know Mrs Mal,' said Sally.

Without warning she suddenly fell asleep, and Lawrie lay cradling her in his arms, then he too fell asleep. Daylight was creeping round the window blind when Sally woke and reluctantly drew away from Lawrie's arms. She crept downstairs and a few minutes later Lawrie followed her. He washed quickly and dressed, while Sally made him watery tea from the well used tea leaves and cut him a slice of bread. The ninepence he had earned the previous day had been spent on bread, sugar and milk, and oatmeal for Matthew's gruel, so there was nothing to spread on the bread, but Lawrie pocketed it cheerfully.

'I don't need any more now, Sal,' he said, 'This'll keep me going. I'm late for the market or the docks, so I'll strike up the other way.'

'You look very smart,' Sally said, surveying him proudly.

'Aye, I feel like a new man,' he said. He kissed her and murmured in her ear, 'Not just with the new clothes either.'

Sally blushed. 'Good luck, lad,' she said. 'We're due some.'

'Always darkest before the dawn, as Mrs Mal says,' he said cheerfully. 'I'll do all right today. I've got that feeling.'

Sally herself felt better able to manage the day. I should be feeling very weak, she thought, but she was filled with an irrational hope for the future, which made her feel better and stronger than for some time.

Matthew was in a good mood when he woke. 'I've had a real good sleep, girl,' he said. Later, when Sally was washing him and tidying his bed, he said suddenly, 'Take me foot outa bed and take me sock off.'

Sally obeyed, wondering whether his mind had gone completely, but he laughed his guttural, bubbling laugh, so rarely heard these days.

'She was right, begod! Cathy said me big toes were overlong. I told her it was a sign of cleverness.'

'You were right then, Da. Mrs Mal always said you were long headed. She said you should have been in Parliament.'

'I couldn't do no worse than what we've got now,' he said, looking pleased.

When the girls came down Sally gave them the weak tea and a slice of dry bread, but she added a small bowl of gruel for each of them.

'Grandad's had his,' she said. 'Watch him for a minute while I slip out. I'll be back in time for school for you.'

A resolve had been forming in her mind. Throughout all their troubles, she had kept her wedding ring, but now she decided to pawn it. What was between herself and Lawrie needed no outward symbol, she felt.

Solly gave her two shillings on the ring, and she bought a bacon shank, a head of cabbage, then a jar of jam and more bread. With the purchase of small amounts of oatmeal, sugar, peas, onions, and two eggs, she was left with sixpence for coal. The girls were waiting on the step when she returned, hopping about anxiously.

'We'll get the cane,' Mary said, but Sally smiled at her.

'Go on. You'll be in time if you run,' she said. 'There'll be a good dinner today.' She boiled the shank and the cabbage, and made pea soup.

Matthew's good mood had not lasted, and several times he summoned her. 'What are yer doing?' he grumbled. 'Never been near me.'

'I'm doing some washing, Da,' she said. 'And making a good dinner for all of us. Can't you smell the pea soup?'

'I don't want pea soup. I fancy tripe and onions.'

Sally refused to be cast down. 'If you try a drop of soup when it's ready, I'll see what I can do about the tripe and onions.'

233

'Aye. That's what you always say,' he grumbled. 'I suppose that means I won't get it.' But later he enjoyed the pea soup and asked for more.

Sally was delighted to give the girls a good, warming meal, when they came home at lunchtime, and she firmly thrust all her fears for the future from her mind.

One day at a time, she thought. That's the way we'll get through.

Chapter Thirty-Five

The morning was raw but Lawrie strode along, his head erect, enjoying the sensation of walking in good, strong boots once again. It was too late for him to hope to be taken on at the market or the docks, so he went across into the town instead of down the hill.

The first three places he tried needed no men for loading or carting, but on the off chance, he tried a butcher's shop, and was taken on. It was a large, busy shop, even busier now that Christmas was approaching, and Lawrie's job was to carry the sides of meat into the room where men and boys were cutting up and boning it before it went through to the shop, and to carry away the entrails which the men threw into buckets.

At first the long months of hopeless tramping and his poor diet made it difficult for him to keep going, but he stuck doggedly to the job, hoping his muscles would soon harden. The man in charge was a stout, florid man, with a red face and a loud voice. He wore a butcher's blue striped apron and straw hat, and a leather belt around his ample waist with a steel suspended from it on which he constantly sharpened his knives. Towards the end of the day he turned suddenly from one of the chopping blocks, and the steel swung out and hit Lawrie on the side of the head as he bent to pick up a bucket.

'Sorry, lad,' the butcher boomed. Lawrie looked up with his ready smile.

'No harm done,' he said, lifting the bucket and carrying it away. The butcher nodded approvingly. He missed little of what went on, and he had noticed how willing and cheerful Lawrie was, in spite of his gaunt appearance.

When the clearing up was being done at the end of the day, he stopped by Lawrie.

' 'Ere, lad' he said. 'Yer missis want a mutton cloth?' pulling out a cloth from the pile which had been wrapped round the meat. He casually slapped a large piece of shin beef on top of it. 'She might use that, too. Wrap it in the cloth and put it in yer pocket.'

'Er, thanks,' Lawrie stuttered. 'She'll be made up.'

When the clearing up was done and the men were going home, the butcher came through from the shop with four shillings which he gave to Lawrie.

'Yer want it be the day, I s'pose, lad?' he said.

Lawrie looked dazed. 'Have I got tomorrow? Am I here tomorrow?' he asked.

'Ye're 'ere till Christmas, lad, if yer pull yer weight, but I don't have no slackers. I want me money's worth, remember.'

'You'll get that, mister,' Lawrie said fervently.

'Right, six o'clock tomorrer, then, lad,' the butcher said.

Lawrie rushed home, feeling as though he was treading on air. He burst into the kitchen where Sally was standing by the table.

'Look at that,' he crowed, slapping down the four shillings and tugging the mutton cloth and the shin beef from his pocket.

'He gave me that for nothing, and, Sally – I'm there till Christmas.' He grabbed her round the waist and waltzed her round the kitchen, as the two girls watched open-mouthed. Mary snatched up the money and looked at it.

'Are we well off again, Mam?' she asked.

'Yes, love, the bad times are behind us,' Lawrie said joyfully. He picked up one of the shillings and gave it to Mary.

'Here, a penny each for you and Cathy, and bring the tenpence back.' The girls ran off, squealing with joy, and he turned to Sally.

'You don't mind, love? They've been so short of things lately.'

She was smiling. 'You'll never change,' she said. 'No, I don't mind. They've gone short for so long and this is a special day.' She went and lifted the lid of the pan on the gas ring, and before he could say anything about the food, told him quietly, 'I popped my wedding ring, Lol. I got two shillings so we've all had a good meal and I got some coal.'

'Oh, love, never mind,' Lawrie said, slipping his arm around her. 'That must have upset you.'

She shook her head. 'No, it didn't, Lol. I decided it was only a symbol, anyway.'

'Well, we'll be able to get it out again now. Just think, Sal. Six weeks at four bob a day. We're made.'

Sally laughed as she ladled out his soup, then picked up the feeding cup.

'I'll just take Da his drink,' she said. 'I won't be a minute.' She came back right away.

'He's asleep,' she said. 'I don't know how he slept through the din we made. He fancied tripe and onions today, but he took the pea soup and enjoyed it in the end.'

'You'll have to coax him to fancy shin beef tomorrow,' Lawrie laughed. 'I tell you what, Sal, when I'm finished, I'll take a walk down to Gell Street and show Mrs Mal the clothes. Tell her how they turned the scale for me today. I'd never have got the job in my old rags with the boots falling off my feet.'

'Take her some snuff, Lawrie. She enjoys her pinch of snuff.'

'Aye, I will,' he said eagerly. The girls came back, giggling together as they came up the yard.

'We both got the same,' Mary said, laying tenpence on the table. 'A ha'porth of kewins, a farthing's worth of stickjaw toffee and a farthing gobstopper.'

'Well, you made the most of your money,' Sally said. She handed sixpence to Lawrie and put the rest of the money in her purse, enjoying the feeling of weight in her purse once again. When Lawrie had gone out, whistling, she sent Mary to the corner shop for some butter and cheese, and a quarter of tea. If Lawrie was going to work with men in steady work she was determined that he would take a proper carry out, and not be an object of pity or derision. Her father was peevish when he woke from his doze.

'What's going on?' he asked. 'What are them two giggling for?'

'They're just happy, Da,' she said. 'They got some sweets because Lawrie's got a job. Do you fancy anything for your supper?'

'No. Just a drink. That soup was too salty. I've got a terrible drouth on me.'

'I'll make you some tea, or would you like milk or cocoa?' Sally asked.

'Tea, tea,' he said irritably. 'Don't go on, fer God's sake.'

Sally was too happy to be upset by his mood. If only Lawrie was right about the job lasting until Christmas. He seemed very sure and he had repeated the butcher's words several times, but all that had happened in the past few years made her afraid to count on good fortune.

Lawrie came back from Mrs Malloy's a little later, and dropped into the chair.

'She was made up about the job, Sal, especially when I said it was the clothes did it. She was made up with the snuff, too.' He yawned. 'I've felt fine until now,' he said. 'But God, suddenly I'm that weary I don't know how I'll climb the stairs.'

'You'd better go right away, love. You'll need all your sleep with a full day's work to come. And Lawrie –' She stopped.

'What, love?' he asked.

'Don't take any chances, sticking up for someone or anything that might lose you the job, will you?'

'Don't worry,' Lawrie said grimly. '*Nothing* will make me risk this job.' He stood up, then laughed at Sally's serious face. 'If I see anyone being chased with a meat cleaver,' he said, 'I'll look the other way, I promise.' He kissed her cheek.

'It all seems too good to be true,' she murmured.

'It *is* true, love. The tide has turned for us, I'm sure of that.' He knelt down before her, and cupped her face in his hands. 'Just believe that, love, and try not to worry.'

She smiled and bent forward to kiss him. 'I do believe it. I'm sorry to be such a wet blanket, always worrying, but as Mrs Mal says, I can't help my nature.'

They both laughed and Lawrie stood up and stretched. 'I only hope I don't oversleep,' he said. 'It's a six o'clock start.'

'Don't worry, I'll be awake,' Sally said. He went upstairs, but the fear of oversleeping had been planted in her mind. Dear God, what if we did? she thought.

Later when her father was dozing she slipped quietly out of the house, and knocked on a door further down the street.

'Will you ask Mr Briggs to give us a knock on the parlour window in the morning, please?' she asked the woman who came to the door, 'My husband's got a job, a six o'clock start, and I'm afraid we'll oversleep.'

'Yis, of course,' the woman said. 'I'm made up fer yer 'e's werkin'. About five o'clock, my feller goes, so 'e'll give yer a knock.'

'On the parlour window, please,' Sally said. 'I've got a little bed in there with my da, you see.'

'How is the ould feller?' the woman asked.

Sally shrugged. 'Just about the same, but he dozes a lot now.'

'God 'elp 'im, 'e must be fed up, laying all these years, and so must you. I'm made up your feller's got werk. Joe'll knock, no danger.'

Sally hurried home, warmed by the woman's words. People were kind, she thought. Mrs Kilgannon was the exception, rather than the rule.

In spite of her fears she was awake the next morning when the tap on the window came at five o'clock, and she moved the curtain to show that she had heard. Quickly she made up a parcel of cheese sandwiches, and was making tea when Lawrie came downstairs.

'I'm going to boil you an egg,' she said. 'I got two yesterday and Da had one, but I can get more today now.' She lifted the tea packet.

'Can you get hot water if I make up a brew?' she asked.

'A lad made a bucket of tea yesterday,' Lawrie said. 'One of the fellers gave me a jamjar to have some of it. I think they all chip in for the tea and stuff.'

Sally was pouring tea, and said decisively, 'You take a mug today, Lawrie, and put some of that money in your pocket so you can stand your corner. We're all right for food for all of us for a couple of days now, so all I need today is the coal order and we're set up.'

'All right, I'll take sixpence,' said Lawrie. 'I'll get another four bob tonight, as long as you're all right today.'

'All right? I feel as though I should keep pinching myself in case it's just a dream.'

The girls had mugs of hot sweet tea, and bread and jam for breakfast, and Mary asked for a second drink of tea.

'It's lovely,' she said. 'Different to what we usually have.'

'That's because the tea leaves are fresh,' Sally said. 'Wait until you come home at dinner time. I'll have something nice for you.'

'Will we get new clothes and boots now, Mam?' asked Mary.

'If the job lasts you will, love. Just say a prayer that everything goes well.'

'I'm not going to say any prayers,' Mary told Cathy as they left the house. 'I'm fed up praying for things I never get.'

'But this time we might get them,' Cathy pointed out. 'I'm going to pray anyhow, just in case.'

Sally stopped the first coal cart that passed, and when the girls came home there was a bright fire in the kitchen grate, and toasted cheese and a rice pudding in the oven. 'Go and talk to Grandad while I dish up,' Sally ordered Cathy, and she went into the parlour.

'Oo, you've got a good fire today, Grandad,' she said. 'Do you feel nice and warm?'

'Aye, I do,' Matthew admitted. 'About time, too.'

'We're having cheese and rice pudding for our dinner,' she said.

'Have you had yours yet?'

'I've had an egg,' he said. 'I suppose that's all I'm getting.'

'No, it isn't, Da,' Sally said, appearing in the doorway. 'Go and get your dinner, Cath. Mary's made toast.' She came to the bedside and lifted her father higher on his pillows and tucked in the bedclothes.

'Do you fancy some cheese, Da, and some rice pudding?' she asked.

'No cheese. I'd be killed with indigestion. I'll have some rice pudden.'

'I'm making a lovely stew for tonight,' Sally said. 'Lawrie got some shin beef, and I've put some on one side for beef tea, if you'd rather have that.'

'I don't know now, do I?' he said irritably. 'Might as well be in a bloody cocoa rooms, orderin' me grub hours ahead.' Sally made no reply, but went out and brought him some rice pudding.

Lawrie came home that night exhausted, but with four shillings and a parcel of breasts of lamb. It seemed to be regarded as a 'perk' of the job that the regular men, butchers and apprentices, took home a parcel of meat if they wanted it, but they despised such items as breast of lamb or offal of various kinds, which were gratefully received by Lawrie. Savoury odours filled the house again, and Sally could afford to keep good fires going in both rooms, and have enough coal for the boiler. It made the constant washing and drying of bedding much easier.

Better diet and ease of mind helped her to bear with her father's moods, but she bitterly resented his attacks on Lawrie. There were unpleasant tasks caused by Matthew's incontinence which Lawrie willingly helped with, and she felt ashamed that his only reward was a stream of abuse from her father. Often he used words and phrases which sounded foul, but which she did not understand. She was sure that Lawrie did because of his heightened colour.

'I'm ashamed of my da,' she said one night. 'He was always so respectable. I don't know how he knows those words. I know they're bad words, Lawrie, the way he says them.'

'He's not himself, love. He probably disapproved of that language when he was well, but it stayed in his mind, and now his mind's twisted it's coming out.'

'It's not fair the way he talks to you, and all you do for him. I know he's my da and I've got to respect him, but I lose patience with him sometimes.'

Lawrie shrugged. 'Can't be helped. God knows, Sal, we don't know how we'll finish up ourselves, do we? I just hope we go off quick, both of us, no dragging the anchor.' He looked at her sad face. 'But not yet, love. Cheer up,' he said, smiling.

For all of them, but especially for Sally, these weeks were a lull in the battle against bitter poverty, but she was always conscious that the job was only temporary. Her wedding ring was redeemed, but no household goods were replaced. She used the money to pay off some of the rent arrears, and to lay in a good stock of coal. All their boots were renewed, and she was able to buy second-hand dresses, and turn and refurbish them for the girls, and to buy warm coats for them.

Lawrie insisted that she had at least a new apron to cover her much darned and patched dress, and one day she returned in triumph from Paddy's Market with a coat and trousers which she altered for him. It meant that he had a spare set of clothes in case he got wet, but while the indoor job lasted there was much less wear on his clothes and boots. He had been given an old apron to throw over his shoulder as he carried the meat.

Lawrie and Sally awaited Christmas with mixed feelings. It would be so much better than they had dared to hope a few weeks ago, and the children were excited about it, but it would mean the end of Lawrie's job.

'Still, I'm not going to worry ahead,' Sally said. 'I was worried to death about this winter, and look what happened.'

'I'm sure I'll get something else,' Lawrie said. 'I look more fit for work, don't I, and with good clothes as well.'

'You do,' Sally agreed. 'It's been a godsend, this job. We're all built up with the good food, and it's put us ahead with the coal and the arrears. We'll still be feeling the benefit in January and February, and we'll have the worst of the winter behind us.'

Sally insisted that Lawrie kept a shilling a week in his pocket. He paid threepence a week for tea money at work, and out of the rest he brought home small gifts. A quarter of a pound of Sally's favourite pear drops, ribbons for the girls, or a penny doll for Cathy and a hoop for Mary, and a newspaper for Matthew, which he and Cathy read aloud to the sick man to help his weary hours to pass. Sally made no protest, knowing that being unable to give small gifts had been one of the hardest aspects of poverty to him.

Just before Christmas Lawrie came in one night, carrying a sack of potatoes.

'Where did you get this?' Sally asked in amazement.

'Give a guess,' Lawrie laughed. 'I've been leaving coppers off it every week. Don't say I can't plan ahead, too.'

'Oh, Lawrie, that's wonderful. I never thought of paying off a sack, but what about something for yourself? All your spend goes on other people.'

'I'll be having some of these, I hope,' he said with a grin. 'The only thing I want is my pipe, Sal, and I daren't start it. It was damned hard when I had to give it up, so I don't want to go through that again when the job finishes.'

'There's sense in that,' Sally agreed. She was glad that he said nothing about the meetings he had dropped, partly because even the few coppers needed for membership could not be spared. It was the one subject on which she and Lawrie never spoke, but she had an uneasy feeling that his views had not changed, and she dreaded any involvement which might make it harder for him to get or keep a job.

Chapter Thirty-Six

On Christmas Eve the shop was busier than ever, and it was nearly midnight when it closed and the clearing up was done. Some of the men would be working the next day, as the shop opened for Christmas morning, but nothing had been said to Lawrie and he braced himself to hear that his job was finished.

The head butcher was supervising a young apprentice as he carried geese and turkeys to a scrubbed chopping block. Lawrie had been given a piece of belly pork the previous day, which Sally planned to cook for Christmas Day, and now he watched, trying not to feel envious, as the butchers collected their geese or turkeys and left.

Soon only the head butcher and the apprentices remained, and as each finished their cleaning, the butcher handed them a parcel of meat and their wages.

' 'E are, lad,' he boomed to Lawrie, handing him a leg of pork and some sausages. ' 'Ere's yer money, and five bob Christmas box. Yer've werked 'ard.'

'Thanks very much,' Lawrie said fervently. 'And thanks for everything. I'm sorry to go. It's the best job I ever had,' he babbled, overcome with gratitude to the man.

The butcher looked astonished. 'Ye're off then?' he said.

'I thought this was it,' Lawrie stammered. 'I thought –'

'I don't want yer termorrer, we'll only be selling off from the shop, but I'll want yer over the New Year an' a couple a weeks after.' He turned suddenly. ' 'Enery,' he roared. 'Put them buckets in proper.'

He rolled off to deal with 'Enery, shouting over his shoulder to Lawrie, 'Merry Christmas, lad.' Lawrie was too overcome to answer.

Sally was as overwhelmed as Lawrie when she heard his news, and saw the gifts of meat and the extra five shillings.

'It's that head butcher, Lol,' she said. 'God bless him. Hasn't he been good to us?'

'Those lads, those apprentices, they're in God's pocket there,' he said wistfully. 'I wish I wasn't too old to learn the trade.'

'Wait till we tell Mrs Mal,' Sally said. 'I've asked Jimmy over the road about the handcart to bring her up.'

'Never mind the handcart,' he said. 'I never liked the idea of bringing her up on that. We'll get a cab.'

On Christmas morning he went down to Gell Street, and brought Mrs Malloy to Egremont Street in a cab, then carried her into the parlour to see Matthew.

'The style of me, Matty lad,' she laughed. 'A cab, no less.' Matthew was propped up in bed, in a new nightshirt, with his scanty hair brushed, and the children had fastened a red ribbon to the bedrail. He smiled at Mrs Malloy as Sally and the girls bustled around her, arranging a blanket over her knees and a pillow behind her.

'That's grand, that's grand,' she said. 'And the fire right up the chimney. Haven't I every comfort?'

'We'll go and see to the dinner, Mrs Mal,' said Sally, 'and leave you and Da to talk.'

'Aren't they all very good, Matt?' she said. 'The children as well. Sally and Lawrie are well blessed, and sure the children take their pattern from them. God will reward them all.'

The children had been amazed to see their grandfather smile, and speak pleasantly to Mrs Malloy.

'I've never seen Graddad smile like that,' Cathy whispered to Sally.

'You have, love, but you were too young to remember,' Sally said. 'He used to be very different. It's just the illness. Come on now, we'll lay up. The dinner's nearly ready.'

Matthew was unable to eat the dinner, but Sally had bought some calves' foot jelly for him as a special treat, and after having that, followed by potatoes mashed with butter and stuffing, and a baked custard, he settled down for a sleep.

Lawrie had carried Mrs Malloy in to the kitchen for her dinner, while Sally looked after Matthew, and it was obvious that the old lady was in great pain with the rheumatism, although she was as cheerful as ever.

'It's just me legs, girlie,' she said, when Sally came back and Lawrie started to carve the pork. 'I'm grand everywhere else, thank God, and I'm going to enjoy me dinner. Sure, the pig must have been hand reared that provided such beautiful pork.'

'What's a pig got to do with it?' the girls asked, and when Lawrie explained, Mary pushed her plate away.

'Augh, I couldn't eat it now,' she exclaimed.

Mrs Malloy looked worried for a moment, but Sally winked at her and said calmly, 'All right, you'd better get some bread and jam. Pity you didn't know before you ate the pork sausages this morning.' She put out her hand to Mary's plate, but Mary quickly snatched it back.

'I've eaten the sausages so I might as well eat this,' she said, with a toss of her auburn curls. Mrs Malloy smiled to herself, but nobody made any comment.

'Have ye heard from Emily at all?' Mrs Malloy asked.

'No. I wrote to her just before Christmas but there was no reply. I suppose they're in mourning for Aunt Hester.'

'Aye. Poor woman, but it must have been a comfort to her to have Emily with her at the last,' said Mrs Malloy. She looked round the table, happy to see the improvement in the family. Sally and Lawrie had lost their hunted, desperate expressions, and both had put on weight during the recent happy weeks. The girls wore fresh-looking brown dresses with white collars, and Mary had green ribbons tying back her glossy curls. Cathy's ribbons were brown, and although so different in colouring, both girls looked pretty and well-dressed.

'I'll write to Emily again,' Sally said. 'She asked to come here but I didn't want her to see the way we were at the time, and the way Da is.'

'Poor Matty, he's travelling a long hard road,' Mrs Malloy said with a sigh. 'Still, it's a mercy he's got back his speech, at least.' Sally said nothing, thinking how shocked Mrs Malloy would be if she knew how he used his ability to speak.

Soon after the dinner was cleared away, Matthew woke and banged his stick on the bedrail, and Sally went in to him.

'Ah, she's a good daughter, so she is,' said Mrs Malloy. 'There's no wooden dish here at all.'

'What do you mean, Mrs Mal?' asked Cathy.

'Did ye never hear about the wooden dish, child? 'Tis an old Chinese story about a woman who was cruel to her husband's mother. She made her sit in a corner and ate from a wooden dish, while they had grand china ones. When the ould one died, the woman was going to throw away the wooden dish, but her own son stopped her. "Do ye keep that wooden dish, Mother," says he. "My wife will be needing it for ye when ye're old." '

'Served her right,' said Mary.

'Yes,' Cathy said with satisfaction. 'She got a dose of her own medicine.'

'Aye, well, what I'm saying is, see how well your mammy does be treating yer grandad, so bear it in mind when she's grown old herself.'

'But she's old now. She's well over thirty,' Mary said. Lawrie and Mrs Malloy laughed.

'Well, be the same token I shouldn't be here at all,' the old lady said, but both girls put their arms round her and assured her that they were glad she was still there.

Mrs Malloy sat with Matthew again while Sally prepared the tea, and Lawrie slipped down to Gell Street to get a fire burning brightly for her return. After tea he whistled up a cab, and rode down with her, to settle with the cabby and carry her into her house.

'Will you be all right, Mrs Mal?' he asked anxiously.

'Indeed, I will, lad. I can manage fine round me kitchen. I just have to take me time getting up, but I do everything when I'm once on me feet.'

'That sofa's not very comfortable,' he said, looking at the pillow and blankets on the slippery horsehair sofa.

'Well now, I have a spell there and a spell in me chair, and I don't need much sleep for the little I'm after doing,' she said. He made her a cup of tea, then walked home, feeling anxious about the brave old lady who had been such a true friend to them.

Sally had been dismayed to see how much worse Mrs Malloy's rheumatism had become, and after Christmas she frequently sent the girls down to help her.

'How is your Granda, Cath?' Mrs Malloy asked one day, when Mary had gone to the shops, and Cathy was scrubbing the floor.

'Just the same,' Cathy said, pulling a face. 'He says things about Dada and he makes Mam cry sometimes.'

'Ah, poor Matt. It's the affliction that's on him, child. He doesn't properly know what he does be saying.'

'He says Dad only got married to Mam because he had no home of his own, and she could sew,' Cathy said. She sat back on her heels, her face troubled, the floorcloth hanging forgotten from her hand.

Mrs Malloy glanced at her shrewdly. 'His poor mind is sick as well as his body, child. Don't take notice now when he says such things. It's only like someone rambling with the fever.'

Cathy looked relieved. 'Is it?' she said. 'I heard Dada say one day when Mama was crying, "It's only a sick old man saying it, not your da." Is that what he meant?'

Mrs Malloy smiled. 'He said that, did he, girlie? Ah, he's a heart of gold, that lad. Have ye been worrying about it, child?' Cathy nodded, her lip trembling, and Mrs Malloy said briskly, 'The ould floor is clean enough, Cathy. Take out the bucket and we'll sit and have a talk.' Cathy took the bucket out and emptied it then drew a stool up beside Mrs Malloy's chair.

'I'll tell ye now about your mam and dad, so you'll know what happened. Your mam was only the age of Mary when her poor mother died, Lord ha' mercy on her. She brought up her two brothers and her baby sister.'

'That's Emily, isn't it?' Cathy said eagerly. 'Mam told us about that.'

'Well, I helped your mam and she was a good hard-working girl, but a terrible worrier. Sure, she was as dear to me as me own flesh and blood, and I was broken-hearted when all the troubles came on her. The two boys died, and Emily was sent away to the grand relations at Ormesdale, so your poor mam was out of her mind grieving for them. She took a job in the Market, and thanks be to God, your dada came to lodge with me with Paddy. Ye remember Paddy?'

'Oh, yes. I liked him,' Cathy said.

'Sure everyone did, Lord ha' mercy on him,' Mrs Malloy said with a sigh. 'God works in strange ways, child. I thought the world of the two lads that were with me, and when they went back home to Ireland, I broke me heart, yet your dad and Paddy came in their place, and haven't I blessed the day that brought them, many and many a time.' She sat looking in to the fire, until Cathy timidly touched her hand.

'What about Dad and Mam?' she asked.

'Ah, yes. The very day the lads came to me, they were stepping out of the door and your mam came down the street. Herself and Lawrie stood looking at each other as if they'd been struck be lightning itself. The next night he went in to ask your grandad, that was her father, could he take her out, and didn't he finish up asking if he could marry her?' She stopped to laugh at the recollection, smoothing back Cathy's hair from her eager face.

'Poor Matt, he didn't know was he on his head or on his heels. Howsumever, he said they had to wait until they were sure, but they were sure from the first minute they saw each other and they were married in no time.'

'And was Grandad vexed?' asked Cathy.

'Not at all, child. He took a great liking to your dad, and no wonder. They were all as happy as the day was long, especially when yourself and Mary were born, until the illness came on your granda. I've lived a long time, child, but I've never seen two people as fond of each other as your mam and dad. And thank God, they feel the same yet.'

Cathy sat entranced. She loved both her parents dearly, and she hated to hear her grandfather saying things about her father. Although she always insisted to Mary that they were not true, she was troubled when her mother snapped at her father, or when they occasionally quarrelled. She was too young to realise that her mother's nerves had been stretched to breaking point by the worry about money, the furtive trips to Solly's, and the exhausting nursing of her grandfather. Her father, too, had been worn down by the constant, often fruitless search for work, and all the humiliations he had endured, and sometimes Cathy wondered if they were sorry they had married, as her grandfather always said.

As though Mrs Malloy had read her thoughts, she said quietly, 'Hasn't it been a great help to them in the terrible times they've had, that they've faced them together? Maybe they've given out at each other now and again, just the way they could relieve their feelings, but they've stood like a rock together.'

Cathy impulsively hugged the old lady, dimly realising that help had been asked for and given. She sang as she did the rest of the housework, and let Mary take more than her share of a ginger cake without arguing. She told her something of what Mrs Malloy had said, on the way home, but Mary paid little attention. She was watching a boy who was strutting along on the other side of the road, and fluttering her eyelashes at him.

Lawrie's job lasted until the third week in January, and when he was paid off, one of the men told him to try the railway goods yard in Great Howard Street.

'Ask for Mr Cannon,' he said. 'He's my brother-in-law, and I'll tell him about you.' Lawrie thanked the man, but he thought he might just have been trying to be kind, to soften the blow of finishing at the shop. He told Sally and said that he would go the following day, but he warned her not to count on it.

'We've done better than we ever expected from this job, haven't we?' Sally said. 'We've enough coal now to see us through the winter, and a stock of sugar and tea and cocoa, and thank God, we've cleared a bit off the book.'

'Yes, and we're all better off for clothes and boots,' Lawrie said. 'I'm sure I'll do better for jobs now. I feel more able for people, not such a failure.'

'Oh, *Lawrie*,' Sally said, putting her arms around his neck and kissing him. 'Don't say such things.'

Cathy watched them happily through the open door, then moved away quickly, before they realised that they were observed.

The next morning Lawrie went to the goods yard and asked for Mr Cannon. A man came out to see him and asked him some questions, then he told Lawrie to wait and went away. A little later he was called into an office, where another man questioned him, and wrote down his replies.

'Well, that seems all right,' he said. 'But of course it doesn't rest

245

with me. I'll put forward your application, and you will be notified in due course.'

'Thank you very much,' Lawrie said with a beaming smile. 'Good morning.' He hurried home to tell Sally.

'I'm not counting on it,' he said, but Sally knew by his shining eyes that he would be bitterly disappointed if nothing came of it.

'Even to get in to see the other man was important,' she said.

'Aye, that chap at the butcher's, he said the railway wages were low but they were steady, and if you got on the railway it was a job for life.' Neither of them mentioned the railway job again but it was constantly in both their minds.

Lawrie got ten days' work with a building firm.

'The way I tried to get building work in the summer, Sal, and never got anything, and now when everyone's laid off, I get this. It's knocking down, not building, but I was dead lucky to get it. I can't go wrong these days, can I?' he laughed.

After that he got a few days at a timber yard, and when two weeks had passed, a man called at the house.

'Lawrence Ward?' he said. He handed Lawrie a card. 'Report to Great Howard Street yard at seven o'clock Monday. Ask for Mr Whiteside.'

'I've got the job then?' Lawrie said eagerly.

'Looks like it,' the man said with a grin. 'Goodnight.' Lawrie dashed into the kitchen waving the card at Sally.

'I'm in, Sal, I'm in,' he shouted. 'I've got to report on Monday.'

'I heard him,' Sally said. Her eyes were shining, but she sounded a note of caution. 'Don't get too excited, love, until you're absolutely sure. Wait till you start. There might be some hitch.'

'Not a bit of it,' Lawrie said. 'We've reached port, Sal. I can feel it in my bones.'

Lawrie settled quickly into the busy goods yard, and even Sally felt confident that the job would last when he was issued with a uniform and a book of rules.

The arrears on the rent book had mounted up so much that at one time she had decided that they must move to a smaller house, promising to pay Mr Jones when they were able. Only the fear of upsetting her father, and Lawrie's unquenchable optimism, made her postpone the move. The recent weeks while Lawrie was getting steady money from the butcher's had made it possible for her to pay off a little, but now she made a definite arrangement with the landlord that she would pay the rent, plus a small amount off the arrears every week.

'I told you, see,' Mr Jones said. 'I knew the bad times would pass, see.'

Sally smiled. 'Thank you for being so patient,' she said, feeling pleased and proud that the landlord's faith in them had been justified.

Until all the debt was paid, she bought only essentials to replace the goods that had been pawned, but she was able to buy all the food and coal that was needed, and small delicacies to tempt Matthew to eat. His appetite had become very poor, and Sally fancied that his speech was more slurred.

One night when Lawrie lifted him he seemed even more helpless, and Lawrie suggested sending for the doctor.

'He might have had another stroke, Sal,' he said. 'His good arm seemed too heavy for him to lift.'

The docter seemed amazed that Matthew was still alive.

'Strange how some of these old people cling to life,' he said. 'Of course he's had good nursing.'

'Do you think he's had another seizure, doctor?' asked Sally.

'Yes. A slight one. Nothing to be done for him really. I'll give you a bottle to make him sleep, give him some ease. Send someone down for it. He won't last much longer,' he said.

Sally paid him and ushered him out, her mouth set grimly. 'He just didn't care,' she told Lawrie angrily. 'It might have been an old dog he was talking about.'

'Never mind, love. Your da didn't hear him,' Lawrie soothed her.

'I'm not so sure. I can't tell sometimes now whether Da's asleep or not.'

Matthew seemed unaware that the doctor had called, but Sally tended him with even more care and gentleness in case he had heard the doctor's words, and been hurt by them. Lawrie bought him a bell to ring when he needed them, as the stick now seemed too heavy for him to lift.

'I never thought I'd wish to hear that stick banging,' Sally told Lawrie, 'but I do.' She tried to spend as much time as possible sitting with her father, reading to him, or listening to his thick speech and answering him. He seemed to have lost his animosity towards Lawrie, and tried to smile with his twisted lips when Lawrie told him funny anecdotes of happenings in the yard.

One Monday morning in early May the girls returned from school at midday to find Sally sitting with an opened letter on her lap, and the tub still full of clothes.

'Is it that time already?' she said. 'I've been sitting here like one of Lewis's dummies since this came.'

'What is it, Mam?' asked Mary.

'Read it,' Sally said, holding it out to her. 'I just can't believe it.'

Mary took the letter and read aloud:

Dear Sally,
I know this letter will surprise you and I hope your feelings will not be injured.

I was married yesterday to Albert Deakin, a business friend of Uncle Walter's. He is a widower. His wife died some years ago, one year after their marriage.

I am sorry that you could not be present at our wedding, and I hope you won't think badly of me for marrying so soon after Aunt Hester's death, but there were reasons which I will tell you sometime.

We are staying in Bournemouth for a week and it is beautiful, but we will return to Liverpool on Friday.

Albert has a house in Aigburth, and he owns a box factory in

Islington in Liverpool, so perhaps I will see you soon.
Fond love to my father, and to Lawrie, Mary and Cathy.
Yours affectionately,
Emily

Mary handed the letter back to her mother.

'I wish I could go to Bournemouth,' she said.

'Fancy Emily a married lady,' Cathy said. 'I didn't think she was old enough, did you, Mam?'

'A widower, a friend of Walter's,' Sally murmured, staring at the letter in her hand, as though it must hold something which would explain the matter.

'I'm glad she's coming to live in Liverpool,' Cathy said. 'Where's Aigburth, Mam?' Sally had stood up and started to stir the fire, but she paused, poker in hand.

'Aigburth,' she said. 'Now isn't that queer? I always wanted her to live in Aigburth.' She put the poker down and began to cut bread for the dinner, and the girls looked at each other, puzzled by her manner.

'Why did you want her to live there? asked Mary. 'Instead of Ormesdale, you mean?'

'No. When Emily was eight weeks old our mother died, so I brought her up. We used to go to Aigburth for days out, and I'd say to her, "Some day, Emmie, you'll live in one of these posh houses." ' She sighed. 'I never thought that this was the way she'd go there.' She went into the back kitchen and brought in some cold spareribs.

'Come on, eat your dinners,' she said. 'You don't want to be late and get the cane.' She folded the letter and put it on the mantelpiece, thinking ruefully, Well, she got there in the end, anyway.

Lawrie was as amazed as Sally had been when he read the letter.

'I wouldn't worry though, Sal,' he said. 'She says she had her reasons, and they must have been good. She's a rock of commonsense. How old is she now?'

'Nineteen last February,' Sally said.

'Well, she's older than you were when we got married, and we managed to convince your da that we were old enough,' Lawrie said with a hearty laugh. 'We proved we were right too, didn't we?' he added, putting his arm round Sally and kissing her warmly.

248

Chapter Thirty-Seven

A month later another letter arrived from Emily, inviting Sally and Lawrie to bring the children to her house in Aigburth, but Sally was unable to leave her father. He had become even more dependent on her, and fretted if she was out of his sight for long.

'You'll have to invite them here instead,' said Lawrie.

'Oh, but Lawrie, I don't want her to see the way Da is now, and a strange man with her too. I think it would shame Da.'

'But they'll have to see him sometime, love, unless you cut yourself right off from Emily,' Lawrie reasoned. 'You'll just have to warn her how ill your da is now.'

'Yes, you're right,' Sally said, 'and at least we're all in better shape than when she wanted to come when Hester died. Dear God, when I think how we were then, and the difference the months of steady wages have made!'

She wrote to Emily, explaining that Matthew was now so ill that she could not leave him, and inviting Emily and Albert to come on Sunday, when Lawrie would be at home. Emily's acceptance came by return of post.

The two girls willingly helped Sally to prepare for the visit, Mary shopping and helping with the baking, and Cathy blackleading the grate and polishing the brass fender, newly retrieved from Solly's. By Saturday night the house was shining and Sally surveyed it proudly, then looked at the cupboard full of food that she had prepared. She said nothing to Matthew about the visit until Sunday morning, knowing that it was unwise to excite him.

Emily and Albert arrived in a cab, both looking very prosperous. Emily wore a dress and jacket of ribbed brown silk, and a large brown hat, trimmed with cherries. Albert's suit of dark broadcloth had braided lapels, and he wore a curly brimmed bowler hat, and a heavy gold watch chain across his stomach. Emily burst into tears as she stepped into the house and hugged Sally, and for a moment all was confusion as they went into the kitchen with Sally comforting Emily, and Lawrie greeted Albert.

The girls were hopping about, their eyes like saucers at the sight of Emily's clothes, but Sally whispered to Cathy: 'Go and talk to Grandad, love. Tell him we'll be in in a minute.'

Cathy went off and they all sat down, and Sally and Lawrie were able to look at Albert. They were even more mystified by Emily's choice of husband when they saw that he was a burly man with a florid face and a heavy moustache, at least twenty years older than Emily. He sat with his hands on his knees, saying little, but glancing fondly at Emily from time to time.

Sally and Emily were a little shy with each other for the first few minutes, but presently Sally asked if Emily was ready to see her father.

'He'll have heard you arrive, you see, and he gets very agitated,' she said.

'Of course,' Emily said. 'How is he, Sally?'

'You'll have to expect a great change in him,' Sally said gently. 'He had another stroke a little while ago, and his speech is very bad. He's a bit confused sometimes, too.'

Emily stood up.

'I'll go in now, shall I? Don't worry, Sal. Aunt Hester was ill for a while so I know what to expect.'

'I'll just slip in and warn him,' Sally said. She went into the parlour to find her father lying with his eyes closed and Cathy sitting quietly beside him, and nodded to Cathy to go out.

'Emily's coming to see you, Da,' she said. He opened his eyes and she lifted him and plumped up his pillows, then smoothed back his hair and wiped the spittle from his mouth.

'There, Da, you look really smart,' she said. 'Here's Emily now to see you.'

She called Emily who came in and stood for a moment, her bright colour fading with shock. Then she bent and kissed her father.

'Hello, Da,' she said, her voice thick with tears. 'How are you?'

Matthew lifted his good hand and clumsily stroked her hair. 'The little runt?' he said, in his slurred speech.

Emily looked enquiringly at Sally, and she said quietly, 'Uncle Walter.' She bent over her father. 'He's at home in Ormsedale, Da. Emily is here with her husband, Albert.'

Albert had been tactfully hovering in the lobby, and Emily beckoned him into the room.

'This is my husband, Albert Deakin, Da,' she said.

Albert held out his hand. 'How d'you do?' he said. Matthew placed his good hand in Albert's and Emily's tears flowed afresh when she saw the contrast between her father's thin, flaccid white hand and Albert's plump one.

'I'm going to give Emily and Albert their tea now, Da,' Sally said. 'Is there anything you want?' He shook his head and Emily kissed him again.

'I'll be back soon to see you, Da,' she said. They left him and went into the kitchen, where Emily sat down and wiped her eyes on a cambric handkerchief.

'Oh, Sally,' she wept. 'I'd no idea he was so bad. Why didn't you tell me?'

'I didn't want to worry you, love. There's nothing anyone can do.'

'Does he suffer much?' asked Albert, patting Emily's hand.

'No, but he gets weary of lying, unable to move about. Mrs Mal showed me how to rub him, so he doesn't have any bedsores, thank God,' said Sally.

'What does the doctor say about him?' asked Emily.

'The doctor,' Sally exclaimed, banging the teapot down on the hob. She was about to give her opinion of the doctor, but she looked at

Emily's sad face and only said quietly, 'He said there was nothing we could do, only make him comfortable. Da had another seizure, you see. That's why we brought the doctor in again.'

'Sally's been a trump,' Lawrie said warmly. 'Changing the bed three or four times a day, and turning Matt every few hours. That's why he hasn't got bedsores. The doctor said it was good nursing.'

Sally blushed and Albert turned to her.

'Must have been good nursing,' he said. 'Paralysed like that and no bedsores.'

Sally smiled at him. Why, he is a nice man, she thought, even though he looks so solemn. Aloud she said, 'Everybody's helped, the girls and Mrs Malloy, and Lawrie most of all. Sit in now, Emily, and will you sit there, Albert? And you two, stop giggling and come and sit down.'

'You still see Mrs Malloy, then?' Emily said, when they were all sitting round the table. 'How is she?'

'As bright as ever,' said Sally, 'but crippled with rheumatism.'

'How's the man with the violin?' asked Emily.

'Paddy Ryan. He died a while ago, so she's on her own in the house now. She was here for Christmas, and Da was made up to see her. She's been a true friend to us, believe me, hasn't she, Lawrie?'

'Aye, she has. Pure gold, Mrs Mal,' he said earnestly.

'I do Mrs Mal's messages and Cathy does her housework,' Mary said. Emily smiled at her and turned to Cathy.

'Are you quite better, love? No more coughs?'

Cathy shook her head, her cheeks pink. She envied Mary's ability to chat easily to anyone, because she found it so hard to do herself. Now she was even more tongue-tied because she was overawed by Emily's magnificent clothes and jewellery.

As soon as the meal was over, Emily went again to see her father but soon tiptoed back to the kitchen.

'He's sound asleep,' she said to Sally.

'Sit down by the fire then, love,' Sally said. 'He sleeps a great deal and it's a mercy. It helps to get the time over for him. Now tell me all about yourself.'

Emily smiled and blushed as she looked at Albert.

'We had good weather in Bournmouth, didn't we?' she said. 'And Albert's house is very nice.'

'It's a good solid house,' Albert said, 'and good furniture. Emily wants to change things but I think it's comfortable as it is.'

'I'd just like to change things round a bit, make it brighter,' Emily said. 'Not buying new things, or not very much.'

'Well, that's natural,' Sally said. 'You've got the summer before you anyhow, so you can take your time and enjoy it.'

'What about you and Lawrie?' Emily asked. 'You haven't told me much in your letters.'

Lawrie gave his hearty laugh, and they all smiled in sympathy. 'That's a good one,' he said. 'What about yours? The food is interesting, the walks are interesting, the lessons are interesting.'

Emily laughed.

'I know,' she said, 'but we were watched over while we were writing, and then the headmistress read all the letters. We weren't allowed to seal them and I never knew what to say.'

'Never mind, at least we knew you were all right,' Sally said.

'And having an interesting time,' added Lawrie.

The girls had been washing dishes in the back kitchen, and when they had finished Cathy slipped into the parlour and came back to whisper to Sally, 'Grandad's awake.'

'I'll go in,' Emily said, and Sally left her alone with their father for a while before going in with a drink for Matthew. Emily's eyes were red, but she kissed her father lovingly, and promised to come to see him again, before she left the room with Sally.

Albert took his watch from his pocket when they returned.

'Time we were off, Emily,' he said. 'I'll get a cab.'

Lawrie jumped up.

'I'll go,' he said, 'take your time with your coat.'

He dashed out and Albert said to Sally, 'I don't bring my horses out on Sunday, you see.'

'We don't seem to have had time to have a proper talk, Sal,' Emily said, in a disappointed voice. 'It's strange. It's so long since we were together yet I feel so close to you still. I'd love to have time for a real long talk.'

'Could you come for the day then?' Sally said. 'Perhaps Albert could leave you on his way to work and come for you on his way home.'

'Yes, I'll do that,' Albert said. 'It's on my way to the factory in Islington, and you could have your meals with Sally.'

'And I could help you to look after Da,' Emily said eagerly.

On the day that she came Matthew was restless, demanding constant attention, but after the girls had had their midday dinner and gone back to school, he fell into a heavy sleep and Emily and Sally were able to settle down for a talk. The house was quiet, except for the ticking of the tin clock on the mantelpiece, as they sat together on the sofa.

'I like Albert,' Sally said. 'I must admit I was a bit worried, love, when you said there were reasons for marrying him – special reasons, I mean – but I think he's a good man.'

'He is,' agreed Emily. 'It isn't a marriage like yours and Lawrie's, but I'll make him a good wife if I can, Sal.'

'I don't know what you mean,' Sally said, looking puzzled.

'Well, I'm fond of Albert and I know he's fond of me, but there's more than that between you and Lawrie.'

'But you'll have a happy marriage, too, love. Albert's older and a bit more settled, but that's not a bad thing. At least you'll never want.'

'That's true,' Emily said. 'But I always remember the day you moved into this house. Everyone was so happy. I'd have given anything to stay with you and Lawrie and not go back to Ormesdale.'

'But I thought you were happy there!' Sally exclaimed.

'Perhaps at first. I liked the farm, and they gave me so much, but even then – Walter used to do sly things and make remarks to make Hester look small.'

'But she always seemed so bossy, and he was such a quiet little man!' Sally exclaimed.

Emily shook her head.

'It wasn't like that really. Especially when he got on, he was a real tyrant and Hester was afraid of him.'

'Good God!' Sally exclaimed. 'Lawrie said as soon as he met him that Walter was deep, and Da never liked him, but Hester afraid of him? I can't get over it! Mind you, that day we went to see you in that posh house we felt there was something wrong. I was glad Miss Blake was there.'

Emily seemed about to say something, then she turned away and began to rub her hand across the arm of the sofa.

'Aunt Hester was very unhappy,' she said finally. 'That day – did you notice Rose, the parlourmaid?'

'The one who was bouncing around? I didn't like the look of her,' said Sally.

'Walter was carrying on with her,' Emily said. 'She was quite brazen about it and so was he. Hester used to sit crocheting and pretending that there was nothing wrong.'

They sat in silence for a moment, then Sally said with a sigh, 'I should be surprised, but I'm not. I felt that there was something wrong, and to think that you were there with that wickedness going on. Thank God Miss Blake was there. Was that why you were sent away to school, love?'

Emily turned suddenly, and put her arms around her sister, burying her head in Sally's shoulder.

'Oh, Sal, if it was only that,' she said, in a muffled voice. 'I've never spoken to anybody about it. I don't know how to tell you, but I'll feel better if I can talk about it.'

Sally's heart began to beat rapidly, and she closed her eyes, bracing herself for what she was about to hear, and holding Emily close to her.

'What is it, love?' she said gently. 'Tell me.'

'It was Walter,' Emily said. 'When I started to grow up, he started kissing me, and hugging me very tightly. I didn't like it, Sal, but I thought he was just trying to make me like him best. There was always that with them, you see, one trying to make me like them better than the other.'

She lifted her head and drew a handkerchief from her sleeve to wipe the tears from her eyes.

'You must think I'm daft,' she said, but Sally drew her back into her arms.

'No, I don't,' she said. 'Go on, love.'

'It was just before I went to Brussels,' Emily said in a trembling voice. 'Walter came to my bedroom one night. He sat on the bed and talked to me, then he kissed me. I was frightened but I didn't know why. He smelled of whisky.'

She stopped speaking, and Sally gently stroked her hair, saying nothing.

After a moment Emily went on. 'He lay down beside me and stroked my face, then he – he lifted my nightdress and began to rur his hands over my body, especially – I was just beginning to have breasts and he said horrible things. He said they were like lemons, then he said – horrible things about Hester's body.'

Sally was trembling with shock and horror, but she made soothing sounds and held Emily more firmly.

'He said I was growing into a woman and I should be more loving towards him. I was so confused and frightened. I'd started my monthlies and Miss Blake said it meant I was becoming a woman so I thought perhaps this was all part of it. I was stupid, Sal. There was a sound outside the door and he went away, but I stayed awake all night.'

'Why didn't you tell Hester?' Sally said, trying to keep her voice steady.

'Walter told me I hadn't got to say anything, but I tried to tell her. She wouldn't listen – just said she felt ill. Miss Blake was spending the day with friends, and she was supposed to stay the night with them, but she came back.'

Emily's tears had started to flow again, and she sat up and wiped her eyes then sat twisting her handkerchief in her fingers, and staring down at her hands.

'He came again that night. I think he didn't know Miss Blake was back. He lay down under the bedclothes and lifted my nightie again and – and –' Suddenly Emily turned to Sally and hid her face on her shoulder again. 'He rolled on top of me,' she whispered, 'then he pushed himself into me, you know what I mean. Oh, Sally, I've never known such pain, and I was terrified. I screamed and he put his hand over my mouth, but Miss Blake came rushing into the room.'

'The swine. The filthy little swine,' gasped Sally. 'If I could get my hands on him . . . God, Emily, if only we'd known!'

They clung to each other, weeping, and now it was Emily who offered comfort.

'It's all right, Sal. I'm just so thankful Miss Blake was there.'

'But where was Hester?' asked Sally.

'Hiding in her room, I suppose. I don't know, but don't blame her too much, Sal. You don't know what her life was like.'

'I do blame her,' Sally said vehemently. 'She schemed to take you from a good home where you were loved and protected, and she let that terrible thing happen to you. What happened to *him?*'

'I don't know. I just remember Miss Blake rushing in, and hitting him as he tried to get away out of the door. She took me to her room and looked after me, then early the next morning she got a doctor to come. He was one of the friends she'd visited and he – examined me, then he gave me something to drink and I slept and slept.'

'And what happened to the other creature?' Sally said, feeling unable to say his name.

'I never found out. I think it was hushed up for Hester's sake, but he evidently had to do what they told him. I had my meals upstairs with Miss Blake and she stayed with me most of the time, but she must have made arrangements for the school after talking to the doctor and the Vicar's wife, because the Vicar's wife took me to Brussels.'

254

'And while all this arranging was going on, did no one think of telling your own family?' Sally said angrily. 'We would have been up there in short order and that swine wouldn't have had it hushed up, believe me. Da would have killed him.'

'I did ask to come here, Sal, but Miss Blake said Da must have let me go to Ormesdale because he couldn't support me, and it wouldn't be fair to come back.'

'That's not true,' Sally said indignantly. 'Da only let you go because the lads had died of fever, and he thought it was healthier for you there. I was broken hearted when you went and so was he, but he did it for the best. Mind you, he'd never have let you go if Hester hadn't pushed him into it. I hated her for that.'

'I know that now, Sal,' Emily said, taking her hand. 'Miss Blake said I would find it hard to live in poverty after a life of luxury and that wasn't true either, but she didn't know that. She had those sort of ideas but she was a good woman, and she did what she thought was best for me.'

'She went to a post in the Lake District, didn't she?' Sally said, feeling soothed.

'Yes, we corresponded for a while, then she married and went to America, and we lost touch.'

'But when you came back when Hester was dying – you were safe then?' Sally said.

'Yes, but things were no better in other ways. Rose ruled the house and she made my life a misery. She's an evil woman.'

'But why didn't you come here then?' Sally began, then she clapped her hand over her mouth. 'Oh, Emily, that wasn't when you asked to come here and I refused, was it?'

Emily nodded.

'Oh, love, why didn't you give me some hint? I was just so ashamed of the state we were in, so ground down with trouble, and half starved and in rags, but nothing would have mattered if I'd known.'

'I *was* feeling desperate,' Emily admitted. 'But Albert asked me to marry him, and I was just so glad to get away from there. I wouldn't have married him, though, Sal, if I hadn't been fond of him.'

'I know you wouldn't, love,' Sally said, kissing her. 'And I'm sure you'll be very happy. You'll just have to put all this out of your mind. Forget it ever happened.'

'I'll try,' Emily said. 'I feel so much better now that I've talked about it, and you don't despise me, Sal.'

'Despise you!' Sally exclaimed. 'Good God, Emily, why should I? I'm just so angry that the people who should have protected you took advantage of you.'

'But I've often thought since – I should have locked my door or screamed sooner or something.'

'Nonsense, you were a child and that swine . . . and Hester, too. I'll never forgive her either, but he'll be paid back some day. Now you forget it, love. I'll never speak of it again unless you want me to.'

Emily gave a long sigh.

'Oh, Sal, I feel as though a weight has rolled away from me. It made

255

it easier, too, that you got annoyed because I didn't come here.'

Suddenly Sally raised her head, then darted into the parlour to attend to her father.

'I didn't hear a sound,' Emily said when she came back. 'You must have sharp ears, Sal.'

Sally smiled. 'It's like when you have a young baby,' she said. 'You hear the slightest sound from them, even if you hear nothing else.'

A little later the girls came home from school, and in no time at all, it seemed, Albert arrived to take Emily home.

'Can I come again?' Emily asked. 'I'd like to help you with Da. You've done it alone long enough.'

'Anytime, love, you're welcome, but if you help with Da you'll need an apron to cover your good clothes. Even giving him a drink can be messy.'

'I'll bring one,' Emily said. 'I want to do everything for him, Sal, not just giving drinks.'

'We'll see,' Sally said, deciding privately that Emily would never face any of the more unpleasant tasks which caring for their father entailed.

Before she left with Albert, Emily drew Sally into the parlour and hugged her.

'Thank you again, Sal,' she whispered. 'I'm so glad that you're my sister.'

Chapter Thirty-Eight

Emily arrived on Friday, with a large white apron and a basket containing calves' foot jelly and grapes for her father. She donned the apron immediately, telling Sally that she was determined to do her share of the nursing. Sally had changed the bed and was washing the bedding when Emily arrived, so she told her that the best help she could give was to read to her father until he was ready to have a meal. She also warned Emily that he might swear or say something about Lawrie, but she should disregard it.

'I can't understand him very well,' Emily confessed.

'Just as well,' Sally said drily. 'He's not so bad now, but he had a spell when he was abusing Lawrie all the time, even to Cathy, and his language was shocking. Lawrie said it was what he had heard but wouldn't have used while his mind was right.'

'I'm sure that was true,' Emily said. 'I remember him as a very respectable man. I'll have to call you if he asks for anything, and I can't understand.' She went to read to her father, and Sally was able to work on undisturbed for a precious hour.

When Matthew fell asleep, Sally was free to sit down when Emily came out of the parlour, and have a cup of tea.

'You've been a great help to me already, Em,' she said. 'I can never get time to myself like that when I'm alone with him.'

'Tell me what you meant the other day,' Emily said. 'Were you really half starved, Sal?'

Sally nodded. 'I didn't mean to tell you, but I had to explain why I put you off from coming here. It was a bad time. Lawrie's firm closed down in the August and Da had his seizure the following February. It was a bad time all round in Liverpool, no work, and prices up and wages down even for people with jobs.'

'Albert has told me about it,' Emily said.

'At first Lawrie got odd jobs, and I was getting some sewing, and Da was still working. We'd had a bad time, with Da and Cathy ill, and I was very weak after I lost that baby, but we thought it was all behind us, and it was just a matter of hanging on until Lawrie got a steady job, then Da had the seizure. He's been bedridden ever since.'

'Poor Da, and poor you, Sally, to have all that worry and nursing. I wish I could have helped.'

'I didn't want to worry you, love, but things got desperate for us. I couldn't sew, and we had to depend on what Lawrie could get, which was less and less, so we sold stuff from the house.'

'I could have helped in that way, Sal. Even in Brussels I had an allowance.'

257

'I was ashamed to tell you. I know it wasn't our fault, but when you're down like that you feel bad about people knowing. Mrs Mal was the saving of us.'

'How, Sal?' said Emily.

'Well, we were at the end of our tether, everything sold and the winter to come. Lawrie's clothes and boots were falling apart, so he didn't have a chance of a job, because he looked so gaunt and shabby. Mrs Mal sent Paddy Ryan's clothes and boots up to us, and the very next day Lawrie got a good job in a butcher's.' She sat for a moment, staring into the fire, and Emily tried to conceal her horror.

'He got meat every night, and the steady money meant that I could buy coal and food, and rig us all out in clothes and boots. He had nine weeks' work, and he got five shillings and a leg of pork for Christmas. To top it all, a man he worked with spoke for him for the railway job.'

'To think of all that going on, and I knew nothing,' Emily said, her voice trembling. Sally took her hand.

'You had worse troubles, love, and had to face them on your own. At least Lawrie and I had each other.'

'He's a lovely man, Sally. So happy and always ready with a joke, and yet so dependable. I think Cathy is very like him, isn't she?'

'Yes, she's been a good help to me, Em. Mary has helped me but Da won't have her near him, so I've had to depend on Cathy a lot.'

'But Da was so fond of Mary when she was little, wasn't he?'

'I think she's partly to blame. She was very impudent to him, and I've caught her putting her tongue out at him, and jumping back before he could clout her with his stick,' Sally confessed.

Emily laughed. 'I know I shouldn't,' she said, 'but she's such a little monkey. I can just picture her tantalising Da.'

'She'll have to alter her ways,' Sally said. 'She'll be working soon. In some ways she's young for thirteen, but in other ways she's far too old. I worry about her.'

'I don't think you need to, Sal. She's been well brought up, and always had a good example from you and Lawrie, so I'm sure she'll be all right. She won't be put on by anybody, that's one thing.'

Sally stood up, and Emily jumped to her feet.

'Are you going to see to Da? You promised you'd let me help,' she said.

Sally hesitated. 'He might be upset if you were there while I changed him,' she said. 'If you could wash the pots for me, or put those dry sheets through the mangle it would be a great help to me.'

Emily willingly agreed, and later she gave her father some of the steamed fish which Sally had prepared for him.

After Emily had gone home, Sally went in to her father and he said immediately, 'Money there, girl. Carriage an' all. That's what you could do with.'

'I've got all I want, Da, and a good husband too. If Emily's as happy as me she'll be very lucky,' Sally said crisply. Warned by her tone, Matthew said no more.

During the following months Emily came twice a week to visit them. Sally still refused to let her help with changing the bed or washing the soiled clothes, but Emily helped to prepare her father's food, and feed him with it, and she spent many hours sitting with him, talking or reading to him. Sally appreciated this. It meant that she was free to do housework or to shop, and relieved the strain she had been under.

She was still not free to visit Emily's house, but Mary and Cathy went several times, and returned full of the wonders of the imposing mansion. Sally smiled wryly one day when Mary told her proudly that they had played in a little park.

'It's not for everybody, Mam,' she said. 'But Aunt Emily's got a key because she lives in the Square, so me and Cathy could go in there.'

A picture rose in Sally's mind, of herself holding four-year-old Emily by the hand and trying to explain why they could not go in the park, and her promise that some day Emily would live in one of the houses. Life was strange, she mused, and it had a way of working out in unexpected ways.

Gradually during Emily's visits, as she and Sally talked and Matthew slept, a clearer picture emerged of life at Ormesdale, and Walter's behaviour.

Much that Emily had been unaware of as a child became clear to her when she returned to Greengates from Brussels, at the end of her schooldays. Local families had long ceased to visit them, and now she realised that this was because of Walter's openly flaunted affair with Rose, and his gambling parties with dubious friends. Hester had steadfastly turned a blind eye to all that happened, and taken refuge in imaginary illness.

'She had a sad death, Sal,' Emily said one day. 'When I came back I was shocked to see how ill she was, and in so much pain, with no one bothering about her. Of course she had pretended to be ill so often, but I was glad I was with her so she didn't die alone.'

'What about Walter?' Sally said.

'He kept out of my way, and I just ignored him if we happened to meet. He never came to see Hester, perhaps because I was with her, but I think his conscience troubled him afterwards because he gave her a big funeral. Perhaps he remembered the good days on the farm,' Emily said. 'Pity they didn't stay there. He might have been a better man, and poor Hester would have been happier.'

Sally said nothing. She was sorry to hear of such a death, but her bitterness towards Hester was undiminished.

'What happened after the funeral?' she asked.

'Nothing changed really. I think Rose had been running the house for years, but she had more power to make my life a misery,' Emily said. 'I was desperate to get away from there, but I'd had no training for a job, not even to go in service, although I'd have done anything. Thank God, Albert asked me to marry him.'

'Thank God,' echoed Sally. 'He's a good man.'

'He is,' said Emily. 'He's been very patient with me, because at first I cried every night if he even came near me.'

'And are things all right with you now, love?' asked Sally.

Emily blushed.

259

'Yes, but I wonder, Sal. Perhaps I'm deformed or something. I was in such a state that night, you see, bleeding and everything. It's strange there's no sign of a baby, and it must be my fault because Albert's first wife died in childbirth.'

'Nonsense, love. Many people don't start a family right away,' said Sally.

Emily sat pleating the edge of the apron she wore, her head bent. 'Perhaps it's a judgement on me,' she whispered. 'I still blame myself for letting that happen, Sal.'

'Put that right out of your head,' Sally said firmly. 'It was *all* Walter's fault, and Hester's for not looking after you. A baby will soon come, and then you'll wonder why you worried.'

She was glad to see Emily smile, but later she told Lawrie about the conversation.

'I hope it won't always affect her,' she said. 'Fancy thinking that she was to blame, but you can't touch pitch and not be defiled they say.'

'Not a bit of it,' he said. 'Her innocence protected her from a lot, and that other business, feeling guilty, it's like after a bereavement. People always blame themselves for something they've done or haven't done, but they work through it in the end. She'll feel better now she's talked to you.' As usual, his words comforted Sally.

On another occasion, Emily took Sally's hand, which was red and puffy from constant immersion in hot water.

'Oh, Sal, your poor hands. They were always so slim and elegant looking. I used to think it was no wonder you could do that lovely sewing,' she said.

'I don't have occasion to do fine sewing now,' Sally said. 'Just before Da was ill I was only doing machining on trousers and that sort of thing. I'd lost the work from Libby's and the embroidery from the clerical tailors, so when the sewing machine went back I was sunk. I couldn't have done anything very intricate anyway, while I was listening for Da all the time.'

'I didn't realise how much attention Da needs,' Emily said. 'I just don't know how you managed all these years, Sal.'

'The girls and Lawrie helped me like I told you, and Mrs Mal used to come and sit with Da, to give me a chance to get something done, but of course she's not able now. I'm very glad of your help with him, Em. He used to want me to sit with him all the time, and he'd get ratty if I left him to see to things.'

'You've been a marvel, Sal. A real devoted daughter.'

'Don't say that, Emily,' Sally said, flushing. 'I've lost my temper with him many a time, and sometimes – well, I almost hated him.'

'You were just tried too far. Anyone can see the care he's had,' Emily said.

'I'll tell you the truth,' Sally said. 'I'd even thought of putting him in the Workhouse Infirmary, but Lawrie went mad at the idea. He said we were family and we should sink or swim together. It was just that I felt so guilty, Em. Lawrie and the children going hungry, so we could give Da what he needed, and me not able to work.'

She stopped, appalled by the look of horror on Emily's face.

'I wouldn't have done it when it came to the point, Em. It was just that we were desperate, and I was tempted. Don't look so shocked.'

'I'm shocked to think that you were in such straits, Sal. I didn't realise that you were actually *hungry*.' She looked around the kitchen at the gleaming grate, the well-scrubbed table now covered with a fancy cloth, and the bright pegged rug beneath their feet.

'It all looks so cosy, just as it always did.'

'Yes, well, those days are all behind us now. Lawrie's job is for life if he's careful, and Da is not so nasty as he was with Lawrie.'

'When did he turn against Lawrie? They used to get on well, didn't they?'

'Quite a while ago, and God knows why. Lawrie's always so gentle when he's lifting him, and he's done any sort of unpleasant job for him, and got nothing but abuse for it. Come to think of it, it started before the seizure.'

'Perhaps it was a warning of his illness,' Emily suggested.

'Maybe, but many a man wouldn't have taken the abuse from him the way Lawrie did. I know we have our differences sometimes, but I'll never forget that Lawrie did that. I really respect him for it.'

'You and Lawrie *quarrel*?' Emily said, wide-eyed.

'Of course we do, love, and so will you and Albert,' Sally laughed. 'I think he's too spendthrift, and I'm sure he thinks I'm mean. He can't keep a penny in his pocket, and he believes any hard luck story. We used to argue about him getting mixed up with politics and trade unions, but he's had such a fright, I think, that he steers clear of them now.'

'He won't have any trouble in this job, will he? He told Albert it's like the Army, officers and men, and lots of rules and regulations, but he likes the job.'

'He'd like any steady job after what he's been through,' Sally said. 'He feels secure now. The money's poor, only twenty-one shillings a week, but it's coming in regularly every week, and it's a job for life, so that's a great relief for both of us.'

'Fancy you quarrelling. I can't imagine it,' Emily said.

Sally laughed. 'We often have a few words,' she said cheerfully, 'but it's soon over. Lawrie takes everything to heart so much – hungry kids, and widows and old people. I feel for people myself, but I don't think I can change the world singlehanded the way he does.'

'It's no crime to be soft-hearted, Sal,' Emily said.

'No, but he goes too far. When he worked in that warehouse in the South End, he was forever walking home because he'd given his fare away. And his carry out, I'm sure he never eats half of it. Even when he only had a dripping butty, he gave it to a child.'

Emily was unconvinced. 'I still think he shouldn't be blamed for that,' she said.

'Do you know he got a black eye once, jumping in when he saw a man thumping a woman? Crowds all round, but bold Lawrie had to be the one.'

'I agree with him doing that, too,' Emily said stubbornly.

'*I* don't,' said Sally. 'He got the black eye off the woman.' They both laughed.

'The best part of a row is making up,' Sally said. 'When we go to bed, I soon forget I'm vexed when Lawrie's arms are round me. We're supposed to live like brother and sister, but we forget all that.'

Matthew's bell rang, and Sally jumped to her feet and hurried in to him. Good job he rang, she thought. I don't know what came over me, talking like that to Emily. It must be because she's so sympathetic.

'What's she sitting out there for?' Matthew grumbled. 'It's me she's come to see.'

'We thought you were still asleep, Da,' Sally said, lifting him higher on his pillows, and wiping his mouth. 'Here's Emily now.'

Emily came in with a newspaper, and began to read aloud all the news, especially the movements of shipping in the river, which always interested him. This gave Sally an idea, and she spoke of it to Lawrie when he came home.

'Da seems to be so interested in the shipping lately, Lol. Why don't you tell him what's in the river, and what's laid down at Laird's now?'

Lawrie agreed, and every night after his meal he went in to tell Matthew about the ships limping in to dock, rusty and encrusted with barnacles, or the great liners, moving majestically down the river with tugs fussing around them. The sick man's attention could only be held for an hour or less, but he often spoke of what Lawrie had told him during the hours when he lay awake at night, and it helped to pass the tedious time for him.

Lawrie was very happy these days. He had made a window box and set it on the kitchen windowsill, and in it he grew mint and parsley and chives. One night he arrived home with two sacks of soil on a handcart.

'I'm going to take up some flags in the backyard for a garden,' he told Sally. 'A fellow in work has done it with his.' For the following nights he laboured until it was dark, taking up the flags and spreading the soil before planting the cuttings from his friend.

'Perhaps Emily will give you some cuttings,' Sally suggested. 'I believe her garden's lovely.'

'The gardener won't let her, Mam,' Cathy said. The two girls were watching Lawrie, and Mary nodded.

'He wouldn't let her give us a peach,' she said. 'Aunt Emily was going to give us one each, but the gardener said Mr Deakin had counted them.'

Sally and Lawrie looked at each other, and Lawrie said easily, 'Probably they weren't ripe enough. Who's going to get me some water?'

Sally said nothing, but she was disturbed by the incident, and even more worried when the girls came in asking for jam butties after their next visit to Aigburth.

'I'm starving,' Cathy said. 'They have awful little dinners, Mam.'

'The dishes are lovely,' said Mary. 'There was a big silver one with a lid on it, but only three tiny little bits of fish, and little dishes of potato and peas.'

'For afternoon tea there were six little sandwiches,' Cathy said, 'so we were glad Aunt Emily didn't want any so we could have three each.'

'That's enough,' Sally said belatedly. 'It's very rude to criticize what you're given to eat.' She told Lawrie about it later.

'It seems very odd to me. Emily can always eat a good meal when she comes here. I wonder if that housekeeper rules the roost, and keeps her short.'

'The girls are exaggerating, probably. Albert didn't get that size on poor meals,' Lawrie said.

'That's true,' Sally said with relief. 'I was just worried in case Emily was bullied by the servants.'

'Put it out of your mind,' Lawrie advised. 'You know what kids are.'

When Emily came again, Sally probed tactfully about the servants.

'Mrs Barry, the housekeeper, looked after Albert when he was on his own,' Emily said, 'but he wants me to take over the housekeeping, so she's showing me how to run the house.'

'You'll like that, won't you, love?' Sally said, but Emily looked doubtful.

'There's a lot to learn, Sal,' she said. 'Mrs Barry is very economical, and very strict with the maids and the cook. I hope I'll be able to balance the housekeeping books as well as she does. Still, I've got another three months to learn before she goes.'

Sally was less troubled, blaming the economical Mrs Barry for the poor meals, but she could not avoid noticing that although Emily was always richly dressed, she seemed to have little money to spend. Her gifts for the girls, or for her father, were always inexpensive, and the present of grapes from the glasshouses was never repeated.

She said no more to Emily about the servants, but talked instead about Lawrie's attempts at gardening.

'He grew that mint,' she said proudly, as they laid the table for dinner. 'I told him he should take up some more flags and grow the potatoes and peas as well.'

'You keep a good table, Sal,' Emily said as she helped to dish up the dinner. 'I don't know how you do it.'

'It's only breast of lamb, twopence a sheet,' Sally said, 'but it's tasty.'

'You could do without finding meals for me as well,' Emily said.

'For God's sake, what's one dinner with all of ours?' Sally said. 'It's as easy to cook for five as for four.'

She turned the subject immediately by telling Emily of some of her early attempts at cooking after her mother died, but she wondered uneasily if Emily had realised why she was asking about the servants.

'Just coincidence,' Lawrie said when she told him. 'Or she's been thinking that for a while, and it came into her mind when she spoke about learning housekeeping.'

Sally was becoming increasingly concerned about Mrs Malloy, but Matthew could now be left with Emily sometimes, and Sally was able to go and help her old friend. She always found her cheerful and uncomplaining, but all her respectable neighbours had left, and the houses about her seemed to be filled with rough and disorderly people.

Rough though they were, none of them would have harmed or upset Mrs Malloy, and several of the women had offered to help with her cooking or cleaning, but the old lady was too fastidious to accept.

'Imagine eating anything cooked be the like of them,' she said. 'Sure they'd bring more than themselves into the house. Every one of them is walking alive with fleas and bugs.'

She managed to make her refusals courteous, however, and the next door neighbour said to Sally, 'I've told the owld lady ter knock on the wall if she wants anythin'. She says she's got youse ter look after 'er, but she might be took bad when she's on 'er own.'

'That's good of you,' Sally said gratefully. 'She's very independent, you know. She won't let us do all we want to do.'

'Aye, owld ones get funny ways,' the woman said, and Sally felt comforted, knowing that help of a sort was available for Mrs Malloy.

Matthew had become very quiet and apathetic, content to lie for hours without speaking as long as someone sat with him, and Emily suggested that she should accompany Sally to Gell Street one day, while Cathy sat with her grandfather. Sally agreed, knowing that Mrs Malloy would be pleased, and they set off together. Sally was as neat as usual, but Emily was dressed in a well-cut brown costume, with a lavishly trimmed hat, and was the object of much attention when they reached Gell Street.

The houses looked dirty and neglected, with slatternly women at the doors, and barefoot ragged children playing in the gutters. The women and a group of barefoot girls chopping firewood outside the end house stared curiously as the sisters passed, arm in arm.

'I feel like an animal in the zoo,' Emily whispered. Sally felt ashamed of the street.

'It wasn't always like this,' she told Emily. 'None of us had much money, but we were respectable. Mind you, a lot of people got drunk so they weren't as well off as us. Da always turned up all his wages.'

They were relieved when they reached Mrs Malloy's house, and pleased by her delight at seeing them.

'Aren't ye the living model of your poor mam, Lord ha' mercy on her,' she said to Emily. 'Ah, if ye're as good as her ye'll do well. Sure, she was mourned be all that knew her.' She wiped her tears away with the corner of her apron.

'Pay no heed to me, girlie,' she said. 'Just seeing ye walk in the door gave me a shock, but I'm delighted to see the woman ye've grown.'

'How do you manage, Mrs Mal?' asked Emily.

'Well, now, Sally and the girls have been as good as gold to me, and Lawrie does be often in to do odd jobs. The little lad across the street comes in and builds up me fire, and gets a message for me.'

'But what about food?' asked Emily.

Mrs Malloy smiled at Sally. 'Doesn't she be always bringin' or sending down food for me, and the odd time young Johnny gets something for me. He got me a bowl of scouse at Flanagan's yesterday, and I told him to get a penn'orth for himself, the way he wouldn't be dipping his fingers in mine,' she laughed.

They stayed for an hour, and Sally did some washing, then swept up the hearth and heated the broth that she had brought. She laid a small table so that Mrs Malloy could eat her meal without rising from her chair, then while Emily said goodbye she slipped away and brought back a jug of stout and placed it with a glass on the table, before making her farewells.

'I'm worried about her,' she confided to Emily as they walked home. 'She always puts the best side out, but life is getting harder and harder for her. The rheumatism is so bad in her legs and back.'

Emily could offer no comfort, and they were glad to go into the house, and hear Cathy's infectious giggle, and the sound that passed for laughter with Matthew.

The weather had become warm and sultry, and the girls told Sally that many of the houses in the Square where Emily lived had been closed for the summer while the owners were away.

Sally noticed that Emily seemed quieter and thinner as the days passed, and when she and Albert visited them one Sunday, Sally took the opportunity of hinting to Albert that Emily should have a holiday, but without success.

'We've had one expensive holiday already this year,' he said. 'I can't leave the business but Emily can sit in the garden or the key park, can't you, chicken?' Emily nodded, and Sally felt it was wiser to say no more, but she raged to Lawrie later.

' "An expensive holiday in Bournemouth",' she said. 'That was their honeymoon in March. Emily needs a holiday *now*.'

Lawrie smiled at her. 'So do you, love, but there's no chance of even a day out for you,' he said ruefully.

'That's different. Emily's used to a different kind of life to us, and he could take her away if he wasn't so mean.'

'Don't worry about it,' Lawrie soothed her. 'At least she can sit in the garden or the key park, as he says.' He slipped his arms around her, feeling a rush of tenderness at her absence of self pity, and her concern for others.

'She's growing up, love,' he said gently, 'and she's got more responsibilities. That's why she seems quieter, so put it out of your mind, and try not to worry.' And Sally was comforted.

Chapter Thirty-Nine

In October Mary left school, and Sally accompanied her to Denby's department store, armed with a good reference and a letter from Miss Carrington. After a lengthy interview Mary was engaged to start work the following day at a wage of six shillings a week, with dinner and tea provided, and a commission of threepence in the pound on her sales.

Mary was greatly excited when she dressed the following morning in the neat dark dress with a white collar that Sally had made for her. Sally insisted that she should eat a good breakfast, then waved her off, feeling that she had done all she could to help her child on her entry into the world of employment.

Mary seemed very different when she returned home at eight o'clock that evening, white-faced, with shadows of fatigue under her eyes.

'It's just the standing, Mam,' she said. 'The other girl said I'd get used to it. She let me sit on the floor behind the counter for a bit, but she gets all the best sales so I won't be earning much commission.'

'You should have a chair to sit on, and more rest breaks with such long hours,' Lawrie said angrily. 'Pity you haven't got a union to stand up for you.'

Sally looked up in alarm. 'Don't be putting ideas like that into her head, Lawrie,' she said.

'No, we'll all keep our mouths shut and our eyes lowered,' he said bitterly. 'Do nothing and say nothing, in case we upset them.'

Sally pursed her lips, but said no more, as she brought a bowl of water for Mary to soak her feet.

After a time Mary became used to the standing, but the petty restrictions on the staff annoyed her, and she was furious when fourpence was stopped from her wages because of a broken pudding basin.

'It wasn't even me who broke it,' she said. 'I saw a woman knock it off the shelf but she rushed away.'

'And they're supposed to be one of the best employers,' Lawrie said to Sally. 'God knows what happens in the worst shops.' Sally said nothing, determined not to be drawn into any discussion about unions.

She was growing more and more worried about her father, who seemed to become weaker every day. Cathy was invaluable to her at this time, helping with the nursing and doing much of the housework, and sometimes Sally worried because the child was indoors so much, but Cathy never seemed to feel put upon. Whenever possible Sally sent her to help Mrs Malloy or left her in charge of Matthew while she went herself to Gell Street.

'Aren't ye well blessed now in Cathy?' the old lady said. 'Sure, I've

267

known hardworking people with miserable gobs on them that take the good out of what they do for ye, and fly-be-nights, always full of laughs but never there when ye need them, but that child does everything so cheerful and willing. It's as good as a bottle of medicine to see her walk in the door.'

'She misses Mary,' Sally said. 'The hours are so long, and Mary wants to go out with her friends for a bit of a break when she comes home, so Cathy's in bed and asleep by the time she comes home again and goes to bed.'

'The job's going well, then. She's still liking it,' said Mrs Malloy.

'Mm, there are drawbacks,' Sally admitted, 'but she's lucky to have a job there. Lawrie goes mad because she's fined something nearly every week, and it's not her fault, but I don't want him putting ideas about a union into her head.'

'Don't worry, girlie,' Mrs Malloy said shrewdly. 'Sure Mary will never fight any battles but her own. Cathy's the one ye need to be worrying about for that, the way she does be always with Lawrie and telling me about his ideas.'

'Does she?' Sally exclaimed. 'I'll soon put a stop to that!'

'Ah, don't be flying off now. Isn't the child not ten years old yet. There's many a long year before ye need to say a word about that.'

Sally took her advice and said nothing to Lawrie, but a few weeks later unions were the cause of a quarrel between them anyway.

Lawrie seemed very subdued when he came home from work, and a little later he said to Sally.

'D'you remember Jack Turner, Sal, from the warehouse?'

'The union fellow who got the sack?' Sally said. As usual at any mention of unions, she spoke stiffly.

'He wasn't a union man. If we'd had a union he wouldn't have been sacked for standing up for a poor feller who couldn't stand up for himself,' he said. Her temper rose.

'Well, what about him?' she snapped.

'He was killed last night. His sister came to tell me,' Lawrie said quietly.

Sally said nothing, and he went on, 'You know the way poor young lads hang around the docks, selling themselves to Lascars, very often just to get food because they're starving? Jack has been trying to do something for them, to save them, and a knife in the back was his reward,' Lawrie said bitterly.

Sally was ironing and she banged the iron down with short angry jerks.

'So I suppose you want to take his place and get a knife in *your* back,' she said.

Lawrie stood up. 'I can admire a man without having the guts to do what he does,' he said. 'Anyhow, as Jack once said and you never forget, I've given hostages to fortune. I've got a wife and children to think of, which he didn't have.'

Tears of mortification stood in Sally's eyes as he walked towards the back kitchen, and she banged the iron down on the jockey, unable to see clearly.

'I'm very sorry we're in your way,' she shouted. 'Maybe *we* should go out and get knifed and leave you free to play Lord Muck.'

Lawrie's face was white as he snatched up his cap from the dresser. 'I'm going out,' he said, his voice shaking with anger. 'I've lost a friend, but I don't expect any sympathy from you. You're only concerned about your own, but everything that happens concerns us all. We're not on a bloody desert island, you know.'

He strode out and Sally sat down and cried, too upset to continue with her ironing, but as she grew calmer she began to think over Lawrie's words.

I'm right to think about my own, she thought, but as she recalled various incidents, doubts entered her mind. She thought of the years of Lawrie's unemployment, the degrading waiting in all weathers like cattle to be selected for the docks, the times when tallies were tossed among them, and men fought like animals for them, for the chance of half a day's work to keep their families from starving. All the other humiliations he had endured, and there were thousands suffering as he did. Even Lawrie's spirit had almost been broken by it, and now Mary. So tired by the long hours of standing, and the petty bullying and the restrictions, and even more upset by the injustice of the fines. Fourpence had been deducted from her first week's wages for the broken basin, and ninepence the following week. When she asked why, she was told that the address she had written down for glasses to be delivered to was wrong.

'But it was the address the lady gave me,' Mary protested. 'She was sending them for a present.' She was blandly told that the customer was always right, and she must be more careful in future.

By the time Lawrie returned, Sally had begun to think that perhaps he was right in wanting changes. Like many easygoing people, Lawrie's anger, though slow to rouse, could be deep and lasting, but he always responded to any overture by Sally after a row. Now she smiled at him, and asked if he wanted a cup of cocoa. He refused, but smiled back at her as he sat down to take off his boots.

'How is he?' he asked, nodding towards the parlour.

'Just dozing,' Sally said with a sigh. 'He's hardly eaten anything all day.'

Nothing was said directly about the quarrel, but later Lawrie said quietly,

'I wish you could see things my way, Sal, about doing something about all the injustice. Rich and poor, it's as if we don't both belong to the human race.'

'I do agree about things being wrong,' Sally said. 'But I don't see how the likes of us can change them. Surely there's clever people to do that.'

'The clever people are well suited with the way things are, and they're busy making sure nothing changes,' Lawrie said grimly. 'No, Sal. Most posh people despise the poor, and think poverty's a sin. Some of them do things to help with soup kitchens and so on, but they're only dealing with the results of injustice, not the cause.'

'Well, I know you read a lot about it and I don't know about these things, but I'm sure no one would take any notice of the likes of us.'

'They would if we stood together, Sally. Suppose all the girls in Denby's threatened to walk out if they didn't stop fining them? The firm would have to agree. They couldn't put new girls in everywhere, and if all the other shop workers joined in it would be better still.'

Sally pondered for a moment, then she said shrewdly, 'Someone would have to be the one to speak up, though, and they'd be the ones who were sacked, like you and Jim Baty.'

'Ah, but that would be a condition of everyone coming back, that no one was sacked,' Lawrie said, but Sally was unconvinced.

'They'd get their own back on the girls some way,' she said.

'Well, it will come someday, Sal, you'll see. The rich have always stood together against the poor. If we stand together now we'll get justice. Get men in Parliament who'll fight for money for people when they're in trouble. When they're too sick or too old to earn, or widowed with children to keep.'

Lawrie's face was flushed and his eyes were shining. Sally looked at him fondly. These were all impossible dreams, she thought, but how fervently Lawrie believed in them.

'I've joined the union,' he said abruptly. 'I'm expected to, because it's strong on the railway, but I'm only an ordinary member. I won't take office, Sal, at least not until we're further in to harbour than we are now.'

Sally laid her hand on his.

'I *am* with you, Lol, as far as agreeing that things are far wrong, but I'm just afraid of you getting into trouble.'

'Don't worry,' he said. 'After the last few years I'm not likely to take any chances, but just to stand together, that's all we need. To make sure that things are better for our children.' He kissed Sally. 'I'm not the hothead you married, love,' he laughed. 'I'm a very sober and staid man these days.'

Sally smiled but said nothing.

Quite suddenly, it seemed, Christmas arrived. Once again Lawrie hired a cab and brought Mrs Malloy to join the family for Christmas dinner. Albert had hinted that he and Emily would like to join them, but Emily said firmly that they should have their first Christmas dinner in their own home, and it was arranged that they would join the family later.

Matthew had been sleeping a great deal, and eating very little, and Mrs Malloy was shocked by the change in him.

'God help him, he's failing fast,' she said. 'Poor Matt. Who would have thought he'd travel such a long hard road, good man that he was.' She wept, and the children hung over her and tried to console her.

'I wish you lived nearer to us,' Cathy said. 'These are nicer houses than Gell Street, too. Why don't you move here, Mrs Mal?'

'Indeed now, these are beautiful houses, girlie, but I'm like an ould snail in its shell in me own house,' she said. Tears spurted from Sally's eyes, as she remembered the time when her father had used the same expression.

'Oh, Mrs Mal,' she said. 'Da said just that – an old snail in his shell – when I'd found this house and wanted to move from Gell Street. When I think of him as he was then, and the way he is now.' She wept bitterly, and Mrs Malloy made soothing noises, smiling reassuringly at the girls. Lawrie came through from the parlour and took in the situation at a glance.

'Have you told Mrs Mal about your commission, Mary?' he asked.

'No, no, I haven't,' Mary said, her eyes shining. 'I didn't ever get commission because the first salesgirl always took over when I'd nearly sold anything, but we've been so busy this week and last, I made one and fourpence.'

'Indeed now, that's grand,' said Mrs Malloy. Sally had escaped into the back kitchen and rinsed her face at the sink. She was drying it on the towel when Lawrie went out to her.

'Sorry, love,' she said. 'I didn't mean to be a wet blanket for Mrs Mal.'

'She's all right,' he assured her, 'the girls are talking the leg off her.' Sally went back into the kitchen, smiling at Mrs Malloy, and resumed the preparations for dinner. After dinner Lawrie took Mrs Malloy in to see Matthew again and Sally and the girls cleared away and washed up. Lawrie built up the fire, and pushed the table back against the wall, then wheeled the sofa round and arranged the chairs so that they could all sit in a semicircle around the fire. Sally laid out glasses and rum and porter on the table, and sasparilla for the girls.

They were just ready when Emily and Albert arrived, and after they had been in to see Matthew they went into the kitchen while Sally settled her father for a sleep, and Lawrie carried Mrs Malloy back to a seat by the fire. Mrs Malloy was rather in awe of Albert at first as he sat without speaking, his feet planted firmly on the hearthrug and his hands on his knees while he puffed at his pipe, but soon she forgot about him as Lawrie told stories about work which made all of them laugh. Sally handed round drinks and the girls sat on stools beside Mrs Malloy and begged her to tell them about her days in service.

'Ah, they're all well told,' she said. 'Ye don't want to be hearing them again.'

'We do, we do,' they chorused, and Emily said wistfully, 'I'd like to hear them, Mrs Mal. I was too young to hear them before I was sent to Ormesdale.'

Two glasses of porter had made Mrs Malloy's eyes sparkle, and loosened her tongue. She told them many tales, some of which they had heard before and some which were new to all of them. There was much hilarity, but Albert sat stolidly, puffing at his pipe without smiling.

'I suppose you saw all this from the other side, Albert,' Sally said. 'Always having servants.'

'I was out of the house mostly,' he said. 'At work or at my Club. My mother saw to all that, then my housekeeper.'

'But what about the young maids?' Sally said. 'Did you hear any funny tales?'

'Funny tales,' he said blankly. 'No, it was always quiet.'

Sally gave up the struggle to involve him, and turned to Mrs Malloy.

'I wonder how those lads got on, who used to live with you,' she said. 'James and John. They were very good to Alfred, and to Da, too.'

'Aye, they were grand lads. I heard through a lad Paddy knew that they did well. John got married and had a string of children, but James was unwed when last I heard.'

She turned to Emily. 'I broke me heart when they went home to Ireland, but didn't I get Paddy and this rapscallion here in their place, so I was a fortunate woman, thanks be to God.'

Albert took his pipe from his mouth.

'Talking of Ormesdale,' he said, as though it had just been mentioned, 'I've heard as your uncle is on Queer Street. He married that woman and went to the South of France for a while, but I've heard he's declared bankrupt now.'

He could tell them no more, although they bombarded him with questions, and Emily looked vexed when she heard that he had known for some days.

'Well now, I'm not sorry for them,' Mrs Malloy declared. 'Isn't it the price of them for the way they behaved,' and Sally agreed with her. She had slipped away from time to time to see her father and to replenish the parlour fire, but he seemed content to lie without speaking, as though dozing.

Later Lawrie quickly restored the furniture to position and brought the table forward again, then Sally and the girls, helped by Emily, laid it with the food she had ready. Albert and Lawrie had gone to talk to Matthew, and Mrs Malloy watched with approval as Mary and Cathy darted to and fro with dishes.

'Ye'll make good wives for some lucky man, so ye will,' she told them, and they laughed heartily at the idea, although Mary turned away and smiled to herself.

The visitors praised Sally's bunloaf, and the trifle which followed the plates of meat with Sally's pickled onions.

'Aye, ye're a notable cook now, girlie,' Mrs Malloy said, as she took a slice of Sally's home made bread. 'Do ye mind the first bread ye made?'

They both laughed and Sally said ruefully, 'I've never told anyone about that, Mrs Mal.' She turned to Emily. 'It was soon after Mam died, and I was very proud of myself at the way I was managing. I decided to make bread but I didn't realise that it had to prove.'

'What's that?' asked Lawrie.

'When the dough is left to rise then put in the tin to rise again, that's proving,' said Sally. 'I put it in the tins and straight into the oven. It rose so much that it filled the oven and came out at the sides. I just screamed when I opened the oven, and ran for Mrs Mal.'

'She was that upset, God love her,' Mrs Malloy said. 'I couldn't keep me face straight when I seen it filling the oven and puffin' out all down the front, but I couldn't let her see me laughing. We just cleaned it up and I gave her a loaf to tide her over.'

'Aye, you've been my standby all my life,' Sally said, smiling fondly at the old lady, 'I don't know what we'd have done without you.'

272

'Amen to that,' Lawrie said, and Albert said solemnly, 'It was a useful lesson to you.' Sally saw Cathy glance at Mary, and knew that the next moment they would be giggling so she hastily sent Cathy to put the kettle on the gas for more tea.

After tea Lawrie rearranged the chairs and sofa again and they sat round talking, until Mrs Malloy asked to go in to Matthew again. Soon afterwards Emily and Albert decided to go, but Lawrie waited until they had left before going for a cab for Mrs Malloy.

'God love him, he knows well I'd be ashamed if he asked them to take me to Gell Street, and Emily shamed, too,' she said fondly.

'They were going the other way anyhow,' Sally said.

'Aye, and he wouldn't like to go out of his way to take me home because of the expense,' Mrs Malloy said. 'Is he a bit tight on the purse strings?' she asked shrewdly.

Sally shrugged. 'I've wondered,' she said. 'Little things, but then Emily has beautiful clothes.'

'She does indeed,' Mrs Malloy agreed, looking at Sally's troubled face. 'Ah well, aren't we all different. Here's one that's never troubled be meanness, more power to him,' she added as Lawrie came striding down the lobby.

'Your carriage awaits,' he said, pretending to bow before picking her up in his arms and taking her in to Matthew again to say goodbye.

Matthew was dozing, and Mrs Malloy just pressed his thin hand as it lay on the cover.

'He's not long for this world,' she whispered to Lawrie. 'And sure ye couldn't wish anything different for him, the way he is.'

Lawrie nodded, his eyes on Matthew's face, so thin that the skin seemed to be stretched over the bones. 'It'll break Sally's heart all the same,' he said quietly.

The kitchen was tidy and the girls were in bed when Lawrie returned. Sally was sitting with her chin on her hand, looking pensively into the fire.

'What's up, love?' Lawrie asked.

'I'm just thinking about Emily. I hope she hasn't gone from the frying pan into the fire, marrying Albert. Mrs Malloy was asking me was he mean?'

'Trust Mrs Mal to weigh things up,' Lawrie said. 'He might be a bit mean in small ways, but he won't keep Emily short.'

'But she was always so generous, Lol, and now she doesn't seem to have any money for little treats for Da or anything. It must upset her, and then the skimpy food.'

'I don't suppose she lived very high in that school in Brussels, and God knows what went on in Ormesdale. Don't worry, Sal, Emily's used to dealing with queer situations – far more than you are – and she'll see his good points and ignore the bad, you see.'

'I hate meanness though,' Sally said. 'I'm glad you're not mean, Lol.'

Lawrie laughed aloud. 'I never thought I'd live to hear that!' he exclaimed. 'How many times have you nearly had my ear off for being spendthrift?'

Sally smiled. 'I know,' she said. 'But when we were hard up, it was things outside that caused it, and we faced it together. I feel sorry for Emily.' Lawrie put his arms around her and kissed her.

'I feel sorry for Albert,' he said. 'Because he hasn't got you.' She clung to him, looking lovingly into his face. The marks of the years of hardship were there, and his thick dark hair was touched with grey, but he still had the ready smile that she loved, and the strength on which she leaned. He could always say the right word to comfort her and to drive away her worries. She held him tight and suddenly the tide of passion rose strongly in both of them, as they lay on the sofa in each other's arms and made love urgently yet tenderly. When their passion was spent, Lawrie held her close, whispering how much he missed her.

The gas had gone out, and in the firelight Lawrie could see that her face was troubled as she whispered, 'I know, love, but what can I do? I must be there to see to Da during the night.'

He said quickly, 'Of course you must, but it's a pity we never thought of the sofa before. First time I've been glad to see the gas run out.'

She smiled as he meant her to do, and he said gently, 'Mrs Mal saw a change in your da, Sal.' He hoped to prepare her, but when she sighed and nodded, he realised that she had already accepted what must come.

Chapter Forty

The New Year of 1906 was ushered in very quietly in the Ward household. It was clear to all of them, even Mary and Cathy, that Matthew was a dying man.

Sally spent most of her time now just sitting with her father. He became fretful if he was left alone, but he was content if Sally sat beside him, not talking, but stroking his hand, and wiping his lips. Sometimes Lawrie brought him news of the launch of a coaster at Cammell Laird's and gave him details of her tonnage, and her name, *St. George*, in an effort to rouse him, or told him of a collision in the river in which all hands were lost from the tug *Sandon*, but neither good news nor bad could rouse Matthew from his apathy.

As the gloomy February days passed, his mind became confused and he seemed not to know where he was or who tended him. One night in early March he had been very restless, muttering all night about jobs in the shipyard, and ships he had worked on which were now sailing the seven seas, but when morning came, and a watery sun shone into the parlour, he became quiet.

Sally sat with him all morning, and rushed through her necessary jobs while Cathy took her place at dinner time. When Cathy had returned to school, Sally sat with him again, and about two o'clock replenished the fire. As she turned back to the bed her father opened his eyes and looked at her. Suddenly he spoke, his voice full and strong.

'The fire, girl,' he said. 'Don't cook the babby, too, as well as the scouse.'

'Oh, Da,' Sally cried, falling to her knees beside the bed. His vacant stare had gone, and his eyes were full of intelligence as he raised his head from the pillow and smiled at her, the old loving smile which she had never thought to see again.

She clasped his hand, her tears falling fast, and he said gently, 'Don't cry, girl. Yer've been a good daughter to me, lass, one of the best.'

Sally could only say, 'Oh, Da, Da,' as she clung to his hand, tears pouring down her face.

'Aye, a good daughter,' he repeated. 'And a good wife. Me poor Julie. I've been well blessed.'

He lay back on the pillow and closed his eyes for a moment, then he opened them again and looked vaguely around the room.

'She'll be in in a minute, Mrs Mal. Never a show without Punch. "I'll help ye, Matty lad," she said.' He withdrew his hand from Sally's and stroked her hair, then his hand fell and he closed his eyes again. Sally knelt on beside him, afraid to move as the afternoon wore on, but he did not speak again.

275

Cathy came home from school, and stood with Sally until Matthew opened his eyes and smiled at them, then he patted Cathy's cheek when she kissed him. When Lawrie came home Cathy went out to warn him, and he came in quietly to join Sally.

'How're you feeling, Matt?' he said, as he often did, but instead of the usual mumbled reply, Matthew said clearly, 'I'm fine, lad. A great day, Mafeking. Jan Smuts.'

He stopped, looking puzzled, and Lawrie said quickly, 'Aye well, never mind. Would you like a drink, Matt?' Matthew nodded, but he took only a sip of milk from the feeding cup, and then closed his eyes again. Lawrie whispered to Cathy to stay with her grandfather while he drew Sally out to the lobby.

'Oh, Lawrie,' she wept, as he put his arms around her. 'He was just – just Da as he used to be. He said about the fire and Emily.' She cried bitterly, and Lawrie held her, making soothing noises.

'And he knew you, Sal?' he asked gently.

'Yes, he said I was a good daughter.'

She could say no more, but Lawrie said quietly, 'You'll have to be brave now, love. This is a sign of the end, but he still needs you.'

'I know,' she said, drawing away from him and dabbing at her eyes. 'I remember when the lads died, Mrs Mal said it was the last flicker before the lamp went out.' She wiped her eyes again and braced herself. 'I'll go back,' she said. 'Should we send for Emily?'

'Yes, I'll send a lad up,' he promised. Sally went back into the room where her father was lying with his eyes closed, breathing peacefully.

'Do you want to go in the kitchen?' she whispered to Cathy, but the girl asked, 'Can I stay, Mam?' and when Sally nodded, she brought in a stool and sat beside Sally, watching the sick man. Lawrie came in to sit with them, and some time later Emily and Mary arrived together.

Sally slipped out to speak to them when they arrived, and was surprised to see that Albert was not with Emily.

'He wasn't home, so I took a cab,' Emily explained. 'I saw Mary walking home from the shop so I called her into it.'

Matthew was still lying with his eyes closed, but his breathing had become shallower. Emily wept when Sally told her what had happened, but when several hours passed, and there was no change in Matthew she became uneasy.

'I'll have to go, Sal, and explain to Albert,' she said. 'I left a message with Mrs Barry, but she mightn't explain properly where I am.' Lawrie called her a cab, and saw her off, promising to let her know if there was any change.

The girls went to bed, after they had kissed Matthew and clung to him. He roused himself briefly, to stroke Cathy's cheek, and lift a strand of Mary's long, bright hair, with a ghost of a smile.

Lawrie made tea, and he and Sally settled down for their vigil with the dying man.

At two o'clock in the morning, Matthew's breathing quickened, then gently died away. Lawrie bent over him and took his wrist, then he turned to Sally.

'He's gone, love,' he said gently. Her tears fell fast but she said nothing, only bent and kissed her father tenderly. Lawrie took her in his arms, holding her firmly, his own throat tight with tears.

A little later, he built up the kitchen fire and settled Sally in a chair beside it, with a cup of tea, while he went to call Mrs Byrd, who lived opposite. She assisted at the birth or death of many of her neighbours, and by some sixth sense seemed to know that she was needed, and came at once in answer to his knock.

Quietly she helped Sally to perform the last sad offices for her father, and as quietly afterwards she whispered advice to Lawrie on what he needed to arrange. When the morning came, he woke the girls and told them of their grandfather's death, warning them that they must do all they could to console their mother.

After sending a boy with a note to Emily, he went to Gell Street to tell Mrs Malloy. She shed a few quiet tears when he told her of Matthew's brief recovery and his words, but she wiped them away.

'Poor Matt, God rest him, he travelled a long, hard road. Sure, death was a friend to him at the end, and thanks be to God, he went peaceful.'

'I'm glad he had that spell with his mind clear, and talked to Sally,' Lawrie said. 'He said she'd been a good daughter to him.'

'Aye, so ye said, lad, and didn't he speak the true word there? It'll be a consolation to her to remember them words,' Mrs Malloy said.

Lawrie called a cab and took her to Egremont Street to be with Sally, and as they clung together and cried, Sally said tearfully, 'I shouldn't grieve that he's gone, Mrs Mal. He suffered so much for such a long time. He was weary.'

'Aye, child, he's better off, but ye'll miss him all the more, for all ye had to do for him.'

'I'm glad we've had these last months though, Mrs Mal. Although he was so much weaker, at least he was friendly again to Lawrie, and he stopped using that terrible language and saw Emily again.'

'True for you, girlie. It'd be a bad thing if he'd gone while his poor mind was twisted. Ye've better memories of him, so.'

Emily and Albert arrived, and they all sat in the kitchen while the undertakers were busy in the parlour. When the men had gone Lawrie took Emily and Albert into the parlour, but he waited until they came out before he carried Mrs Malloy in, and left her alone with her old friend. Later when he carried her back to the kitchen her eyes were red with weeping, but she only said quietly, 'Twenty years to the day very near, since your poor mam died, Sally. Lord ha' mercy on the two of them. Well, they're together now, and their lads with them.'

Sally was surprised when several elderly men called in the course of the day, explaining that they were old workmates of Matthew's, and had heard of his death. All were taken in to see him in his coffin, then they were given a glass of whisky and a slice of cake, and departed satisfied that they had paid their respects.

'Wouldn't it have been better now, if they'd come to see him while he was alive, to cheer him up,' Mrs Malloy said. 'Sure, men have no sense at all, even the best of them.'

Albert and Lawrie glanced at each other but said nothing, and Sally said quietly, 'I don't think Da would have wanted them to see him as he was, Mrs Mal.'

'Maybe not, child. He was ever a proud man,' she agreed.

Mrs Kilgannon arrived dressed in her best, and cried in loud gulping sobs when Lawrie took her into the parlour. He gave her a glass of port when she came out, and she was disposed to linger, saying how much she admired Matthew and his family, but Mrs Malloy cut her short.

'The family have things to discuss,' she said, nodding at Emily and Albert, 'It was good of ye to come in. Goodbye to ye.' Mrs Kilgannon left hurriedly, and even Sally had to smile.

'You have a rare talent, Mrs Malloy,' Albert said ponderously, and Lawrie added, 'Aye, you'd make a great chucker out.' Several neighbours called to whisper condolences, and Emily opened the door to them, and showed them into the parlour and directly out again, without bothering Sally, who seemed to be sitting in a stupor of fatigue and misery. She was persuaded to go upstairs and rest for a few hours. Emily and Albert had gone when she came down, much refreshed.

Lawrie was sitting at the table with Mrs Malloy and the girls, and he jumped up to get her a cup of tea, but she shook her head.

'Finish your meal, Lol,' she said. 'I'll go in to see him now.'

'By yourself?' he asked.

'Yes, love,' she said quietly. She went into the parlour, where the bed had been taken down and her father's coffin lay on trestles in the centre of the room.

Matthew lay in his coffin, his hands folded on his breast, all the signs of his long illness smoothed away, and a look of quiet dignity on his face. He was the father Sally had always known until his affliction came upon him, and she was shaken by a storm of weeping.

Oh, Da, Da, she wept, how could I have lost my temper with you, and said such things? She forgot all the years of patient nursing, the devoted care she had given her father, and remembered with anguish the times when she had been driven to scolding him. Presently she grew calmer, and when she had made her own loving farewell to her father, she returned to the kitchen, quiet and composed.

Late in the evening Mrs Malloy said to Lawrie, 'Will ye take me in to the parlour again, lad? I'll sit up with him.'

'No, no, I'll stay up,' Lawrie said, but he was overruled by the two women.

'Ye need yer rest,' Mrs Malloy said, 'and I want to do it.' Eventually Lawrie settled her in a chair beside the coffin, and Sally took the other chair while Lawrie went upstairs to sleep in readiness for the next day's work.

It was very quiet in the parlour. Mrs Malloy sat with her lips moving silently, and her rosary beads slipping through her fingers, and Sally's mind roved over the past.

She remembered the days when she was a young child, and she would run to meet her father coming home from work, and be hoisted up on to his shoulder. Then the years after her mother died, when she felt so proud when her father praised her for being such a help to him. How happy they'd been when the first sharp grief for Mam had worn

278

off, and Emily had been such a delight to all of them. She thought of her father pretending to cut Emily's toenails every night, before carrying her up to bed, and the boys pushing her in the swing in the doorway. Other images passed through her mind in the long quiet hours. Herself and her father visiting the cemetery. The first happy years of her marriage when Mary and Cathy had been born, and had brought them such joy, and Lawrie and her father had become good friends.

Later Sally made tea, and she and Mrs Malloy talked in whispers, until Mrs Malloy suddenly fell into the light sleep of the old. Sally dozed too, and she was surprised to hear Lawrie's footstep on the stairs, and to realise that it was six o'clock. Mary went to work wearing a black armband on her dress. She was sad at her grandfather's death, but she enjoyed the attention she received, and the sympathetic enquiries from the other girls.

Sally kept Cathy at home to help her. There were several callers during the morning, but in the afternoon, Mrs Malloy told Sally to rest on the bed.

'Me and Cathy will see to things, won't we, Cath? We'll call ye if ye're needed.'

Sally was easily persuaded. Her eyelids felt so heavy that she could scarcely keep her eyes open, and her body felt drained and heavy. She slept for several hours, only coming down in time to make the evening meal. Afterwards, Lawrie insisted on taking Mrs Malloy upstairs to sleep on their bed.

Mrs Cassidy and her daughter Kathleen arrived a little later, offering to keep watch during the night with Matthew's body.

'That's very good of you,' Lawrie said quickly, before Sally could refuse. 'Mrs Mal and Sally sat up last night, but two nights are too much.'

'Sure, it will be a comfort to me,' Mrs Cassidy said, adding obscurely, 'yiz were very good to me poor girl.'

When Mrs Malloy came downstairs, she insisted that she had had all the sleep she needed, and would sit up again, so Kathleen was sent home and the older women shared the vigil. Wreaths arrived from friends and neighbours, but nothing came from Ormesdale, although Albert had told Walter.

The funeral was quiet and dignified, as Matthew would have wished. Mrs Malloy stayed until it was over, then she insisted on going home. Lawrie and Sally had talked things over in bed one night, and decided that they would fix up the parlour for her, so that she could be cared for by them, but she refused.

'No, yiz want some time to yerselves,' she said firmly. 'The summer's before us, and thank God, me legs is always better then.'

'But we'd bring your own furniture, and your own bed if you liked,' Sally said. And Lawrie added, 'And you could please yourself, and see as much or as little of us as you wanted, as long as we were within reach if you needed us.'

But Mrs Malloy was adamant. 'Ye're kindness itself, now,' she said, 'and sure it's a great comfort to me knowing I can come next winter if things get beyond me, but I'll see the summer out in Gell Street.'

'I know you're always better in the summer,' Sally said. 'But I wish you had better neighbours. I hope you'll be all right.'

'I'll be grand. When the good weather comes I'll take me chair to the door, and watch the children playing, and have a jangle with the women.'

'But what about that rough fellow next door?' Sally protested.

'He wouldn't harm a hair of me head. Sure the neighbours'd lynch him entirely if he was to harm an ould woman like me. There's no harm in them without the drink, and I'm inside me four walls be the time they're drunk.'

Sally went the next day to prepare Mrs Malloy's house for her return, building a bright fire, and cleaning the kitchen and the back kitchen. When she was satisfied that she had done all she could to make the house warm and welcoming she went home, and found Emily sitting with Mrs Malloy.

'I got the horse 'bus to London Road and walked across,' she explained. 'You don't mind, Sal?'

'Mind!' Sally exclaimed. 'I'm delighted to see you.'

'It's just that there's no reason for me to come so often now,' Emily said wistfully, but Sally urged her to come as often as she could.

'We've a few years to make up,' she said. 'Isn't that right, Mrs Mal?'

'Indeed it is, girlie, and I hope ye'll come to Gell Street too if ye have the time. Sure, none of us are short of things to talk about.

Emily stayed until after Lawrie came home, explaining that Albert would be late, then they all shared a cab to Gell Street. Lawrie jumped out and had a quick word with the driver before he lifted Mrs Mal out, then he said quietly to Emily, 'He's taking you home now, Em. I've settled with him so don't let him try to charge you again.'

Sally had said goodbye to Emily and gone into Mrs Malloy's house, to light the lamp and stir up the fire.

'Now haven't ye made me very comfortable?' Mrs Malloy said, as they fussed around her, leaving all she needed within reach. 'I'll be grand now, but I'll not forget the way ye wanted to bring me to yer own place. Sure, ye've hearts of gold, the pair of ye, and God will surely bless ye.'

Later they walked home, arm in arm.

'Seems strange for us to be out together again, doesn't it?' Lawrie said. 'You know what, Sal, I'm glad Mrs Mal can manage for a bit longer, so we can be on our own.'

Sally leaned her head against his shoulder as she had in their courting days, and squeezed his arm without replying. Cathy was lying on the sofa reading when they went in, and she told them that Mary had gone to see her friend in the next street.

It seemed strange to Sally, to sit before the fire, her hands idle in her lap, and know that there was nothing she needed urgently to do. No need to listen for a summons from the parlour, or snatch moments to catch up with the endless washing. She could hear sounds as Lawrie moved about the parlour, tidying up, stacking trestles to be collected by the undertaker, but nothing was required of her, and she could sit tranquilly for as long as she wished.

Later when the girls had gone to bed, she and Lawrie sat together in the firelight.

'How odd it was, Lol, that Da should go exactly twenty years after Mam. It seems like an ending somehow.'

'It is, love,' he said. 'The end of one part of our lives and the beginning of another.'

'Twenty years,' she said. 'In some ways it seems such a short time, and in others like a thousand years. So much has happened.'

'Aye, we've had some rough times, Sal, but we've been luckier than your poor da, losing your mam so young. At least we've always had each other.'

'Luckier than Emily, too,' Sally said sadly. 'I don't think she's happy, Lawrie. I don't think Albert really cares for her, except the way Hester and Walter did, as someone to dress up and be proud of, not for herself.'

'Never mind, we'll love her for herself,' Lawrie said, drawing her close. A coal fell in the grate and the fire blazed up. By the light of it Sally looked at Lawrie's beloved face, and thought what he meant to her. Like a rock she could lean on, and yet with the same cheerful, optimistic approach to life that had charmed her from the first. She held him closer.

'I wonder what sort of life Mary and Cathy will have?' she wondered.

Lawrie laughed. 'I can just see Mary,' he said, 'queening it in a big house, with a pair of matched greys in the stable.'

'As long as she doesn't have a stalled ox, too,' she said. Then as Lawrie looked puzzled she added, 'Do you remember what Mrs Hart said on our wedding day? "Better is a dinner of herbs where love is, than a stalled ox and hatred therewith." How truly she spoke, Lol.'

'Aye, she was a clever women,' Lawrie said. 'But never mind looking back, Sal. Look forward to twenty years from now. Things are getting better all the time. There'll be no more poverty, no division between rich and poor. Mary and Cathy will be living in a better world altogether.'

Sally smiled. 'Twenty years from now,' she said. 'That'll be 1926. Life should be good for everyone then. I wonder what the girls will have to look back on, what will happen in the twenty years to come?'